THE SVALBARD PASSAGE

THOMAS KIRKWOOD
GEIR FINNE

The Svalbard Passage

A Novel

AN AUTHORS GUILD BACKINPRINT.COM EDITION

AN AUTHORS GUILD BACKINPRINT.COM EDITION

Published by iUniverse.com, Inc.

For information address:
iUniverse.com, Inc.
5220 S 16th, Ste. 200
Lincoln, NE 68512
www.iuniverse.com

Originally published by Macmillan

ISBN: 0-595-15146-9

Printed in the United States of America

For Rayanna Simons, our incomparable editor, and for John Hawn, who believed in this story from the start

Svalbard

Svalbard is an archipelago in the North Atlantic. Until well into this century, it was a no man's land. Today it is under Norwegian jurisdiction, but there are traces of its former status everywhere. Russian inhabitants, for example, outnumber the Norwegians two to one.

Appropriately, Svalbard means "cold coast." It is six hundred and fifty miles from the North Pole and a somewhat shorter distance due north of the northernmost tip of Norway. Of the nine islands, Spitsbergen is the largest, Bear Island perhaps the most legendary.

Once one leaves the few small settlements huddled along the banks of the Ice Fjord, there are few signs of civilization. One is more likely to encounter a polar bear, reindeer, or arctic fox than another human.

Night falls on Svalbard in October and does not lift again until February. The

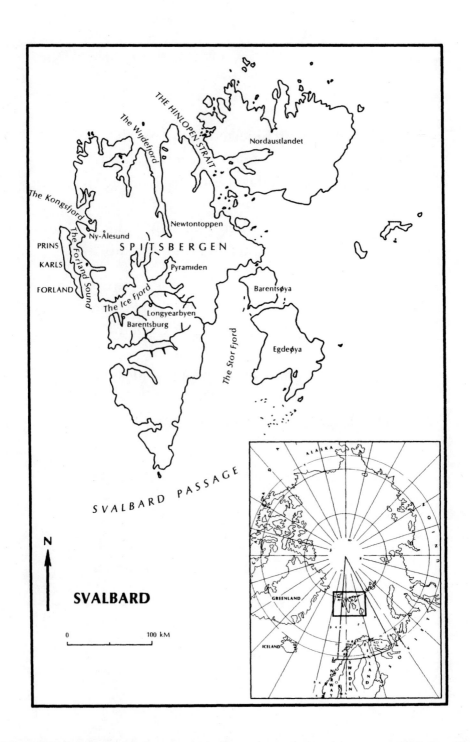

THE HINLOPEN STRAIT

The Wijdefjord

Nordaustlandet

The Kongsfjord

Newtontoppen

Ny-Ålesund

PRINS

S P I T S B E R G E N

KARLS

The Forland Sound

Pyramiden

FORLAND

Barentsøya

The Ice Fjord

Longyearbyen

Barentsburg

The Stor Fjord

Egdeøya

S V A L B A R D   P A S S A G E

N

SVALBARD

0   100 kM

thermometer hovers around forty below; the snows come, driven by the arctic gale; the ubiquitous glaciers thicken; and the Svalbardians grow resigned and glum. The only break in the darkness occurs when the northern lights cast their eerie glow across the barren terrain.

Then the sun rises. At first it scarcely peeks above the surface of the sea. But it steadily gathers vigor until, in April, it no longer sets at all. For four and a half months, the fabled midnight sun trudges out its great ellipse along the horizon, touching all points of the compass every twenty-four hours. Whether resting on its fiery perch in the north at midnight or hanging lackluster at its low apex in the south at noon, it is at work round the clock illuminating the unearthly landscape of Svalbard: jagged peaks and towering rock steeples, huge granite domes and desolate gravel flats, ice cliffs which rise in awesome blue and green formations from the fjords.

In the protected valleys, the constant sunlight of summer pushes the mercury above the freezing point. The top few inches of earth, frozen to a depth of a thousand feet, turn soft. In the shallow mud, a small miracle takes place: shrub-like growths—the polar willow, the dwarf birch —appear on the treeless wastes, and colorful grasses create a patchwork of miniature meadows. The archipelago's flowering plants—the yellow ranunculus, the light-blue mountain phlox, the white Svalbard poppy, the purple saxifrage—stage a brief celebration which brightens the ugly, menacing face of the land.

Today this bleak cluster of arctic islands is a focal point of great power politics. More than the coal deposits, more than the reputed oil reserves under the coastal waters or even the uranium known to lie beneath the permafrost, it is Svalbard's immensely strategic location which makes it so important. For nature has given the archipelago one gift among all her curses: the Gulf Stream passes so close that the waters to the west and south, though clogged with ice, remain navigable the winter long.

A glance at the map will reveal the result: an ice-free passage between Svalbard and northern Norway which links the great Soviet naval installations on the Kola Peninsula to the open seas. Since this is the Soviets' only secure window to the Atlantic, it is not surprising that they have concentrated most of their nuclear navy in and around Murmansk. Nor is it surprising that they take more than a casual interest in the Svalbard Passage.

PART ONE

Prologue

The lead climber slammed his ice ax into the glacier wall and lifted himself another few inches. A crystalline shower of tiny fragments exploded in the air and fell glittering into the sea. He felt a rush of exhilaration: they were ready, this would be the last practice climb, the real work could begin soon.

He glanced up the vertical, aquamarine face of the glacier . . . another couple of hundred feet to the top. He saw his route in the folds and creases of the ice as clearly as if it had been penciled in on a photograph.

It was cold, well below freezing. But the sun had been out all afternoon and tiny rivulets of water were beginning to trickle down the cracks in the ice. It poured into the sleeves of his wind parka and soaked his wool sweater. His muscles tightened from the chill. Better get moving.

The view held him a moment longer. A thousand feet below, the blue-green sea stretched to the horizon—quiet, immense, dotted with gently bobbing floes. The low sun glowed across the water. Its rays glinted off the ice screws he had twisted into the wall, off the helmets and ice axes of the other climbers.

He was about to move when he caught a glimpse of his own shadow. It sliced across the ice wall and disappeared into the gray crevasse that ran parallel to their ascent.

A dark force—the kind he often experienced climbing—seemed to pull him along the line of his shadow toward the crevasse. With powerful blows of the ice ax and delicate steps of the

3

spur-like crampons on his feet, he moved sideways and slightly downward toward the point where his elongated shadow melted into the bottomless void.

"Heinz!" yelled the girl who hung from the wall below him. "Heinz, for God's sake! Put in another screw!"

"Losing your nerve?" he shouted back.

"Shut up and put in another screw if you want to traverse! Why take chances now?"

He ignored her. His shadow drew him onward toward the darkness.

"Heinz! Put in a screw!"

He reached for the pocket of his belt. Suddenly, a rivulet of freezing water gushed down on him. His hand cramped around the ice ax; panic stabbed him. He saw the sea far, far below. He saw the yawning gray fissure. He looked up—a vertical mirror of ice and a vast empty sky.

Pressing his chest against the wall, he tried to flex the fingers of his frozen hand. Nothing. A splash of water hit him in the mouth. He choked violently. The cough jolted him away from the wall, tearing his hand from his ice ax. As he tumbled backward, he felt the crampons twist his ankles and break free.

She caught him at the end of his sixty-foot cascade with a perfectly timed belay. Miraculously, the top ice screw withstood the force of his fall, leaving him helpless but alive as he swung back and forth across the sheer face of the glacier.

She pulled out her transmitter and called the rescue helicopter. He hung below her now, his eyes to the sea, his back toward her, held only by the rope around his waist. . . .

1

Tromsø, Norway

PROFESSOR ORVIK droned on and on.

"We in Tromsø," he said, "consider it a very special honor that the Ministry of Education has chosen our university to host the Institute for Disarmament."

I know the type, thought Martin. Loves conferences, loves titles. This could go on forever.

He checked out the audience: town dignitaries, stiff and attentive in their dark suits; students, fidgeting and whispering to one another; a few members of the press, jotting down a perfunctory note or two to combat the boredom.

He felt a growing irritation. Another windbag at the podium, an entire evening of vacuous ceremonies—precisely the image he had wanted the Institute to avoid. The sun, still high on the horizon in spite of the late hour, glared through the tinted windows that lined the west wall of the conference room.

"It gives me great pleasure," continued Orvik, "to introduce to you the first Director of the Institute for Disarmament, Dr. Martin Dodds from Stanford University. I am sure you are all familiar with his brilliant new book, *Obstacles to Disarmament*. We are fortunate enough to have Dr. Dodds with us here in Norway for an entire year, thanks to the generosity of Stanford."

Orvik paused to study the watch he had slid from his vest pocket. Undaunted, he went on, as energetic as when he had begun over an hour ago.

"Now I'm sure all of you will be interested to know that Dr. Dodds is. . . ."

But Martin had already bounded to his feet, grasping a golden opportunity to cut the introduction short. He was ambling toward the podium when Orvik caught sight of him. The old professor gave a start and shuffled the pages of his text together. For a brief second he froze, as though considering a defense of his beloved turf.

"Thank you, sir," said Martin, pulling up to the podium. "A most comprehensive and flattering introduction." There was a moment of awkward silence during which Orvik—diminutive, erect, immaculately dressed—stared in disbelief at the tall, disheveled American. But, alas, there was nothing he could do. He grabbed his notes, muttered something under his breath, and sat down.

"Ladies and gentlemen," said Martin in flawless Norwegian, "it would be difficult to improve on Professor Orvik's excellent description of what we at the Institute hope to accomplish." He turned deferentially toward the deposed speaker; Orvik responded with a stiff nod.

Martin surveyed the room. The younger guests were cheerful, but many of the older people in the audience seemed offended. To them, Dr. Martin Dodds, in cotton slacks, a maroon turtleneck, and rumpled cord jacket, must have looked like one of the radical students the new university had attracted in droves . . . and about whom the staid citizens of this provincial town in northern Norway had very few good things to say. They'll just have to get used to me, he thought, pushing his unruly brown hair from his forehead.

"I'm enthusiastic," he said, "about the prospect of working with the people of Tromsø on so important an endeavor. I would like to encourage each of you to come by and chat with me at the Institute. We're always looking for ideas to further the cause of disarmament and, as you can well imagine, such ideas often originate outside the university. If you have information that might aid us in our work, or if you have a lead you would like us to investigate, don't hesitate to contact me personally."

He put a hand on either side of the podium and leaned forward. His disingenuous warmth was chipping away at the last vestiges of hostility in the audience.

"Now, I'm not a great one for speechmaking," he continued. "About the only insight I have to offer tonight is this. Hunger and thirst should never be underestimated as obstacles to disarmament. I suggest, in the name of peace, that we move to the buffet. Whatever questions you have, I'd be happy to answer over a drink."

There was some subdued laughter as the guests filed off in polite groups to the makeshift bar at the rear of the hall. A young woman with shoulder-length honey-blond hair caught his eye. She looked at him and smiled, shaking her head in disbelief. He watched her leave the room through a side exit, her light fawn dress clinging to the backs of her thighs. When he descended the steps and headed for the bar, the image of her face, her hair, her lithe body still swam before him.

Washing down a morsel of herring with a large swallow of aquavit, Martin glimpsed a tall blond man in a superbly tailored suit standing by the same door through which the woman had left. The man's features were angular and handsome; he radiated self-assurance. Composed and elegant, he studied the crowd. When he saw Martin, he smiled pleasantly and walked toward him.

"Professor Dodds?" he asked in American English, his accent more American East Coast than Norwegian.

"That's me," answered Martin, piling more herring on his plate.

"I'm sorry I missed your speech."

"You did yourself a disservice. It was brimming with subtle insight, astute analysis, and high moral purpose." He winked at the stranger with a hint of mischief.

"So I hear," said the man. "I met a friend in the hallway who brought me up to date."

"A blond woman?"

"A very pretty blond woman. Let me congratulate you on your discerning eye. And also on your speech. Really, that's just what my countrymen need—a little spirit, a little defiance of custom now and then. I'm Bjørn Holt, with the Foreign Office in Oslo."

7

He extended his hand but retracted it when he saw the American had his hands full—a plate in one, a glass in the other.

Martin looked at him, puzzled. "Well, Mr. Holt, what brings you to the Northern Cape?"

"You," answered Bjørn.

"That's what I was afraid of." Martin spoke Norwegian now, the tongue they would speak for as long as they knew each other. He filled his glass with aquavit.

The predictable metamorphosis of Scandinavians in the presence of alcohol was already under way: they were becoming animated. Bursts of laughter mingled with the din of conversation. In a corner, two silver-haired elderly men in formal attire were toasting one another repeatedly. A student, bottle in hand, was lecturing a group of colleagues so loudly that disjointed fragments of New Left rhetoric could be heard above the noise.

Martin looked away, noticing for the first time how plush the SAS Hotel's conference room was. Not at all my taste, he thought, but plush just the same. Thick blue carpeting, chrome and leather chairs, a row of sleek contemporary sculptures in front of the great tinted-glass windows that formed the west wall, linen and Bunderose china on the buffet. . . .

"Professor Dodds," said the Norwegian, "I must discuss a matter of some importance with you. Prime Minister Danielsen has—"

"For Christ's sake, Mr. Holt, one of the reasons I came here was to avoid the meddling of governments in my work." He glowered angrily at Bjørn.

"I'm sorry, terribly sorry. You have every right to be peeved. But I assure you it's most urgent."

Martin said, "Well, if it has to be, let's get it over with. What time is it?"

"Ten-fifteen."

"That rules out tonight. There's going to be no early closing here." He peered around the room. "The serious drinking's just beginning, and I've got a lot of socializing to do to make up for the speech they all came for and didn't hear. Tomorrow morning is as soon as I can talk."

"I'd prefer tonight."

"I'm afraid, Mr. Holt, that it will be too late by the time the reception is over. Now, if you'll excuse me. . . ." He turned, about to walk off, but the authority in Bjørn's gentle voice detained him.

"Professor, you haven't spent a summer this far north before, have you?"

"I haven't. Why?"

"Because on the seventieth parallel in summer, no one talks about its being 'too late.' Do you know tonight is the last night of the midnight sun? Starting tomorrow, the sun will dip below the horizon. It will only stay there for a few minutes, you understand? Nevertheless, it's the beginning—the beginning of a relentless succession of ever-longer nights. Winter here is a bad time, a wretched time, Mr. Dodds. Something you can't really imagine until you've lived through it. But for now we've got the sun, we've got twenty-four hours of daylight. And believe me, people up here make the most of it. Sleep? That can wait for the winter. There's a lot of living to be hoarded, and those who hoard too little pay the price when the darkness closes in. How about after the reception?"

"If it's that blasted important to you." Martin looked around impatiently. "When and where?"

"Where are you staying?"

"The Grand Hotel."

"I take it you've stumbled into the Polar Bar, the all-night bistro on the ground floor?"

"In and out."

"Is two o'clock acceptable?"

"Yes."

The reception lasted longer than Martin had expected. It was almost three as he neared the hotel. The rays of the midnight sun exploded through a space between the buildings and dazzled him. In the lobby, he waited a moment for his vision to clear, then opened the door to the bistro. He was greeted with bursts of drunken laughter and clouds of tobacco smoke.

Bjørn rose when he saw Martin and smiled warmly. "And how did it go?"

"Passably, considering how it began." His eyes followed one of

9

the drunks who was weaving toward the men's room, ghastly pale, one hand over his mouth, the other slapping the air as if to beat back the laughter which pursued him. "Mr. Holt, let's get this little session over with."

Bjørn dropped ice cubes into the two glasses. "Scotch?" he asked, nodding toward the bottle on the table. "Or should I order you something else?"

"Scotch is okay."

"To put matters bluntly," said Bjørn, pouring each of them a large drink, "Prime Minister Danielsen wishes an assurance that your work will not antagonize the Russians."

Olav Danielsen, the Norwegian Prime Minister, had been causing quite a stir with his bold—some would have said reckless—shift in foreign policy. He maintained that a small nation wishing to protect its independence must not take sides with either of the superpowers. He called his approach the "third way." Recently, he had begun to loosen his country's military ties with NATO and the United States.

At first the growing anti-American sentiment in Norway had made Danielsen's "third way" very popular. But in recent months, a vague malaise had gripped the tiny country. Had the government gone too far in distancing itself from the Western alliance? Might the Soviet Union interpret this as an opportunity to coerce Norway into its sphere of influence?

Martin set his glass down with a bang. "Look, how in God's name can I guarantee that our work will or will not antagonize anyone? We attempt to expose companies, nations, leaders bent on furthering military causes. That tends to antagonize."

"I assure you," said Bjørn softly, "that I respect your position. In fact, if it's of any interest to you, I think Danielsen is looking for trouble with his foreign policy. I think he's naive about Soviet intentions. But, Professor Dodds, that's another matter altogether. Danielsen is in power now, he's funding the Institute and—given the realities of the political universe—he's going to have a say in how it's run."

"I'm starting to feel right at home, censorship and all," said Martin sarcastically. He gave Bjørn a long, hard look. "You know, Mr. Holt, this really is rather ironic. I've been an enthusiastic supporter of Danielsen's 'third way.' I've cheered him from across the sea. Damned right, I've agreed, it's a pity for an idealistic country like Norway to have its destiny tied up with an unprincipled military colossus like the United States. So I come to Norway, and what happens? One of Danielsen's men, who doesn't even agree with Danielsen, tells a visitor who *does* why Danielsen has to muzzle him."

Bjørn smiled and filled the glasses. "Yes, it's ironic. And I'm sure it's very frustrating for you. But try to understand Danielsen's predicament. The people of northern Norway have the Russians at their doorstep. Murmansk is the largest concentration of military hardware in the world, and it's just over the hills. When the Russians get angry and protest, the people up here get scared, regardless of who's right or wrong. At the present time, the situation is particularly delicate. We've got a misunderstanding of some sort over Svalbard. The Russian Ambassador insists that we're playing with fire on the archipelago, and we haven't the slightest idea what he means. If *that* becomes public, Danielsen is in real trouble, Svalbard being the potential bone of contention it is between Russia and the West."

"What do you care if Danielsen's in trouble?"

"I don't. But you should."

"Oh?"

"Because the message I've been asked to give you is this: If your Institute in any way antagonizes the Russians, your funding will be cut—not reduced, but eliminated."

Martin fished in his coat pocket for his pipe and tobacco. He sighed as he packed the bowl. Suddenly, he was ashamed that he had been so rude, so hostile to a man who was only carrying out an assignment, who had even shown some concern for his feelings. Of course it was wrong for the Norwegian government to interfere in his work, but in politics there were always concessions. After all, he, Martin, wasn't interested in what the Russians were up to. It would be easy for him to avoid antagonizing them. Not that the Soviets weren't as arms-crazy as the West. But they had an excuse. They were responding to the threat from the West, just as they had done at so many points in their history. And that threat was emanating from the Pentagon, the CIA, American industry. That's what the Institute had to make clear, what the people of the United States and Western Europe had to understand. Here in Norway, he had a magnificent opportunity to advance his cause, an opportunity so perfect only a fool would jeopardize it.

He wanted to say something but could not. He lit his pipe instead, inhaled deeply, and stared out into the smoke-filled room. God, he thought, what's wrong with me? I've become so crotchety, so cold and miserable. Perhaps it's the fatigue. Jet lag, hardly any sleep for the last two days, one party after the next, a series of minor irritations. . . .

"Holt," he said, "I've been a prick."

"I'll drink to that," answered Bjørn lifting his glass.

Martin chuckled, suddenly feeling better. "Tell Danielsen I'll cave in to his wishes. You know, Mr. Holt . . . Christ, why are we being so stiff? May I call you Bjørn?"

"Please do, Martin." They clinked glasses.

"What I wanted to say, Bjørn, is that my work isn't really concerned with militarism in the Soviet Union anyway. It's aimed at the United States. Don't know why I made such a fuss about your request in the first place."

"Why don't we not worry about it anymore? Are you free tomorrow evening?"

"I am."

"Excellent. My very dear friend, Christina Sollie, lives in Tromsø. Dransveien 52. We're giving a little dinner party for some friends. Can I expect you around eight?"

"Delighted." He contemplated Bjørn's handsome face for a moment, marveling at the patience behind those cool blue eyes. "Christina . . . is that the friend of yours with the blond hair?"

"Blond she is, but that doesn't narrow things down very much this far north. You're referring to the woman at the reception?"

"Yes, that one."

"No, that's not Christina, but she'll be there too. And if I were you, I'd watch out. She's a West German journalist, she wants to do a story on the Institute, and she'll be out to interview you."

"In depth, I hope," said Martin, drawing on his pipe.

2

Barentsburg

MIKHAIL OBRUCHEV paused on the steps in front of his office building and looked about. At the end of the street, a black cloud billowed as dump trucks emptied coal into a storage bin. Through the coal dust he watched a yellow crane at work on the pier, its mast tottering above the corrugated roofs of the warehouses that lined the harbor. The clatter of machinery came to him in nervous bursts from all directions—from the busy waterfront and from the steep brown hills above the town where the mines were located. The screech of a steam whistle signaled the end of the night shift; a departing ship wailed a ghostly response. He looked up at the sky as he did every morning. It was blue, a washed-out blue hardly distinguishable from the white of the fleecy clouds that thickened to the north and west. Gulls circled and swooped over the harbor, and the light breeze that wafted inland carried no hint of a chill.

It usually calmed him to see how well the city functioned, but not today. "Damn," he murmured to himself, taking a deep breath of the sooty air. He lowered his head and kicked at a pile of filthy snow left from last week's storm. Chunks of ice scattered about on the mud or hit the puddles on the street, ruffling the smooth water. "Damn," he hissed aloud. Monday morning was bad enough without being visited by those KGB bastards from Moscow.

Mikhail Obruchev was the Consul of Barentsburg, a Russian coal-mining settlement on the south shore of Spitsbergen's Ice Fjord. He had lived in the town for the past seventeen years and, since the death of his grandfather nine years ago, had not bothered to return to the Soviet mainland. There was, in fact, no reason that he should have. Both of his parents were long dead, he was not on speaking terms with either of his brothers, and he had lost contact with relatives and old friends. No matter: he preferred Svalbard to any other spot on earth, even the sunny coasts of the Black Sea, which he had once visited during his student days in Novgorod. He was a tough man who thrived on harshness. A fire, a bottle of vodka, a few hearty male companions, five minutes with a woman now and then, a bear hunt—these were his pleasures.

As Consul, he was the highest official in the tiny settlement of twelve hundred souls. He lived in a green stucco house just outside town. It was a bleak, dilapidated structure, but in comparison to the claustrophobic apartments of the lower officials or to the barrack-like quarters of the miners, it was almost luxurious. His work was routine: he saw that the mines were safe and productive, that the Workers' Center offered an adequate variety of entertainment, that supplies from the mainland were ordered in proper quantities. The more tedious tasks he delegated to those beneath him, just as the previous Consul had done. Until now, the authorities in Moscow had intervened very little in his affairs, and this was much to his liking.

He had first heard of Svalbard when he was a child. His grandfather, a self-styled historian with a keen interest in the Arctic, used to take him on his knee and tell him wonderful tales no one else in the family would listen to. The boy's favorites were about the Pomor Russians, who the old man—Russian patriot that he was—insisted had discovered Svalbard long before the time of Willem Barents.

Obruchev had been thirty-four years old, employed as an engineer in the state mining company in Novgorod, when he saw the announcement for a job on the archipelago. Svalbard! The long-forgotten tales of his childhood, tales of hardship, adventure, and heroism, came back to him. He applied and was accepted at once—the sole applicant, no doubt, but his mood was as triumphant as if he had won a competition among a thousand of Moscow's brightest engineers.

For eight years he had worked his way up the administrative ladder of Barentsburg, joining the Party to facilitate his ascent. In the ninth year of his service, he was chosen to succeed the deposed Consul. It was clear that he had the skills needed to govern: coal production soared and complaints from workers all but ceased to be registered in Moscow. After the first year, he was left to his own devices—so much so that he could not determine how his performance was being judged. This annoyed him greatly, and he soon got into the habit of submitting unsolicited reports on almost anything to assure the authorities on the mainland he was hard at work. It was just such a report that was responsible for his current troubles.

Like enterprising men everywhere, Obruchev had sought to turn the privileges of his position into private gain. He had built a thriving little business in timber—a valuable commodity because trees do not grow on Svalbard. The timber came from the Barents Sea east of Spitsbergen, which periodically filled up with stray tree trunks from the logging rivers of northern Russia.

Whenever he decided enough logs were adrift to make a haul worthwhile, he organized his task force. Two helicopters flew from Barentsburg to the floating treasure, fished the logs out of the sea, and loaded them onto a waiting trawler. Back in Barentsburg, the Consul pressed into service the vintage sawmill in a shed behind his house. When he had first acquired the rusty equipment, he intended to produce only firewood. But he was a good businessman, and he was soon looking for directions in which to expand. Not a year had passed before he found his golden opportunity. He learned to position the saws to cut rough planks, and from these he built all kinds of rustic furniture. Perhaps this branch of his enterprise was so profitable because of the surplus of cheap—or, rather, free—labor. When he was ready to manufacture, he replenished his vodka supply and summoned a contingent of workers from the mines. These "productivity trials," as he liked to call them, were carefree, boisterous occasions; no amount of difficult work could convince the lucky miners that a day above ground with a liberal supply of drink was anything but a party.

The chairs, couches, tables, and beds were shipped, along with

15

tons of firewood, to his Norwegian business partners. Payment was rendered in Western goods, with whiskey, vodka, and foodstuffs at the top of the list. The demand for anything made of wood seemed to grow as Obruchev produced, and he might have sold his wares in Barentsburg as well if he had not deemed it too risky. As it was, only his own home contained evidence of his enterprising spirit. The furniture was of his own making, and coal from the mines rarely blackened his hearth.

There was nothing specifically illegal about the timber business, at least not according to the Norwegian law that was supposed to be in force on Svalbard. This was not so with his other business. For the killing of polar bears had long since been banned, and there were stiff penalties for offenders. But the combination of excitement and profit lured Obruchev outside the letter of the law.

Over the years, his drunken polar bear hunts had become a colorful part of the archipelago's folklore. Perhaps it was their longing for good stories that kept the more honest Norwegian officials from putting an end to the practice with a report to Moscow; or perhaps they had a greater stake in the lucrative affair than anyone suspected. In any event, the hunts continued. When the weather cooperated with his moods, Obruchev called his cronies—Nisjezov of the Mines Administration and Belov of the Workers' Center. They would load a helicopter to the hilt with food and drink, fly to some remote area, and kill and skin several of the huge white bears. When they returned, exhausted and hung over, they would transfer the valuable hides to their Norwegian accomplices, who treated them and, in stealthy transactions far out on the Ice Fjord, peddled them to Western tourists.

Of course, Obruchev feared that one day the stories of the hunts would get back to the mainland. Each fall he resolved to mend his ways. But a bottle of vodka and the first rays of the spring sun conspired annually to dissolve his good intentions, and off he went again, with all the exuberance of a naughty child.

These were hardly great offenses. Nor was his relationship with his secretary, Olga Surovsky, who on her first day of work had run her hand inside his baggy trousers while she stood beside

16

him reading a report. Hardly great offenses, especially in light of his flawless performance in more important aspects of his post. But he realized that the authorities in Moscow would take a different view of his petty crimes. Perhaps they expected certain "irregularities" in the behavior of officials stationed at distant outposts, but their leniency had its limits. And he was well beyond those limits, whatever they were. If they found him out, they would send him away. Not to Sibera. That, perhaps, would be tolerable. No, they would send him to some dismal industrial city on the mainland; they would banish him to a factory job—a fate that, for Mikhail Obruchev, would have been worse than death.

He was fifty-one years old and looked his age. He had a massive bald pate surrounded by an even band of closely cropped gray hair, identical in color to his moustache. He was squat and powerfully built, with great rounded shoulders, a protruding stomach, and short legs as stout as the tree trunks he hoisted from the Barents Sea. His eyes were brown and often bloodshot from too much vodka; when he smiled, they seemed to retreat into his skull and disappear, making the two gold teeth on the upper right side of his mouth the center of attraction of his broad Slavic face.

Mikhail Obruchev was not an evil man, at least not intentionally. He was opportunistic, to be sure, crude and, if provoked, sometimes violent. He had a peasant's wiliness and a nasty temper. But there was something warm and a trifle touching about him as well. He was as generous as he was clumsy, like the well-meaning uncle who arrives with gifts for the children and ends by frightening them. And he was a fair boss, a great drinking partner, a good companion. Obruchev was a man's man, and his colleagues on Svalbard adored him.

He kicked the pile of snow once more, glanced under the bell at the brass plate with his name and title on it, and yanked open the door. Olga Surovsky was at her desk. Her smile faded when he mumbled a curt good morning and trudged up the stairs to his office. Christ, he thought, what in the hell does she want? Just Friday afternoon he had spread his coat out on the conference table in the workroom, very politely undressed her, and made love to her for almost half an hour. He had even helped her get back into her clothes and, although he felt silly doing it, escorted her down the stairs to her desk. He should have known better; now she would be expecting the same treatment day in, day out, regardless of the occasion. Why, he asked himself, was it so goddamn impossible just once to be nice to a woman without her chalking it up as a personal victory? Women! They were only good for one thing, and you'd better make damn certain they knew it.

In his office, a copy of the telegram still lay on the desk. His irritation with himself rose, a tide he could not stem. "Fool," he yelled aloud, "stupid, blundering fool."

A month ago, while hunting on northern Spitsbergen, he had come across a supply depot. He found nothing really suspect: food, clothing, snowmobile parts, camping supplies, radio equipment. All of the printed matter he could locate was in German or English, and he concluded the depot must belong to some sort of Western scientific expedition.

Two weeks later, it occurred to him that he had not submitted one of his unsolicited reports for several months. They mustn't think I'm slacking off, he reasoned, as he drafted a routine description of the depot. He exaggerated a few things—the size of the depot, the complexity of the radio equipment—to keep his report from appearing trivial. He sent it off to Moscow, with a note that eavesdropping operations should not be ruled out and that the KGB might want to glance at it. Two days later, he had the uneasy feeling he had erred. The KGB might take the document seriously or, even worse, use it as a pretext for snooping around Barentsburg. When the telegram arrived from Moscow last Saturday, he did not have to open it to know that the KGB would soon be at his doorstep.

He slammed a heavy book of Norwegian mine regulations—a volume he kept in his office because he didn't know how to dispose of it—onto the floor. With clenched fists, he walked to the window and peered out. Just in time.

They approached rapidly along the wooden sidewalks he had ordered built above the muddy streets. Their dark business suits and stiff bearing might have contributed to their anonymity in the capital, but here the unwelcome visitors stood out like emissaries from another planet. From windows, doorways, and street corners along the route to the Consul's office, curious stares followed them. "Mikhail's finally been found out," the townspeople would be whispering. "Wouldn't want to be in his shoes today." The thought exasperated him yet more; he was hard-pressed to control his rage. He began to pace the length of his office, picking up the book of mine regulations and pausing twice to straighten the picture of Lenin behind his desk.

The intercom buzzed.

"Yes?" said Obruchev.

"Mr. Consul," answered Olga, "Comrades Karnoi and Nikovski are waiting to see you. I will send them up."

The stupid bitch, he thought, as incensed by her cheeriness as he earlier had been by her frown. KGB agents barge into the office and she acts like she's dealing with a couple of tourists. He would have a word with her later, on the appropriate way to greet those troublemakers. "Tell the gentlemen to be seated for a moment. I'll call for them when I'm ready."

But the two agents were at his door before Olga could convey the message.

"Good day, Comrade Obruchev," said the shorter of the two. "General Koznyshov sends you his regards." The Consul's heart began to pound wildly. Koznyshov was the head of the entire KGB, the last person in the world he wanted to have anything to do with. "I'm Lieutenant Karnoi. This is my colleague, Lieutenant Nikovski."

Karnoi was a short, wiry man in his late thirties. He had olive skin and black eyes. His hair was combed straight back and glistened like an oil slick. When he spoke, his thin lips drew taut in a faint sneer. Nikovski, on the other hand, was pleasant-looking, even handsome. He had curly brown hair, brown eyes, and a warm smile. He was the same age as Karnoi, four inches taller, and more solid-looking.

"Welcome to Svalbard, Comrades," said Obruchev, trying to sound cordial. "May I propose a toast to your health?"

"*No* thank you," shot back Karnoi. "We must begin immediately. General Koznyshov awaits our report with the greatest urgency, and, as you well know, we must return to Longyearbyen

19

for the flight home. Let us hope our government isn't too long building a Russian airport in Barentsburg."

Just what I need, thought Obruchev, as he led his visitors to the metal conference table in the adjoining room.

"First," said Karnoi, "we wish to convey to you the satisfaction of your superiors. Your duty is to protect at all times Soviet interests on Svalbard, and this you have done most commendably." The agent's high voice and jerky mannerisms revolted Obruchev and forced him to look away. He felt his blood pressure rise as he fixed his gaze on a crack in the mauve plaster wall. "The Western presence you describe," continued Karnoi, "is a serious violation of Soviet interests in the area, more serious perhaps than any of us is aware."

Obruchev dug his fingernails into his arm under the table. This was worse than his worst nightmares. Not only had they taken his report seriously; the top echelons of the KGB were involved. A stupid blunder, his own goddamn fault, and there was nothing for him to do but play along—at least until he could devise a way out. Now he was trapped; the sanctity of his little private world was in danger. He rubbed his hands together just as he did during an unsuccessful bear hunt when he was trying to ward off discouragement.

"I'm glad," he lied, "that the KGB has heeded my warning." He looked at Nikovski and gave a start when he realized he was readying a tape recorder on the chair beside him.

"Yes, yes," said Nikovski. His deep voice was pleasant after Karnoi's grating monotone. "We're waiting for a Norwegian response to our charges. As it was explained to us, it is important that our intelligence people have as much information as possible on the supply depot. General Koznyshov asked us to tape the interview."

"We will begin," said Karnoi. Nikovski smiled as he placed a small microphone on the table in front of the Consul. Obruchev leaped to his feet. If there was anything he could not tolerate, it was some pretentious bureaucrat from the mainland ordering him around in his own office.

"We will begin when I'm ready," he growled, stalking out of the room. The tape recorder hummed on.

He returned carrying a bottle of vodka and a single glass. Still on his feet, he poured himself a healthy shot and glared at the microphone, which looked up at him from the spot where Olga's head had lain not long before.

"Begin," he commanded, crashing into his chair.

Karnoi glared at him. "Comrade Obruchev," he said, "two weeks ago yesterday, July fourteenth, you drew up a report to Comrade Bakalov in Moscow and wisely suggested that it be forwarded to the KGB. In it you state that you discovered large stockpiles of German equipment, including, you write, 'what seems to be some type of sophisticated monitoring equipment, possibly listening devices.' "

"What I stated was that—"

"No need to repeat what's already in the report. We have a copy right here." Karnoi snapped his fingers at Nikovski, who dug into his attaché case, produced the document, and slid it across the table. Karnoi picked it up but did not look at it, as if to imply that he had committed its contents to memory. He continued in a shrill whine: "What you have failed to explain, Comrade, is just how you came upon the site. Quite a coincidence, I must say, for you to be up on the banks of the Wijdefjord. Now, do not think we are asking you this for no good reason. We must consider the possibility that you were directed to the depot in order to distract Soviet intelligence from operations in progress elsewhere."

"I see," said Obruchev. He had to think of an alibi; his mind was blank. If only he could find some way to draw their attention to a set of circumstances that might corroborate the existence of some other operation. But he could only do so with an outright lie. He would leave himself no escape. It would be fatal. The hum of the tape recorder sounded like a roar; the vodka he was pouring into his glass, like water gushing from a tap. Perhaps he should reveal part of the truth. He could, for example, tell them he was hiking when he stumbled across the German supplies. He might be forgiven. After all, there was no law against leisure activities of that sort. But he was quite simply unwilling to give the intruders any satisfaction in the battle he conceived himself to be waging against them. Suddenly, he had an idea. He remembered an American couple who had entered Barentsburg by accident last summer. A perfect pretext for a story the KGB would have difficulty checking. Vodka glass in hand, he leaned back in his chair.

"About four weeks ago," he began, "an American couple—"

"Would you give the exact date, please."

"It was a Saturday evening. Must have been . . . let's see. . . ."

"One moment," said Nikovski. He pulled out a calendar and began counting. "Four weeks ago last Saturday, you say?"

"Yes."

"That was . . . the twenty-eighth of June."

"Yes. Thank you. I received a call from Belov at the Workers' Center. He said two Americans had landed in a small boat near the coal docks and had signaled to some of the workers. Evidently, they had had a mishap and lost their supplies. Belov said the woman looked exhausted and asked me what he should do with them. I told him I would come to the waterfront. He and I then took them to the Workers' Center, ordered them a meal, and sent them on their way to Longyearbyen with some provisions."

Karnoi narrowed his eyes to slits behind the thick lenses of his wire-rimmed glasses. "And what, Comrade Obruchev, gives you the authority to admit Americans to Barentsburg? It's strictly forbidden by regulations. It's precisely the type of slovenliness that Western powers count on in their attempt to destroy us. We should get this matter cleared up here and now."

The vodka had made Obruchev bold. He slapped the table with both hands, causing Karnoi to blink and the microphone and bottle to jump. "You know, Comrades," he bellowed, "the Arctic is not Moscow. The Americans were escorted by me personally to the Workers' Center and back. You see, when people are in trouble up here, you come to their aid. Acting any other way is what arouses suspicion. For example, if one of them had died—"

"Very well, very well," said Karnoi. "We will let others decide on the correctness of your behavior. The tape will be heard by others, including Koznyshov."

Obruchev glowered at him. The little worm, he thought. I'd break every bone in his body if I could get away with it. His eyes returned to the ugly crack in the wall and followed it to the top of the, window frame. Outside, he could see the harbor and the waters of the Ice Fjord beyond. He felt claustrophobic, impatient to get the interrogation over with and take his daily walk about town. Don't get careless, he admonished himself. If you don't slip up, you might take the first round. "All right," said Obruchev, "we will let the others decide. Would you like me to continue?"

"Please."

"During lunch with the Americans, we carried on a conversation as best we could. I speak a very few words of English, as does Belov. Now, knowledge of the English language is not one of the requirements of my job. It wasn't until a week or so later that Belov and I were able to piece together enough of the conversation to figure out what they were talking about. 'Supply depot,' " he said in English. "We kept repeating it, looked under everything we could think of in the dictionary, guessed. Finally we understood—supply depot, Germans, the Wijdefjord. This is why my search and my report came some time after the initial clues were in our hands." Obruchev beamed, pleased with his story.

But Karnoi did not seem impressed. Quite the contrary. He glanced at his colleague; it was time to spring the trap. He said, "In conclusion, we must ask you to describe the type of search you conducted."

A silence ensued during which Obruchev felt a stab of terror. He fought to remain calm. Did they know something he wasn't aware of? Had he made a mistake? "Comrades," he stammered, "quite clearly a search by air was called for." The sound of his own voice relaxed him; he recovered his momentum. "We loaded a snowmobile aboard our helicopter and flew to the west coast of the Wijdefjord. We sighted the depot about forty miles inland. There were no signs of activity around the site, and we found nothing within a twenty-mile radius. Participants were myself, Belov, and Nisjezov of the Mines Administration."

"Did you make any stops along the way?" asked Karnoi.

"Yes, of course. We landed in Pyramiden to refuel and rest."

A triumphant sneer spread over the agent's face. "Comrade Obruchev," he squawked, "our investigation in Pyramiden indicates that on July fourteenth you and your colleagues spent several hours in the Workers' Center pub. It appears that your

23

refueling applied to more than your craft. We have good reason to believe that your heroic mission was nothing more than a chance occurrence, that you stumbled onto the depot while you were on some kind of a drunken excursion. Such grossly irresponsible behavior does not sit well with either the Party or the KGB. Nor does an attempt to conceal the truth through lies."

Karnoi had played his trump card. Brimming with self-satisfaction, he sat back in his chair and smirked. He thought of the accolades with which Koznyshov would undoubtedly smother him upon hearing the tape of this skillfully conducted interview.

But he had underestimated his wily foe. Obruchev stood up and pummeled the table with his fists. "Christ," he roared, "I pray for the sake of Mother Russia that not everyone in intelligence is as naive as you. Something as critical as this search is best kept secret. What the hell did you expect me to do? We had to stop for fuel. Should I have announced with a bullhorn why we were in Pyramiden? Not even Nisjezov was told the objective of our search until we were on the final leg of the journey." He let himself down in his chair, praying that they had not yet spoken with either Nisjezov or Belov. When he looked at Karnoi, he could see that they had not. The agent was flustered. Inwardly Obruchev rejoiced. He was going to survive; these two shitheads from the mainland were being taught a lesson. "Excuse my outburst," he said, feigning contrition. "I took great care planning the necessary stops so that they would stir no suspicion of irregularities on Svalbard. I believe I succeeded."

Karnoi and Nikovski knew he was lying. They also knew that they had been outmaneuvered. There was nothing to do but return to Moscow with the tape and make their suspicions known. Revenge would have to wait.

Nikovski, reacting like a robot to an awkward flip of the hand from Karnoi, packed the recording equipment into its case. They stood up and walked to the door. Nikovski bade the Consul farewell and hurried onto the landing. Karnoi hesitated for a moment, his hand on the door knob, his eyes on Obruchev. "Just one more thing," he said. "You will soon receive a visit. A very important visit from Moscow. Be in your office by seven o'clock Friday morning and do not leave until you have been so advised."

24

3

RAIN was in the air as Martin walked up the steep, twisting road. Faded blue and yellow wooden houses dotted the green hills on either side. High above the town, he looked down at the banks of fog that lay motionless on the bay. Finger-like white clouds raced inland beneath an unbroken gray sky. He turned his face into the brisk northwest wind and felt its dampness on his cheeks and forehead.

By the time he reached the wrought-iron gate in front of Dransveien 52, a light drizzle was falling. The muffled lament of a ship's whistle wafted up to him from the harbor, and from the city came the chiming of a bell tower. He glanced behind the gate. The shrubs, cobblestone path, and garden rocks glistened with a cold sheen, and the moisture painted drooping, mysterious figures on the white facade of the old wooden house. A solitary car drove by, and he listened for a long time as the sounds—the sloshing of tires over wet pavement, the changing of gears—receded into the sodden murmur of the city.

Standing in the rain, the peacefulness of the north about him like a cloak, he vowed that this year things were going to be different. There would be time to live, time to enjoy. He would simply not allow it to be otherwise.

A tall blond woman in her early thirties waved to him from the door. He pushed open the heavy gate and walked up the path.

"Good evening," she said. Her voice was reserved but friendly.

"Bjørn saw you standing out there and sent me to fetch you. I'm Christina Sollie."

She wore no jewelry and no make-up. Her hair was piled casually atop her head in a loose bun. She was dressed in a white sweater and tan skirt that hung limply to midcalf. Martin found her extraordinarily beautiful, her grace effortless and unstudied.

"Martin Dodds. Delighted," he said, searching her green eyes for a response. "Most kind of you to invite me."

She smiled at him, amused. He knew what she was thinking: So *this* was the crazy professor who had scandalized the good citizens of Tromsø at the Institute last night.

"I trust Bjørn's told you about me."

She laughed. "A bit. Now please come in out of the rain, won't you? I've got to get back to the kitchen this second. My friend who promised to help with the dinner is late, and I've got a real logistics problem on my hands."

"Need some help?"

"Don't be silly. Get in there with the others and have a drink." She took his raincoat and umbrella and pointed him toward the parlor. "Bjørn will be down in a second. He's on the phone."

Martin recognized some of the people who had been at last night's reception. But the young blond woman Bjørn had promised would be there was not in the room. His disappointment reminded him sharply of how much he had been looking forward to meeting her.

"No, really, I can't say that I do." Perplexed, Bjørn sat on the edge of the bed. A quick burst of static garbled Marianna's words. "Run through that one more time. This is a lousy connection."

"Mr. Holt, you know I'd tell you more if I could. The Minister simply said for you to be here at eight tomorrow."

"But he just sent me up here to handle this thing with the American. Did he forget, or is it really something serious? Svalbard again?"

"Well, he didn't forget. I'm sure of that. He booked you himself on the last flight from Tromsø tonight."

"Himself?"

"That's right, Mr. Holt."

"Marianna, don't you find that strange? How long's it been since he's lifted a finger to do something he could delegate to someone else?"

"It's strange, I agree. And he does seem upset about something."

"I think I should call him. Is he at home?"

"Probably. I don't know where else he would be."

"All right. Thanks, Marianna. If I don't reach him, I'll be in Oslo in the morning."

"I think you'll be here in any event, Mr. Holt. I'll have the coffee ready."

Bjørn tried for fifteen minutes to get through. When the phone finally rang at Foreign Minister Skogan's home, it took another minute or two for him to answer. Their conversation was brief and tense. By the time he'd hung up, Bjørn had learned nothing; he knew only that he had awakened an elderly man who was in a foul mood.

He stood and straightened his tie in Christina's bedroom mirror, then cast a wistful glance at the big antique bed. Not only was he going to miss that, he mused. There was also going to be a scene. It had been over a month since he had been in Tromsø, and last night had been sacrificed to Martin. He decided to wait as long as he could to tell her.

The rectangular table in the dining room was spread with sumptuous platters: shrimp and mayonnaise, smoked salmon with scrambled eggs, a whole cod smothered in a white wine sauce, herring and sour cream, and a mound of caviar. There were Swedish meatballs in a silver bowl, baskets of breads and crackers, and wines and liqueurs at the small bar.

The evening was proceeding splendidly until Bjørn pulled Christina off into a corner and whispered something in her ear. She grew tense and her tension fell like a pall on the warmth and gaiety in the room. They excused themselves and went upstairs.

Martin settled back and lit his pipe. He was relishing a rare sense of well-being and couldn't have cared less about the concerns of the others. He looked about the room through the big indolent clouds of tobacco smoke he puffed out: a few bright watercolors and a cluster of African artifacts on the white plaster walls, a parquet floor with small but very exquisite red oriental rugs, unobtrusive modern furniture, high ceilings, high narrow windows, an enormous fireplace. He thought: like Christina's style of dress, like the conversation tonight, like Scandinavia itself —modest, uncluttered, efficient, and pleasing. Yes, by God, this was going to be a good year, maybe even a great one.

"Hello, everyone," called a cheerful voice from the kitchen, its owner apparently unaware of the problems plaguing the host and hostess. "I'll be with you in a second. Just one quick phone call."

Martin heard a slight German accent and felt a twinge of excitement. He stood up and sauntered to the kitchen door with exaggerated carelessness. Leaning against the doorframe, he watched her dig around in her purse, shrug her shoulders and, without warning, dump its entire contents onto a counter. Coins, pencils, hairclips, make-up, a wristwatch, and several items he did not recognize landed with a clatter and scattered in all directions. A few scraps of paper fluttered lazily through the air, and a five-krone piece that had evaded her lightning grab fell to the floor, careening to a stop at his feet. He picked it up, inspected it briefly, and threw her what he hoped was a casual glance. She was leafing through a tiny black address book, too absorbed in her search to notice him. He pocketed the coin and watched her furtively as she dialed and talked.

Ulrike: her face mirrored everything. She frowned, her brow furrowed, and her expression grew somber. She laughed—a clear, hearty, uninhibited laugh that seemed to bubble up from the depths of her being. The next moment she looked perplexed. With the receiver clamped between her cheek and shoulder, her arms hanging flaccid at her sides, head slightly cocked, her straight blond hair falling vertical as a plumb line, she sighed almost inaudibly. Then she spoke: softly, intently, her full lips drawn just a trifle taut, her inquisitive blue eyes darting from the window to the coffee grinder to the heap she had spilled on the counter. . . .

She slid her foot under a nearby chair, pulled it toward her, and sat. He watched her, studying the curve of her hip as she flung one leg over the other. He wanted her to stay just that way for a long time, long enough for him to capture an image of her he would not lose: her delicate fingers around the receiver, the profile of her fine straight nose, the muscles in her slender calf flexing slightly as she moved her foot back and forth. Instead, she sprang to her feet. With a curt "adieu" she hung up and began tossing the debris back into her purse.

He circled the counter and approached her from the other side, feeling happily ridiculous as he fished the coin from his pocket and flipped it into the air.

"Heads or tails?" he asked.

She looked up at him, not at all startled. "Tails, Professor. Quite beyond question." She stared at him with mock gravity as he stretched the back of his hand with the coin on it toward her. It was heads.

"I knew you'd try to cheat me," she said, breaking into a grin. "I'm Ulrike von Menck. Nice of you to save me the trouble of tracking you down."

"Tracking me down?"

"Yes. You see, I'm a journalist with the *Zeit.* I assume it's one of the weeklies a scholar like yourself is familiar with?"

"Sure. I carry it under my arm to faculty meetings to impress my colleagues. Works, too."

She pushed the remaining odds and ends over the edge of the counter and into her open purse. "Glad to hear it, Professor," she said ironically. "Without your type of reader, we'd have long ago gone under. But, alas, we're still in business, and I'm up here doing a series on the Cape. I thought it would be a good idea to include something on the Institute for Disarmament. With your permission, of course."

"I'll have to think about that one for a moment. Care for a drink while I mull it over? And something to eat? My God, you came in after dinner. You must be famished."

"A drink in any case, Mr. Dodds, but the dinner I think I can skip. Seven months of shrimp, herring, salmon, and cod. . . ." She looked up at him, her lips rounded to imitate a fish. "Sometimes I think I'm sprouting fins. I mean, the dear girl is a wonderful cook, but, really. . . ."

"What will you have?"

"There should be a St. Emilion around somewhere," she said, nodding in the direction of the bar. "A '73, to be exact. You see, Professor, they bought several cases of it a while back. I've monitored the rate of consumption and found it very low. A consequence of all the fish. There just never seems to be an occasion to serve it. But from time to time, Christina has been known to put a bottle or two of it out there with all that horrid German *Zuckerwasser*. She knows I adore it."

"At your service. I see you haven't limited your investigative talents to journalism."

"It would be a pity, wouldn't it?"

He started for the buffet, trying to piece together a tentative impression of her. She seemed playful, warm, direct. But he sensed other, more complex qualities. She must be extremely intelligent, he thought, to have the job she did with such a prestigious paper. No doubt she was strong-willed, perhaps even a bit callous if you scraped away the pretty veneer. To hell with it: he would just have to wait and see.

"Meet you at the kitchen table?" he called back to her.

"Okay," she answered in English.

"I'm terribly sorry," said Bjørn, standing at the entrance to the parlor with Christina. His suitcase was beside him and his trenchcoat was over his arm. "No, no. Believe me, I tried. He wouldn't hear of it. He even threatened to hang up if I went on. No, Jon, nothing serious, I'm sure. Just the usual minor crisis which requires immediate attention if it's not to grow."

"But can't it wait till Monday?" asked Jon in a slurred and pleading voice.

"Probably. But the Minister's a little overwrought these days. He gets worked up far more than he needs to. Unfortunately, all I can do in those instances is try to humor him."

He lifted his valise and glanced at Christina, who made no effort to conceal her anger. "I'd better be off," he said. "The last flight to Oslo leaves in forty-five minutes. I'm sorry everyone, but I fear the worst if I'm not in my office tomorrow at eight."

Christina glared at him, her green eyes icy. "You tell the Foreign Minister I'll have a word with him the next time I'm in Oslo. This is outrageous."

"Christina, please."

"All right, I'm upset. Do you blame me? Now go on if you must. Take my Volvo and leave it at the airport."

He kissed her on the cheek and headed for the door, exchanging goodbyes as he went. Before he could get past the kitchen, Ulrike lunged forward and grabbed him by the arm. "Christina," she called into the living room. "I'll bring the car back. I want to have a word with this *Lump* of yours on the way to the airport."

"He's all yours," snapped Christina.

The young man named Jon struggled to his feet. "Listen, Bjørn, I'll come along. That way Ulrike won't have to drive back alone."

"Sit down, Jon," ordered Christina. "Didn't you hear her say she wanted to talk to him? I thought I told you to get off her back. Enough is enough."

Jon sighed. Oh, well, he thought, I'll just tell them I followed her to the airport and back. They'll never know the difference. He smiled meekly at Martin, who was standing beside him with a full glass of red wine in each hand. My kind of drinker, he mused, lumbering back to his chair like a tottering giant.

Jon Lellenberg was beginning to detest his new employers. When they had approached him over a month ago, he had taken them for Norwegian tax investigators. How relieved he had been to find out they were only private detectives. They had been friendly and generous. "In a little trouble with the tax people, Mr. Lellenberg? Well, who isn't these days? Now listen carefully. We've got a very lucrative and painless proposal to make you. We need Miss von Menck watched. Watched closely in a way only a friend or acquaintance could do it."

He was in deep trouble with the tax people; the compensation these men offered him was a windfall. Ten thousand krone a month to keep track of a woman he would have given his left nut to climb in bed with. But the "detectives," whoever the hell they were, had turned out to be more demanding than he had anticipated. When he had let her get away for an afternoon, they had paid him a visit at home. He had decided to give up the little game then, for he sensed he had blundered into an arrangement with a couple of very unsavory and dangerous characters. But

31

they would hear nothing of it. He could have more money if he wanted—twenty thousand a month, in fact. But he had to stay with it. He had to or else.

He hadn't asked what the "or else" meant. He had rationalized his consent by telling himself over and over how much fun it would be to pay off the tax people just when they thought they had him by the balls. But now he was tired of trooping around after Ulrike, taking shit from everyone in Tromsø for being the world's number one lovelorn fool. And he was scared.

At least things would be easy tonight, he thought. A private party, no one here to monitor his actions. When she got back from the airport, he would pick up snatches of her conversation here and there. He would also get good and drunk. He knew her habits well enough now to know she would go straight home after the party. As long as he could still walk, he would accompany her. Either at her side if she consented, or a couple of hundred yards back where she couldn't see him if she didn't. The next morning, he would deliver a flawless report, the kind that would keep those two asses from getting weird.

From time to time he wondered who they were, why they were willing to pay so much to have her watched. One of these days when he got up the nerve, he was going to ask them. Maybe they had some ties to the German government and wanted to keep her from writing certain things. Or maybe they had been hired by a jealous ex or something. Oh, well, he thought, scanning the party through half-drunken eyes, it really doesn't matter anyway. As long as they don't start getting weird again like they did at my place the other night. . . .

4

"In a hurry, Bjørn? Perhaps you should let me drive. You know how we drive in Germany. It would be a shame if you missed your flight."

"For Christ's sake, Ulrike, do you have to be so aggressive? Of course you're not driving." He opened the car door for her. She shut it with an angry crash.

They backed out of the garage in silence, but as soon as they were on the open road, she erupted. "Bjørn, you know goddamn well there's a crisis over Svalbard. You don't really believe I'll buy that crap about the Minister's mood. Why won't you even—"

"Listen, what if there is? So what? You go publishing a bunch of irresponsible nonsense and you might really stir something up. Ulrike, listen—"

"Irresponsible, eh? Irresponsible not to want the Germans to start another war? I'd say your values are a little screwed up."

"The Germans? What in hell's name have the Germans got to do with this?"

"Come on, Bjørn, don't play dumb. Don't take me for an idiot. You know as well as I that Arnheim and his boys are up there mining uranium."

Bjørn sighed. "Are you ever going to get over that obsession of yours? Germans this, Germans that. Do you think your countrymen have a monopoly on evil? You don't—"

"You don't know what you're talking about. First, Bjørn, it's not a question of my obsession. I don't even see how you can say a thing like that. Six million Jews, countless others, including—"

"Ulrike, please! I know what you're getting at. But in this case the Germans are not involved."

"You think not, eh? Well, wait until you read next week's—"

He slammed on the brakes, sending her forward. "Look here, I'll not have you publishing one word about Svalbard until this—"

"How do you plan to stop me?"

He pulled off the road and took her by the shoulders, trying to control his irritation. "I'd like to think you'll listen to reason."

"Go on, drive. I don't want you to miss your flight."

"What *do* you want?"

"I want you to tell me everything you know about the Svalbard crisis."

He pulled back out onto the wet, empty road, trying to decide if he should submit to her blackmail. There didn't seem to be much choice. "I'll tell you what I know. But only if you promise not to print anything on Svalbard until we've had a chance to discuss your article. Can I trust you?"

"You can trust me, Bjørn, but you can't censor me. What I'm writing is too important for anyone to tamper with. But if you talk now, I won't publish a word until we've gone over the draft together."

He said nothing.

"Better start talking, Bjørn. We'll be at the airport in a few minutes."

"When will you want to go into print?"

"Depends. On the situation, on how it develops. Also on how long it takes me to assemble my evidence. Now talk, Bjørn. Otherwise you can forget about my cooperation."

Hesitantly, he began to tell her what he knew.

Christina had evidently decided not to let her lover's departure spoil her evening. She was taking part in an animated discussion around the coffee table, laughing, her eyes sparkling. Her cheeks were flushed, and a few strands of yellow hair hung about her face in unruly wisps. She waved to Martin, and he came over and sat down beside her.

34

"A wonderful meal, Miss Sollie. I'm sorry Bjørn—"

"Shhh. Let's not even mention it. Just one of those things a woman who likes ambitious men learns to tolerate. It's hardly the first time, you realize."

While the wine and brandy glasses were refilled, Martin looked around the room to see if Ulrike had returned. All the while he admonished himself to get his mind off her. Christina must have sensed his restlessness, for she tried to draw him into the conversation. "Well, Professor Dodds," she said charmingly, just loud enough to get the others' attention, "why don't you tell us a little about yourself? Where in heaven's name did you learn such beautiful Norwegian?"

"Amazing indeed," chimed in a young man, the only male guest other than Martin who wasn't wearing a necktie. "It's a treat, I must say, to encounter an American who speaks Norwegian fluently."

Martin cleared his throat. "Ladies and gentlemen, it would give me the greatest satisfaction to be able to take credit for my substantial linguistic abilities. But. . . ."

He was imitating Professor Orvik, and those who had been at the reception roared. "Frankly," he continued, this time in his own voice, "I must confess that I'm half-Norwegian. My mother was born and raised in Oslo. Father was working there during the interwar years as a radio engineer. They met and married. We didn't even visit the U.S. until I was three. Mother and I spoke Norwegian until the day she died. In fact, even as a teenager up there in Minnesota where we lived I had ample opportunity to speak Norwegian. There was always somebody's grandmother around from Bergen or Bodø or God knows where who could hardly get out a word of English. Then I spent two years in Oslo as a graduate student and two more as a visiting instructor. And let me tell you something—it's great to be back. It's been almost ten years."

There was a flurry of appreciative nods. Someone was asking him a question when Jon rambled up brandishing an unlabeled bottle. He crashed on the sofa and passed it around. "Yes, sir," he said, "I make the best bootleg in all the northern provinces. The authorities who came by to put me in the slammer said so themselves. Got so drunk, they did, couldn't even initiate proceedings for fear I'd expose them. Yes, sir, swear it's true. I've got 'em wrapped around my little finger."

He gazed at Christina drunkenly. "Say, honey, what's with your little Kraut friend? Running out like that with. . . ."

"Oh, for Christ's sake, Jon. Quit blabbering about Ulrike. She's not interested in you and never will be. Accept it—she's not your type. Or to put it more bluntly, you're not her type."

He grinned like an embarrassed schoolboy.

"Come on, Jon," urged a tipsy middle-aged woman, "don't worry about it. It's time for a story. Pulled anything new on the tax people?"

She turned to her husband, who was cleaning his glasses with his handkerchief. "He's a treat, dear, don't you find?"

"Not particularly," the man said without looking up.

"Matter of fact," bellowed Jon, "I taught 'em a lesson just this last week." His cloudy pink face brightened as he unscrewed his bottle and sniffed the contents. He took a loud gurgling drink and began. But he wasn't more than a few words into his tale when he yawned, tried to get to his feet, then tumbled sideways onto the floor.

"Thank God," whispered Christina to Martin. "It'll spare us having to listen to any more of that."

Martin gazed at the massive figure sprawled out near his feet. "Isn't anyone going to help him?"

"Forget it. It's his normal party posture. He'll be there for hours, harmless and happy. Come on. Let's go somewhere and chat."

"Who is he?" asked Martin at the bar.

"Our mechanic. Not a bad guy when he's sober and not chasing my friends. Bjørn's a born diplomat, and Jon's the only man north of Ålesund who can fix his British car. Bjørn loves the drive up here when he's got the time."

"Does he ever have time?"

"No. But he always thinks he will. Some wine, Professor?"

"Please."

She poured them each a glass of Mosel.

"Skoal."

"Skoal."

"Miss Sollie," he said, ignoring the inner voice that told him he was about to make a fool of himself, "have you known von Menck, the journalist, for long?"

"Why do you ask?"

"From the little I've seen of her, I find her most . . . fascinating."

"That she certainly is. Yes, I've known her long, almost as long as I can remember. We first met back in Gymnasium days. On one of those programs the Germans never tire of organizing. Youth-ambassador summer exchange, or some such thing."

She held her glass to the light for a moment and took a sip. Her green eyes shone warmly when she smiled. "The first day I saw her sticks in my memory as though it were yesterday. I went to the train station to pick up the German girl who was to spend the summer with us. The group had just arrived, and the director, a fat, pompous German, was talking down to the exchange students, lecturing them on how programs like this one were necessary to heal the wounds of war, to teach German youth respect for foreigners.

"Suddenly, a feisty blond girl shoved herself to the front of the group and interrupted. She called him by name, no title, just Herr So-and-So. 'Unlike you and your generation,' she snapped, 'we don't need to be taught how to respect foreigners. As for the war, that was your doing, not ours. These programs are for old Nazis like yourself, not for us. They make you feel less guilty, don't they?' "

"And that was von Menck?" chuckled Martin.

"It was. And she turned out to be the girl staying with our family."

"I see."

"She came back the next summer too. And when university time rolled around, I decided to go to Munich, where she was studying. I had planned to go abroad anyway."

"How long were you there?"

"Oh, God, it must have been almost six years. She and I got involved in radical politics. We became part of a tight little group —all good friends, all idealistic as hell. We thought we'd always stick together. Do with friendship what the bourgeoisie wanted to

37

do with money . . . save it, treasure it, build a life around it. Then we grew up and got practical, as they say. We all went our separate ways."

"But you two have remained close?"

"Quite." Reflecting, she made circles on the floor with her foot. "It was wonderful when she got the assignment to come up here. I was really doubting my own decision to leave Oslo for the teaching job in Tromsø, wondering if I hadn't made a terrible mistake. But since she's been here, things have been better. She's a wonderful friend, Professor Dodds." She paused and looked away. "But I do worry about her."

"Worry? But she seems to be on top of things."

"And usually she is." Their eyes met. "I don't know why I'm telling you this. If she wants you to know, she'll tell you herself."

"No, please. Please go on."

She leaned over the bar and sorted through the bottles until she found the one she wanted. Suddenly, her face saddened. Holding the wine bottle limply at her side, she spoke in a hollow, distant voice.

"Ulrike's not had an easy time of it. You can't imagine what it was like to visit her parents' home. They lived in Kiel. We went there often. It was very painful, unbearable almost.

"I don't know exactly what happened to him . . . her father. First it was something with the Nazis, then the East Germans, then, after the whole family had fled to the West, something else, something more dreadful. She told me once, but she was too upset to finish. It had to do with a mistaken internment of her father by the West German authorities. They had him confused with someone else, an East German spy, I believe. I guess that was the last straw. When I knew her father, he'd already been destroyed. He would sit at the window, hour upon hour, and stare into space." She grimaced, moistened her lips with her tongue.

"He had the most horrible emptiness in his eyes. He seemed dead to me long before his body gave out. Ulrike would sit with him for hours. I know they must have been very close at one time. I think she always believed he would come around. Sometimes at night or in the morning I heard her crying. It was dreadful. I wanted so much to help, but there wasn't much I could do."

"Is he still alive?"

"No. One day he just slipped away. No pain, Ulrike said, and I'm sure no regrets. Things went from bad to worse after that. First it was her mother. She came unraveled from one day to the next. Ulrike took a semester off to be with her, but it was no use. She finally had to be institutionalized. I don't know whether she's still living or not. Then Ulrike lost her fiancé—"

"Jesus."

"*Berufsverbot,* is that something you're familiar with?"

"Vaguely. When someone is excluded from the teaching profession for political reasons, isn't it? One of those dubious laws enacted in West Germany during the days of student radicalism?"

"Exactly. And we *were* a pretty radical little group. Georg was barred from teaching. That's what he had wanted to do all his life."

"And?"

She jerked her head back toward him. "And she found him in his room. Not a pretty sight, Professor. He'd talked of suicide, but . . . but, anyway, she's had quite a time of it. I can't believe how well she holds up. But scars, Professor, she has plenty of them."

Martin took the bottle she was still holding and filled their glasses. He watched Christina intently for a while. "Is she with anyone now?" he asked. "I mean—"

"I know what you mean. No, she's not. I think half the men in Tromsø have tried. I'm talking about intelligent, attractive men too. Jon's no indication. It's *not* a good idea, Professor. Not a good idea at all."

When he saw Ulrike again, she was at the other end of the smoky room, nestled into the recessed well of a window. Her back was propped against the wall and her lovely legs were stretched out on the marble sill. Quickly, he found a bottle of St. Emilion, spilling a few drops in his haste as he filled a glass. Keep it light, he admonished himself, she's not likely to welcome a panting and smitten forty-five-year-old jackass among her suitors.

She was asleep. The air was warm and heavy. He reached gently across her lap to turn the window crank. She did not stir when his arm brushed her skirt or when the stubborn window opened with a pop. It was raining hard now. The staccato of windblown drops on the glass deadened the sound of the party. A slant of gray light fell across her face, exposing the first tiny lines of age around her eyes. He head was tilted back against the wall and her lips were slightly parted. A gust of damp wind blew in from the open window, tousling her soft hair and ruffling the lace of her blouse. She sighed and awoke.

"Your St. Emilion," he said, handing her the glass.

"Thank you." She slid around on the sill and let her legs dangle. Putting the glass down, she stretched her arms above her head and yawned. "What time is it?"

"We could dig the wristwatch out of your purse."

"What?" she asked, puzzled. Then she smiled at him, the same impertinent smile she had given him at the reception.

"It must be close to midnight."

She cranked the window all the way open and peered out. "Must be. Do you realize this is the first night the sun dips below the horizon? It doesn't look any darker out there, does it?"

"Not really. Miss von Menck . . . I thought. . . ."

"Yes?"

"The reason I awoke you," he lied, "was to ask if you wanted that information you asked for earlier. I must be leaving soon." He cursed himself for his clumsiness.

She slid down from the sill and looked at him. "Very thoughtful, Professor. If you're in such a hurry, I suppose we should get right to the point."

"Not that great a hurry. I'm more than glad to discuss with you whatever you wish. Besides," he joked, "I know better than to try to put off a German."

"Careful now. You wouldn't want to jeopardize your already slim chances with the press."

"Are they really that slim?"

"If your last book's any indication of how you plan to conduct the Institute."

"You've read it?"

"Yes."

"And?"

"Professor Dodds, it was a piece of shit."

"I see," he stammered. "Must have been the German translation. You did read the German translation, did you not?"

She smiled. "Indeed I did. But what I'm referring to are oversights and faults that have nothing to do with the translation. Of course, the translation was also bad."

"That's a great consolation. Willing to share your critical insights with the author?"

"Quite. I object first to your naiveté for taking disarmament seriously. But if you insist on fantasizing . . ."

If she only knew what I've been fantasizing about all evening, he thought vengefully.

". . . even a bad fantasy about disarmament would have to include an analysis of the role of the new West German regime. Which brings me to what I wanted to talk to you about. Professor Dodds, how could you be so dense, so blind? Just like—"

"Jesus Christ," he yelled, "we've known each other for a few hours and you've already got total war on your mind. What the hell have I done to deserve this?"

She stared at him aghast, suddenly aware of how the nasty fight with Bjørn at the airport had frayed her nerves. "I'm sorry," she whispered, her eyes lowered. "Of course you don't deserve that. I've—"

But he was not ready for her apology. "Just a minute," he interrupted. "My mistake. How idiotic of me. And how ungrateful. Here I am with an aggressive German and I'm fool enough not to acknowledge my debt. After all, there'd hardly be a job market for us disarmament people without aggressive Germans."

"Professor, that's a mean thing to say. And I apologize, I really do." She seemed genuinely sorry. "Now, truthfully, am I that aggressive? It's what Bjørn keeps telling me, and it worries me to think—"

"Cut the bullshit. You know damned well you're aggressive. If it's any comfort to you, I don't find it that unattractive."

"I'm glad. And you had every right to blast me. I'm very unstrung tonight. There's one thing that upsets me more than any other, and it's been on my mind a lot lately: Germans in world politics."

41

"I can certainly understand that," said Martin, remembering what Christina had told him. "I have problems coming to terms with the role of my own country in the world. Look, why don't we make peace even if you don't believe in disarmament? Want to go back to where we began?"

She was calm now, but intent. "Yes, agreed. Tell me, Professor, were you serious last night when you said your Institute would look into all suspected acts of militarism?"

"Of course." He smiled wryly. "We'll even take on cases brought to us by our detractors."

"Well, you've got a customer. And a potentially very grateful detractor."

"Oh?"

"Listen, to hell with the interview about the Institute. That's not what I wanted to see you about anyway. You saw Bjørn leave tonight?"

"How could I have missed it?"

"You don't find it strange?"

"Things like that are routine in his line of work, Miss von Menck."

"Perhaps. But Professor, I'll tell you something." She paused, biting her lip.

"Go on, I'm listening."

"If it weren't for my friendship with Bjørn, I'd be blowing the whistle on Arnheim right now. Look, there's a crisis brewing on Svalbard. The Russians are irate. I don't blame them. Professor, my countrymen are mining uranium on the archipelago right under Ivan's nose."

She was tense again. Martin could sense the depth of her rage, her agony; he felt a wave of sympathy for her.

"Just listen," she continued. "Don't ask me where I get my information, just listen. Those bastards are at it again. They're Neanderthals, Professor, those new men in Bonn. If we don't stop them, the Russians are going to take military action. I promise you, my dear countrymen are about to plunge us into another holocaust. We've got to do something about it. No one will listen. Not Bjørn, not . . . not. . . ." The life seemed to go out of her. With slumped shoulders, she turned toward the window. She looked out into the night, laying her hands on the marble sill. It was wet with rainwater.

However groundless her claims were, Martin felt it would be both cruel and futile to take issue with her. In the weeks ahead, he would learn just how correct he was. He stood beside her at the window. "And Bjørn?" he asked. "What does he say about this?"

"He says I'm out of my mind." Abruptly, she spun and faced him, resting her hand on his. Her touch, soft and cool with rain, filled him with a desire to be close to her, to kiss away the tears he imagined on her cheeks, to hold her until she trembled with pleasure.

"Professor, I'm asking you to help me. Will you investigate the information I have, even if you think it ill-founded?" Her words were cold, but not cold enough to erase the lingering excitement of her touch.

"Really, I . . . this isn't exactly—"

"Professor Dodds, I'm asking you for a personal favor."

"Yes, of course. Of course I'll look into it. But secretly, you understand? Everything must remain between the two of us. I've already told Bjørn—"

"You mean he's muzzled you too?"

"I guess you could say that."

"Fine, Professor, not a word. This is very kind of you, very kind. I can guess what you think of my contention at this point. But I'm going to prove you wrong."

Her changes in mood were hard for him to keep up with. Now she was happy. Her eyes were warm and her face was open to him.

"When can we get together to work out a line of attack?" she asked.

"How about Sunday afternoon in the Café Norge?"

"For God's sake, Professor, anything but *that*. Sunday afternoon in a café? Do you want me to feel like a fifty-year-old Bavarian hausfrau?"

"Careful, now. I'm not that far short of fifty myself."

She looked up at him, delighted. "How about some place that will make you feel younger?"

43

"Any suggestions?"

"As a matter of fact, yes. The best restaurant in Norway happens to be in Tromsø."

"You're kidding?"

"Absolutely not. I'd love a dinner invitation . . . but not before Tuesday. I'd like a few days to gather more evidence. The place is called the Peppermøllen. It's just across from the Grand Hotel."

"Seven sharp on Tuesday evening?"

"Seven sharp. And, Professor, I really can't tell you how much your help means to me."

When they parted, he stood at the door and watched her walk along the cobblestone path. With her black umbrella held into the wind, she hurried toward the wrought-iron gate, which she opened and clanked shut without looking back. After she disappeared around the wall, he stepped outside and listened to the sound of her footsteps as they faded in the soggy, half-lit night.

5

EARLY the next morning, Bjørn sat behind his immaculate oak desk at the Foreign Office. Looking for a clue to the events that had cut his weekend short, he thumbed carefully through the documents before him. Nothing here, he mused, waiting for the Foreign Minister to arrive.

Bjørn Holt was a civilized man—patient, understanding, and pleasant. He also had a brilliant mind, the type that threatens and offends. But he threatened very few and offended hardly a soul. His charm, sense of humor, and modesty were so unmistakably a part of his nature that one forgave him almost anything, even his intelligence.

It had been less than a decade since he had completed his graduate studies at Harvard. His work had been admired, and he had counted among his friends in the Department of Government students of many persuasions. Whenever one saw pathologically cynical New Yorkers at the same table with bright-faced Californians, it was a cliché that Bjørn must be somewhere in the group. His graduate years were carefree, distinguished, and happy—just as he had expected.

After graduate school, he had joined the Norwegian Foreign Service. He was first sent to Washington, where his resourcefulness and professionalism made their mark. "He's got the Americans figured out," said his boss more than once. "Just goes to show what a Harvard education will do." But there was more to his success than that.

It was during his five-year tour in Moscow that his reputation began to blossom in earnest. Russians and Norwegians alike came to respect him for his honesty, intelligence, and skill as a strategist and negotiatior.

Now, at forty-one, Bjørn was in his second year as chief adviser to the Norwegian Foreign Minister. He lived in a comfortable villa outside Oslo, drove a cream-colored Lotus sports car, dressed very stylishly, enjoyed good food, the arts, beautiful women. . . . But it would be misleading to think of him as frivolous. If anything, he worked harder now than ever. Kristen Skogan would have been hard-pressed to find a more loyal, serious, or competent assistant.

Bjørn was quite content with the course his life had taken. To be sure, he had his regrets, his minor bouts of depression, and an occasional longing to flee from the weight of his responsibilities. But he took such things in stride. "Any game," he was wont to say, "be it life or politics, would be boring without some obstacles."

"Mr. Holt?" said Marianna over the intercom, her voice fresh and clear in spite of the early hour.

"Yes?"

"In already, I see."

"Of course." The clock in his office pointed to seven-fifty-five.

"Wouldn't you know? You've come all the way from Tromsø and still have arrived before the Minister."

"Listen, Marianna, have you found out yet what this is all about?"

"No. But—" The bang of a slammed door reverberated through the intercom. "Good morning, Mr. Minister," he heard her say.

"Good morning," mumbled Skogan. "Is Mr. Holt in?"

"Yes, sir. It's—"

"Good, Marianna. Thank you. Would you be so kind and bring two cups to Mr. Holt's office? And the cakes, did you pick up the cakes?"

"Certainly, Mr. Minister. I haven't forgotten once in eleven years, you realize—"

"Of course, Marianna. How silly of me. Would you cart them down to Mr. Holt's office too?"

"Yes, sir."

Bjørn switched off the intercom and waited. He listened to the Minister's footsteps beat a hollow rumble in the hallway. Odd, he thought, how every little noise seems so loud when the building is empty. During the week, a hundred typewriters clattered, doors slammed, the din of conversation echoed everywhere. And yet one was never more than vaguely aware of the sound.

The Minister knocked and entered. Kristen Skogan was a tall, slightly overweight man in his sixties. Today, as usual, he wore a dark, conservative suit, complete with vest and watch chain. His white hair, thinning on top, was combed back in elegant waves. His manners were impeccable, his bearing formal, his appearance quintessentially respectable.

Skogan was a career civil servant of the old school, nurtured on the tradition of European diplomatic politesse. But while he was no convert to the informal practices of the Foreign Office's bright young men, he accepted the waning of old-world mores with equanimity. He even managed a bit of good-natured irony from time to time. "Well, Mr. Holt," he had said recently, "I saw the spread they did on you in the fashion section of Saturday's *Aftenposten*. Now, Mr. Holt, I've indeed come to view the decline of Western civilization as one of the givens with which we must work. But do you really believe we at the Foreign Office need to accelerate the process by parading our contempt for all the standards of good taste in dress? Honestly, those jeans they showed you walking around in!"

Bjørn had smiled with affection. He respected Skogan and was immensely fond of him. Of late, he had also come to worry about the elder statesman's health, a concern magnified by the closeness of their friendship.

Skogan let himself down in the only other chair in the office, a chrome and leather sling affair he hated. He rubbed his forehead, looking tired and irritable.

"Mr. Holt," he said. "I'm sorry you had to return on so little notice. And I apologize for my rudeness on the telephone."

"Quite all right, sir. If there's a job to do, it must be done. Now what has—"

47

"Just a moment. Just one moment. First the cakes and coffee. You know how the absence of cakes and coffee in the morning can distort and darken one's perception of events."

He smiled at Bjørn, then at Marianna, who had just come in with a tray of pastries, a coffee pot, and two cups. "Thanks, dear," he said. "And can I talk you into one more favor? See if you can get someone to straighten up my study. I spent half the night creating havoc. Mr. Holt and I will want to work there later this afternoon."

"Now, now, Mr. Minister. Do you really believe I'd find someone else to put your study back together when I'm sitting in the room next door doing nothing? Is there anything else?"

"Marianna, you are a treasure. No, nothing else for the moment. As I said, we'll most likely need to get into the Svalbard archive later in the day."

Bjørn watched her slip unobtrusively out of the room. Thank God for Marianna, he thought. The Svalbard archive? If he had to go in there, it would take him a week just to orient himself. God, how many claims for mining operations, how many permits for scientific expeditions must have been filed since Norway was granted jurisdiction over the archipelago in 1920!

Skogan downed his last swallow of coffee and wiped the corners of his mouth with his handkerchief. "It's that Cossack again," he said.

"Ivanov?"

"Ivanov." Skogan glanced at the clock on Bjørn's wall. Then, as if he did not trust it, he pulled out his pocket watch. "Yes, Ivanov. That's why I was in such a nasty mood when I talked with you last evening. He demanded a meeting this morning at nine just before I rang you up . . . sounded like thunder coming through the receiver."

"His Svalbard obsession again?"

"Of course. But now he says he's got something concrete."

"Well, Mr. Minister, we'll get to the bottom of it today. I think I can determine from observing him what he's up to. I had many dealings with him when we were both in Moscow."

"That's what I had in mind, too. But listen, Mr. Holt. You know how he despises you. About the only man I'm aware of whose ire you've irrevocably raised. Some day, young man, I insist you tell me what you did to him during that Barents Sea conference. But given his animosity toward you, I've decided it would be wise to let you sit out today's meeting. Let's not give him any excuses for jumping on us."

"Hmmm," said Bjørn, "I see what you mean. In fact, it's a very good point."

"Look here, Mr. Holt, if we're in agreement on this morning's meeting, I'd like you to do something else in the interim. While I'm in the lion's den, take Marianna with you and collect all of the mining claims and expedition permits we've issued for Svalbard this calendar year. Leaf through them and see if you come up with anything unusual. Ivanov yelled something on the phone about our turning Svalbard into a NATO base. I think we would be well advised to determine exactly who is on the archipelago and for what purpose."

"I'll get right on it, Mr. Skogan. And good luck with the . . . what did you call him? . . . The Cossack?"

"Yes," said Skogan. "And thank you most kindly, Mr. Holt. I really don't know what I'd do without you." The Minister paused. "There's one more thing I wanted to ask you, Mr. Holt . . . can't seem to recall what it was . . . oh, yes. That American in Tromsø, did you locate him?"

"I did indeed. Seems to be a fine fellow. A little bit dogmatic, but you know how academics are. And stylishly anti-American. That much you will have guessed. But I don't think he's completely devoid of reason. No, I don't believe he'll give Danielsen any trouble."

"Well, I certainly appreciate your handling the matter." Skogan glanced at his watch. "The hour of battle has arrived. Don't get lost in there with all those claims and permits."

Mining claims and expedition permits for Svalbard: how clearly those documents revealed the curious international legal status of the archipelago. Svalbard was discovered by the Dutch navigator Willem Barents in 1596 while he was searching for a northeast passage to China. He first went ashore on the southernmost island and named it Bear Island when his crew killed a polar bear. Later, Barents landed on a larger island to the north, which he named Spitsbergen ("Pointed Mountains"). After Barents came the hordes: fishermen and hunters of a dozen nations in pursuit of a seemingly inexhaustible stock of whale and walrus. Nowadays, a wanderer might still stumble upon the ruins of a whaler's cottage above some desolate gravel beach, or the skeleton of a whale. Neither wood nor bone decomposes quickly in the Arctic.

After the whale and walrus had been hunted almost to extinction, interest in Svalbard waned. However, that interest suddenly revived in the last decades of the nineteenth century with the discovery of rich coal deposits. Again, a northward migration was underway, a consequence of industrial Europe's expanding appetite for energy.

Svalbard was a *terra nullius,* a no man's land without any laws to resolve the conflicts among the nations and parties mining there. On paper at least, the situation was improved by the Svalbard Treaty of 1920, a piece of the victors' work at Versailles. The treaty preserved the right of the forty-odd signatory nations to exploit the archipelago's resources and to use the area as a base for scientific work, but it placed the territory under Norwegian jurisdiction. Today a group or nation with interests on Svalbard must register with Norwegian authorities; hence the existence of the documents Skogan asked Bjørn to locate.

The changes brought about by the treaty were in many ways more symbolic than real, and Ivanov's onslaught made this uncomfortably clear. In spite of the formal rule Norway enjoyed over the archipelago, it was the Russians who had settled there in the greatest numbers. Russians outnumbered Norwegians two to one, and they lived in open defiance of every provision of Norwegian law—including the law of taxation.

There were those who argued that Svalbard was more Russian than Norwegian, that it was only a matter of time until Russia made its de facto hegemony official with a military takeover. Yet such voices were seldom heard among government officials. In Danielsen's administration, it was considered a minor treason to mention anything more specific than "Soviet interests in the Svalbard–Norway–Murmansk triangle" or "the vulnerability of NATO's Northern Flank."

,"Thank you, Marianna," said Bjørn. "Now why don't you take off and enjoy the rest of your Saturday?"

"The Minister said he wanted me here."

"I know, but only to fish these documents out of the archive. Now run on. I'll take the blame."

"All right, Mr. Holt. It would be a shame to spend a day like this indoors."

Yes, thought Bjørn, yes it would be. When she had gone he tore a sheet of paper from the note pad on her desk and wrote:

Mr. Skogan,

I assume you survived your interview. I will be waiting for you with the documents at the Café Leopold. If you would prefer that I return to the Foreign Office, please call and leave the message with Alois, the waiter with whom you had the debate about Swedish unemployment insurance last week.

B.H.

"A pilsner, if you please."

"Anything to eat, Mr. Holt? We've got a new man in the kitchen, a Frenchman. A real ass, but he certainly can cook. He makes the best sandwiches you've ever eaten. Guaranteed. My favorite is one he calls a 'croque monsieur.' Just a treat, sir. Ham, Emmentaler—"

"Not just yet, Alois. It sounds good, but it's only eleven o'clock."

"Very well, sir."

Weekend Oslo was throbbing with life under a cloudless azure sky. A steady stream of sun worshippers filed by on their way to the Slottsparken, the Frognerbadet, and a hundred other city parks to soak up the welcome sunshine. Bjørn watched the girls. Not one in the whole town, he thought, who has the legs of Christina. But just the same. . . .

The sidewalks were overflowing with gaily dressed shoppers and sightseers. He listened to the cacophony of languages rising from the crowd like a joyful chorus. Groups of enthusiastic partisans were warming up for the afternoon soccer matches, chanting slogans as they plowed through the crush. Cyclists in smart numbered jerseys darted in and out of the heavy traffic. He imagined Ivanov arriving in his Mercedes limousine with diplomatic tags. What would the old battle ax think of all this youth, all this glamour and nonsense? Did he abhor it or secretly long to be part of it? Or was he so involved with politics that he just did not notice it?

Alexi Ivanov, mused Bjørn, what a strange bird, what an unlikely choice for Soviet Ambassador to Norway. His predecessor had been so refined, so conciliatory. Then one day two years ago, for reasons that were perhaps only now becoming clear, he had been replaced by this vulgar sixty-year-old dynamo from the region of the Don. Bjørn could picture Ivanov in action, consuming enormous quantities of greasy food so that the equally enormous quantities of liquor that disappeared down his gullet would not make him drunk; yelling, threatening, intimidating and, if all else failed, pleading mawkishly; a consummate actor, a formidable negotiator. Bjørn was perhaps the only person in the Foreign Office who had a good word to say about him: Bjørn liked a scrap and relished a challenge, and Ivanov never failed to oblige him.

Poor old Skogan, he thought, sipping his beer as he leafed through the claims and permits. Skogan is a complete gentleman. He's tough, he's quick, he can take care of himself in any situation. But, by God, how it must hurt him to have to stoop to Ivanov's way of doing business. Especially now with his health failing. . . .

The day wore on; the documents revealed nothing that struck him as significant. The heat became oppressive. Bjørn was sweating under his wool turtleneck; the prickly collar annoyed him. He looked with envy at a table of teenage boys. Several of them had shed their shirts and thrown them over the back of an empty chair. Naked to the waist, they laughed, hooted, and swilled beer. I should do the same, he thought. He conjured up a scenario in his mind: Skogan arrives, Norway is under assault by the Soviet Ambassador, the course of history might be influenced by the manner in which Skogan responds. He needs an intelligent arena in which to discuss his alternatives, he needs help from his brilliant young adviser. And what does he find? Bjørn Holt, chief assistant to the Foreign Minister, shirtless in public, brandishing a stein of beer, hardly distinguishable from the noisy kids around him. He ordered a "croque monsieur," still laughing inwardly.

It was four-thirty when Skogan emerged from a crowd across the street. The Foreign Minister looked angry. Ignoring the traffic signal, he jaywalked toward the café and motioned Bjørn to the sidewalk. Bjørn nodded and paid the waiter who had relieved Alois.

"Good afternoon."

"Good afternoon."

The two men walked in silence toward the Foreign Office. The air around Skogan was charged with tension. He did not break the silence until they were seated next to each other in the two leather armchairs in his study.

"Mr. Holt," began the Foreign Minister, "if you've made any plans for this evening, or for the next few days for that matter, I'm going to have to ask you to cancel them."

"Of course, sir. Is it serious?"

"I'm afraid so."

Bjørn waited for Skogan to continue, but the Minister said nothing.

"What did Ivanov throw at us this time?"

"He claims, Mr. Holt, that West Germany is mining uranium on Svalbard. Of all the ridiculous things! And he accuses Norway of being an accomplice! He has given us an ultimatum of sorts: either we get them out of there or, as he puts it, the Soviet Union will take matters into its own hands."

How the hell, thought Bjørn, did Ulrike come up with her information? Of course she always interpreted it falsely, but that uncanny ability of hers was absolutely mystifying.

"Bjørn, you're such a self-righteous fool," she had cried out at him last night at the airport. "If you *really* don't know what's going on on Svalbard, it's because you listen to no one who isn't part of that myopic little team of yours. You're deaf and you're blind!"

He had scoffed at her. Not that he had been wrong. It was obvious that the new administration in Germany would not jeopardize its tenuous position with an act of reckless adventurism. But it was startling that her charges should coincide with those of the Soviet Union. He would have to look into the matter.

He was about to say something, but Skogan lifted his index finger to his mouth. "Shhh," he whispered. "Not a word until we've had our drinks. You realize, Mr. Holt, that events viewed in

53

the absence of afternoon cocktails tend to appear unnecessarily somber. Now tell Marianna I'll have my usual—double Scotch on the rocks. And by all means get something for yourself."

Bjørn sensed that the Minister was dangerously close to the breaking point. When he was like this, a trifle could set him off. Bjørn did not mention that Marianna had left. He slipped into the office and made the drinks himself, fumbling around behind the bar until he found glasses, ice, and Scotch.

When he returned, Skogan was at the window. His hand was on the latch, but he seemed to lack the strength to turn it. Bjørn saw him grimace and totter as if he were about to crash to the floor. He gasped for air, and his face turned ashen. Then, as if nothing had happened, he smiled. Color flowed back into his cheeks.

"Don't distress yourself, Mr. Holt. It's nothing. Nothing at all. A touch of asthma, you know. I used to have it as a child and it creeps up on me from time to time when I'm fighting mad." He brushed Bjørn aside and opened the window.

The warm evening breeze blew into the room, redolent of the city. It brought with it the carefree chatter of the crowds and the din of heavy traffic. Bjørn handed Skogan his drink, trying to hide his distress. It wasn't the right moment to talk of health.

"If they only knew what goes on up here," said Skogan, gesturing with his glass toward the street. He sighed; his brief spell had washed away some of his aggravation. They clinked glasses. "Well, Mr. Holt, what are we waiting for? Let's get to work." He led the way back to the armchairs.

Skogan took a large swallow of Scotch and shut his eyes. He said, "I want to go over the contents of the meeting with Ivanov. When I've finished, we'll see if we can make something of it."

"All right, sir. I won't interrupt."

"Thank you." He wrung his hands and, with his eyes still closed, began to grope around for his drink. "The insults, Mr. Holt. Insults leveled at Norway, at me personally. I find such behavior inexcusable. And the physicality of that man is downright nauseating. Have you ever seen the beginning of a prize fight, the little ritual where the two fighters glare at each other while the referee recites the rules?"

"I have. It's the same look you see when two Harvard law students having dinner together find they don't agree on something."

"Yes, yes. I've heard how competitive it's gotten over there." He opened his eyes and looked at Bjørn. "And that," he said, "is exactly the stare I got from Ivanov when I walked into the conference room. No greeting, no handshake, nothing but that ugly stare. So I thought to myself: To hell with it, he's the one who wanted to talk. If he's going to sit there like a tree stump, I'll just be on my way. I didn't get far, though. I'll tell you, Mr. Holt, it was a real circus. When I started for the door, he leaped up so violently he knocked over his chair. I don't want to speculate on what would have happened if I had tried to go around him and out the door. Perhaps—yes, perhaps—that's exactly what I should have done."

"Jesus, he's really outdoing himself."

"Yes, you could say that. And what worries me is that his rage is genuine."

"Sir, that cannot be. He's a most accomplished actor, but—"

"All right, we can discuss that later. But first let me get to the heart of the matter."

"By all means."

"Our nasty little confrontation at the door put an end to his mute act. He began to shriek that hideous KGB cant of his before I could get back to my seat. 'Why have you not seen fit to inform us of the German mining activities on Svalbard? You know precisely to what I am referring. We will not tolerate a German presence on Svalbard. If the situation is not remedied at once, we will take the matter into our own hands.'

"Mr. Holt, he must have repeated that phrase fifty times today: 'If this is not done, if that is not done, the Soviet Union will take the matter into its own hands.' You can imagine the rest. The Soviets will not allow their security to be jeopardized by the likes of Germany, Norway, or any other of the capitalist warmongers; if we think we can fool him with our soft talk, we're in for the surprise of our lives, on and on ad nauseam."

"Jesus," said Bjørn again. "Did you make any headway at all?"

"On the contrary." Skogan emptied his glass and slammed it

55

on the coffee table, then apologized for acting like a "Cossack." "You know, I used every bit of ingenuity I could to pin him to some specifics: How large is the alleged operation? How did you discover it? Where is it taking place, on which island? What proof do you have that uranium is being extracted? All to no avail."

"But it does seem like the proper thing to have done."

"Proper, Mr. Holt? What makes you think there is a proper way to deal with a man like Ivanov? Instead of answering my questions, he screamed like a lunatic: 'You know very well what I mean! Neither I nor the Soviet Union will be duped by your denials!' Over and over like a broken record. I tried to assure him that Norway had no more interest than the Soviet Union in what he called a 'German presence' on Svalbard. He ignored me. I promised we would give his charges immediate attention. He chided me. Finally, after hours of this, he up and left without a word. In short, not a very pleasant day."

Bjørn fixed more drinks. Skogan thanked him in a weak voice; the description of the meeting had drained the last of his energy. Bjørn did not push the conversation. If the Minister could relax or catch a few winks, so much the better. He watched Skogan settle back in his chair and close his eyes.

The complex design of the oriental carpet in the study suddenly captured Bjørn's attention. There's symmetry and order beneath all that seeming chaos, he thought as he paced quietly back and forth. No, one mustn't allow oneself to be deceived by surface appearances. It was like that in politics, too. Down deep, there was always some sort of internal order; every game had an underlying set of rules. If you wanted to win, you had to discover those rules and play by them. You had to make them serve you rather than the other way around. If you got bogged down in passions and values, you were asking for trouble. He, Bjørn, would unravel Ivanov's motives with cool, rational analysis. And in the same fashion, he would devise an appropriate counter-strategy. Of course it was a game. But it was not one he intended to lose.

He paused at the window. The traffic had died down; the crowds were smaller and more subdued. The breeze carried the first chill of night; the sky glimmered coldly like polished steel. Across the street, a man in a white apron was grilling sausages at a stand. The man noticed Bjørn watching him and raised in succession one, two, then three fingers. Bjørn was about to wave him off when he felt the Minister's hand on his shoulder.

"Son," said Skogan, "are you trying to deny one old man his dinner and put another out of business? Now run down there and pick us up some sausages." He waved four fingers at the man, pulled a hundred-krone note from his pocket, and smiled. Bjørn took the bill and hurried down to the street, feeling vaguely like a kid at a soccer match with his father.

He returned minutes later with the sausages, a bottle of red wine, and half a dozen pastries—the Minister's great weakness. "We must take care," he said, "that our perception of events is not darkened by the absence of certain essentials."

"You're learning," joked Skogan. "Some day, you might yet prove worth your salary." They ate and drank in silence.

Bjørn was making coffee in the adjoining office when Skogan signaled his readiness to begin what they called a "strategy hour."

"All right, Mr. Holt," he snorted, "speed things up out there. It's time we took the bull by the horns."

"I'm on my way, sir."

They resumed their discussion, seated again in the two massive armchairs. "First of all," said Skogan. He nodded at Bjørn.

"First of all, Mr. Minister, there isn't a chance that the Germans are mining uranium on Svalbard. Are we agreed on that?"

"Yes."

"Which leaves two possibilities."

"Correct."

"One: The Russians, paranoid about a German military resurgence, have mistaken a scientific expedition or some other peaceful German activity on Svalbard for uranium mining. Or two: They are using the charge of uranium mining—a charge they know could stir up a good bit of confusion in the West if it became public—as a pretext for pressuring us."

"And why, Mr. Holt, do you suppose they'd want to pressure Norway?"

"Good question. They have only to ask and that weak-kneed Danielsen and his Labor Party colleagues will be stumbling all over each other to hoist the white flag."

"Now, now, this is hardly the time for personal venom. And

Mr. Holt, not all of us Laborites are as soft on the Soviets as you'd like to believe."

"I was half kidding, sir."

"I know. But would you kindly answer my question?"

"Mr. Skogan," said Bjørn, turning to face the Minister, "I'm not sure I have complete confidence yet in my own perception of the affair. But I have been able to come up with only one hypothesis."

"Well?"

"I believe that the Soviet Union is feeling us out. I have the impression the Russians want to seize the islands and that they'll do just that if not convinced we'll fight tooth and nail—fight so viciously that the U.S. would appear utterly impotent if it failed to come to our aid."

"A dismal analysis, Mr. Holt. And one which I share with you completely."

Bjørn was impatient to continue. "Sir," he said, "we must concentrate our efforts on Ivanov, at least initially. He's the one who will suggest to the Soviet leadership how Norway will react to an invasion of Svalbard."

"Exactly. And that is a problem in its own right. What do you know of his past?"

"Before we met in Moscow seven years ago, very little."

"May I fill you in?"

"Please."

"He was captured around Kiev during the German offensive of '41, escaped the same winter from a prison train, and went to work with the partisans in White Russia. He became an organizer of guerrilla raids on German supply convoys—a good one, too. So good, in fact, that the Nazis rounded up the inhabitants of his hometown and shot them. He lost his father and two sisters."

"I see," muttered Bjørn. "Are you thinking what I am?"

"I don't know. What are you thinking?"

"That the Soviet government might be *using* Ivanov. That they've told him the Germans are mining uranium on Svalbard —concocted a lie, if you will, knowing that he will believe it with a passion. This will give the attack he has been directed to make on us the force that only conviction can provide. We, they reason, will perceive the genuine nature of the threat. And we, consequently, will show them how we intend to respond to a Russian takeover of the archipelago. If they sense weakness, they'll strike like lightning."

Skogan grumbled something under his breath and began to gnaw on the last pastry.

Bjørn was wrapped up in his own scenario. "We must act as if we take Ivanov's charges seriously," he went on, paying the Minister no mind. "Otherwise, we'll end by making him even madder. We've got to use every intelligence option we have, including the CIA if it will cooperate, to determine exactly who is on Svalbard and why they are there. We will have to get official assurance from the Germans that the charges are unfounded. And we must avoid leaks to the press. I don't think the Russians will make their accusations public until they have a better picture of how we intend to meet them. But if the whole world is screaming about the Germans, they might see the opportunity to move as too good to pass up."

"Which brings us to your work today. What did those documents reveal about who's up there?" Skogan looked up with a start. "By the way, where the hell is Marianna? I forgot to send her home. Is the poor woman still sitting next door?"

"Heavens, no. I sent her home at eleven."

"Good, good. You are on the ball, I must say. And the documents?"

"There's only one registered expedition now on Svalbard. Wouldn't you know it's sponsored by the German government? It is a very international group of glaciologists. The U.S., Great Britain, etc. They'll be in the northern part of Spitsbergen up around the Wijdefjord until mid-September. Now, Mr. Minister, there isn't a chance that this particular group could have been mistaken for anything except what it is. It's hardly an area where anyone would be looking for uranium. But it would be wise to alert them, to tell them to leave Svalbard as soon as possible. If we're right about the Russians planning an invasion, they're not going to want any witnesses on the scene."

The Foreign Minister drummed his fingers on the table. "No,"

59

he said. "As much as I agree with you that they are in danger, we cannot contact them."

"But sir—"

"I am sorry. The moment we make contact with a German-sponsored group on Svalbard, we will incriminate ourselves in Ivanov's eyes. We must tell the Russians exactly what we know. More we cannot do."

"Yes," mumbled Bjørn, "you're absolutely correct. The game gets brutal at times, doesn't it?"

"Game?" asked Skogan with raised eyebrows.

It was after midnight when they left the Foreign Office. Tomorrow, they would begin to assemble every piece of information they could about German activities on Svalbard. Anything to gain a little time, to deny Ivanov an excuse for lashing out. They would also gather intelligence information about Russian military activities on the Kola Peninsula. But the essence of their strategy was yet to be conceived. For they had to find a way to convince Ivanov that Norway would fight the giant alone if attacked, just as Finland had done many years ago. And that impression would be difficult to convey while Danielsen was spurning NATO and the need for the American nuclear umbrella.

The mountain air, thought Bjørn, will clear my head. He drove away from the city until the roads became narrow and steep. He loved a crisis; the challenge invigorated him. His mind was overflowing with ideas, hypotheses, strategies; the prospect of success mingled with the ever-present shadow of disaster produced in him a pleasant intoxication. He parked beside a noisy stream, lowered the convertible top, and tried to concentrate on the crisis. But Skogan's parting words plagued him.

"I noticed," the Foreign Minister had remarked, "that your analysis tonight contained the following astute observation: Ivanov's beliefs, you said, will give his attack on us 'the force that only conviction can provide.' Now Mr. Holt, it is at times like this when I sometimes ask myself what *your* convictions are. For example, whether you love Norway as a man in your position should? Or whether, were dark days to descend upon us, you might simply up and leave, go back to the States, to Canada, to

Latin America? It would mean a lot to me to know that you shared my own dedication to this land, Mr. Holt, because this crisis might place a greater responsibility on your shoulders than you realize."

PART TWO

6

THE STREET where Martin found the Peppermøllen
is typically Norwegian: some of the buildings are very old and
charmingly rustic; some are stunningly modern. The Peppermøllen was once an apothecary shop. On the ground floor there is a
crowded oyster bar, and at the top of a slanting, creaky staircase,
in a maze of small rooms where generations of chemists, their
wives, and children had lived, is the restaurant. The old wooden
building still holds the lingering warmth of its past.

At the bar, Martin sipped his whiskey. He wore a tattered
sports coat and yellow wool turtleneck. His hair was shaggy, his
shoes scuffed . . . hardly the Norwegian idea of how an interna-
tionally renowned scholar should dress. Yet, for all his indifference to how he looked, he was a very handsome man. He had a
high forehead, thick brown hair going gray at the temples, and a
fine, aquiline nose. His smile was irresistible, and when he was
amused his brown eyes danced with wit and warmth.

He looked around—no sign of Ulrike yet. Summoning her
image, he recalled the pretty stranger as he had first seen her at
the reception. She was walking away from him, her dress clinging
to the backs of her legs. He saw her on the phone at Christina's:
a vibrant woman with honey-blond hair. The images multiplied.
He recalled her as the angry fanatic, her penetrating blue eyes on
him as she attacked; as the demure coquette begging forgiveness;
as the impertinent and supremely self-assured beauty. . . .

He was about to order another drink when he saw her come

in. Her hair was tousled from the wind, a few strands blown forward into her face. With a quick motion of her hand—a gesture that was brisk and blasé at the same time and seemed to capture a very essential part of her—she brushed the hair away from her forehead.

She carried a trenchcoat over her arm. From the same shoulder hung her big leather bag, with whose contents he felt oddly acquainted. She wore a lavender blouse with elbow-length sleeves, which followed closely the lines of her breasts and shoulders. A slender gold necklace sparkled when she moved under the light. Her flowered skirt hung loosely over the tops of her tan leather boots. He found her more beautiful than ever.

She stopped the busy maître d' and spoke. He took her coat, looked at her keenly and, after a moment's pause, pointed to the bar. Martin stood up, bumping into the man beside him, and waved. She started forward without a greeting. They met in the center of the room.

"Forgive me, Professor," she said, approaching with her hand out. "Punctuality isn't one of my virtues."

"Are you late? Didn't even notice. Nice to see you again." He shook her hand warmly.

"Let's get a table," she said. She seemed preoccupied.

"Something wrong?"

"Svalbard. It's even worse than I had expected."

The walls on three sides of the tiny dining room were lined with large photographs of the great arctic explorers whose expeditions had left from Tromsø in the days when the Peppermøllen was still dispensing syrups and pills. The rugged faces of the men, framed in great fur hoods, stared harshly into the room, as though reproaching the diners for their easy lives. The wooden walls beneath the pictures were painted a deep rich red; above, they were covered in a soft, green, flowered cloth.

They sat at a small table on the windowed side. Ulrike pulled back the curtain and peered out. He watched her fingers play with the white lace.

"Take a look at this, would you?"

She opened the curtain further, and he leaned forward to get a better view. Three swans were gliding about on the silvery water of a pond in the park below. A group of children stood on the bank, laughing and tossing them morsels of bread. A narrow slice of harbor was visible through the trees—a tangle of masts, cranes, and smokestacks. Between islands in the bay, languid banks of fog had settled in. The sky was colorless and dreary; the dying sun struggled to pierce the high overcast.

Georg, her former fiancé, was still on her mind. Yesterday would have been his thirty-fifth birthday. She had spent a night of bittersweet remembrances interspersed with periods of rage. The rage was directed at *them*—those Germans she held responsible for the deaths of her fiancé and her father, those Germans who now were in power in Bonn and were perpetrating this latest outrage. Those Germans, the other Germans, the bad Germans. For her they had become a symbol of all that was despicable in this world. And her private struggle against them was consuming her.

It had been a hot intense rage, and at moments she had felt as if she would explode or go mad in some unbearably grotesque fashion. But when her rage had subsided, the memories returned, poignant and shattering.

She recalled moments of closeness when he had looked at her fondly while she teased him. Then the wild, burning moments of sexual release; or the warm, close mornings in bed together drinking the strong coffee he loved and reading the newspapers while the snow fell softly outside.

Her isolation in Tromsø, she knew, had increased her feelings of loss and emptiness. There was Christina, thank God for that. And Bjørn, too, when he could get away from Oslo. But the others—Christina's friends, university and government people, local journalists—all very pleasant, meant little to her. And this new thing with Jon following her around was just depressing.

Last night, in the throes of a passionate memory, she had made a firm decision: she must force herself back into the normal world of men and women. Her life had been tragic, the global political situation was tragic, the bastards in Bonn were preparing still another tragedy. But, in the name of God, must she continue down a road that promised only more loneliness and despair? No, what she had been doing was self-destructive, understandable but perverse. With the passage of time, her stifling sense of loyalty to

67

Georg had become ridiculous, a transparent defense to shield herself from new wounds. Certainly, he would not have wanted it that way.

She had thought about *him* that night, too, the professor at Christina's party. An odd man, a playful man, and someone who seemed to have both the toughness and flexibility to withstand her savage swings of mood. To her surprise, she had even imagined herself lying naked beside him, and her body had tingled at the thought of his hands touching the inside of her thighs.

She was nervous about seeing him tonight. Perhaps it was only the startling new information on Svalbard and her dangerous plan to confirm what she now knew. She would have to talk to him about it. If he ridiculed her, she sensed how violently she would react. But perhaps it was something more, her premonition that if he treated her in a certain way, she would let him come closer to her than any man since Georg.

She let the curtain fall and turned toward him with her eyes lowered. She ran her fingers across the linen tablecloth. "It's so deceptive. You look out on an idyllic landscape like that and you begin to believe you're in a more hospitable region. Denmark, Austria, England, perhaps." She looked at him sadly. "But when the darkness comes, you think you're on another planet. I do dread it, Professor. One black winter was quite enough."

"You're staying the winter?"

"It certainly appears so." She was about to add something when the waiter, a small lithe man with bony cheeks and a black moustache, appeared at the table.

"Good evening," he sang out, his accent unmistakably Italian. "An aperitif?" His eyes remained on Ulrike a bit too long.

"Yes, Dubonnet," she said. "On the rocks and with a twist."

"Likewise," said Martin. "And please bring us the menu and wine list. We'll want to order shortly."

The drinks and menus arrived. Her earnest eyes on Martin, Ulrike took a swallow of Dubonnet. "And, Mr. Dodds, I must stay because my countrymen are on the brink of—"

He was determined to steer her away from politics for as long as possible. It would be risky to oppose her, that much he knew from the party at Christina's. But his instinct told him that their relationship wouldn't go anywhere if he allowed it to be smothered by her obsession.

"Please," he interrupted, "can't we postpone business until after dinner? You do realize it isn't every night I have the good fortune of dining with a beautiful woman? And please, Ulrike—call me Martin."

She swished the ice around in her glass, perplexed. To his surprise, she said, "Of course."

He ordered her another drink. She smiled at the Italian waiter, who was causing quite a stir across the room. With graceful gestures, he prepared a chafing dish and poured hot Pernod over shrimp in the copper skillet. The flames leaped into the air; the young Norwegian couple at the table giggled shyly.

"This is lovely," said Ulrike. "The smells, the colors, that marvelous Italian's strutting around. God, how I miss the Mediterranean. Silly of me, isn't it? But do you realize, Martin, that I've been stranded up here since January?"

"That's a long time. Shall we order?"

"Yes, let's do." Suppressing a sudden urge to laugh—for what reason she didn't know—she propped her menu against the window sill where they both could see it. "Let's have something exquisite. We deserve it. We've got a long evening ahead and a lot to discuss." All the while she did not take her eyes from his face.

Their waiter brought the second bottle of Pommard with the châteaubriand. Ulrike seemed to have forgotten Svalbard completely. She ate and drank lustily.

After devouring her sherry cream dessert like a greedy, happy child, she spoke of Georg. Smiling, she described the first days of their long relationship. She hadn't talked about him to anyone, not even Christina, but once the dam burst, she could not stop.

"Do you believe," she said, turning the empty wine glass in her hand, "that the stodgy old moralist refused to sleep with me that whole first year we were together?"

He filled her glass, amused and a little shocked at her frankness. "Saving himself for better things, I take it?"

"Indeed. And he didn't relent until we went to Italy together for the summer. Italy, wouldn't you know it? He was a model of self-control in Germany, but as soon as we crossed the Alps he went wild!"

"The south does loosen one up. . . ."

"And we Germans have a problem dealing with that. We go there to revel in what one of our poets called its 'sweet sensuality' and end up feeling overstimulated and lascivious. We don't know whether to rejoice or crawl back home and do penance. With Georg, it was terribly funny. Our first time was in a little pension in Verona. Afterwards he growled a lot about Southern decadence. I really thought I'd die laughing. He dozed off for a while and when he awoke . . . well, you know? It was so new to him to be unable to control his emotions with an act of will."

"The poor boy."

"I couldn't resist a joke, he had been so delightfully absurd. I said, 'No, Georg, not again, I'm a reformed woman. You've convinced me it was depraved. Besides, I don't want to contribute to your moral downfall.' "

"Was he angry?" asked Martin, laughing.

"Oh, no. Heavens, no. He simply tried to attack the problem *intellectually*. I knew just what he was thinking: Faust. You see, we had all studied *Faust* at the Gymnasium until we knew it by heart. The soul strives upward, the body downward, and Faust, poor wretch, realizes he is a victim of this dilemma and must suffer into all eternity. So there he sat, convinced of his own damnation. We Germans and our philosophy. We really are hopeless."

"Yes. That you are," he said, bemused. "Don't leave me hanging. What happened?"

Her cheeks glowed from the wine. She grinned, brushing the hair from her forehead. "I stretched out beside him and put my hand on his knee and asked him nonchalantly what he was thinking about. 'Faust,' he said. He sort of giggled at himself, then we both started to laugh and then we made love. We stayed the rest of the summer in Italy. It was the happiest time of my life."

She paused and stared at her hands. "You know, Martin, he was the serious type. He worried even when there was nothing to worry about, and when there was, things got very bad. I steered him away from his *Weltschmerz* whenever I could. I almost had to teach him what was fun, what was beautiful in life as opposed to what was beautiful in art and literature. But when he had learned to appreciate something sensual, I think he enjoyed it more deeply than most people. Lovemaking, nature, food, luscious indolence. . . .

"He sounds like a wonderful guy."

"Yes, he was. What happened to him was a tragedy, one from which I fear I'll never recover. But of that we'll talk another time. It's much too pleasant an evening."

Martin feared she would become sad, but she remained cheerful. He told her a little about his career: the bitter Cold War years when he had been harassed and even branded as a traitor; the sixties, when he had made his mark as a champion of the new humanism in international politics; the seventies, when the warnings of the disarmament people had fallen on deaf ears; and now his struggle to make people aware of how dangerous the new arms race was. He skirted the subject of his failed marriage deftly, then regaled her with funny stories about the Scandinavian community in Minnesota where he had grown up. The feeling between them was warm and light-hearted.

The espresso arrived. Their eyes met over raised cups. For a long time she did not look away, and in her gaze he saw a flicker of desire. He recalled Christina's words and wondered if it were really true that she, Ulrike, had had little interest in men since Georg's death. Already, he felt protective toward her, as though he must shield her from himself. The evening had gone well, better than he had dared hope. But now things were moving too rapidly; he felt uneasy.

"It's been wonderful to get to know you a little in such an informal way," he said.

She smiled broadly. "I couldn't agree more."

"Well, what do you say? Shall we talk about Svalbard?"

She didn't answer but pulled back the curtain and twisted in her chair to face the window. The park and harbor had disappeared in a heavy fog. Patches of condensation had formed on the glass, and the tiny drops glistened in the candlelight. "That helps," she said listlessly. "A reminder we're on the seventieth parallel where all is not rosy. It was a pleasant escape, Martin."

When she looked at him again, her expression was almost hard. She needed only to think about Arnheim's plans to secure an independent supply of uranium for Germany to bring her blood to the boiling point.

"Martin, I told you I worked for the *Zeit*. Perhaps you should know that this isn't my only professional liaison."

"Oh?"

"I also write for the *Frankfurter Rundschau.* Georg's brother is editor for foreign affairs. Helmut Griem. Perhaps you know the name?"

"No."

"You're familiar with the paper, though?"

"Unfortunately not."

"Shame on you. It's the only reputable leftist daily in West Germany. Even gave your book a decent review. It's been under a hell of a siege since Arnheim and his Conservatives came to power."

"Does your working there have anything to do with Georg?"

She sat up straight in her chair. "Maybe I was paying homage at the beginning. But Martin, it's been almost four years since his death. Yes, his death. I didn't intend to mention that tonight, but *la voilà.* No, that's not it. It's a case, a quite clear case, of my believing in what the paper is trying to do. We offer the type of resistance to a thoroughly evil regime that my knee-jerk liberal colleagues at the *Zeit* cannot. For want of courage, if you wish my opinion."

"And how do the knee-jerk liberal colleagues respond when they see your pieces appearing elsewhere?"

"They don't. I write under an alias," she said, coolly matter of fact. "Not even Bjørn and Christina know."

"Why, may I ask, are you telling me? You hardly know me."

"Because, Martin Dodds, I need your help. There is no one else I can turn to. Under our noses here in Norway the Germans are about to start a war. A war, do you hear me? There isn't a soul in the entire place who will listen. Self-deception goes hand in hand with fear."

The Germans in world politics: as he had seen at Christina's, the mere mention of it triggered a rage in her so violent it blinded her to all else. He saw the same Sibyl-like transformation he had witnessed earlier. Her features hardened, her lips grew thin and tight, her anger filled the space between them like the churning water of a cataract.

"The important thing about my working for the *Rundschau* is the contacts."

"Oh?"

"Yes. Sources from outside Germany."

"I'm afraid I don't quite follow."

"From East bloc intelligence organizations, if we want to be precise. You know how the East bloc countries suspect Arnheim." She had turned inward again, as if Martin no longer existed. "Some of what we receive is garbage. Small-time functionaries after a little Western money. But some of it isn't. One contact has been especially trustworthy, and he's the one who is my source on the Svalbard affair. Of course, I need indisputable facts before I go public. The *Rundschau* won't risk printing the story unless it's properly documented. Anyway, it's our best chance to enlighten the German people—assuming they want to be enlightened— about Arnheim."

She was so disturbed she seemed on the verge of losing control. Martin wanted to help her, to calm her. He hardly recognized her any longer; the demons of her past had taken possession of her.

"Dodds," she blurted out.

"Hush, not so loud."

"It's a fact," she cried, fighting to keep her voice down. "A fact. The Germans are up there mining uranium. The Russians have found them out. They're not going to take it sitting down. They'll invade, Martin, I swear to God they'll invade!"

A shocking piece of information indeed, but not shocking enough—even if it were true—to diminish Martin's concern that he bring Ulrike back to her senses. He attempted to distract her with irony and committed a monumental blunder—his first and last on the issue of Svalbard.

"Then, my dear," he quipped, smiling a wry smile that deepened the crow's feet around his eyes, "your problem is solved. Let them invade. The Russians will know damn well how to put an end to Arnheim's adventurism."

She looked at him, too stunned to speak. Her hurt was all the deeper because she liked him. Or thought she did. It seemed an act of incomprehensible brutality that he should attack her in this way. Just an hour ago she had begun to tingle with excitement. She was going to try at last to sleep with another man. Her fear had vanished; she had let him come close to her, at least in her fantasies, and had experienced only pleasure. And this was her reward.

Martin saw his mistake. Horrified, he tried to stammer an apology. But he was too late. She jumped to her feet, enraged.

"I was a fool," she hissed, glaring at him. "You're a pig like all the rest. No, worse. Worse because you're false on top of everything else."

She turned to walk away. He grabbed her by the wrist and held her. "Pig," she shrieked, wrenching herself free. A shocked silence filled the dining room. He leaped up and caught her from behind, holding her so tightly by her shoulders that she could not escape.

The Italian waiter rushed up with a colleague. "Something no good, Signor? Something we can help?"

"Yes, indeed," said Martin, smiling politely as he held her with an iron grip. "It's the espresso. My wife is upset about the espresso." He put the emphasis on "wife" hoping that the marital status would make their quarrel less interesting to the onlookers. "She's very temperamental and she finds bad coffee a terrible insult coming on top of such an exquisite meal."

The waiter looked Ulrike over from head to toe, torn between anger and incredulity. Martin felt her go limp. She seemed to recover a little of her composure. She nodded. The waiter seized her demitasse—which for some inexplicable reason was empty—and stalked off, muttering under his breath.

Martin pulled out her chair and stood over her as though she might bolt. He put a hand on her shoulder, more gently this time, and touched her hair. She turned toward the window, staring at the drawn curtains.

"You're crazy," she whispered. "Absolutely insane."

Martin shrugged his shoulders and sat down again. "How about a good cognac? It makes me even crazier."

"Thanks, but—"

74

"Tell me, Ulrike, who *is* that man who's been staring over your shoulder at me all evening?"

Puzzled, she twisted around, shuddering involuntarily at the grizzled face and intense eyes in the photograph behind her.

"You really don't know, Herr Professor?"

"I really don't."

"Roald Amundsen," she said, feigning indifference. "Discovered the magnetic North Pole, starting from here. First man to reach the South Pole. Sailed over the Polar Cap to Alaska once in a dirigible. He finally met his end trying to rescue his rival explorer, Nobile."

"Whereabouts?"

"Svalbard," she answered angrily.

7

MIKHAIL OBRUCHEV sat brooding in his office, the state of his nerves going from bad to worse. Typical, he mused. Typical of those KGB bastards to keep you waiting, to let you stew in your own anxiety. "Be in your office by seven o'clock Friday morning," that little worm Karnoi had admonished him, "and do not leave until you have been so advised." Well, he had been here since seven, pacing around like a fool. What was he supposed to do about lunch? It was almost noon and his colleagues at the Workers' Center would be expecting him. He had a good mind to defy his "orders" and join them. An important visit from Moscow? Probably another team of pipsqueaks sent up to make things difficult for him. If they had the gall to keep him waiting for five hours, let them come and look for him. For Christ's sake, he was the Consul of Barentsburg. Why should he let himself be shoved around?

A knock at the door put a quick end to his momentary bravado. "Yes?" he bellowed, trying to disguise his fear.

"Mikhail, it's me," said Olga Surovsky. "Please come and let me in. I've got my hands full."

He stalked to the door and opened it. Her smile irritated him. Didn't she have the sense to understand his predicament?

"I thought you might be getting hungry," she said, handing him a tray of sandwiches, which she balanced on one hand. "And coffee, too, Mikhail. See here. I've made you a whole pot of fresh

76

coffee. I heard that man telling you the other day to stay in your office on Friday."

Olga Surovsky was a hefty woman of twenty-eight. Before coming to Svalbard, she had lived all of her life in an industrial suburb of Leningrad. But with her high cheekbones, jet-black hair, and dark eyes, she looked more like a gypsy than a city dweller.

Obruchev stomped to his desk with the tray. She followed with the coffee pot, careful to remain as unobtrusive as possible.

The telephone rang. "Answer it," he barked, glaring churlishly at her.

Olga picked up the receiver and listened for what seemed a long time. "Please," she said, "wouldn't you repeat that to the Consul? He's in his office. I can connect you at once." But the caller had already hung up. She put down the receiver gently.

"Well?"

"Mikhail . . . I—"

"Speak up, goddamnit. What the hell is wrong with you today?"

"Mikhail, that was . . . General Koznyshov." She looked at him, aghast. "Oh, Mikhail, what have you done? Mikhail, I'm so afraid."

Stunned, he dropped into his chair. "Can't be," he whispered. "Koznyshov? Koznyshov phoned here?"

"And, Mikhail, he acted so odd. He said you were to meet him in your home in an hour. Why would he want you to. . . ."

"I'm done for," mumbled Obruchev, "done for." He glowered at his secretary, fists clenched. "It was those filthy little bastards who were here the other day. Do you understand me, Olga Surovsky? Those filthy little KGB bastards. They laid a trap for me with their tape recorder."

Had Obruchev been thinking clearly he would have recognized his good fortune. For the head of the entire KGB, one of the most important and feared officials in the Soviet Union, would hardly come all the way to Barentsburg to punish a middle-level functionary. But he was far too agitated to be lucid.

Olga moved close to him and tried to draw his head against her chest to comfort him. But he was already in the throes of a blind rage. He leaped to his feet, shoving her away with such force that she almost fell. His right hand raised above his head, palm open, he started toward her. She was too terrified to move. In the last second he came to his senses, grimaced, and slapped his thigh with an awesome blow. The sound reverberated in the room like a gunshot; the sting spread to his loins. His rage turned to frustration, then to uncontrollable desire. He shoved her against the wall and thrust a hand under her skirt. The more she struggled, the more excited he became. When she began to respond, he dropped to his knees and, gripping her buttocks, dragged her down to the floor beside him. There was no time to undress, to spread a coat across the cold linoleum, to extinguish the bright overhead light that shone directly into her eyes. . . .

He left her at her desk, weeping inconsolably, and walked out onto the street. The driving rain that had begun to fall the previous night stung his bald head and sent streams of water down his forehead and cheeks. He waited to open his umbrella, hoping the cold would ease his nausea. Lifting his eyes upward, he watched the monotonous drift of the rain clouds as they hurried southward over a frothing gray sea. Then he took a deep breath and trudged off to his home along the familiar half-mile path he feared he might never walk again.

Obruchev's green stucco house on the outskirts of Barentsburg was as drab inside as out. The living room was dominated by a large hearth on the north wall whose stone facade was blackened by the soot of many decades. When the fire was not burning, the hearth resembled a great, shadowy cavern. On the scuffed and lackluster linoleum floor was a polar bear rug, the fur soiled and matted from years of wear. Around the rug in a semicircle stood the monuments to his entrepreneurial spirit: a sofa, two large chairs, and a coffee table—all of roughly hewn pine. The cushions on the sofa and chairs had once been bright yellow, but had long since faded into a lifeless ash gray.

Obruchev went straight to the kitchen and downed a quarter bottle of vodka. His eyes closed, he waited for the warmth from the alcohol to spread across his chest and down his arms and legs.

Was there really no hope for him? No hope whatsoever? He set a teakettle on the stove, shed his wet clothes in the bathroom, and dressed in his only suit—a double-breasted antique with baggy trousers.

Time was growing short. He hurried into the living room to see what might need doing. But he saw instead how futile it would be to lift a finger. Everything incriminated him: the rug, the furniture, the split pine logs that lay in a neat pile beside the hearth. As he built a fire, his hands trembled. He returned to the kitchen for another drink.

From the window above the sink, he saw a lone man approaching the house. Koznyshov looked like anything but the terrifying martinet the Consul had imagined. He wore an elegant English-style trenchcoat, and from the looks of his shoes and his trousers, he was in civilian dress. His gait was relaxed, almost insouciant, and he appeared to be whistling.

Obruchev rushed to the front door and opened it. "Good day, Comrade," the General called out in a pleasant voice. "Sorry to keep you waiting in your office this morning. We were unable to get through to you earlier because of the storm." He bounded up the steps and embraced the bewildered Consul. "I'm General Koznyshov. Delighted finally to make your acquaintance. We in Moscow give you boys out on the front line too little credit."

Obruchev mumbled an awkward greeting, ushered Koznyshov inside, and took his coat and umbrella. The General smiled at him with a calm, reassuring smile, then nonchalantly looked around the living room. He was a tall, handsome man about ten years the Consul's elder. With his trim physique, artfully cut dark hair, and well-tailored vested suit, he could have passed for a film celebrity.

Koznyshov did not wait for an invitation to sit; perhaps he sensed his host's clumsiness. He strode directly to the chair nearest the fire and let himself down. "Fine weather you've got up here, Consul," he said, rubbing his hands together. "Don't know how they got around on such days in Barentsburg before you had those wooden sidewalks built over the mud." He smiled up at Obruchev, who was standing in the doorway to the kitchen at a loss for what to say or do. "Well, let's not waste any time getting that vodka out here, my friend. And some hot tea as well. I see you've got the water boiling already. Most thoughtful, indeed."

Obruchev took refuge in the kitchen. As he fumbled with cups, saucers, sugar, lemon, vodka, and glasses, he tried valiantly to compose himself. When at last he arrived with the tray, Koznyshov was making notes on a scrap of paper. The General looked up, waving his pen like a small conductor's baton.

"Thank you, Consul. I've been looking forward to this ever since we lifted off. Hell of a helicopter ride it was across the Barents Sea. Felt too wretched even to take a drink." Koznyshov helped unload the tray. "Just let me jot this last thing down," he said. "I was watching you out there making tea. That's when it struck me. What your otherwise delightful home is missing is a samovar. We'll get it taken care of at once. When this whole mess with Svalbard blows over, we'll get one sent up. I'm writing a memo this minute. You see, Consul, I like to do things on the spot. Don't care for procrastination."

He folded the paper and stuffed it into his breast pocket. "That aide of mine, he's always on the lookout for those things. The real old ones, you know, from the days when power and luxury went hand in hand. Brutal days for the masses, of course, Consul. But they did have their charm."

"Thank you, sir," said Obruchev, more perplexed than ever. He poured the tea and vodka. They toasted one another and drank.

"Smoke?" asked the General after the third round of drinks.

"Yes, sir."

Koznyshov tossed a light blue package of cigarettes onto the table. "Try one of these. Gauloises. French. You see, Comrade, we've come a long way in the Soviet Union. Used to be we were too insecure to admit that certain other peoples did certain things better than we. Today, we admit, give credit where credit's due. Admit and enjoy. I find that a much healthier attitude, don't you?"

"Of course," agreed Obruchev. He got up to put another log on the fire. The General was examining him keenly.

"Consul, I understand your apprehension over my visit."

"Yes, sir, maybe I am a little nervous. You see, it isn't every day we have—"

"As I was saying, Consul, I understand your apprehension and I wish to reassure you that it is wholly unnecessary. You see, we are well informed as to your little, shall we say, indiscretions."

Koznyshov lit another cigarette, filled both vodka glasses, and watched his host turn white as a sheet.

The moment of reckoning has finally come, thought Obruchev. His stomach tightened into a knot and his heart began to pound. He wanted to blurt out some sort of an apology, some neat little explanation—but what was there to say?

"Consul, you don't appear to grasp what I am saying. I said your little indiscretions are not at issue here. At least not directly. Is it so hard for you to accept what you should regard as happy news indeed?"

"Sir, I . . . I'm afraid I—"

"Then let me make things very clear. I understand that Miss Surovsky is a most attractive woman. Haven't had the good fortune of meeting her myself. Now, certainly, Comrade, no one begrudges you your friendship with her."

The bastard knows everything, thought Obruchev, even what goes on in the office. He imagined Koznyshov in possession of a detailed account of today's events there.

"And the bear hunts," continued the deep, calm voice, "the stories of the bear hunts caught my fancy. Perhaps I'll even join you some day when I'm retired. After all, it isn't Soviet law which forbids the hunting of polar bears." Obruchev felt he was being mocked, the way to his final humiliation paved with sarcasm. Why didn't he just come out with it? What was the point of all this indirect garbage? His unruly temper began to stir.

The General took a deep draw on his Gauloise, exhaling with a sigh. "Now, the furniture business. . . ." He paused and drummed his fingers on the table. "The furniture business is, what should I say? Imaginative. Yes, that's the word. Imaginative. Most imaginative, indeed. The Soviet Union would do well with a little more of that type of creative boldness."

He turned in his chair to face the fire. Staring into the flames, his hands clasped together and a cigarette stuck between his lips, Koznyshov looked serious now. "Consul," he snapped, "it would be a mistake, of course, for me to say that your record is acceptable. On paper you look pretty miserable. I can imagine some

Party official reviewing the file we keep on you. 'What sort of commitment does this man have to socialism? What? Do you mean to tell me he has used his position as a Soviet official to operate a number of profit-oriented businesses? Out with him, he must go. His case doesn't even warrant a hearing.'

"But Consul," he said, spinning around in his chair. "I take a different view. A radically different view."

Obruchev glanced at him, befuddled. "You see, Consul, I personally have studied your past. More thoroughly, you can rest assured, than our hypothetical Party official. Of what period shall we speak? Of your days as a student at the Novgorod Technical Institute? Of your years in the Mines Administration? Of your tenure as Consul? And, Comrade Obruchev, it would be a mistake for you to think this is a new development, a result of the taped interview with Karnoi and Nikovski. No, Comrade, don't do that. Could well be you haven't seen the last of them. Could well be you'll soon be working together. What we know of you, we've known for some time. That interview merely reinforced my opinion of you. And, Comrade, that opinion is quite high."

Koznyshov ground the butt of his cigarette into the ashtray, blowing smoke through his nostrils. "Of course, you have sinned. So much is understood. Back in the days of Beria, they would most likely have had you shot. But today, Comrade, we've become much more sophisticated. Perhaps it's more a question of efficiency than of ethics. You see, we have found that reformed sinners make the best zealots." He raised his eyebrows. "And, Consul, I *need* a zealot."

Obruchev felt a tingle of excitement. Could it be? Had he understood properly? Was Koznyshov offering him a chance to redeem himself? God, if it were only so, if they would give him just one last chance, he would do anything, anything at all. They would never find a more loyal supporter, never in a million years. He filled both vodka glasses and in a booming voice he said, "General, I wish to propose a toast to your health." He wanted to proclaim his love for the Soviet Union, to fall to his knees and weep at Koznyshov's feet, to leap into the air for joy. Instead, he lifted his glass and downed its contents in one exuberant gulp.

For the next two hours, General Koznyshov subjected Obruchev to a barrage of pointed questions. "I am satisfied," he said at last, "that your knowledge of Svalbard is as extensive as it is reputed to be."

"Thank you, sir."

"Now, Comrade Obruchev, I realize I've kept you in some suspense as to what your role in Svalbard's future will be."

"Quite all right."

"Let us get to the point. From this moment, you are to be Chief of Security for the entire archipelago. Answerable only to me, of course."

"Chief of Security? But, General, I. . . . What I mean is . . . what the hell would someone that important do up here?"

Koznyshov held up a hand. He rose to his feet as if he were about to take leave. Obruchev followed suit. "Sit down, Comrade," commanded the General. "I have much to say. Much to explain. Before I go, you will have a better grasp of what all of this is about. An excellent grasp, I should hope."

Obruchev, not wanting to appear overly obsequious in his first moments as "Chief of Security," marched to the hearth and placed two more logs on the fire. When he had taken his seat again, Koznyshov was pacing the length of the room. He seemed lost in thought.

Outside, the storm intensified. The wind howled above the chimney as rain and sleet lashed against the north window. The General paused before the battered glass to peer out. "You don't know war, do you, Mikhail Obruchev?"

"No, sir. I was too young. But my older brother—"

"In war, my friend," interrupted the General, "there are many variables." He glanced at Obruchev, then nodded toward the window. "But none in our own military history has been as consistently decisive as the weather." He stood motionless, his hands on the window ledge, his gaze fixed on the storm. When he spoke again, his voice had become deeper, softer, more distant. "Let me give you an example. In the fall of '41, I was engaged on the central front. It didn't look as if we would be able to save Moscow, so furious was the Nazi offensive. Comrade, they would encircle whole armies of our men before we could organize our retreat.

We lost our tanks, our trucks, our will. The weaker we got, the bigger the hunks the beast would tear off of us. Sometimes they'd take a hundred thousand prisoners in one maneuver."

Koznyshov looked out at the storm in silence. Obruchev wished to add something about his brother's experience on the front, but he was mesmerized by the General's reminiscences. There was something awe-inspiring about the man—a depth, a strength, a complexity—which made Obruchev feel insignificant. He had no idea why the General was talking as he was, but he knew there was a reason. He waited in silence.

"You see, Comrade," said Koznyshov, "the elements just then were on the side of the enemy. In peaceful times, you would have called it a splendid autumn. For weeks on end, the sky was azure. Where the peasants hadn't had time to set fire to their crops, the wheat fields stretched as far as the eye could see, glistening in the sunlight like a golden carpet. At night, the moon would swim up and the fields would look even softer, even more luxuriant. The wind would create little waves in the wheat, tiny waves that would start up in the distance and roll toward you. When they got close enough, you could hear the rustling in the grass and then you'd feel the breeze—that mild and fragrant evening breeze—on your face and in your hair. It made your senses come alive, it made you want to live. But it was that gentle breeze which bore disaster, which delayed the winter and made us helpless against the invader."

He lit a cigarette, still facing the window. A violent gust of wind shook the house and drove the sleet against the glass so fiercely it sounded as if the pane would shatter. But Koznyshov seemed not to notice. "You would say to yourself in those peaceful moments, 'How wonderful it is, how beautiful.' But those moments never lasted. The rumbling would start up in the background. Flashes of light would appear on the horizon, and pillars of smoke would darken the moonlit sky. Their battalions would come across the fields just as the waves had come. We were powerless against them. The sky would fill with planes; artillery shells would turn the earth around us into a volcano; the smell of explosives and of blood would cling like glue to our nostrils. Whenever there was a lull, you'd hear the growl of tank motors in the distance. And with each lull, that distance would be less. They'd surround us, they'd slaughter us like animals. Some of us would escape, I don't know how. We'd be joined by hordes of poor green country boys. We'd wait and watch the wind ruffle the fields and wonder if we'd live to see another sunset."

For a long time he peered out in silence, his hands resting on the windowframe. "It was then, Consul, that the rains came, weather like today. The mud got so deep a horse could hardly walk in it. And on top of the rain came the cold. I remember sitting around in an abandoned farmhouse, watching the first big wet snowflakes tumble down. When we had first holed up there, the weather was like summer. From the loft, we could see the spires of the Kremlin on the horizon. We had all but given up. No one said it, of course, but everyone thought it: Moscow would be in enemy hands in a week.

"But the snow continued to fall. We cheered, we made a fire, laughed as we hadn't laughed in weeks. Because, Comrade, we knew that Mother Nature had switched sides. The mercury plummeted, the ground froze up like steel."

Koznyshov strode in front of the fire and warmed his hands, as though the memory of that winter had chilled him to the bone. "And then," he said, turning to Obruchev, "then came the order to attack." A tremor of excitement shot through his last words. "And attack we did. On foot, on horseback. With rifles, swords, bayonets; with scythes and pitchforks.

"They fled in terror, sensing the change in our morale. And nature's wrath took care of the ones we couldn't get our hands on. We found them frozen in tanks that had refused to start; frozen like slabs of granite in the fields and in the rubble; frozen inside the carcasses of horses they had slit open for warmth."

The General returned to his seat and filled both vodka glasses. "Which brings me, Comrade Obruchev, to the point. There are times when the Russian soldier has no equal, when he becomes ferocious, indefatigable, thirsty for revenge and for victory." His voice trailed off to a whisper. "And, Consul, should it come to war on Svalbard, the world will again be reminded of this fact. I'll tell you quite openly, Comrade, that I do not share the prevailing opinion in Moscow: the opinion that we shall get through this without a fight."

Koznyshov refused to be more specific. After alluding to the possibility of war, he added only a few vague remarks about "provocations" from the capitalist–imperialist bloc. These, he said, had forced the Soviet Union to take defensive measures. The army had been ordered to undertake the militarization of the two Soviet mining towns on Svalbard—Pyramiden and Barentsburg. This would be accomplished, beginning immediately, by moving crack Soviet units to Svalbard. The troops would arrive disguised as miners; the real miners would be transferred to "better positions" on the mainland. Unfortunately, Olga Surovsky would no longer be needed in Barentsburg. She would receive an excellent job in Odessa with opportunities for rapid advancement. Her exact whereabouts would be communicated to Mikhail Obruchev after the "crisis" had been resolved.

All of this, of course, seemed somewhat obscure to the Consul. After all, he had good friends in Longyearbyen, friends who were well informed on international political developments in the West and who had mentioned nothing of an impending crisis, or even of any abnormal friction between the NATO powers and the Soviet Union. The furniture business was booming; the demand for polar bear hides was as strong among Western tourists as ever; and increased orders from Norwegian officials for Obruchev's firewood were pouring in. Everything pointed to another long calm winter.

From his seat near the fire, Koznyshov gestured toward the window. "As you see, Consul," he said, "my prediction of snow was correct. I think you will find that my predictions are usually correct."

The two men watched the big flakes stick to the pane and slowly ooze downward. A stream of water gushed from the roof, blew against the glass, and cleared away a long strip of slush. The vodka bottle on the table was empty; the fire had died to a bed of embers.

Obruchev, still uninformed of his first task as Chief of Security, felt restless. He got up and walked to the hearth where he gathered up a load of kindling and tossed it onto the coals. The dried wood burst into flames at once, and he struggled to set a log on the grate without burning himself. For the hundredth time that long afternoon he cursed himself for his clumsiness.

"Mikhail Obruchev," said the General, "let's get to the point." He stiffened, clapped his hands, and smiled a thin smile. "I regret I am unable to discuss in more detail with you the causes of the great tension between ourselves and the West. You will have to content yourself for now with the knowledge that the situation is perilous. You know from what I have already told you that troops will take the place of miners in our cities here. We must be prepared for armed conflict. Now, Comrade, should such a conflict occur, we should not wish to involve the citizens of any country other than Norway. The reason for this is obvious, is it not?"

Obruchev grunted.

"Good. Now, that report of yours on the Western supply depot. . . ."

There was a moment of tense silence. "Relax," he whispered, aware of Obruchev's discomfort. "For all its distortions, it was a good report. Good, Consul, because that expedition you discovered is limiting our freedom of action in dealing with the provocations to which we are being subjected. It's a German-led expedition, a glaciological survey of some sort. Wouldn't be such a blasted problem if all of the participants were German. But no. There's at least one Englishman along, and several Americans. Americans, Consul! Do you see what I'm getting at? No, of course you don't. How could you?"

Koznyshov slammed his fist on the table in an uncharacteristic display of anger. "Mikhail Obruchev, that expedition must return home at once! Americans and Englishmen, that's all we need! There's trouble brewing over Svalbard; things are going to get nasty. But there's a chance, still a chance, we'll get out of this thing lightly—if we don't start out by killing a few prominent American scientists. Obruchev, I know I'm not making much sense to you, but listen. That expedition must be forced off the archipelago at once. I don't care how you do it. But you, Comrade, are the man I've hand-picked for the job. You know the country like no other Russian alive. I don't care how you do it. But I want it done, and done smoothly. . . . Tell me, Mikhail Obruchev, expeditions up here are quite frequently forced to leave ahead of schedule, are they not?"

"Of course, sir."

"This blasted bunch we've got up there now is supposed to stay into September. That's too long. Much too long. What, in your opinion, would be the most likely cause of such an expedition's premature departure?"

"Weather."

"How bad is a storm like today's farther north?"

"Not that bad, General. Anyone with plans to stay into September comes prepared for much worse."

"Yes, of course. Silly of me. Now what else might make them close down shop? We've obviously got little control over the weather."

Obruchev was at last in his element. In a gesture similar to the one Koznyshov might have made, he leaned forward and placed his palms flat on the table. As he spoke, a sense of well-being settled over him, just as it did on those evenings when a bunch of his cronies dropped by to drink and swap tales.

"General, accidents in the Arctic are not unheard of."

"For example?"

"For example, people get lost and freeze. Or get attacked by the bears. Snowmobiles fall into crevasses, climbers fall off glaciers, avalanches bury campers and hikers. I could tell you some stories you—"

"Another time. What type of accident might cripple an expedition?"

"Anything I've mentioned, if key people were lost or if equipment were damaged."

"Can you stage such an accident?"

Obruchev struggled to hide his shock. "I believe so, sir," he answered, forcing himself to look Koznyshov in the eye.

"And do it in such a way that no possible suspicion of foul play might arise?"

"Yes," snapped Obruchev. "I'll find a way."

"You are aware, I assume, of how important your success is? To me, to the Soviet Union, to your own future."

"Of course, sir."

"How many men do you need?"

"Sir, I'd prefer to do it alone."

"Alone? No. Impossible. Out of the question. If something were to happen to you the mission would not be completed. Besides, you never hunt alone, do you?"

"No."

"How many are you on your hunts?"

"Four or five."

"Good. Fits with the provisional plans we've made. You are to equip yourself exactly as if you were going on a hunt. A week-long hunt, let's say. Don't worry about any special equipment. That will be taken care of. You will be picked up at five o'clock tomorrow morning at the helicopter pad and flown to a predetermined spot near the Wijdefjord. You will receive at that time detailed information and some very carefully prepared instructions."

Koznyshov chuckled briefly. "I have only one bit of unpleasant news. After listening to that tape of yours, I almost hate to break it to you."

Obruchev crossed his arms and waited.

"When you land, you will rendezvous with agents Karnoi and Nikovski." The smile vanished from the General's face. He cleared his throat and contined sternly. "You will learn to work with them, Consul. They are trained in ways that are not immediately evident. Make use of them. You will be pleasantly surprised."

"I will try," grunted Obruchev.

"No. You will not *try*. You will do it. You are in charge. You have the authority to discipline them, if that makes you feel any better. But I don't want one iota of abuse. We in the KGB no longer work in that manner. Now, Mikhail Obruchev, my coat and umbrella. I'm an hour late already."

Koznyshov extended his hand. "My friend, the best of luck to you. I'm predicting success, success for you, for us, for the Soviet Union. Report to me immediately upon your return. You'll know me as Comrade Velovsky. I shall be in Belov's post at the Workers' Center."

"Belov?" he asked, startled. "Where will Belov be?"

"Don't worry about your colleague. Don't give it another thought. He is being promoted as a reward for the excellent job he has done here. There are better opportunities on the mainland for someone with his administrative talents."

"How can I reach him?"

"Comrade, after we've brought this affair to a conclusion, we'll discuss such matters. Now, please. My coat. I must go at once."

The Consul stood on his front steps in the heavy wet snow. The sooty ground was already hidden under a white blanket. The wind had died down, but the sea still churned angrily. He watched Koznyshov disappear around the corner, his footprints a trail of compressed slush that shone silvery in the pale light. In some places water gurgled up and turned the footprints into muddy pools. But the storm soon mended the flaws in the blanket of white.

Mikhail Obruchev scuffed away the snow before him with his foot. His hands in his pockets, his gaze fixed on the nearby horizon where gray sky and gray sea met, he began to whistle an old Pomor folksong he had loved as a child.

8

It is not unusual that a quarrel between two people who are very fond of each other will bring them closer together. That, precisely, was what happened to Martin and Ulrike at the Peppermøllen. He explained to her carefully why he had made his idiotic remark. He apologized. Ulrike admitted she had behaved badly.

He reassured her that he took his responsibilities at the Institute very seriously indeed: it was his job to find out what was going on in the north, and he would help her in any way he could.

"One condition, however," he said, and she knew she would be wise to listen—he was quite stern. "You must allow me to ask questions, you must control your temper, and you must treat me like someone as determined to get to the truth as you are, not like a knee-jerk liberal from the *Zeit*. Agreed?"

"Agreed." She looked angelic. "Pax. And I really don't mind your skepticism—you'll become a realist soon enough. I'm sorry I screamed at you like a fishwife. If it happens again, a few words of warning will straighten me out."

They lifted their brandy snifters and drank to peace.

"I have a car of sorts outside," said Martin. "How about a change of scenery?"

"No. Let's not budge until we get this thing hashed out. Then, perhaps, a drive would be nice."

"Fine."

She put her hands on the table, palms down and fingers

91

spread, and took a deep breath. "Will you make me an initial concession?"

"Depends on what it is."

"Will you for a moment pretend my information is accurate?"

"Yes, but only for a moment."

"Okay—Arnheim has a German crew on Svalbard mining uranium. The Russians know this and are planning to invade the archipelago." The warmth vanished from her voice; she stiffened in her chair.

"First, a Russian invasion will bring with it the risk of an American nuclear response. The U.S. has no conventional forces in the North Atlantic that could defend the archipelago. Nor does any other NATO power. Which means that if the West responds at all, it must use tactical nuclear weapons. Do you find that line of analysis correct?"

"So far."

She went on: "Assuming we're spared that hideous scenario, assuming the Soviet Union invades and there is no nuclear response, what then?"

"Go on. What are you getting at?"

"This: No one will believe the Germans were really the cause of the Soviet invasion. They'll see the Russian charges as a shrewd pretext for gobbling up a strategic hunk of territory. Arnheim and Company won't suffer at all. They'll be involved somewhere else in no time. With heightened arrogance, no doubt."

Anger flashed across her pretty face. "Martin, I've said this before and I'll say it again. Germany can't be trusted. Those bastards will do anything to get the bomb. They're pushing us headlong into another war. The only way to stop them is to expose Arnheim for what he really is. Svalbard is our chance, Martin. NATO *has* to be interested. Even if it doesn't give a damn about Germany becoming a nuclear power, it's not going to welcome the clash between Russia and the West which Arnheim's making inevitable. We've got to get out the word. We've got to shock the public. We've got to make them believe us."

She waited impatiently for his reaction.

He lit his pipe and watched her fidget with her napkin. "The only problem I have with your analysis is with the credibility of your information. Not with the part about an impending Soviet invasion. That may well be true, and I certainly intend to use all of the means at my disposal to find out if it is. But with the part about Soviet motives. Maybe the CIA is building a major eavesdropping facility up there. They'd certainly have more of a motive than the Germans, given the importance of the Svalbard Passage to the Soviets. Why your East bloc contact would leak a story to you about Germans and uranium—on that I won't speculate, although I can think of a half-dozen good reasons."

She listened without looking up. He could sense her frustration. But she forced a faint smile and slid her hands over his. "Very conventional," she murmured softly.

"Which doesn't make it false."

"Martin," she said gently, "I don't want to sound self-righteous, but you don't know Germany as I do."

"I can't argue with that. But supposing they *are* mining uranium? How the hell do you intend to get the proof you need? Some nameless source isn't going to stir much interest. Maybe a few radicals here and there—"

"*Finally,*" she said. "You're finally getting the point."

"The point?"

"The point: I'm going to Svalbard."

"You're what?" He shook his head, incredulous. "What in hell's name do you expect to accomplish by that? How in the hell is one person going to do a job the CIA would have trouble with?"

Her hand began to shake, forcing her to set down her glass.

"Ulrike, please." He waited for her to regain her composure.

"I don't know, Martin, I don't know. I only know two things. First, the *Rundschau* will foot the bill. And second, I know some people on Svalbard. I conducted an interview tour there in May."

"Who?"

"I'm thinking of one man in particular. Obruchev is his name, Mikhail Obruchev. He's the Soviet Consul in Barentsburg. He'll know what's going on. I'll trick him into giving me a hint. You'll see, Dodds. Don't underestimate me. It would be a big mistake."

She leaned forward on her elbows, bracing herself with her fists against her temples. Tears streamed down her face and her voice faltered. "I'll find them. I'll find the bastards, whatever it

93

takes." She bowed her head and her hair slid over her hands and into her eyes. "Forgive me," she choked, "I'm terribly upset."

She pushed her hair back with both hands and managed a smile. "Do you feel privileged, Martin?" she asked, sobbing. "Not many people get to see me like this, not even my oldest friends."

He reached across the table and put his hand on her wet cheek.

She said, "You're probably wondering what kind of help I expect from you. Whether I want you to accompany me up there or some such absurd thing."

"No. I—"

"Well, relax. All I want from you is this." She yanked a handkerchief out of her big leather bag and blew her nose. "I want you to promise that if something happens to me on Svalbard . . . if something should go awry . . . that you and the Institute will look into the circumstances. If you'll only promise me that, I'll know my efforts won't be in vain. Martin, the truth is going to come out, and you're going to be one of the first believers. Will you promise me that much, Martin? Can you promise me that?"

"I'll gladly do that. More if you wish."

She took his hand in hers and laid her forehead upon it. "God bless you," she whispered. "Let's go now. And, shhh. Not another word about Svalbard tonight." She looked up at him, smiling, and lifted his hand to her lips.

He helped her into the driver's side of his old VW van—the other door didn't open—and climbed in after her. The clatter of the engine replaced the whine of the starter.

"Will this thing go up hills?"

"There's one way to find out."

"Are you game?"

"Always, my dear."

"Then back across the bridge. Head north on the coastal road, the one that runs out past the whaling station. Do you know the one I mean?"

"Of course not. I've only been here a week."

"Uncanny, Martin. I feel I've known you for years."

He pulled out of the parking lot, bumped over a curb, and

turned in the wrong direction on a one-way street. There was no traffic; they drove on, laughing.

On the long bridge over the Sound, Martin saw in his rear view mirror a lone car behind them, a tan Saab 900. He could barely make out a big blond man behind the steering wheel; he suspected it might be Jon. That guy, he thought, must really be hooked. Understandable. He, Martin, wasn't doing so well himself. But did he have to make such an utter ass of himself, following her around like that? Martin felt angry: if she saw him, she'd get upset, and that could ruin a promising evening. He hoped the fog would thicken and he could lose him.

The night was dim but not dark. An occasional scrawny pine came into view, a forlorn skeleton suspended in the mist. The damp russet surface of the road faded into the grayness around them.

"Where are you leading me?" asked Martin after a long silence.

The question startled her: she really didn't know. She knew only that she was glad to be with him and felt warm and happy.

She remembered a spot she was especially fond of.

"I think I'll take you on a little journey into the last century."

"It has to be an improvement on this one. Where are we going? Looks like we're already at the end of the world."

"I had in mind a cluster of abandoned peasant cottages from the pre–World War I days. How does that sound?"

"Romantic."

"It depends on who you're with." She grinned. He was watching the road and didn't see her smile.

The route became mountainous; the air took on a chill. In the fog, the steep grades appeared level, and only the wail of the overworked motor told them they were climbing. He shivered, glanced at her. Her silhouette in the half-darkness excited him; he struggled to suppress his desire. Why in God's name, he wondered, is she taking us to some remote spot at this hour? He tried not to think about it.

"Aren't you cold?" he asked.

"No."

"Ha! I should have guessed. You're one of *them*, aren't you?"

95

"One of whom?"

"Those Germans who swim in Lake Geneva during Easter vacation. I saw them doing it once as a young man and haven't gotten completely warm since."

"Do we do that? We do, don't we? I remember a friend. . . . Damnit, now you've made me cold. Turn on the heat, will you?"

"I would if I could, but the heater died three years before the door latch on your side."

"Bastard. You're putting me in training for Svalbard, aren't you?"

"Someone has to look after you," he said, fishing around behind his seat for a blanket. She shivered and curled her legs under her.

"Hurry up. You're as slow as when you're packing your pipe."

He pulled off the road. While he fished a thick tan army blanket out from behind his seat, he heard the sound of the approaching motor. He watched her wrap the blanket around herself and twist it into a knot under her chin. She did not see the car slip by and vanish in the fog. Relieved, Martin was about to drive on. But he heard the car stop and turn around.

"Look to your right, directly into the forest," he said cheerfully. "I'll be damned if I'm going more than a foot from home base in this weather for my *Pinkelpause*."

She laughed. "Go on. I'm not looking."

He jumped out and stood in the middle of the road, flipping Jon an obscene gesture with his free hand as the Saab cruised by. The Norwegian gaped, then hit the accelerator. Martin knew he and Ulrike wouldn't have to worry about *that* creep for a while.

They drove on in silence. A break in the fog appeared. Ulrike let go of the blanket and leaned over him to see out of his window, resting a hand on his thigh to support herself. He touched her fingers but she seemed not to notice.

"Let's pull over for a second," she said. "That's quite a view."

He stopped in the middle of the road and they peered out the window. He slid his arm around her shoulders, knocked the blanket off by mistake, and draped it gently back around her. Her hair brushed his lips as she strained to see something in the distance.

They were in the middle of a huge fissure in the fog which ran down the mountainside to the sea below. A swarm of small rocky islands stretched across the greenish-gray water to the near horizon. A trawler plowed northward and disappeared into a towering wall of mist.

"Heading for Svalbard, perhaps," said Ulrike. "It's not a trip I look forward to." He pulled her to him and she did not resist. The fog swirled up from the sea. She twisted loose from his arms and looked at him. "Still want to see the cottages?"

"I do. But can you find them in this soup?"

"If I can't locate a group of buildings half a mile from a paved road, there isn't much chance of my finding a group of Germans in an arctic wilderness the size of Saxony, is there?"

"I don't know. Germans do tend to be conspicuous."

She laughed. "Just drive. There's a straight stretch of road. Can't be too much farther. After that there's a turnoff. You can't miss it. It's just before a caved-in church right beside the road."

They found the turn, half-hidden by drooping pine branches, blocked by a pile of mud and rocks. The van broke through the barricade and landed with a crash on the tiny road. As they inched along, the bottom of the old VW scraped on the rocks, and the sides and roof rasped against the overhanging limbs of the pine forest. A clearing emerged where the ground became grassy and the trees receded into the fog.

They got out and walked. Ulrike was still draped in her blanket. Martin held her arm. A cabin loomed before them in the thick fog. They circled it, their hands on the weather-beaten wood, until they found the door. Martin pushed, and it opened with a screech of rusty hinges.

An old wooden bench stood beside the gigantic hearth. A rusty iron pot hung overhead. In the corner was a pile of split logs covered with dust and cobwebs. Milky light filtered in through two windows in the south wall. The mist entered like steam, pushed its way into the cabin, and dissolved.

Without a word, they began stacking kindling into a tepee inside the hearth. Martin returned to the van for some newspaper and got lost in the fog. He called to her, and her voice wafted to him, muffled and alluring, through the dampness. He entered the cabin, kneeled on the blanket she had spread out, and began crumpling the paper. She kneeled beside him, smiling, her eyes lowered.

The fire caught with a burst of golden light. He piled on larger logs. The room became warm, almost hot. For a long time, he stared into the fire. When he looked up, she was sitting on her heels facing him. She had taken off her coat and laid it neatly beside her. He watched her. Her eyes still lowered, she unbuttoned her blouse. "It's been a long time, Martin, a very long time."

He remained absolutely still, as though any movement might frighten her. She raised her eyes to his and smiled. Without looking away, she slipped off her blouse and let it tumble onto the wooden floor beside the blanket. The glow from the fire shimmered roseate and orange on her slender arms, her neck, her tight, shapely breasts.

She lifted her hand and brushed the hair from her forehead, then waited motionless, delicate and lovely as a Dresden nymph, while the light from the fire danced on the golden chain around her neck and sent the shadows of her torso darting across the floor and up the wall behind her.

He slid close to her and, taking her head in both hands, kissed her eyes, forehead, cheeks. She stretched her arms behind her and shifted her weight to her hands, and he kissed her neck and breasts. Then she lay down on the blanket and wrapped her arms around him.

When he awoke he knew they had been in the cabin a long time. Their legs were still entwined, her head was on his chest. The fire had died down and crackled in uneven bursts. The wind moaned in the trees; fog filtered through the slits in the south wall.

She twisted about, sighed and was still. Careful not to awaken her, he slipped away and put another log in the hearth.

9

A STEADY RAIN had begun to fall. The soft drumming on the roof awoke Ulrike. She was cold. She twisted about in her blanket, moving closer to the hearth, and slid Martin's coat, which he had rolled into a pillow and placed beside her, under her head. She raised herself on her elbows and looked at him. He was sitting on the old wooden bench, staring into the fire.

Something about him reminded her of her father. Memory swept her back to the autumn of 1954. Her father, too, sat staring into a fire, the fire of the coal stove in their tiny flat in Dresden. It was the last evening they would spend there before their escape to the West. Mutti was already in Berlin with Aunt Lena; Ulrike was still in school and had stayed behind with her father. The big oak in the courtyard creaked in the breeze, and one of its branches rasped against the window.

"It won't be long until the snow comes," he said. She remembered his voice, how sad it had been. "I think the Elbe will freeze this winter."

She gathered up her schoolbooks from the sofa and tried to run into the kitchen before he saw she was upset. His quiet voice stopped her.

"Put your books down and come over here to me. There's something very important I want to talk to you about." He dried her eyes with his handkerchief, then picked her up and carried her to the window. Across the river they could see the streets of the business district, crowded with pedestrians and streetcars.

Piles of rubble as high as the stark new buildings lined the main boulevard. Night was falling, and the silhouette of the bombed-out cathedral towered black and jagged above the glow of the city. A smokestack on the distant hills belched orange flame, illuminating the roofless brick walls where a factory once had stood.

He hugged her gently. "Tonight I'm taking my little princess away from Dresden. We're going to find you a better place to grow up. Somewhere in the Western Zone. In Kiel, maybe, way up on the sea. . . . I have a brother in Kiel you've never met. . . . And don't worry about Mutti. She's waiting for us in Berlin."

She stood, motionless, hands on the window sill, her eyes moving from his kind, sallow face to the rubble-strewn city. He wrung his hands and looked at her. "Nine years, my sweet, it's been nine years since the end of the war. I don't know what's happened in those nine years. . . . They went by before I even noticed, before I had a chance to take you and Mutti away. . . .

"You see, I couldn't leave. I just couldn't. It was so beautiful once. . . . I always dreamed that one morning I would awake and find it the same again—all gardens and parks, red and green roofs. I loved the colored storefronts, the pretty little display windows, the cafés, the cathedral. Dear, the cathedral! People used to come from hundreds of miles to see it." His eyes filled with tears. She hurt for him with an unspeakable hurt, remembering how helpless she had felt.

Her father propped a hand against the sill to steady himself. "Old Dexter, you never knew old Dexter. Died in the bombing. He had his tobacco shop right down there on the first corner." He nodded in the direction of a massive office building with rows of narrow windows and an unadorned gray facade. The corners of his mouth quivered as he forced a smile. "Yes, princess, it was a wonderful city.

"Every Friday," he chuckled, "your Opa would give me money for his tobacco. He'd always say, 'Son, we're not made of gold these days. Now I've counted the money out to the penny, so don't you go spending one cent or you won't be able to pay for the tobacco.' I'd do as he said, stop at Dexter's after school, and lo and behold, there would always be enough change left over for me and the other kids who walked home with me to stop at the candy shop next door. It's funny . . . to this day I don't know if the extra money came from Father or Dexter. . . . I was always too embarrassed to ask."

She moved closer to him. He put a hand on her cheek and hugged her again. Falling leaves brushed against the window. A narrow band of frost stretched across the bottom of the pane.

"The river froze in 1933, too," he said. "That was the year we moved to Dresden from the country. We would sit right here, Oma and Opa and Aunt Lena and I, and watch the Nazis. They would march all night to the sound of drums. They carried torches and beat up anyone they didn't like."

He turned his back to the window and looked into her eyes. "You hear a lot about the Nazis in school, I know. But there's a lot they don't tell you. They tell you about the leaders, men whose hearts were black, men who were evil to the marrow of their bones. Now that's true, princess, everybody agrees on that. But they don't tell you about the puppets. They can't, you see, because most of them are puppets themselves. Governments have come and gone: the Kaiser, Hindenburg, Hitler, the Communists. But you see, my sweet, nothing has really changed. 'Why?' people ask until they're blue in the face. They keep on asking even though the answer is so clear. Nothing has changed in our land because there are too many of these people I call puppets among us. They follow, they do what they're told, they let others decide what is right and what is wrong."

She watched him place two coal bricks on the fire. She was frightened. He took her hand, led her to his chair, and lifted her onto his lap.

"Ulrike," he said, "perhaps you don't understand all of these things yet, but someday you will. The puppets are the ones who make it possible for evil leaders to have their way. Now you wouldn't want to call the puppets totally evil; that would be going a bit too far."

He coughed. A siren howled on the street below, and she felt his body tense. "What makes them what they are is not any strong wish to do bad. It's just that something is missing in their souls, something that gives the rest of us love and respect for our fellow human beings.

101

"In peaceful times, these puppets seem like perfectly normal people. They are loyal friends, good parents, helpful colleagues. But let the crisis come, let them fear for their jobs, their security, and they forget everything but themselves. They forget all kindness, all pity, all simple human decency. In their fear they line up in the parade of the one who commands, they march to the tune he has ordered, and force others to follow. They become ruthless, they carry out the leader's will even if it means striking down their own families. I wouldn't believe it myself if I hadn't seen it happen before my very eyes."

She opened her eyes and saw Martin. He was still looking into the fire. She tried to blot out her memories. . . .

"Ten minutes," he murmured, "ten more minutes in this old hovel where I've spent the last twenty years." That was the moment she knew they were leaving Dresden.

He smiled at her. "And, princess, we can't take a thing with us, nothing that might arouse the suspicion of the puppets. A coat, gloves, a hat. Well, we don't have much anyway. It wouldn't bother me a bit, leaving it all behind, if I could only be sure. Sure that we would be rid of the puppets. But I have an uneasy feeling they'll be waiting for us on the other side. They'll be harder to spot over there, better disguised, more subtle, but I can't bring myself to believe. . . . Oh, Ulrike, don't listen to me. Don't be frightened. Everything will be fine. I'm just rambling because I'm. . . . Ulrike? Are you asleep?" Martin's voice, mingled with the sound of the rain on the roof, sounded far away. She lay motionless, and he did not call to her again.

A sense of helplessness and futility overwhelmed her. What was the use of all her idealism, of all her fierce determination to see justice done, if the world was and would always be filled with weak unprincipled men—men who would turn on their own brothers for no better reason than the crack of a whip? She tried to think of Martin, of his tenderness, of what it might mean for her future. But her past was too powerful; it pulled her down into the vortex of wild, distorted, terrible dreams. . . .

Later that same evening she was with her father on the streetcar, riding into town for the borrowed auto which was to take them to Berlin. As they crossed the Elbe she looked downstream. The charred remains of the old railroad bridge rose from the shimmering water, a monster of twisted steel which glared menacingly at her. A mysterious force seemed to pull her into the icy current below. She gasped and grabbed her father's arm.

Driving out of town they encountered a policeman who was cordoning off the intersection through which they had to pass. They stopped. She heard the roll of drums, faint at first, then so loud it vibrated through her body. A column of troops arrived at the crossing; the light from their torches flickered across their faces and shiny boots. The leader of the procession—an officer in a regal white uniform—bellowed an order at the drummer, who pivoted toward the car. He drew in his massive stomach. Leering, he hammered out an eerie rhythm. He smiled a lustful smile, exposing two gold teeth on the upper-right-hand side of his mouth. She clasped her father's arm in terror and found it rock-like and cold as the cobblestones of the street. The drummer laughed and threw back his head; his cap went careening into the air. He started toward her, his bald pate reflecting the tongues of flame from the torches, his short, stout legs moving to the beat of his drum.

Aghast and pleading, she looked up at her father. But he stared emptily into space, as if she were not there at all. The drummer was at the car now. She buried her face in her hands and waited for him to strike her.

The world around her became utterly silent. Thinking he might be gone, she peeked through her fingers. But he had merely stopped drumming; his face was pressed against the window glass beside her, his distorted features danced in the torchlight. Fear paralyzed her; she was unable to look away. She could see the soldiers approaching behind their leader. They surrounded the car; the officer opened the door and dragged her father onto the street. He lay motionless on the cobblestones. The drummer, on command, beat furiously on his drum and ordered her father to stand. When he did not, he kicked him viciously in the side, then in the head. Her father struggled slowly to his feet. She tried to cry out to him but the words stuck in her throat. He looked at her with sad, lifeless eyes. Blood trickled down his temple. He turned his back to her and, with bowed head and stooped shoulders, walked off into the darkness.

The soldiers fell into formation behind the officer and the

drummer, shouted three times a booming "hurrah," snapped to the left and marched back in the direction from which they had come. The policeman lingered at the crossing, smiled at her as he took down the cordons and, as if nothing had happened, strolled away.

Panic-stricken, she jumped from the car and ran after her father. A mountainous pile of rubble blocked the street down which he had disappeared. Her legs were almost too heavy to move, but she struggled to the summit, convinced that he would be waiting for her on the other side. But the street was a deadend; the rubble heap plunged almost vertically into the river. The water lapped gently at its bank; her eyes followed the sagging wreckage of the railroad bridge to the pine forest on the far shore. Not a sound came to her from the city. She spun around. The streets were deserted; the ruins of the cathedral towered into the heavens, thrusting a jagged shadow across the moonlit water. "Father!" she screamed. "Father!" But the vast emptiness of the night swallowed up her words.

Awake now, she struggled free of the nightmare. *No,* it had not been at all like the dream. Not at all. They had arrived safely in Kiel, everything had turned out well. But now she relived the real horror: her father's face on the day it happened. He stood at the door with the West German undercover agents who came for him, his look the same as when he had walked away from her in the dream. It was seven years after the family's happy arrival in Kiel. They charged him with spying, spying for the East German regime he hated with such a vengeance. *That* was his reward for refusing to cooperate with the East Germans, for refusing, earlier, to cooperate with the Nazis. They accused him of spying for those he hated, threatened to send him back to East Germany in a spy-swap deal, took him away.

Later, of course, they discovered their mistake. But the damage had already been done. They had destroyed him, they had destroyed her father with some irreversible act of cruelty whose exact nature she would never know. When he came home after six months in custody, he no longer recognized her or anyone else, had no recollection even of his own past and no interest in anything. For ten years he sat, gazing blankly into space just as in the dream. Ten years for her hatred to grow. Then one day the kind gentle man with the stooped shoulders died, quietly and modestly, just as he had lived. The loneliness and abandonment she had felt in the dream returned; she realized how true to her life her feelings in sleep had been.

Without warning, she was filled with rage: those who had destroyed her father, who had struck down Georg, were puppets. Germany was filled with puppets. It had been bad enough before; the deaths of her father and her fiancé attested to that. But what would happen now that Arnheim had come to power? The puppets would have a field day again just as they had under Hitler. Someone must fight. "Bastards," she hissed aloud. "Bastards."

She felt Martin's hand on her back. "Ulrike, are you all right?"

She stammered his name and burst into tears. He wrapped the blanket more tightly around her and lifted her into his arms. "Ulrike, I've been thinking," he whispered. "I can't let you go like this. We've just begun, you and I. I know this might seem a little crazy, but . . . but I'm going to Svalbard with you."

10

"Put this thing down on that big ice floe out your left window," yelled Obruchev over the din of the turbine and whirring blades.

"What, boss?"

"I said land, for Christ's sake. Right over there on that floe." He stuck his hand in front of the helicopter pilot and pointed.

"Sorry, boss, can't do it. Got my orders, and they don't call for no ice floe landings. No stops, altitude two hundred feet, ten miles out from the coast."

"You got new orders. Or do I have to land this thing myself?"

"Eh?"

"You heard me. Now get this thing down. Didn't they tell you who was in charge of this mission?"

Lydov flung the craft into a sharp banking descent to the left. "Sure, they told me who was in charge," he said, smiling. "But they didn't tell me you was crazy."

"Shut up and land," growled Obruchev.

Grinning, Lydov accelerated the descent. The surface of the floe rushed up toward them. At the last moment, he pulled back on the controls; the helicopter slowed as if it were on the end of a giant rubber band and came to a stop a few feet above the ice.

"How's this?" he asked.

"What do you mean, 'How's this?' I said land. Put her down and shut her off."

"No way, boss. Look at that mush. We'll break through. Get ourselves stuck."

"Then you'll dig us out."

"Ain't got no shovel on board, chief."

Obruchev reached across the instrument panel and shut off the power. The helicopter dropped the short distance to the surface of the floe, stopping with a jolt on the solid ice beneath the slush. "Break through, eh?" he scowled as he flung open his door and jumped down.

Lydov leaned out behind him. "I'll be damned," he chortled, "and all that just to take a piss. You could have done that from two hundred feet. I'd have hovered up there for you."

Obruchev, who was relieving himself with his back to the helicopter, twisted his head around and snickered. "For all I know, you'd have pushed me out. Now, come on, son. We've got work to do."

"Work?"

"You heard me. We're going hunting. Grab my rifle from behind the seat and get your ass down here."

Lydov eyed him suspiciously for a moment, then handed him his rifle and clambered down from the other side. He strolled around the helicopter and took up station next to the Consul, who was savoring the brisk sea air with his head thrown back and his nostrils flared. For a moment, the two men stood in silence as the floe bobbed gently in the swells.

Yesterday's storm was over; all that remained of the overcast were a few puffy white clouds which drifted lazily eastward. The sky and sea were deep blue, and the sun shone brilliantly. In the distance, the shoreline of Spitsbergen was visible. Enough of the snowcover from the storm had melted to expose vast areas of gray stone on the jagged walls of the peaks. To the northeast, the vertical face of a glacier rose glistening from the sea.

Suddenly, not more than fifty yards from where they stood, two baby seals struggled up onto the ice. Obruchev swung his rifle around. Before he could aim, the seals slid, squawking, back into the water.

"Damn," he whispered.

107

"Heh, boss," chirped Lydov, "don't take it so hard. We got plenty of explosives in the 'copter. If it's seals you're after, I'll rig us up some depth charges."

"Idiot!" boomed the Consul, seizing him by the collar and shaking him.

"Heh, boss, only kidding."

Obruchev stared at him angrily for a moment, then broke into a smile and shoved him away.

Oblivious to the danger, the seals returned. Lydov shuffled back and forth in the slush, looking uneasy.

"Here," said the Consul, "have a try."

"Love to, boss." The pilot grabbed the rifle and blazed away without taking aim. Slivers of ice flew into the air, hung glittering in the sunlight, and tumbled down around the seals. The startled creatures vanished without a sound.

Obruchev stared ahead at the spot where his quarry had lain, shaking his head in disbelief. He held out his hand for his rifle. Lydov was tiptoeing away with it. With a lunge so sudden it caught the agile youngster off guard, he snatched the weapon and pushed the butt into Lydov's chest. Lydov stumbled across the slush off balance. A broad smile spread across the Consul's face.

"Crazy Ukrainian. Should have known they'd try to screw me up some way or other." He feigned a scowl and roared, "Now shut up before I use you for target practice. Go on, go on. You're headed in the right direction. Get us some coffee. You know where the thermos is."

Lydov stumbled backwards to the helicopter, making comic faces. His smile transformed half his face into rows of gleaming white teeth; a shock of sandy blond hair stuck out from his cap; the exaggerated movements of his small supple body and his bright hazel eyes radiated mischief. Yet there was something about him that Obruchev found irresistible, and the more outrageous Lydov became the more the Consul liked him.

Lydov was in the helicopter searching for the thermos when the seals again dragged themselves onto the floe and stretched out in the sun.

"Look out, kids," shrieked the pilot, watching from the window. A gunshot echoed above his muffled cry. One of the seals slipped unharmed into the water; the other shuddered and collapsed on its side. A trickle of blood gushed from its snout and swelled into a scarlet pool on the ice.

Obruchev waved. "Come on," he commanded. He drew his hunting knife, squatted beside the dead seal, and dragged the carcass farther up onto the floe. Quickly, he made incisions in the hip and tore loose a strip of blubber the size of a shoe. The flesh, still warm, steamed when it touched the cool air. He smiled at Lydov, who had been watching from a distance, and flung the fat directly at him. Bewildered, the pilot caught it and clutched it, as if paralyzed by revulsion.

"Wrap it up real good," snapped Obruchev, cleaning his knife in the snow. "Real good, understand? In polar bear country, you don't want the scent of seal fat around unless you're looking for company. Go on, go on. Don't stand there like a blasted fool. Get that thing wrapped up and into your pack. I want you to carry it wherever we go. Could come in real handy." He kicked the carcass off the edge of the floe.

Lydov stood by for a moment, dazed. Another shove from the Consul brought him back to his senses, and the two men fell into stride together. Soon, Lydov was whistling, clapping, twirling about and juggling the fat as he imitated a Ukrainian folkdance. Half-amused, half-irritated, Obruchev snatched the fat from the air. Lydov lost his balance and landed with a splash on his rear. Obruchev helped him to his feet.

"Thanks, boss," said Lydov, brushing the slush from his pants. "Can't tell you how good it is to get away from those KGB pricks and have a little fun. But don't you worry. When the flying gets tough, no one can hold a candle to me. It's the only reason they keep me around, boss. I'm not their type. Don't like shooting, don't like checking up on people. But I like to fly. And let me tell you, boss, in this organization they got flying jobs you wouldn't believe."

Obruchev smiled at him as they climbed aboard. "Head due north, kid," he said. "You'll get your flying in."

"See that break in the coastline?" yelled Obruchev over the clatter of the motor. He tapped on the plexiglas pane beside him. "Know what that is?"

"One second, chief, and I'll have your answer." Lydov studied the map. "Let's see. We just passed the end of the Prins Karls Forland out there on the left. Which means we're talking about the mouth of the Kongsfjord."

"Right. And inland a ways on the fjord's south bank is the Norwegian settlement of Ny-Ålesund. One woman and a bunch of drunks. I drop in when I'm hunting."

"How is she?"

"Who?"

"The woman."

"Want to go find out? She likes young men, Lydov. She's about twice your age and three times your size."

"No thanks, boss. Let's stick with the bears. How much longer we got to fly?"

"Depends on the route we take. Your orders were to hug the coast all the way around?"

"Yep."

"Which means fifty miles north, another fifty east, and fifty more south to reach a point that's just over those mountains." He tapped the window again, pointing to the mountains. "Why do you suppose they don't want you flying over land?"

"We're not supposed to be seen, I guess."

"Correct. And there's not a soul north of Ny-Ålesund. No danger of being spotted. I know a route between the peaks that'll have us where we want to go in time to relax and have a drink before those two shitheads get there."

"Shitheads?"

"You heard me. Don't you know what's going on?"

"Can't say I do, boss. They just told me to fly you up here and stick with you till the job's done. They never tell me nothing. Must know I don't like their kind of games." He winked at the Consul and made a clicking noise with his tongue. "So who are these two friends of yours?"

"You'll meet them soon enough. You might even know them already. A couple of intelligence shits I'd like to have stuffed and mounted."

"Heh, boss," exclaimed Lydov, grinning broadly, "that's what I like to hear. You know, for an old fart, you're all right. Not like the guys I usually fly for. All they ever do is sit around trying to look important."

The sun shone directly on Lydov through the plexiglas. Obruchev watched him with affection as he lifted his hat and wiped the perspiration from his forehead with the back of his hand. A good kid, he thought, a damn good kid. The kind you don't run into much anymore. Nowadays they were all so serious, so career-crazy. . . .

They flew into a band of turbulence over the coast. Obruchev screwed the top onto the thermos—some of the coffee had sloshed out onto his pants—and concentrated on the breathtaking view before them. Lydov had descended to within several feet of the water and was flying toward one of the towering walls of ice which ran along the coast. It formed a sharp boundary between the ocean and the massive glaciers which covered the land. He edged up the wall and, from the point where it jutted from the sea, began a gradual vertical ascent parallel to its face.

The ice, cracked and furrowed, glimmered incandescent emerald in the sunlight. They watched, awe-struck, as the shadow of the helicopter skirted along before them, plunging from time to time into a bottomless gray crevasse, only to reappear in another spot—nervous, wispy, and insignificant.

From the top of the wall, they looked inland over the horizontal surface of the glacier. It stretched endlessly toward a range of distant peaks, a vast desert of ribbed and sequined snow. Lydov cast one last glance down the resplendent facade of the ice wall, then flew eastward over the glacier, taking on altitude as he neared the mountain range.

In half an hour, they were inside a narrow gorge which sliced through the peaks to the Wijdefjord. Obruchev settled back and watched the dark cliffs on either side rush by. His mind was hard at work, trying for the hundredth time to make sense of Koznyshov's visit. The events of the previous day confused him, and the more he tried to piece them together, the more frustrated he became.

A clash over Svalbard which might lead to war? Certainly, he would be the first to recognize the telltale signs of crisis—and there had been none, none at all. Something fishy was going on.

He was being kept in the dark. The wily peasant in him began to stir; his mind groped around for clues in the hidden folds of his memory.

His frustration was about to erupt into rage. Provocations from the West? That, if he had half his wits about him, was most certainly bullshit. Then it dawned on him: Koznyshov was planning an outright invasion of Svalbard! It was so obvious he couldn't understand why it had taken him a sleepless night and half a day to figure it out! Troops disguised as miners in Pyramiden and Barentsburg; a clearing operation to get foreigners out of the way; the arrival of the chief of the KGB on Svalbard.

For a golden moment he bathed in the glow of satisfaction. He'd figured it out at last. But wait! A Soviet Svalbard? His revulsion grew as he pictured how the police, the bureaucrats, and the officers would come, how they would bring with them the awful regimented life of the mainland. They would be invading *his* territory, denying him the things he loved. Briefly, he hoped that the invasion might fail or be called off; his hope swelled to an ardent wish.

But he soon saw that this was no solution, either. His crimes were too many and too well known. If he were not able to redeem himself, if he were not able to become part of a great Soviet victory, they would have little use for him. Karnoi and Company would call the shots, and he, Obruchev, would find himself defenseless against them.

More clearly than ever, he saw he must please Koznyshov—and please him unconditionally. If he succeeded, the powerful man would protect him; if he failed, his head would become one more stepping-stone for some ambitious young agent's advance up the KGB's organizational ladder. It was useless, he told himself, to reflect any longer on his predicament: he had no room to maneuver, no alternatives to choose from. There was but one course open to him, and the sooner he got that through his thick skull, the better.

"Wake up, boss," Lydov said. "I think we're getting close." Obruchev watched him clip a more detailed map into the holder and glance down at it.

The gorge had widened. Ahead, its mouth was visible, and

through the opening they could see the blue-gray waters of the Wijdefjord. Obruchev took another swig of coffee and handed the thermos to his pilot. Lydov sloshed the liquid around, looked at the map again, and handed the thermos back without taking a drink.

"Take her down to fifty feet," ordered the Consul. "Let's get our bearings while we've still got the coastline in sight."

"Yes sir."

In minutes they were hovering just above the water. They studied the map together, then flew northeast until they reached the far bank of the fjord. From there they followed the shore northward, searching for the two egg-shaped boulders and the sheer rock cliffs which marked the spot where they were to meet the KGB agents.

When Obruchev gazed back across the water the glare of the sun blinded him. For what seemed a very long time the fiery colors of the low sun on the water exploded behind his closed lids. He took note of this, for his mind was already hard at work devising a strategy to force the glaciological expedition off Svalbard.

They were sleeping on the desolate beach, backs propped against a boulder, when the clatter of the approaching helicopter woke them. The craft landed so close it knocked over the half-empty vodka bottle on the rock between them and sent Lydov's cap bounding crazily over the sand and melting snowbanks.

While the chopper hovered a few feet above the ground, Karnoi and Nikovski jumped down. Obruchev had half-expected them to arrive in business suits, but in their olive green jackets and tattered cords they looked like ordinary hikers or hunters.

From the helicopter a soldier handed down several large boxes, a canvas duffle bag, backpacks, and two high-powered rifles. While the agents stacked the supplies in a neat pile, the helicopter lifted and turned its nose toward the open water. In seconds, it had disappeared into the huge orange sun which hung just above the mountains across the fjord.

Obruchev leaped to his feet, dragging Lydov up after him. "Know them?"

"Not them two, boss." He scratched the back of his head as he studied them. "But I wouldn't worry if I was you. They don't look so bad. At least not the bigger one."

"They're all pricks, Lydov."

"Boss, you probably don't know what a real prick is. No one can spot 'em like me. Otherwise, I'd sure as hell be working in the mines." He gave the Consul a friendly clap on the shoulder and started after his cap.

"Lydov," hissed the Consul, "get back here. Let that cap of yours go for now. I'm not joking."

Obruchev grabbed him under the arm and, staring toward the two agents, whispered: "For the time being, I'm one of those pricks, got it?" He lowered his voice to a low growl and tightened his grip on Lydov's arm. "Those two are working for me. They're going to need some filling in on who's running the show. Until that's established, you'll get the same treatment they do."

Karnoi and Nikovski, who had just finished arranging the boxes, looked up. The four men met on a barren stretch of beach.

When they had exchanged greetings, Obruchev examined his young friend from head to toe. "Lydov," he snapped, "you look like hell. Fetch your cap. And, for Christ's sake, get that bottle off the beach. What kind of an operation you think I'm running, anyway?"

"But, sir, I was only—"

"Go on, on the double," bellowed the Consul.

Lydov scurried off, more amused than frightened. Karnoi watched him for a while, muttered something under his breath about insubordination, and pivoted to face Obruchev. "Comrade, let us stop wasting time." His grating high-pitched monotone made the Consul's blood boil.

"Get to the point."

"The point, Comrade Obruchev, is this: since your report arrived at KGB headquarters, our job has been to gather exhaustive data on the expedition in question." He nodded toward Nikovski with a stiff jerk of the head. "Before Comrade Nikovski and I go any farther, we would like to discuss that data with you."

Obruchev looked away, unconcerned. "Lydov," he yelled, and

114

his voice echoed among the boulders. "Lydov, bring your bottle over here. I think we should drink to a successful mission before we get down to details. I'm sure my subordinates here feel the same way."

Lydov swung on the wheel struts of the helicopter like a schoolboy. With his free hand he lifted his cap and waved it. "Yessiree, chief, comin' right up," he cooed cheerfully.

Karnoi's narrow lips tightened. The veins on his neck stood out as he spoke and his voice quivered with rage. "Consul, this is not another one of your drunken hunts. This is a matter of crucial importance to the Soviet Union. I—"

"For that very reason, you will join me in a toast. Or do you wish to start defying orders immediately? If so, I'm sure my *friend*, General Koznyshov, will want to hear about it."

Lydov's arrival with the bottle broke the tension. He opened it and handed it to Karnoi, who took a quick drink and passed it on. Obruchev drank last. He took the largest and noisiest gulp, as if the gesture would establish his dominance. Then, like all good leaders, he sought to temper his harshness toward those who would serve him.

"Now, Comrades," he said, wiping his chin with his sleeve, "let's go over that data of yours. General Koznyshov assures me you two have done a hell of a good job gathering it."

There had been very little wind all day, but a sudden gust sent Lydov's hat skipping across the beach again and swallowed up Karnoi's mumbled words.

The wind continued to gust and the sun glared at them from across the fjord. "Wind and sun," shouted the Consul, draping his massive arm around Karnoi's shoulders. "Wind and sun could make our job very easy."

"Yes. Therefore let's speed things up. Let's use our advantage before it disappears." Karnoi twisted loose. The reflection on his lenses made his eyes invisible, but there was no mistaking his sneer.

Huddled in the shadow of the supply boxes, they spread out their maps on the sand. The wind tugged at the corners of the paper and whistled among the boulders. The waters of the fjord had begun to stir, and the rhythmic sound of waves breaking on shore mingled with the cawing of the gulls.

Nikovski produced a fat bundle of documents. "Glaciology, as you perhaps know, Consul, is a branch of—"

"Cut the shit," yelled Obruchev. "What the hell are those Westerners doing up here?"

"They're glaciologists, Consul. They take samples of ice from glaciers at different depths. They choose glaciers where man has most likely never set foot. That's how they hope to get samples free of any contamination."

"Go on, go on. What I don't understand is why they give a damn about digging up ice that's been buried for hundreds of years."

"Because, Comrade Obruchev, hundreds of years ago that ice was not buried. It was exposed to the earth's atmosphere. Hence, if they are able to analyze the glacier properly, they know when a sample taken from a depth, say, of one hundred feet was in contact with the earth's atmosphere."

"So?"

"So, by analyzing the chemical content of that ice, they are able to gain a clear picture of the pollutants in the earth's atmosphere in the period when the ice in question was on the glacier's surface."

The Consul picked up several rocks, tossed them up onto the beach, and watched them bounce about. "It'll be a shame to interrupt such imaginative work." He grinned.

Lydov, who had been etching figures on the sand with his finger, sat bolt upright. "What?"

"Don't worry," said the Consul. "It's for their own good."

Lydov went back to his etching, unconvinced. Nikovski knelt over the maps and papers as he spoke.

"Since the sample must be totally uncontaminated, the method and the place chosen for the extraction are both of crucial importance. Which brings us to the most interesting part of our report." He paused and rubbed his hands together.

"Well?" said Obruchev impatiently.

"They cannot use helicopters in their work because the pollutants from the engine exhaust might find their way into the samples. Also, it is impossible to fly close enough to the sheer ice faces where the best samples can be taken."

"Come on, come on. Out with it. How do they get to the samples?"

"Ice climbers, Comrade."

"Ice climbers? Are you sure?"

"Absolutely. And they are often away from the base camp for several days. Their system seems to be to work several glaciers each trip. They sometimes take snowmobiles to within a couple of miles of where they begin their climbs, but no closer. That's how concerned they are about contamination."

"Holy shit," whispered Obruchev, pounding his open hand with his fist. "It's perfect, isn't it?" He did not see Lydov saunter away.

Karnoi snickered. "We've worked against far greater odds and succeeded. If we plan well, we shall succeed again."

"Where are they now?"

"The base camp is approximately fifteen miles north of the Newtontoppen. Before yesterday's storm, the climbers had just set out to the northeast. It seemed to us that they were headed for the glaciers inland from the Hinlopen Strait. Do you know the ones I'm referring to?"

"What do you mean, 'Do I know them?' " Smiling, Obruchev turned to Karnoi. "I've been hunting bear in that area for as long as I can remember. On those glaciers, they'll get their uncontaminated samples. No one's ever been up one of those. Vertical walls a couple of thousand feet high. If they can get up there, they'll get their samples. But, Comrades, it's risky business climbing around on that ice. You go up there, seems to me you're asking for trouble."

Lydov was perched on a distant rock, dangling his legs. "Kid," yelled the Consul, "get over here." But the wind hurled his words back at him.

Karnoi raised his rifle and fired two shots in the air. Without looking up Lydov ambled toward them. "What's up?" he asked, shuffling back and forth in front of the Consul. The sand he kicked up blew against Karnoi's trousers.

"Comrade Lydov," shrieked the agent, "what do you—"

117

"Silence, Karnoi," commanded the Consul. "I'll take care of this. Now get those maps put away and load this stuff onto the helicopter. We're lifting off in five minutes."

"Comrade Obruchev," snapped Karnoi, "I wish to object. We've yet to make plans for forcing the expedition off the archipelago."

"Wrong," barked Obruchev. "If the climbers go, the expedition goes. True or not, Nikovski?"

"Yes, that is correct. The climbers are indispensable to the expedition. And they could not be replaced for months."

"So there, at least we're agreed on that. The details of staging the 'accident' you will learn soon enough." Lydov started to wander off again but Obruchev caught him by the arm.

"No, Comrade Obruchev, that will not do," said Karnoi shrilly.

"That will have to do. Now, not another word. That's an order."

Obruchev, still holding the pilot with a vise-like grip, took a step toward the KGB official. "You see, Karnoi," he snarled, "I know what I'm doing. You do what I say and we'll get along just fine. If I fail, shoot me, arrest me, do what you want. But don't count on that happening. Now, on the double! Get this stuff loaded. I want to have a word alone with Lydov here about how we'll fly in."

Minutes later they were in the air, following the coastline around the northeastern tip of Spitsbergen toward the Hinlopen Strait. Lydov tried not to think of what he knew lay ahead; he struggled to concentrate on the beauty of the wild country below. In vain. Again and again, an image swam up before him: he saw the baby seal the Consul had shot. The carcass was far out to sea, blood pouring crimson from its snout and turning the clear green water for miles around a dull sickening red.

Early that evening they landed at the end of a narrow gorge that wound its way inland from the Hinlopen Strait.

Obruchev pointed to a semicircular ridge just ahead which blocked their view toward the west. It was the boundary, he explained, between the rugged country over which they had just passed and the great high plain which stretched westward for several miles to the high peaks and glaciers where he expected to find the climbers.

He assured Karnoi and Nikovski that their arrival by helicopter could not have been detected by anyone much farther inland from where they now stood. Their approach route up the gorge had kept them deep in the shadows, he said, well below the level of the high plain.

He pointed to the ridge. "See there. It's a couple of hundred yards higher than this basin. And this basin is as high as we've flown the whole way up here. There's the wind to help us out, too." He grabbed Lydov's cap and tossed it into the air. It flew off like a seagull and looked for a moment as if it might plunge down the dark canyon up which they had flown. Lydov made an obscene gesture and trotted off good-naturedly. "That wind," continued the Consul, "would gobble up the engine noise of a whole armored division."

The sun had already begun its northward journey along the horizon. It must have ducked behind one of the high peaks to the west which were invisible from their vantage point inside the gorge. Although they were already in the shadow of the ridge, the sky above them darkened and the air grew colder.

Obruchev asked for the white nylon coveralls which Nikovski had packed in the duffle bag. The ground at that altitude was still covered with a shallow but unbroken blanket of snow from yesterday's storm. There would be some reconnaissance work to do that evening, and there was no use taking a chance on being spotted.

The Consul climbed into the helicopter to get his rifle. As he clambered down, he shouted at Lydov, who was silently stretching the white tarpaulin over the craft. "Leave that for now. Get your field glasses from the cockpit, put on one of these cute little outfits, and come with me."

Lydov, clowning, tried to jump into the coveralls with both feet at once. Obruchev ordered the two agents to finish camouflaging the helicopter.

"And dinner," he added. "You might as well get a few things laid out. No fire, of course. Not even the butane stove. Bread, butter, whatever else your Moscow gourmets sent along. A man works up an appetite in this country."

"And a thirst," chirped Lydov.

Karnoi fixed a reproachful stare on the pilot and his boss. Lydov snapped to attention. "We'll be back in an hour," said Obruchev hurriedly. "Wish us luck. If they're there, tomorrow's work will be easy."

When they reached the rim of the gorge, the sun was emerging from the shelter of the peak which had hidden it. The glare on the high plateau—a vast meadow of dazzling white—blinded them.

"Damn," whispered Obruchev. "Damn, damn, damn. We were too slow getting here."

"Eh?" said Lydov, out of breath.

"Don't act so blasted dumb. Can you see into that?"

"Sure, boss. There's a park, two restaurants, a. . . ."

Obruchev slapped him on the back of the head. "Here," he said, handing him his sunglasses. "Put these on and look straight out there. Tell me what you see."

Lydov put on the glasses, closed his eyes behind the dark lenses, and stared directly into the glare. It took the Consul an anxious moment to see through his ruse. "Open your eyes, wise guy. Do you want me to feed you to Karnoi for dinner?"

"All right, boss, all right." He blinked and whistled. "No way no one's gonna see into that, chief. Listen, I've been thinking. That game of yours, you know the one. Sneaking up on people and letting them have it. You'll be able to walk up to those poor devils about twelve hours from now and hit them over the head with a hammer before they see you coming. Anyone on those glaciers in the morning will have the same view of you you got of them now."

"It doesn't take genius to figure that out, kid. Why do you think I brought us up this way?"

Lydov handed him the sunglasses and looked at him. He was subdued and serious now. "Didn't think about it, boss," he said earnestly. "Like I told you, I fly where they tell me to and that's it. Don't like that other stuff. No, sir, don't like it one bit. Say, boss, how did you ever get mixed up in—"

"Shut up, Lydov. We've got work to do. Look here, the sun's moving north along the horizon now. You can't see anything, but

I know what's out there like I had a picture of it right here in front of me. There's a row of high narrow peaks straight ahead. The sun will slip behind one of them before long. That's when we've got to get our scouting done."

"And then?"

"Depends on what we find."

Silently, they waited. The wind stung their faces and frayed their nerves. But when the blinding glare began to fade—slowly, almost imperceptibly at first, then so swiftly it seemed night would engulf them in the next instant—a sense of tranquility fell over them. The snow meadow appeared, a giant billowy eiderdown, strangely inviting in its forlorn immensity. Beyond, the outline of the jagged mountain range cut a sharp figure against the reddish-blue sky. The ice walls that joined the meadow to the high peaks looked dark and forbidding, like the hull of a gigantic freighter in dock at twilight.

Obruchev snatched the field glasses from Lydov, slung his rifle over his shoulder, and surveyed the desolate expanse before him. Suddenly, he froze in place, focusing the binoculars nervously. "Son of a bitch," he exclaimed, still peering through the glasses, "looks like we're in business."

He had spotted two bright blue alpine tents at the base of one of the glaciers. On the ice wall just above the campsite hung the tiny figures of four climbers. They were dressed in orange, and they appeared to be practicing mountaineering techniques. First, the lead climber moved laterally across the wall for several yards, then the others, one at a time, followed. The third climber fell a short distance; the rope, invisible to Obruchev, caught him. The Consul's heart almost leaped from his chest. A treacherous climb, he mused, the kind on which an accident could easily happen.

He handed the glasses to Lydov, who hung them around his neck without bothering to look. Obruchev studied him for a while, irritated that the young man refused to share his excitement.

"Look here, kid," he pleaded, "this is a job that's got to be done. Now, for Christ's sake, quit acting like a schoolgirl. You're up here to help me, aren't you? Or are you with those KGB bastards? What's gotten into you? I thought we were pals."

Obruchev's voice faltered as he felt for the first time the

enormity, the brutality of the assignment he had been given. Those were *men* on that mountainside, not bears or deer.

But he knew at that moment that all pangs of conscience, all sentimentality, all weakness must cease. Those were the things that crept up on you before you could defend yourself. They changed nothing, they only made whatever you had to do more difficult.

He grabbed Lydov by his bony shoulders and shook him. "Make up your mind this minute," he growled. "Either you're working for me or I can't use you. You know, son, I can fly a helicopter, too. Wanted to come up here on my own in the first place."

Lydov tried to free himself but the Consul's grip on him was too strong. He hung his head and kicked the slush beneath his feet despondently. "Why, boss, do you have to go around killing people? You're not like all the Karnois I work for. All I want to know is why you go around doing that."

The Consul released him. The sun was again emerging from behind a lofty summit, and the meadow to the north gleamed brilliant white. Fists clenched and eyes pressed shut, he conjured up a vision of Koznyshov. The General was sitting across from him, spelling out what he was to do as Chief of Security on Svalbard—and what would become of him if he failed. No sooner had the image of Koznyshov faded than he saw the repulsive face of Karnoi. The agent, dressed in a business suit, was sneering triumphantly. He led Obruchev out of his office, past Olga Surovsky, who didn't even bother to look up from her desk, and onto the street. As they walked along the wooden sidewalks of the town, his friends and subordinates moved aside and pretended not to see him. He felt himself begin to tremble with rage and humiliation.

"I'm doing it," he blurted out, "because they've got me by the balls. Lydov, kid, listen. They've got me nailed down cold. I do as they say or else. What am I supposed to do? I don't like it any better than you, but it's got to be done. Now answer me. Are you with me or not?"

"Sure, boss," said Lydov wearily. "What am I supposed to do?"

The four Russians set up camp a hundred yards below the rim of the gorge. From their observation point just above the campsite, they could look out across the snow meadow at the glaciers and peaks beyond.

Obruchev had assumed the first watch. He noticed a vaporous pall of smoke rising from the vicinity of the glaciologists' tents. It was, he thought, a good omen. The smoke indicated that they were preparing a meal; no doubt they would want to sleep, too, before undertaking the difficult climb.

Instinctively, he began his calculations, tracing with extended arm the elliptical course the sun would follow, glancing occasionally at his wristwatch. It was now almost seven in the evening. The sun was between two of the higher peaks, hanging low and orange just above the saddle that connected them. At midnight it would reach its nadir to the north. From there it would begin to rise gradually as it followed the horizon in a clockwise direction. Early in the morning, it would be in the east, still low enough to produce the glare on the meadow that would hide their approach.

He etched some lines in the snow, studied the angles they created and calculated that, should the climbers appear on the wall at any time between four and eight o'clock, it would be safe to move on them.

Moments later, Karnoi crawled up the slight incline to the observation point and stretched out beside him silently. The Consul handed him the field glasses.

"Take a peek," he whispered. The wind had died down to a gentle breeze, and Obruchev had ordered complete silence. "Looks like they're cooking up an evening meal. My guess is that they'll turn in for a good night's sleep afterwards. Which means they're likely to be on the wall when we've got the sun at our backs. I'd say, Comrade, that this little affair is pretty much wrapped up."

Karnoi observed the smoke plume with the naked eye, then pushed his wire-rimmed glasses onto his forehead and studied the camp through the binoculars.

"Luck has been with you so far, Comrade Obruchev," he whispered. "I must grant you that. But early success can make for carelessness. This, indeed, seems to have happened. Comrade

Nikovski and I are agreed that you have overlooked some very critical details. I would wish to know how you plan to deal with these."

Obruchev had an urge to grab the agent by the ears and hold him face down in the snow. He looked at his wristwatch. "You have thirty seconds to make your point."

"Comrade Obruchev, I—"

"Twenty-five."

"First, we'll leave tracks in the snow. Second, autopsies will reveal that the climbers have been shot, regardless of how badly their bodies are mutilated from the fall. Therefore—"

"Time's up." Obruchev snatched the binoculars and stared menacingly at Karnoi, whose glasses had dropped into the snow.

"Comrade Obruchev, you seem not to—"

"Comrade Karnoi, shut your mouth. Or do I have to do it for you?"

They glowered at each other. Karnoi reached down to retrieve his glasses, drying them off as best he could on his nylon sleeve.

"As for your first objection," Obruchev went on, "the snow will not be on the meadow by the time the bodies are discovered. Lydov assures me the temperatures will stay above freezing for the next twenty-four hours. Here, feel." He pushed a pile of slush toward Karnoi. "It will give us our protection by creating a wicked glare. And then, Comrade, it will melt. It will take with it all the evidence of our presence. And if the temperature should drop? That happens. Sure it happens. But nine times in ten at this time of year, it happens in the wake of a storm. And more snow is as good as more sun, isn't it? Comrade, there are risks in this line of work. You must know that as well as anyone. But in this case the risks are very small."

"Very well," said Karnoi, looking past the Consul. "That much I'll concede. But what about the bodies?"

"You mean the bullet holes?"

"Precisely."

"Karnoi, there will be no bullet holes."

"What do you mean, no bullet holes? How else are you going to get them down? Look here, Consul, if you're playing games with us, you'd better reconsider fast. You'll regret it later. We're not an organization that takes kindly to that sort of thing."

124

Obruchev shoved the field glasses back toward Karnoi. "It's time for your watch," he said, smiling. "I'm going for another liverwurst sandwich. You boys do a better job with the food than I expected."

"Tell me at once how you plan to get them off the mountain!"

"Shhh. You talk like that and they'll hear you in Longyearbyen."

"You've got no right to plan a joint expedition without consulting us. I'll tell you now, Consul. You'll either follow the rules of this organization or you'll—"

"I said there will be no bullet holes. Hard for you KGB boys to imagine, isn't it? Now excuse me. You'll learn soon enough what it means to do a job properly."

The Consul slid backwards on his belly until he was below the observation point, stood up and strode off to the tent.

At half past four in the morning, Nikovski, who had been at the observation point, burst into the tent. "They're going up," he said crisply.

Obruchev lurched to a sitting position with his sleeping bag still around him. "The weather, how's the weather?"

"Not a cloud in the sky. Gusty wind from the southwest."

"The temperature?"

"The snow is melting, but the meadow is still covered."

"Let's make quick work of it," snapped the Consul. He crawled out of his bag, gathered up his pack and rifle, and jostled Lydov, who was still asleep beside him.

The youngster began to stir at last. "Come on," he groaned, "let me sleep. You don't need me yet." He rolled over onto his stomach and wrapped his arms around his head.

Karnoi pulled on his boots. "Bravo, Consul," he said with sarcasm. "The excellent results of your lax way of doing things." Karnoi stared at the mummy-like figure in the sleeping bag for an instant and, with the point of his boot, kicked Lydov in the side. "On the double," he screeched. "You're not in a French brothel."

Obruchev dragged himself out of the tent, leaving his friend at Karnoi's mercy.

Five minutes later they were hurrying westward across the

snowfield toward the face of the glacier, four men united in a common endeavor for vastly different reasons. The slush was shallow in spots. Clumps of greenish-brown grass and patches of pale blue mountain phlox poked up through the silvery mantle. The wind was brisk, the air pure.

A mile from the glacier Obruchev signaled a halt. He surveyed the towering wall of ice through his field glasses. The lead climber was already about two hundred yards up. The other three were stretched out in a straight line below, each about fifteen yards from the other, following the steps in the ice which the lead climber was chopping with an ice ax. The rope to which they were attached ran like a hair between them; a second rope ran from the last climber to an oddly shaped gray container at the base of the precipice. Obruchev assumed this held the equipment for drilling into the ice and would be hoisted up when the climbers had found a secure place to begin their work.

He handed the glasses to Nikovski, who studied the wall for a moment.

"How close can we get without being detected?" whispered the agent.

Obruchev pointed with his thumb in the direction from which they had come. Nikovski looked back and covered his eyes, blinded by the unearthly brightness of the sun on the great mirror of snow behind him. It took him a full minute to regain his vision.

Less than three hundred yards from the ice wall, the Consul stopped. He squatted, slid his rifle from his shoulder, and stretched belly-down in the slush. The others followed. He inched toward Nikovski and whispered: "Watch through your scopes. Don't fire for any reason. That's an order. Pass the message on."

The Consul fought back his revulsion as he propped himself on his elbows. He had talked himself into thinking of the mountaineers as a species of exotic game. Yet he could not rid himself of the presentiment that something would go wrong. He gave a start. Perhaps one of the climbers was an American? Had not Koznyshov said that the whole point of getting the expedition to leave was to avoid harming Americans? But no, how silly of him. This was going to be an accident, this little episode he was staging.

What difference would it make who came to harm? None, of course, none whatsoever. . . .

Lydov! That's what was bothering him. The kid had done everything possible to scare off the seals the other day. God knows what he might try now. The Consul looked at Lydov and found him lying face down in the snow, his arms wrapped around his head, just as he had lain this morning in the tent. Better get it done, he told himself, before he gets loony again.

Through his scope he concentrated on the second climber. He almost cried out in rage when he saw that it was a woman. Why, at this moment, did fate seem so intent on conspiring against him? Until now everything had gone so well. Just another minute, just one more minute and it would all be over. What was this horrible foreboding that choked off his breath?

He closed his eyes, felt calmer when he opened them. He watched her for what seemed like an eternity. She was young, perhaps in her late twenties. Her curly brown hair was tucked into her orange windbreaker. She glanced down the treacherous incline and jerked her head immediately back toward the wall. He sensed her anxiety.

He lifted his rifle past her and focused in on the lead climber. He had just banged a long ice screw into the wall and was twisting it with the handle of his ice ax. When it was screwed in all the way, he clipped a carabiner through its eye, fastened a loop of blue nylon cord to the carabiner and, with another carabiner, hitched the rope into which he was tied to the whole apparatus. He looked up and, without wasting a second, began to chop a hand hold in the ice above him with precise, powerful blows of the ax.

The sunlight flashed from the metal screw he had just inserted and from the spur-like crampons on his feet which dug into the ice and held him securely. Obruchev followed the rope downward, keeping it in the cross hairs of his scope, until he reached another ice screw. It was about three yards beneath the first screw. He paused to calculate.

He moved his scope down to the next screw. That should do it, he told himself. He's a big fellow. Ten yards of free fall and a piece of steel halfway through the glacier wouldn't hold him.

With the third ice screw from the top still in the cross hairs, he exhaled, took in a deep breath and steadied himself. He shifted his aim an inch to the right and pulled the trigger. The crack of the rifle echoed among the peaks and glaciers. He watched a fissure appear in the ice around the screw. He moved up the rope and fired again. Once more, the ice cracked between the screw and the bullet hole a few inches away.

"Mein Gott, was war denn dass?" cried the woman climber, her voice filled with terror. There was another shot. The woman shrieked. Her scream hung in the wind, primitive and hideous as the death rattle of a great beast. This time, Obruchev had hit the top ice screw directly. It exploded from the wall in a shower of glittering ice.

The lead climber slipped and tottered but managed to stabilize himself long enough to plung his ice ax into the wall. The jolt tore his crampons loose, and for a time he dangled from the ax handle, clutching it desperately with both hands. Obruchev saw cracks appearing in the wall all around the ax but somehow it held. The man sank his crampons into the ice, steadied himself and pulled a device which looked like an emergency transmitter from his pocket. In a frenzy, the Consul fired at his torso.

For a moment, the climber continued to cling to the ax. He tottered again, his feet broke loose from their holds, and then the ax, too, tore free. He plunged downward, his long blond hair flying wildly about where it hung out of his helmet.

The two screws which Obruchev had loosened did not slow his fall. They ripped from the ice, leaving craters the size of melons. By the time the safety rope reached a firm screw, the momentum of the cascading body was so great that it tore the screw from the wall, sending another resplendent shower of ice fragments into the air. The remaining screws zippered in sequence, as if the ice wall were being blasted by a machine gun.

Silently, the four climbers plummeted in a great cartwheel toward the boulder field below, still bound to one another by the rope. Ice axes, ice screws, a pack that had ripped from the girl's back, and a helmet that had broken free fell with them.

Minutes passed before the stunned Russians could speak.

"Goddamnit!" roared Obruchev. "The bastard would have to

have a radio along." He began to rummage frantically through his pack. "Lydov, the seal fat! Hurry!"

The pilot seemed to have gone a little mad. With a diabolical smile, he bounded to his feet, tore open his pack, unwrapped the blubber, and began a Ukrainian folkdance, more frenzied than his last. He shouted, whirled, kicked, and clapped, tossing the fat into the air and catching it.

Obruchev ignored him. He was readying a butane stove above the slush. "Someone get me a skillet," he ordered. When he looked up he was staring down the barrel of Karnoi's rifle.

Lydov fell silent. He turned in search of Nikovski and found himself covered. Shuffling back and forth, he began again to juggle the blubber.

"Mikhail Obruchev," rasped Karnoi, "the farce is over. Get up and move back." The Consul did as he was told. Karnoi signaled to Nikovski to take away Obruchev's rifle. "Remember, Consul? You said no bullet holes. You've left evidence. You've botched the mission. Our instructions are to take command in such a case."

The Consul winked at Lydov. "Toss me the fat, kid." Lydov pitched it over. Karnoi stiffened, about to fire.

"Easy, Comrade, easy," said Obruchev. "Let's not get carried away by a minor mishap." He held up the fat as if it were an item to be sold in a shop. "This, my friends, is seal fat. Now I hadn't intended to shoot. You saw what happened. It was unfortunate. But we've got an out."

The agents eyed him suspiciously. "It better be a damned good one," said Karnoi. "You've got thirty seconds to explain it."

Obruchev cleared his throat and spoke in a grave unruffled voice. "I knew an old sailor once. After his retirement, he took to carting tourists around up here. They were always wanting to see a polar bear—"

"Time's up," screeched Karnoi. But the Consul went on as if he hadn't heard.

"Now, the old bear's a pretty smart creature. He doesn't always show up just when you want him to. And sometimes he comes around at bad times. He's a natural predator of man, you know. Stalks us, eats our flesh, even prefers it to seal meat. You heard about the two campers who were dragged from their tent and eaten last summer, didn't you?"

"Of course not. We in Moscow have more important things to do. Get to the point."

"Well, anyway," Obruchev went on, "one of the captain's tourists shot a seal one day and chopped it up into little pieces. He spread them all around the ice floe where they had landed. 'This should get one of your bears over here,' he said. A real pushy tourist, you know the kind. German or something. Wouldn't let the captain leave until the bear showed up. So the captain, after a couple of hours, gets the idea to burn a chunk of the seal fat. And lo and behold, in fifteen minutes there were bears swimming for the floe from all directions. They had to get back on board like a herd of panicked steer to keep from being eaten themselves."

Obruchev paused. He was all business. "We burn the fat," he barked, "and we'll have a bear here in fifteen minutes. I know. I've done it many times right in this region. There's a fjord three miles north of here. They'll come inland that far for the fat."

Karnoi seemed unable to make a decision.

"And, Comrades," added Obruchev, trying to help him out, "if you back off and let me complete the mission, there won't be a word about your little insurrection to anyone. On the other hand, if you kill me and Lydov, you'll have a lot of explaining to do to Koznyshov. Not a very pleasant position to be in."

Karnoi continued to struggle with himself.

"Heh, boss," blurted out Lydov as if he were greeting a friend in a pub, "how the hell does—"

"For Christ's sake, kid, will you shut up."

"No, boss, listen. What if that bear decides he's going to eat *us* instead of the climbers?"

"He won't. First, when we see him coming, you're going to carry the blubber up to where the bodies are and trot back here real fast. And second, the smell of their blood will be the first thing he'll home in on when he gets close."

"Very well," shouted Karnoi. "You've got an hour. If you haven't produced results, you're under arrest. Go to work."

The agents laid their rifles in front of them, sat in the snow, and opened their packs. Obruchev watched them from the corner of his eye as he lit the stove. Suddenly he sprang at them. He smashed Nikovski in the nose with a blow that sent him flat on his back and, with the other arm, unloaded a vicious elbow punch on the side of Karnoi's head.

"Lydov!" he shrieked, "get their rifles!"

Nikovski lay unconscious; a stream of blood flowed from Karnoi's ear. Obruchev, on his knees in front of them, drew his hunting knife and pressed it to Karnoi's throat.

"Miserable little worm," he growled, "you'd better hope that bear shows up. I'd hate to have to announce to Koznyshov that you two started shooting at the climbers against my orders . . . hate to have to tell him that you two turned on me when I tried to stop you . . . that I had no other choice but to put a bullet through your heads. Now flat on your back, Karnoi. Not one move or one peep out of you. I've got some cooking to do and I don't want any disturbances."

PART THREE

11

THREE WEEKS had passed since the Russian Ambassador to Norway, Alexi Ivanov, had charged that the Germans were mining uranium on Svalbard. The world knew nothing of these charges, thanks to the desire of both the Soviets and the Norwegians to hush them up. Even the rumors that had sprung up around the time of the initial meeting between Ivanov and Norwegian Foreign Minister Skogan had dissipated. The "Svalbard Affair" seemed over almost before it had begun.

In northern European diplomatic circles, nothing disturbed the humdrum of daily routine. But in the Norwegian Foreign Office an air of muted urgency prevailed.

Skogan had dispatched three search parties to Svalbard. They were to report any unregistered mining operations, for it was necessary to give the Russians a careful account of the measures the Norwegians had taken to answer Ivanov's charges. Skogan had also instructed the search parties to look for any abnormal military activity that might signal a Soviet buildup. They had found no evidence that the Germans were mining uranium or that the Soviets were preparing an invasion.

But a shocking piece of news had just landed on Bjørn's desk. The Western glaciological expedition whose permit he had dug out of the Svalbard archive was no longer on the archipelago. The expedition had been forced to suspend operations because of a mysterious incident involving the disappearance of its ice climbers. The Norwegian government had been asked to conduct the search for the missing. . . .

One of the search parties already on Spitsbergen had been sent to the area where the glaciologists had been working. On the verge of turning back empty-handed, the helicopter pilot had spotted scraps of orange material scattered over a boulder field at the base of a glacier. Finally, two days ago, a sack of shredded clothing and a box of crushed and splintered bone fragments had arrived at the police laboratories in Oslo.

On this Friday afternoon, August 15, an official from the Police Department's Homicide Division sat in a private meeting with the Foreign Minister. Bjørn waited nervously for Skogan to summon him.

Marianna, who should have begun the weekend several hours earlier with her boss's blessing, greeted him in a low, worried voice. She led him into the Minister's study without a word.

Skogan stood at the window, a coffee cup in hand instead of his usual afternoon Scotch.

"Mr. Holt?" he said, not lifting his eyes from the rush hour traffic below.

"Yes."

"Mr. Holt, I don't quite know whether to rejoice or despair."

"As we expected, sir?"

"Indeed, indeed. A bullet hole in a rib. No doubt at all among the pros at the lab that it *was* a bullet. Can't say I followed all of Lieutenant Svensen's technical talk, but if he and his colleagues are convinced, that's good enough for me."

Shaking his head, Bjørn sat down in one of the leather chairs. "I'll be damned," he mumbled.

Skogan took a case of Havana cigars from a side drawer of his desk. He offered one to Bjørn, who refused, found one that suited him and lit up. He paced the length of the room, inhaling deeply and blowing out great fragrant clouds of smoke. He seemed in turn resolute, nervous, discouraged, angry. Skogan almost never smoked. "Special occasions only," he quipped, holding up his cigar. Yes, thought Bjørn, this certainly was a special occasion; but in just what way he wasn't sure.

Both men were now utterly convinced that the Soviet Union was planning an invasion; all remaining doubt had been swept away by the discovery of the bullet hole in the shattered rib of a climber. Everything hinged now on the success with which they could convey to Ivanov two impressions: that Norway would fight viciously if attacked; and that the United States, in spite of its strained relationship with Norway, would not stand idly by while the Soviets gobbled up Svalbard.

If the Norwegian Prime Minister met with Ivanov—which he no doubt would at some time during the next weeks—Danielsen would try to be conciliatory to protect his "third way." Ivanov would interpret this, quite correctly, as a sign of weakness. It was imperative that Bjørn and Skogan get Danielsen to see that the Soviet danger was real—and do it in a hurry. This, they both knew, would not be easy.

It would also be necessary to make key American government officials aware of the Soviet threat. But this must be done in a way that would not draw attention to the present friction between the United States and Norway. For if the American public got wind of a Russian threat to Norway, its first reaction would be self-righteous. The Norwegians would be derided for their "naiveté." "Turn your back on us and see what happens!" would be a popular sentiment in a country grown weary of rebuffs from abroad. This attitude, so contrary to American as well as Norwegian interests, would not persist for long. But it might not take long for the Soviets to become convinced that the United States would *not* intervene to protect a wayward ally. And the invasion itself could be completed so rapidly that a stunned Western world would not have time to unite against the aggressor.

For Bjørn and Skogan, therefore, it was essential to prevent the invasion in the first place. To accomplish this, the brunt of their attack had to be directed at Soviet *perceptions* of how the United States and Norway would respond to a Soviet invasion of Svalbard. The reality was far less important.

The two men sketched out a rough strategy: the Foreign Minister would concentrate on Danielsen; Bjørn would attempt to involve the Americans in the crisis as quietly as possible. They gave themselves a week. The next meeting with Ivanov wasn't until the following Friday, and they were both certain that the Russians would not move until they had a clear picture of how the Norwegians were likely to respond to an invasion of Svalbard . . . and until the KGB had planted stories of German uranium mining in the Western press. There was time, but not much.

The thought struck Bjørn like a hammer blow. Ulrike! Where in the hell was she getting her information? Why hadn't he grasped that possibility sooner? Jesus, could it be that she had been duped by the Russians? Might they be aware of her fierce hatred of the Arnheim regime? Might they be priming her with false information in the hope that she would give their alibi its needed debut in the West?

He knew he had to see her, and fast. If she started the ball rolling, it might lead to an uproar against the Germans which would provide the pretext for the Soviet attack. He would call her, he would insist that she keep her promise, that she remain silent on the Svalbard situation until they had talked again. He would bring her to Oslo and fill her in. That woman! She had to be set straight even if it meant divulging top secret information. Thank God he hadn't forgotten about her in all the confusion. He was about to tell Skogan about her but decided not to. There were so many angles to this whole mess, and the old man already had quite enough on his mind. Ulrike was *his* problem.

"Mr. Holt," said Skogan tartly, "how are your contacts with the lower echelons of the CIA operating in Scandinavia?"

"Very good, sir. But why 'lower echelons'?"

"Because I'm afraid we'll have to begin there. The big CIA boys are presently too much under the political yoke to do us much good. You know that they've been instructed to avoid cooperation with us ever since our good man Danielsen initiated his 'third way.' Now, who do you know?"

"I'm thinking about one man in particular. You wouldn't exactly call him a friend, but during my Washington tour we worked on several major projects together. He's now with the Scandinavian branch of the CIA and is stationed around Stavanger. His name is William Johnson."

"Stavanger, that's your hometown, isn't it, Mr. Holt?"

"It is. That's probably why I'm still in contact with Johnson.

You see, he's recruited an old Norwegian friend of mine to work for him, a retired sea captain named Turk. Whenever I'm in Stavanger, I look up the old guy—he was sort of an uncle to me when I was growing up—and Johnson joins us if he's not out snooping. Turk's one of those men who'll do almost anything to stay at sea. I suspect that's how he got mixed up with Johnson."

"This Johnson. Can you trust him?"

"Absolutely. He's very ambitious, bent on making a career for himself in the CIA. If we can convince him that the Soviet danger is real, he'll risk his neck to be the man who brings the scoop to his superiors. And if the information comes from the bottom up like that, it will be *American* information. Johnson would never mention that the tip-off came from us. The CIA brass will listen to what *their* men discover. If the press can only be kept from finding out, I think we've got a good chance the U.S. will take some sort of secret preemptive action. I don't care how upset the American leaders are with Danielsen. I can't imagine they would be willing to sacrifice their own interests just to spite him."

"Interesting, indeed. Tell me, Mr. Holt, is your father still in Stavanger?"

"He is."

"Will you be staying with him?"

"Yes." Bjørn jotted down a phone number and handed it to the Minister. "And Mr. Skogan, if you call me and get him on the line, for God's sake don't tell him who you are. He knows you're a Laborite, and . . . well . . . he might just hang up."

"Hang up?" Skogan shot him a sharp, disgruntled look, but smiled when he remembered old Jens Holt. He hadn't thought about him for years, and could never picture him as Bjørn's father.

"I won't tell him," Skogan smiled. "Now, let's jump on this Johnson thing. Can you by any chance leave tonight?"

"Of course."

"You're not tired?"

"At a time like this?"

"And you like driving that Italian toy of yours, don't you?"

"It's British, sir."

"Oh, I see. Now listen, Mr. Holt. I don't think we can rule out the possibility that we're being shadowed. I'd feel more comfortable if you didn't travel on public transportation. Are you up to driving to Stavanger? I know it's a hellish stretch of road."

"I think it will be a nice change. And if there is a tail, I don't think he'll have much luck trying to keep up with me."

"Yes, yes. I see." Skogan looked as if he doubted the wisdom of asking Bjørn to drive. "Well, do be careful. I'll need you back here for that meeting with Danielsen. I'm going to try to get him to agree to Monday afternoon. And Mr. Holt, if you can fit in a little rest, by all means. . . ."

"And the same goes for you, Mr. Minister."

They shook hands warmly. Skogan accompanied Bjørn to the door, arm around his shoulders, and wished him a good trip. He sent him off with a pat on the back. The crisis was eroding his formality.

Summer nights in southern Norway are different from those on the Northern Cape. The sun sinks entirely below the horizon for several hours. But when the sky is clear, darkness never really falls. Rather, a long twilight melts gradually into an extended dawn. In the forests or along deserted mountain roads, these nights have a peaceful, dreamy quality about them. It was through such an enchanted night that Bjørn longed to drive.

Dressed in French jeans, a khaki army shirt, and leather sandals, he sped out of town and into the countryside. The convertible top of his Lotus sports car was down, and the warm wind was heavy with the smell of newly mown hay. It whipped his face and chest and tugged at his hair, coaxing his senses back to life.

He glanced at the large plastic bag on the passenger seat. In it was his dinner, which Mrs. Erlandsen, the proprietress of a small pub near his home, had prepared for him. There would be cheese, butter, dark bread, Westphalian ham sliced thin as paper, tins of marinated herring, fruit, and an ample supply of pilsner. That was what she always packed for him when he went driving in the mountains alone.

He felt famished now, after weeks of tension during which he had had no interest in eating. But he was enjoying the driving so much he would not stop just yet. He downshifted to pass a lumbering truck, slid around a late-model Volvo, and urged the willing engine to the red line before shifting. A glance in the rear view mirror assured him that he was not being followed.

To the left the deep green waters of the Oslo Fjord faded into the evening haze. To the right, a hilly quilt of farmland lay framed by the purple silhouette of the mountains. He had forgotten how beautiful the summer landscape around Oslo was, how fragrant and soft the evenings were, how much he loved to get out of the city. While he drank in the wonders around him, he thought of Christina. If this thing dragged on much longer he would have to invite her to Oslo. Three weeks had passed since he had run his hands over her exquisite body, had listened to her sigh, had felt her legs tighten around him. Much, much too long. . . .

The road veered sharply and ran along the fjord for a stretch before heading into the mountains. A pang of hunger replaced his yearning for Christina, and he pulled onto the shoulder. Bag in hand, he scurried down the rock bank to the water's edge, hoisted himself onto a huge flat boulder, and spread out his evening meal.

A luxury ship was passing. The ship was close enough for him to see passengers on the deck, drinking, chatting, watching the banks of the fjord glide past.

Someone must have seen him in the waning light of the evening. A group of elegantly dressed people on the aft deck stared in his direction. A woman in a low-cut white gown lifted her glass toward him and waved. He toasted her with his beer bottle, not knowing whether she could see him. He grew pensive as he waited for the swells from the wake to lap at the rocks below. He knew that ship well. It was the famous Kieler Ferry, on another of its carefree voyages between Norway and the continent.

Bourgeois Europe, he mused. How good-natured and banal everything seemed. Poverty and mass suffering had long since vanished; so had greatness in the arts and in public life. Something had been lost in these affluent postwar years, something of the toughness of his father's generation, of its willingness to defend its ideals, to fight, to sacrifice. Just as well, he thought.

Times certainly had changed. He stood up and stretched, taking a deep breath of the damp evening air. As he watched the lights of the luxury liner recede into the haze, he wondered what it would have been like to peer out over this same stretch of water on the day that the *Blücher* had steamed toward Oslo. That was in 1940, and the great German battleship was on its way to the Norwegian capital. Orders had gone out not to oppose the Nazi fleet, but—at least according to legend—a cook in the Home Guard had failed to get the message. He fired one of the giant guns guarding the fjord at the steel behemoth, sending it and its fifteen-hundred-man crew to the bottom of the deep, icy waters.

Bjørn felt a touch of pride over the obscure Norwegian's deed. A senseless act, no doubt, one almost certain to lead to the cook's death, one that was to have no lasting effect on the course of the war. And done in the name of that questionable ideal, nationalism. Why then, he asked himself, was he moved tonight by the cook's idealistic and meaningless sacrifice for Norway?

He of course knew the answer: the Svalbard crisis was forcing him to grapple with issues he preferred not to face. He was playing a diplomatic game with the Russians and playing it well. What allowed him to be so effective—of this he was quite sure—was his freedom from strongly held ideals, ideals that committed *others* to rigid and easily discerned positions. It was ironic, but in this instance it was the absence of any great love for Norway that allowed him to stand up to Ivanov without fear. His detachment gave him the advantage; he could do more in deterring the Russians than a thousand of his country's most devoted patriots. The Russians wouldn't know what cards he held, wouldn't know from which position he would strike next, or how they should prepare to meet him. He was dedicated only to the game, and because of this his politics were almost flawless.

But what if something went wrong? What if there were a war? What if the loss of Svalbard were the first step in a gradual Soviet takeover of Europe? If that were to happen, might he feel differently about the cook's sacrifice? Or about his own philosophy of politics? And was it such an unlikely possibility? Nineteen forty, the sinking of the *Blücher*, five tortured years under the Nazi boot —all of that was hardly the distant past. War and occupation were commonplace in the history of the old continent. How easy it was to forget after a few short decades of peace.

The Soviet boot suddenly seemed to him a real possibility. It would be just as harsh as the Nazi boot, harsher perhaps, and it

142

would last a hell of a lot longer. Was he really playing a game with Ivanov? Was it as simple as that? He suppressed his thoughts; they would only diminish his effectiveness in the coming confrontation.

He drove on into the serene night. He sped through lush and fragrant pine forests, climbed above the timberline toward rows of dome-shaped mountains whose pale phosphorescent glaciers peered back at him through the half-darkness, descended in tight curves to the banks of still, narrow fjords, crossed trembling bridges over noisy streams, and watched waterfalls in the distance glowing like white ribbons on inky black cliffs.

It was shortly before noon when Bjørn reached the outskirts of his hometown. He drove through orderly rows of nondescript suburban houses and on toward the harbor.

Sleepy old Stavanger—with its narrow cobblestone streets, quaint wooden houses, open-air markets, and Gothic cathedral —had become a bustling operations center for oil drilling in the North Sea. From here the offshore rigs were supplied with everything from food and clothing to heavy equipment. The families of the oil workers had moved to Stavanger in droves, and the huge drilling platforms—some costing over a billion dollars— were built in special shipyards along the waterfront.

One of the platforms was being towed out to sea. He stopped for a moment to watch. The huge edifice of concrete and steel towered above the placid blue waters beyond the harbor, dwarfing the dozen tugs that pulled it. Business is good, thought Bjørn.

Downtown, shining glass and aluminum office buildings had sprung up all around in the two years since his last visit, and the hills to the northwest were dotted with high apartment towers. He drove under an enclosed pedestrian bridge, which arched gracefully between two of the new buildings, and turned right on the Ibsensgata, the street where he had grown up. On his left, an enormous American-style shopping mall was under construction. A little farther, the old park where he had played soccer on Sunday afternoons was now a modernistic playground. White, blue, and yellow cubes stood on end, clustered around chrome slides and monkey bars.

143

It was not until the street became narrow and bumpy and the sun disappeared behind the boughs of overhanging trees that he began to recognize the city of his childhood. His heart beat a little faster when he passed the old yellow schoolhouse with the twin chimneys. It didn't seem so long ago that his mother had walked him here for his first day of school that rainy September morning. A moment of sadness took hold of him as it always did when he became acutely aware of the passage of time.

He pulled up to the iron gate in front of the big white house where he had grown up, shut off the engine, and jumped out. His father was asleep in a rocking chair on the porch. Bjørn slammed the car door, grabbed his suitcase from the trunk, and called out, "Nap's over, Father. There's not a second to waste."

The elder Mr. Holt awoke with a start. He ran his fingers through his mane of white hair and sprang to his feet. He was tall and trim from the five-mile walks he took, rain or shine, through Stavanger's hilly streets. His face was reddish-bronze from constant exposure to the elements, and his bearing was rigid, almost military. He bounded down the steps two at a time and met his son halfway to the gate. They shook hands and embraced.

"Crazy bastard," growled the old man jokingly, "why in hell's name didn't you take the train?"

"Father, you forget not everyone's in your physical condition. I wasn't sure I could survive the walk from the station."

Mr. Holt looked him over, scowled with mock disapprobation at his dress, embraced him again and led him inside.

"Bjørn, is something wrong?" asked Mr. Holt. "You look tired. Come on, out with it. There's nothing you need to hide from me."

"I know, Father. I trust you to hold your tongue. You'll see what I mean about secrecy being crucial after we've had a chance to talk."

Bjørn closed his eyes and rubbed his forehead.

"Son, you're not ill, are you?"

"No, no, Father. Just tired. I'm as fit as you." He reached over and squeezed Mr. Holt's sturdy arm. "Well, maybe not quite."

"That girl of yours? She been giving you grief?"

"Christina? No, not the slightest. It's politics, Father. . . ."

"I should have guessed it right off. Working for those Labor

Party clowns would drive anyone to despair. Are they after your head because you've stuck to the Liberals?"

"Worse, Father. Some of us in the Foreign Office think the Russians—"

"Hell, Bjørn, I could have told you a thing or two about the Russians back in '45. Now what is it? Are they finally coming after us because of that donkey ass of a Prime Minister? Wouldn't surprise me one bit. Not one bit."

Bjørn stood and stretched, not ready just yet to begin a detailed explanation of the crisis.

"Father, is the beer still where it used to be in the cellar?"

"Sure, son. But check the refrigerator first. I put in a few bottles last night when you called. I don't think I've drunk them all yet. And bring me one while you're up, would you?"

Bjørn laughed when he opened the refrigerator door. The top two shelves were loaded with several dozen half-liter bottles of his favorite pilsner. Two frosty bottles of Gewürztraminer were wedged in the vegetable bin between heads of lettuce and a big yellow squash. He knew this was his father's way of welcoming him home, for the old man drank very little. Touched, he took down two mugs and filled them, watching the thick foam climb to the rim.

The big tidy kitchen filled him with memories of his youth. It hadn't been especially pleasant growing up in the shadow of a domineering, powerful man. But since his mother's death eight years ago, a lot of things had changed. He had seen his father grief-stricken and vulnerable, and had realized there was more to him than his granite-like facade. Certain things simply weren't discussed in the Holt family—emotions for one. But he had sensed in his father's clumsy attempts at tenderness a wish to apologize for the severity with which he had raised his only child.

Jens Holt's life had been far from easy. In the late thirties, he had been the youngest member of the Storting, the Norwegian Parliament. As a member of the minority Conservative Party, he had made quite a nuisance of himself speaking out in favor of emergency military preparations to deter the "German aggressor." Politicians in the governing Labor Party had branded him an alarmist. He had replied in speeches, articles, interviews, and shouting matches in the Storting that his accusers were cowards, too full of fear to face up to the Nazi threat.

The invasion he had predicted came, of course, and Jens Holt left his wife and baby to help organize a post-surrender resistance in the mountains. He was captured by the Germans in 1943, deported, humiliated, tortured, and almost worked to death. But he survived the war to return to politics, no less outspoken than before. In the sixties, however, as the gap narrowed between the political parties, his Conservative colleagues decided he was a liability. His quick mind, sharp tongue, and uncompromising values were disrupting their attempts to work more closely with the Laborites. He was forced out of the Party and, feeling bitter and betrayed after a lifetime of service, he gave up public life.

Mr. Holt sat attentively through Bjørn's analysis of the Svalbard affair.

"Son," he said afterwards, "you've got a damned good head on your shoulders. What's more important—mark my words—you've got the patience and the tact to deal with both the Russians and the Laborites. I don't know how you do it. I know how I'd react. I'd speak out too soon. My feelings would be too strong to contain. I'd botch the whole damned thing the first day."

"Not true, Father," said Bjørn, knowing that it *was* true. "In fact, I'd like to hear your opinion on how we should proceed. Why don't we go out to dinner tonight? We'll get a private table and talk about the problem from every conceivable angle."

"Son, we've got the private table already. The Hotel Atlantic at six."

"Splendid, Father, excellent."

"And, Bjørn, we'll make a real evening of it. What do you think? Can we spend a thousand krone in one night?"

Bjørn twisted uncomfortably on the sofa. "We can give it a hell of a try. But listen, I didn't come only to visit. There's some very important work I've got to handle in Stavanger, beginning tonight. We'll have to make an early evening of it."

"What?"

"Not that early, Father. Let's say nine o'clock. I've got to—"

"Got to get yourself a girl?" joked Mr. Holt to disguise his hurt feelings. "Well, you won't have any trouble. Stavanger's become a

146

pretty wild place. All those foreign women are just hanging around looking for something to do while their husbands are out on the rigs. You know, son, I might even join you myself if I were a few years younger. Now out with it. What's there to do tonight that can't wait till morning?"

"Do you remember old Turk?"

"Yep. A hard one to forget. Just saw the rascal at the fish market yesterday. He was with a bunch of foreign oilmen. Said he had just gotten back from running supplies out to a Caltex platform."

"Father, Turk isn't running supplies. He works for the CIA. Those foreign oilmen you saw with him were probably the agents I've come to Stavanger to talk to. Anyway, I've got to meet him at the Golden Horn at ten and make a couple of calls before I go there."

"Well, Jesus Christ," boomed Mr. Holt, slapping his thigh and laughing. "So old Turk's retired in style. Should have known he's up to something, that sly dog. Okay, Bjørn, well and good. We'll make an early night of it. Run on upstairs and get a shower and change. If we have to call it quits at nine, let's see if we can get into town soon." He smiled and shook Bjørn by the shoulder. "It isn't often I have my son here to entertain me."

"Bjørn, I'm sorry," snapped Christina. "I don't appreciate being treated like a secretary, understand? I told you I spent my entire day trying to track her down."

"Did you try Jon?"

"Of course. That was one of the first places I went. He seemed as anxious to find her as you are. Maybe you two should team up."

"Christina, I apologize for being so insistent. It's just that I've got to find her before she does something stupid."

"You don't approve of her relationship with your American friend? Why the sudden change of heart? You said last week you were happy for her."

"It's got nothing to do with him. And I can't talk much longer. If you hear anything, call me at my father's, will you? Do you have the number?"

"Of course, Bjørn. You gave it to me yesterday. Now when do I get to see you? It's been a long time, you know."

"It's been a hell of a long time. Can you come to Oslo next week?"

"Bjørn, sometimes you act like you're the only one who has a job. . . . Let me see if I can cancel some classes. I'll call you as soon as I find Ulrike."

"Thanks, love. It's a marvel you put up with me."

"It is indeed."

He hung up and pushed open the door of the phone booth. For a moment he toyed with the idea of flying to Tromsø in the morning. But what would be the use? If Christina wasn't able to find her, he wouldn't be either. He would just have to wait . . . and hope. Perhaps, too, Christina had been right. If Ulrike had promised him that night on the way to the airport not to publish anything on Svalbard without at least discussing it with him, she would certainly not do otherwise.

He glanced at the clock on a bell tower across the street. It was twenty after nine. Enough time to walk to the Golden Horn, he thought, time to relax and work off the heavy meal.

He loosened his tie, put both hands in his pockets, and strolled toward the waterfront. Across the street, two chic couples in evening dress were leaving an exclusive restaurant. Tipsy businessmen in suits were milling around a taxi stand like teenage boys, pumping a driver on where the best prostitutes could be found. Everywhere, oilmen caroused like soldiers on leave, descending in droves on the few women who dared come out unescorted. A few drunks staggered by, and an ambulance with flashing blue lights and howling sirens pushed its way through the heavy traffic. His mind was wrapped up in the crisis; the scene hovered on the periphery of his awareness.

In fifteen minutes, he reached the modern playground he had passed on the way into town. He leaned against a scrawny tree and propped a foot on a neighboring bench. The bustle of the city grew quieter. Overhead, the leaves swished in the breeze, and in the distance a dog barked plaintively.

The sky diffused a chalky light. A row of streetlamps came on. Faint shadowy patterns of the playground's strange, angular structures appeared on the grass. The cubes that stood on end became great elongated parallelograms spilling over onto the street. Climbing bars became busy overlapping grids, linear and brittle. Abstract stone monuments became elegant ellipses. Sweeping curves intersected the straight lines at a thousand points.

Confusion and order, thought Bjørn, taking in the scrambled geometry with an odd sense of fascination. The pattern was always the same. If you looked only at the shadows, you saw a meaningless tangle. But as soon as you glanced at their origin, they seemed an extension of logic itself. Look, analyze, piece together the missing parts . . . and then act!

12

Oɪʟᴍᴇɴ, sailors, and harbor workers sat in noisy groups around rough wooden tables. They were drinking, back-slapping, boasting—a Saturday night like any other on the waterfront.

Bjørn pushed his way to the back of the pub and entered a small private room without knocking. Johnson and Turk smiled; two younger men interrupted their pool game and stared at the stranger.

Trygve Torsvik, whom Bjørn had never seen in a hurry to do anything in the thirty-odd years of their friendship, stood up slowly. The old sailor's leathery face brightened and the crow's feet around his wistful blue eyes grew deeper. He scratched his stubby white beard, shook his head, and puffed on an oversized pipe with a long curved stem. "My, my," he mumbled, "your father sure was wrong about you. You've amounted to something after all."

"Hardly, Turk," said Bjørn. "I'm just another one of those uppity Oslo bureaucrats your townspeople are so fond of. Your bartender asked me on the way in if I was the tax inspector."

"What did you tell him?" laughed the old sailor.

"I told him I was indeed. Turk, *you're* the success story if I've ever heard one. Sixty years old and on the rise in the world's toughest business."

"My business is the sea, Bjørn. Always has been, always will be. Now if what I'm doing happens to help out the U.S. or Norway, so much the better. But my friends here are the pros. I'm just the captain, no different from thirty years ago."

The two young men at the pool table stiffened at the allusions to the CIA. Although they had been briefed by Johnson for tonight's meeting—Johnson didn't know enough himself to tell them much—they reacted to Bjørn's presence with the instinctive suspicion of intelligence agents. William Johnson must have noticed his men's distrust of the Norwegian, for he motioned them to join him.

"Bjørn Holt," said Johnson to his colleagues. He spoke in Norwegian. "Chief adviser to Norwegian Foreign Minister Skogan and a very good friend of mine from my old Washington days at the State Department."

The two young Americans—Bjørn guessed them to be in their late twenties—seemed to relax. Johnson draped his arm around the one nearer him, a short, slightly plump man with shaggy dark hair and a baby face. "Bjørn, this is Andy Wheeler from Tulsa. They grow a crazy breed down there, as you probably know."

"Howdy, Be-yorn," drawled Wheeler in English. He went on in fluent Norwegian with the same Oklahoma twang. "I hope we'll be able to help you out."

"I hope so too." They shook hands.

The second agent shook Bjørn's hand.

"Jim Duncan," he said formally.

"Jim," said Johnson, "is the linguist among us. He's got several of the Norwegian dialects down pat. Not bad for a boy from Toledo, Ohio."

"I should say not."

"Jim is so fluent in Norwegian that he has to practice making mistakes. We pose as American oilmen, and no American oilman speaks Norwegian like Jim. You can't be too good without blowing your cover."

Duncan smiled but said nothing. He was a tall man with short flax-colored hair and the gaunt face of a distance runner. The competent, dreary type, thought Bjørn, the type you had trouble liking but were glad to have around when there was trouble.

Bjørn tried to size up all three agents. He was going to have to ask them a favor that would put their lives in jeopardy, even

151

under the most favorable circumstances. If any one of them were not convincing in the disguise of an American oilman, the chances of the mission's success—and of the agents' safe return—would be zero.

About Andy Wheeler he had no qualms. Andy reminded him of a thousand characters he had seen in the southern and western United States. There was an Andy Wheeler lurking around somewhere inside every gas station; frying ham and eggs behind every short order grill; sitting behind the wheel of every pickup that passed you on a dusty side road. He was also from oil country. There must be a good number of Okies working out on the American-owned platforms.

Duncan was no less convincing. He was the clean-cut sort who would drink Coca-Cola at a smorgasbord, wear his trousers much too short, and defend United States foreign policy with the moral fervor of a Baptist. That he spoke fluent Norwegian might surprise people at first, but it wouldn't give him away. Americans were such a mixed bag that Europeans and Russians almost expected an occasional surprise.

It was *Johnson* who was worrying him. He, like the others, wore scuffed boots, faded jeans, and a grease-splotched denim workshirt. His hands were calloused, his face well weathered, and he looked tough. But Bjørn saw only the smooth bureaucrat he had known in Washington. He remembered him as he had seen him one fine April morning almost a decade ago, dressed in a light-blue shirt and wide, trendy tie, his sport coat flung over one shoulder and his attaché case in his free hand, bounding up the staircase of an imposing public building.

Johnson was a good-looking man with curly brown hair and what the Americans called a winning smile. He was Bjørn's age, forty-one, of medium height, athletic and well muscled. He was pleasant and witty, and had been no stranger to the capital's sophisticated social circles before his curious change of career.

Bjørn decided his memories of Johnson were causing him unnecessary doubts. The man would do; he would *have* to do. Suddenly, he was anxious to begin the meeting.

Turk spoke up as if he had read his mind. "Well, Bjørn, your call yesterday put us in quite a bind. We're supposed to leave tonight in the trawler. We'd better get to the heart of the matter. It wasn't easy getting your friend William here to postpone the departure, not even for a couple of hours."

They sat down at the sturdy wooden table. Johnson gestured toward the ice, glasses, and assorted bottles. "We've gotten wind of a sabotage operation out on one of the offshore platforms. The British think a group of left-wing terrorists has infiltrated the work force. We're sailing to the platform tomorrow, supposedly to do some repairs on a valve. Time's a factor, Bjørn, because this is a highly coordinated joint operation with the Tommies."

Bjørn poured himself a small Scotch. "Thanks for waiting. I'm sorry I wasn't able to speak to you personally, but Turk didn't know where you could be reached."

"Professional caution, Bjørn. Now let's hear what's on your mind. I've got to be out of here before midnight."

Wheeler was rubbing chalk on the end of a pool cue. He looked up and smiled at Bjørn. "A shame we don't have time for a little game."

"Perhaps next time we meet."

Duncan seemed suspicious again. He shot Bjørn a furtive, unfriendly glance before pouring a bottle of Coke into a beer stein packed with ice cubes. Turk gazed off into the distance, puffing on his pipe. Peals of laughter from the tavern clashed with the tense silence in the room.

"Let me lay it on the line," said Bjørn. "We have good reason to believe the Russians are preparing an invasion of Svalbard and northern Norway."

"But, Bjørn, really!" exclaimed Johnson. "With all due respect, this is something you should take up with Wilson in Oslo. For Christ's sake, you've worked with him before. With very good results, I understand."

"I realize this sounds a little rash, but. . . ."

"A little," Wheeler joked, taking aim with his pool cue at Duncan's fizzing stein of Coke.

"Shhh," said Johnson. "Let him talk."

Bjørn crossed his arms and leaned forward until his elbows rested on the table. "William, you know as well as I that Danielsen's 'third way' has wrecked relations between Wilson and our people. From what I understand, he has orders not to cooperate with Norwegian intelligence in any way, shape, or form."

"Right. And I work for Wilson. Do you see the position that puts me in?"

"I'll tell you right now, William, that I'm going to be asking a lot of you and your men. If you'd prefer . . ."

"Do you have some sort of concrete data—pictures or something—from your own boys? If we had something to go on, I might be able to approach Wilson without pissing him off."

"Our intelligence people know nothing of this. It's a long story. Long, complicated and, I'm afraid, rather tragic."

The three Americans stared at Bjørn, incredulous. Turk relit his pipe.

"In other words," said Duncan, "you want us to follow your hunch and do your intelligence work for you in defiance of our orders? Sounds like you're taking up where your Prime Minister left off."

"Mr. Duncan, I don't really think you quite—"

A loud knock at the door silenced Bjørn. Johnson picked up the deck of cards and dealt them around. "Come in!" ordered the American.

The bartender entered with a bottle of Cutty Sark, fresh ice, and clean glasses. Smiling, he set them on the table. "On the house, Mr. Inspector. Made any arrests yet?" He winked at Turk and walked out without another word. Duncan locked the door.

"No more interruptions," said Johnson. "We've got to get moving."

Bjørn knew how essential it was that his performance in the next hour be flawless. It would not be an easy matter. With Americans, if you appeared too polished, too sophisticated, they pegged you as a talker, someone incapable of decisive action. If you came across too blunt, they dismissed you as dumb. If you were too aggressive, all they could think of was dealing you a few hard blows to put you back in your place. And if you were too polite, they thought you spineless. Hard people to deal with, these Americans, harder in many ways than the Russians.

He began by confiding in them that Danielsen's "third way" had been a drastic mistake that neither he nor Skogan had ever

154

supported. He explained some of the domestic political reasons for Danielsen's folly—reasons, he said, that did not excuse the statesman's blunder but at least made it clear he had not been out to humiliate the United States. He then explained very precisely his and Skogan's dilemma: if Danielsen were confronted with any public suspicion of a Russian danger, he would rush to deny it, cozying up to the Soviet Union to create the image of a Russian–Norwegian friendship his "third way" required. The result would be catastrophic. The Russians would see in Danielsen what Hitler saw in Chamberlain in '38. They would strike; Svalbard and northern Norway would be in Soviet hands before the West had time to develop a defensive strategy.

He next revealed his suspicion that the Soviets were passing false information about German uranium mining on Svalbard to a few unwitting Western journalists—information that, if widely published in Europe and the United States, would give the Soviet Union a pretext for the invasion. Such lies would also divide NATO internally, with most member countries siding against Germany. Finally he told them his suspicions about the fate of the glaciological expedition.

Johnson, Duncan, and Wheeler looked at each other, speechless.

"And you can't go to Wilson," said Johnson, at last, "because that would politicize the matter, is that it? Your Prime Minister would get wind of the crisis, would openly try to placate the Russians, and would thus squander every chance you have of making Soviet Ambassador Ivanov believe a Russian invasion will not go unopposed. Is that it, Bjørn?"

"That, precisely, is it."

"I think we've got to do something," said Johnson.

While a roar of laughter from the tavern shook the walls, the two agents nodded their silent agreement.

"I might be able to get hold of some satellite pictures of the area," said Johnson. "Landing craft, supply ships—all of those things would show up. Only problem is that I can't possibly get loose for a couple of weeks without letting the cat out of the bag. As I explained, we're working together with British antiterrorist squads out on the rigs. If we weren't to show up, you can imagine the kind of stink that would cause."

"Yes, of course. And even if you were free, the satellite pictures would do us no good."

"What do you mean?"

"William, the Russians aren't dumb. They know exactly what type of monitoring capacity you possess. And in any event, they won't take Svalbard with an amphibious assault from the mainland. There would be no reason to. There are only a thousand Norwegians on the archipelago. A few hundred Russian troops smuggled into Barentsburg would be able to do the job quite nicely. And with no advance warning."

"We can detect the movement of a few hundred troops, especially if there's heavy equipment involved. Which I assume there would be."

"There will be. But neither the troops nor the equipment will be moved in one operation. Norwegian intelligence has known for some time of a Soviet contingency plan—"

"Well, let's hear it."

"The main activity in the town of Barentsburg is coal mining. Exchanges of mining personnel are routine, and heavy machinery for the mines arrives weekly at the Russian port, usually crated up in some type of standard industrial wrapping. Over a period of several weeks, soldiers disguised as miners and military hardware disguised as mining equipment could be smuggled into Barentsburg without any risk of detection. In fact, it's possible they could bring in intercontinental ballistic missiles right under our noses. An SS-20 with an added third stage could be carted up to the mine shafts in components and assembled underground. Since Svalbard is on the shortest ballistic path from Russia to the American heartland, I would be surprised if they *didn't* have that in mind. And all of this could happen right under the blind eye of your satellite."

"But we'd pick up the radiation from the warheads."

"No, William, because they won't risk arming the missiles until Svalbard is theirs. And as for the second prong of the attack, the one against northern Norway, what is there to detect? Every kind of ship, tank, gun, missile, and aircraft is already stationed around Murmansk. How are you going to distinguish between that massive concentration of hardware and the type of buildup needed for an invasion?"

Duncan, whose opinion of Bjørn had skyrocketed, said, "Then what are you asking us to do? Sail right through the Northern Fleet and into Murmansk, find a pay phone, call Moscow and ask what's cooking?"

Bjørn laughed: humor from Jim Duncan was a good sign. "Let me start over from a different angle. If you three were able to convince yourselves that the militarization of a Russian mining settlement on Svalbard was underway, would you be able to rouse Wilson's interest in Soviet activities on the Cape? Certainly, Wilson is as aware as anyone of the critical strategic importance of the Svalbard Passage for American security."

He could almost see the wheels of Johnson's mind turn—the old political wheels which had made him so successful in the bureaucratic jungles of Washington. An intelligence coup on Svalbard, he was no doubt thinking, would catapult him high up the Agency's ladder. He must also be picking up the scent of adventure hanging heavy in the stale air of the room, the same scent that had lured him away from civilian life. Bjørn was right on both counts.

"How would Wilson *react*?" groaned Johnson. "Christ, Bjørn, if we came up with solid evidence of a Russian move, he'd pour every resource we've got in Scandinavia into the area." He seemed pleased. "But answer me something, friend. How are you suggesting we get into the place? And out again alive?"

"I don't know just yet. It's a problem, obviously. You'll have to give me some time to work on it. But if I can find a means acceptable to you, are you willing to give it a go? It's a lot to ask, I'm aware of that."

"If you come up with a plan that gives us half a chance, I'm willing," said Johnson.

"I, also, of course," added Duncan.

They all looked at Andy Wheeler. "Come on, fellas. I didn't join you old dogs to pussyfoot around. Hell, yeah, I'm in. Goddamn sure as hell!" These were the first English words spoken in over an hour. For some reason, Bjørn found them exhilarating.

Turk poured himself an aquavit and tossed it down in one

157

swallow. "Norway's my country," he said. "I've fought for her before. I'll fight for her again. Now, I've known Bjørn Holt for most of his life. Ain't a finer fellow anywhere. If he says there's a danger, you can be damned sure there is. I just want to be good and sure of one thing before I drag these men way up north. Sounds like it might be into September before we sail. That right, Bjørn?"

"It's almost September now, Turk. Most likely it will be."

Johnson rapped on the table with his knuckles. "Two weeks," he said, "is the minimum time we'll need to get our little affair with the British wrapped up. Unless, of course, you want us to go to Wilson at this point for permission."

"No," said Bjørn. "Two weeks is all right. We're running a risk, but a lesser one, I think, than if we tell Wilson. So I guess that answers your question, Turk. September it will be. Why?"

"Why, eh? Have you forgotten, my boy, all the stories I used to tell you about fall storms up there?"

"Of course not, Turk. You used to scare me to death."

"Well, the ole *Utsira*'s a sturdy ship. My American friends'll vouch for that. But you should all be cautioned. If it starts a blowin' up around Svalbard like it did in '42, the Russians'll be the least of our worries."

"Turk," said Bjørn, "if you don't want to take the *Utsira*, we'll arrange—"

"Hush, boy. The *Utsira* and I've been together too long for swapping round like that. She'll be all right. I just want these men to know what they might be gettin' into before I take 'em north." He smiled, and his watery blue eyes danced with mischief. The sea was his life; the prospect of a long voyage filled him with excitement.

Johnson sprang to his feet and reached across the table to shake Bjørn's hand. "We've got to be off, friend. I'm glad we've reached an accord. Let's hope Ivan waits on us. I'll call you at the Foreign Office as soon as we get back."

"Better not."

"Then at home."

"No. Go to a booth and call my father here in Stavanger. He and I will work out a communications system in the meantime.

He'll put us in contact. The number is under Jens Holt. Tell him you're an old friend of mine from the States and are trying to find me. I'll have him give you my address and number in Oslo. Ignore them. Go directly to the Wesselstuen on the Ibsensgata. That's near his home. I'll instruct him to meet you there day or night fifteen minutes after you phone."

"You're really worried about being watched?"

Bjørn didn't want to confuse them by explaining that Danielsen as well as the Russians might have a burning interest in what he was doing. "Professional caution," he said, and left it at that.

He opened the front door and closed it without a sound. The sight of his father asleep on the couch in his wrinkled green pajamas startled him. It was two in the morning—well past the old man's bedtime. He walked quietly across the dimly lit living room.

"Father," he whispered. "What are you still doing up?"

"Waiting for you," answered Mr. Holt groggily. He sat up. "That girl of yours called about an hour ago. Got me out of bed. She wanted you to get back to her tonight."

"Christina Sollie?"

"Yep. Now if you'll excuse me, son, I'm going to bed before I wake up all the way. See you bright and early."

"Thanks for waiting up, Father. Good night."

He watched the old dynamo tackle the staircase and march up. Sheer will power, he thought. That man would do almost anything to deny a weakness, even an ordinary weakness like fatigue. He felt a sudden burst of anguish over his father's tortured life; he was glad he would be able to give the old warrior a minor role in the crisis.

He waited until he heard the bedroom door close, then rushed to the telephone in the kitchen.

It seemed forever until Christina answered.

"Bjørn?" It was the same sleepy voice with which she greeted him when he crawled into bed long after she had gone to sleep.

"Love, are you awake?"

She cleared her throat. "Hardly. You got your father's message?"

"Yes. He said you called an hour ago. I just got in and he was waiting up for me."

"An hour ago? Bjørn, I called you at ten. The poor devil must have been up all this time."

"I think he was. Christina, is something wrong?"

"Oh, Bjørn, I don't know. Ulrike called just after I talked to you last."

"Where is she?"

"Oslo."

"Oslo? What in hell is she doing in Oslo?"

"I don't know and she wasn't eager to explain. All she would say is that she had some research to do on uranium deposits on Svalbard."

"Christ! Where is she now? Where's she staying?"

"I don't know that either."

"What?"

"Bjørn, she wouldn't tell me. Don't you find that strange?"

"Indeed. And the Professor?"

"He's with her. I made her promise she'd keep trying at your place until she got you. She knows you're due back Monday and she knows you want to talk to her. Bjørn, listen, I'm very upset by this whole thing. Can't you—"

"Christina, I want you to come to Oslo Monday morning. Cancel your classes or find someone else to teach them. It's important. Can you get the early flight?"

"I'll try. Will you meet me at the airport?"

"If I can. If not, I'll leave a message with SAS. Take a taxi to the house and wait. Does anyone else know Ulrike's in Oslo?"

"No. I mean, no one except Jon."

"Jon? What the hell does he have to do with this?"

"Oh, Bjørn, I don't know. He's so desperately in love with her he can't stand not seeing her for more than a day. I felt sorry for him, I guess. I promised him I'd ring him up if I found her, that's all."

"All right. The fool should give up on her. I'll see you Monday."

"I'm glad, Bjørn, very glad. It's time we talked about a lot of things. If she leaves, I don't know if I can really stand staying up

160

here much longer. Especially if you keep disappearing for weeks on end like this."

"Christina, I promise you everything will be fine. Now listen, we'll be together in two days. Let's be happy about that."

"I am," she whispered. "Goodnight, dearest."

He hadn't the energy to reassure her further. If he seemed cold and preoccupied, she would soon understand why. Or perhaps she wouldn't. But that was something he would deal with later.

He grabbed a beer out of the refrigerator and went up the stairs. He dozed off wondering what Ulrike could possibly be doing in Oslo. The same question was going through his mind hours later when Jens Holt banged on his door and announced it was time for breakfast.

13

ULRIKE had been unable to sleep most of the night. Shortly after six that morning, she climbed out of bed and slipped on her light robe. Careful not to awaken Martin, she opened the louvred doors to the balcony.

The sun had already risen above the rooftops of the neighboring buildings. Its rays shimmered on the dew-laden foliage of the trees and bushes and washed the walls of the courtyard below in dappled golden light. Birds chirped and twittered; two squirrels were at play on the courtyard lawn.

It was going to be another scorching day, she thought. The rain and fog a thousand miles to the north in Tromsø seemed far away. Here in Oslo it was summer, a good honest summer like the ones that came to Munich every second or third year. She remembered the serene walks through the English Garden on warm, fragrant evenings, the noisy sailboat races on the Amersee, the sunburn from which no amount of lotion protected her fair skin. And she shuddered at the thought of Svalbard.

She was troubled. Something had been eating away at her since they arrived in Oslo two days ago. Not the frustration over their delayed departure for Svalbard—that was bad enough—but something deeper, more elusive.

Ten days ago everything had been set. They were to sail from Tromsø to Longyearbyen, the Norwegian settlement on Svalbard, on the coastal steamer. From there, she and Martin planned to bribe a boatman to take them to Barentsburg. There were plenty of crooks, as she knew from her previous visit. The Ice Fjord was swarming with peddlers of polar bear hides and other illegal goods. Barentsburg was, of course, off limits to Western tourists. But if she and Martin paid one of the shifty boatsmen enough, he would find a way to get them in. Perhaps he could develop engine trouble or feign serious illness—how didn't really matter. Once their presence attracted the Soviet Consul's attention, she was sure there would be no further difficulties.

Indeed, she had every reason to believe that Mikhail Obruchev would receive her warmly. A few months back, he had given her a long, clumsy interview and had taken her on a tour of his domain. She had written glowingly of Barentsburg, and she was certain that the Soviets would have read her article in the *Zeit*.

Nor was that all. She had noticed—and it had been quite disturbing at the time—that Obruchev was strongly attracted to her. Once, in a dimly lit mine passage, she had even felt a stab of panic, turning to catch him staring at her backside with thinly disguised lust. Now, however, she realized that his attraction to her might play into her hands. . . .

When she was again inside Barentsburg, she planned to trick Obruchev into giving her information about the German uranium mining. The facts she got would start the ball rolling. The *Frankfurter Rundschau*, as soon as it had something more concrete to go on than hunches and leaks, would launch a full-scale investigation. An expedition would be sent to Svalbard. Arnheim would be unmasked, his neo-fascist government would fall, the puppets would be defeated, and a new lease on life given the other Germany—the good Germany of Mozart and Goethe, Grass and Böll, her father and Georg.

That had been the plan. But things had gone wrong almost from the beginning. Two days before their scheduled departure for Longyearbyen, she had come down with a nasty case of bronchitis. Her fever climbed to one hundred three, and the doctor warned her that she risked developing pneumonia if she traveled before the antibiotics had a chance to work. Martin convinced her to postpone the trip for a week. Neither of them had realized that the tourist season on Svalbard ended September first. To her dismay, all of the remaining cruises to Longyearbyen were booked solid. She comforted herself with the knowledge that, if there were no cancellations for the ship passage, they would be able to get a flight on short notice.

She had been dead wrong. The biweekly flights to Longyear-byen were booked until mid-October. All she could do was request two places on the waiting list.

Her health mended. She and Martin spent two days combing the Tromsø harbor for a seaman who would take them to Long-yearbyen. Some were willing but none seemed trustworthy. There was much frantic telephoning, frustration, and anger; precious time slipped away.

And time was of the essence. If the Russians invaded Svalbard before she was able to expose Arnheim, all would be lost. The Americans, French, and English would never understand why the Soviet Union *had* to move. How could they understand? The Russians were the ones who had lost twenty-six million people to German arms in this century alone. It would be impossible to convince the West that the Soviets could not sit around twiddling their thumbs while Germany amassed huge supplies of uranium for God knows what purpose. Indeed, the tragedy was that the Soviet move would force the West into a tight alliance with Arn-heim's Germany for fear of Russian aggression.

In her desperation, she let Martin persuade her to drive to Oslo. He had found a passage to Svalbard aboard an old coal transporter which was undergoing repairs in nearby Moss. The ship, he had been assured, would be ready to sail between the twentieth of August and the first of September.

The sun climbed above the tallest tree in the courtyard and shone warmly on her. In the distance, she could hear the din of Monday morning traffic.

A powerful longing to give up seized her, a longing to melt in Martin's arms, to have him take her far away where just the two of them could live their days in perpetual sunshine. God, how happy she had been these last weeks in spite of all the problems. The intimacy, the wonderful nights of love, the moments of close-ness when not a word was spoken. . . . How had she been able to live without these things for so long?

But her longing to give up filled her with bitter self-loathing.

164

The golden opportunity was within reach; it might never come again. She had the chance to avenge the deaths of her father and Georg, to join forces in some significant fashion with all of her countrymen who, over the centuries, had laid down their lives fighting the German "evil." In that moment she knew that if she surrendered now, her life henceforth would not be worth living —with or without Martin.

Suddenly she sensed that the journey would separate them in some unknown way. An anguish arose from the depths of her being and sent a searing pain through her heart. But her suffering had an unexpected effect: it returned her to that tortured state from which her initial resolve had sprung. She was once more certain of what she had to do. Something akin to joy and yet so different surged inside her, something blissful and hauntingly tragic, a vivid realization that henceforth nothing, not even the highest sacrifice, could deter her from the pursuit of her goal.

Calmly, she returned to the room and telephoned for breakfast. She carried the tray to the night table and sat on the bed beside Martin, who was half-awake now, grumbling something about her misplaced Teutonic efficiency. She piled two big down pillows against the headboard, helped him sit up, and poured him a cup of coffee.

"What time is it?" he groaned.

"Late. Almost seven."

He managed a smile. "My, how people's notions of 'late' differ. Good coffee."

She took a taste from his cup, poured her own, and slid the breakfast tray closer to the bed. His mood improved; he was hungry. After studying a roll as if it were some kind of exotic fruit, he sliced it down the middle and buttered the bottom half.

"Did you ever get hold of that German friend of yours at the Polar Institute?" he asked.

She laughed. "You *are* tired today, aren't you? Was I too much for you last night?"

"Probably." He piled ham and cheese onto his roll. "Why?"

"Martin, I went downstairs and called him last night. Don't you remember?"

He chewed thoughtfully for a moment, scrutinizing her. "Sure

I remember. But you didn't tell me what he said. Or even if you'd reached him."

"You didn't give me a chance. You were lying in wait when I got back to the room."

"I will be tonight, too. Well, what *did* he say?"

"He wants me to come by the Institute at ten. He's going to sketch for me the areas where uranium has already been discovered and the areas where it would be geologically possible to find other deposits."

Martin emptied his cup. She poured him the rest of the pot and telephoned for more. He had a sudden urge for a smoke. "I always pick the worst time for my annual kick-the-habit drive," he muttered.

"What?"

"Nothing. Just talking to myself again. What does your Polar connection want in exchange for all this information? He'll probably ask you out tonight."

"You sound jealous."

"I am. Madly. Who is this clown?"

"He's hardly a clown, Martin. I'm sure he'll want to do all he can to help when he hears what Arnheim is up to. . . ."

"I doubt he'll be *that* interested in Arnheim."

She gave him a mock scowl and kissed him. "Oh, shut up. We're lucky I found him. I need the information."

"Then my little detour to Oslo might pay off after all."

"If we don't get to Svalbard too late."

"Tell you what. While you're with that friend of yours, I'll drive down to Moss and see how the repairs on the old barge are coming. When do you expect to finish with him?"

She laughed and toasted him with her coffee cup. "When he's so sick of my questions he throws me out."

At about the same hour, Bjørn sat under a pine tree a hundred miles southwest of Oslo, cursing British workmanship. His Lotus was parked beside the road, hissing angry white clouds of steam into the still morning air.

All night he had been driving a few miles, stopping to let the engine cool, filling a big plastic container with water from a stream or fountain, topping off the radiator, and driving a few more miles. But now the leak had sprung in earnest. As far as he poured the water in, it came trickling out down around his toes.

Why in hell's name, he fumed, couldn't the British build a water pump? This was the third time in two years! It was disgusting.

Next time he would listen to Christina and buy a Volvo. Hers was still clunking along after eight years, and she hardly even bothered to change the oil. But what in the hell was he going to do now? He glanced at his watch, reassured by the tiny letters on its face that spelled out "Made in Switzerland." It was already eight o'clock and he was due in Oslo at eleven. Skogan had explained yesterday on the phone that the meeting with Prime Minister Danielsen was set for one, and it would be "nice" if they could chat over lunch beforehand.

Hell, yes, it would be nice. But now he was worried he might not even make the one o'clock meeting. This wasn't Britain. There was a job to be done. He couldn't don a jungle helmet, long socks, and short pants and phone in that he had decided to hunt instead of work.

The sound of a car brought him to his feet. A Rover 2000 rounded the bend so slowly it appeared about to stall. But it continued at a snail's pace past the shipwrecked Lotus, then stopped as if it had recognized an old friend. It backed up and stopped again. A tall elderly man with a ruddy face and white moustache climbed out and stretched, then rubbed his hands together. He was wearing a two-piece khaki outfit—the standard garb, Bjørn thought, of that hearty breed of adventuresome Englishman out to explore exotic foreign realms like the European continent.

Folding his arms in front of him, the man made a slow circle around the Lotus, leaning over from time to time to peer into the windows. At last he looked up and saw the car's owner standing under a tree twenty feet away.

"A mite of trouble, eh, lad?" he called out in English, quite oblivious to the possibility he would not be understood.

"A mite, yes," Bjørn answered, hobbling down the rocky slope. They stood silently shaking their heads.

"Well, well," said the Briton after a time, "nice morning to get stuck, anyway. The name's Harrison McBride. I'm from Coventry."

"Bjørn Holt. From Oslo, unfortunately. This is a hell of a thing to happen a hundred miles from home when you've got a meeting at—"

"Now see here, mate," scolded McBride. "You've got to learn to relax. Type A behavior, I think that's what the Yanks call it. Won't do the heart any good. Shall we drag the old girl up to the next town and get that radiator fixed?"

"It's the water pump."

"Now, now. If that isn't something. I'll tell you, Mr. Holt, it's these roads of yours. They must be hard on the little pumps. I've been laid up in Kristiansand for the last week with the exact same problem. A lovely place to spend a week, lovely. I almost wish they hadn't got the old girl repaired so soon."

"Yes, very lovely. Are you vacationing in Norway?"

"Oh, no, my lad, wish I were. Here on business. Strictly business. Selling hydraulic pumps for water purification plants. Hydraulic, mind you, not mechanical. I'm not an engineer, nothing like that. But you don't really have to be. You just explain what the pumps do and how much they cost. Quite easy, really. Well, what do you say, mate? Can I give you a lift? I've got an appointment in Oslo at one and I'm already a week late. I suppose I ought to be getting along."

Bjørn did some fast thinking. If he crept along at thirty miles an hour with the Englishman, he would just make the meeting with the Prime Minister but would miss the eleven o'clock strategy session with Skogan. A fast driver could have him in Oslo by ten-thirty, but he couldn't count on flagging one down. He decided to play it safe. "That's most kind of you indeed, Mr. McBride. Let me fetch my suitcase out of the boot."

Mr. McBride opened his trunk and waited calmly. He took the luggage from Bjørn and laid it gently beside his golf clubs. "Well, let's hope she holds up," he said. They climbed in, the motor sputtered and caught, and they inched back onto the road.

Bjørn's sense of humor was not at its best. "Holds up? Jesus, it should. The pump's brand new. You talk like Oslo's on the other side of the Sahara."

"Well, mate, you never know about these things. Tough terrain for machinery, even the best of it."

"Yes," said Bjørn, with resignation. "It certainly is. By the way, Mr. McBride, how do those hydraulic pumps you sell perform in these rugged northern lands?"

McBride slowed down to twenty miles an hour to answer the question. "Well, lad, the pumps themselves are good, best in the world. But sometimes we can't get the parts for them. First there'll be a lorry strike in Manchester, then the boys over at the bearing plant will decide to walk out for a couple of days, then we'll have a dockworkers' strike and the fellows over at the foundry will go out in sympathy. Nothing serious, you see. Just the normal everyday things everyone has to put up with these days."

He pulled off the road and stopped to let a truck pass. Bjørn watched in a mild state of shock as McBride applied the parking brake and twirled his moustache. "Our real problem's the Jerries," he grumbled, his tone melancholy. "They come up here with the same pump, ask three times the price, and end up taking most of our business away from us. You don't suppose, Mr. Holt, that your people have something against us, do you?"

"Would you like me to drive?"

"What? Oh, no. Here, here. We'll get her rolling again. I prefer to talk when I'm not moving, that's all." He gave gas, but the car did not budge. Bjørn released the brake with a quick clandestine snap and they shot onto the road. "Oh, my," said McBride, slowing down again. "Well, what is it, Mr. Holt? How do you explain our troubles with the pump sales?"

"Hmmm," said Bjørn, "if I think about it, I'd have to say it's a result of some bizarre perceptions. People must perceive the German pump as being better and buy it for that reason. It's the same way in politics, you know. People act according to how they perceive things. Sometimes reality takes a backseat to what people think is reality. I'd say you've got to work on changing people's perceptions here. That should solve your problem."

"Indeed, my boy. Just what I keep arguing in the firm. I tell them it's got nothing to do with our pumps. It's the bloody Jerries. Politics? Did you say politics? You're not in politics, are you?"

Bjørn slumped down in the comfortable leather seat and closed his eyes. He didn't mind chatting, but the more they talked, the more McBride slowed down. If things continued at this pace he might not reach Oslo in time for dinner, much less for the meeting with Danielsen. "Me in politics?" he asked sleepily. "No, thank heavens."

At ten minutes after two Bjørn burst into Skogan's office. He had changed into his suit during Mr. McBride's third stop for tea, but his grooming fell far short of his usual standards.

"Where is Mr. Skogan?" His gruff tone startled Marianna.

"Why, Mr. Holt," she said, looking up from the typewriter, "you *have* had a nasty time getting back here, haven't you?"

"It's been rather trying, Marianna. Were you able to get my message through to him?"

"Yes, of course. He took it in stride. He's a little depressed today, but he was before you called. They're in there right now if you want to join them." She nodded toward the door.

"They're here? Why did Danielson come to the Foreign Office?"

"I don't know. Mr. Skogan called him this morning."

"Well, I guess I'd better go in. Do I look awful?"

"You look fine. Don't give it another thought." She led him to the door, cracked it an inch and knocked. "Mr. Foreign Minister, your adviser is here."

"Send him in," came the reply.

The two men were sitting in the armchairs where Bjørn and his boss held most of their strategy sessions. A third chair was glaringly empty. With some difficulty, they both struggled to their feet.

The Prime Minister was a big, energetic man, bigger now, thought Bjørn, than when he had last seen him. He was bald, with bushy eyebrows and a massive double chin. His exuberance was contagious.

"Good to see you, Holt," boomed Danielsen. His voice was full and resonant, like a good bass. "I understand you've been having some automobile problems. Glad you could get here."

"Yes, so am I. Nice seeing you again, Mr. Prime Minister."

Danielsen was still pumping Bjørn's hand when Skogan interrupted. "I told you, Mr. Holt, that you should give up on that Italian toy."

"It's British, sir," said Bjørn apologetically.

"Oh, yes, so you've told me. Well, I don't suppose there's much difference anymore."

The three men sat down. Danielsen took his enormous, half-smoked cigar from the ashtray, stuck it in his mouth, and lifted his glass of bourbon. "Now I think we should get back to business. With your consent, of course, Mr. Skogan. I don't have all day to spend with you gentlemen, although I must say I wouldn't mind." He pointed to the glass with his cigar. "Well?"

"Mr. Holt, I suppose I should fill you in on the latest before we go any further," said Skogan wearily.

"That would be most helpful."

"Evensen from intelligence was in to see me first thing this morning. Finnish authorities have uncovered a trailer filled with Soviet electronic equipment in a forest north of Ivalo. All indications are that it is the type of equipment used to coordinate armored attacks."

"Fine, fine," roared Danielsen. "I admit that's odd. But tell him that other nonsense you were telling me. I want to see what conclusions he draws from it."

Skogan did not doubt for a second that Bjørn would come up with an interpretation of Evensen's data similar to his own.

"Mr. Holt, the sightings of unidentified objects in the northern fjords have increased tenfold in the last week. The reports that have been checked out have revealed the objects to be old bathtubs, kitchen sinks, and the like."

"All right," interrupted the Prime Minister, "that's enough. Holt, what conclusions would you draw from all these bathtub sightings? Come on, speak up. Let's at least return this discussion to an intelligent level."

Bjørn tried not to show how startled he was by Skogan's revelations . . . the trailer of electronic equipment, the flood of sightings. He laced his fingers behind his head and looked up at the ceiling, where the smoke from Danielsen's cigar hung in inert wisps. "Mr. Prime Minister, I'm sure Foreign Minister Skogan has brought you up to date on our suspicions regarding a Soviet invasion plan. Is that correct?"

"He's brought me up to date on *his* suspicions. I remain wholly unconvinced."

171

"Of course. It's not a conclusion one wishes to jump to immediately. But if we for a moment accept the hypothesis that a Soviet invasion is in the making, then it is clear what the debris in the northern fjords signifies."

"Clear, Mr. Holt?"

"The debris has most likely been planted so our conscientious citizens along the fjords will call in the authorities and repeatedly make fools of themselves. You know the northerners—as shy as they are intelligent. Imagine the embarrassment of having your report checked out only to be notified you had sent the good officials of your community in pursuit of a floating bathtub. It won't take the people long to wise up. And the authorities will become skeptical of the remaining reports that trickle in. They will become less watchful. What better strategy to prepare the way for sneaking in a few contingents of pre-invasion saboteurs? Small amphibious craft enter our northern fjords some foggy morning . . . the same morning, in fact, that other Soviet forces are seizing Svalbard. You see, Mr. Prime Minister, if you can get the people to cry 'wolf' too often, you can quite effectively deprive them of their scream. Which is what I would suspect is happening right now in the north."

The Prime Minister grunted and emptied his glass. "Do you suppose, Skogan, old boy, that you could scare me up another bourbon and water? Well, Holt, you and your boss certainly think alike. I'll give you credit for that."

Skogan rang for Marianna.

"By the way," continued Danielsen, "what kind of bourbon is that? I consider myself a connoisseur of bourbons, but this one's got a taste I don't recognize."

"Wild Turkey."

"Wild Turkey . . . oh, yes, Wild Turkey. I'll have to make a note of that. Why don't you ask your secretary to make that a double, Skogan? Wild Turkey, interesting taste indeed."

He lit another cigar and blew the smoke skyward while he waited for his drink. Marianna slipped in, placed the glass on the table, and faded from the room.

Bjørn watched the Prime Minister take a long swallow of the bourbon. Appalled, he realized that the future of Norway might hinge on how the second glass of Wild Turkey affected his mood.

172

"Holt," said Danielsen at last, "I don't like your analysis. Typical of that Foreign Office–army–intelligence way of thinking. Take a bunch of harmless data and twist things around until you've got a national emergency. Now, Holt, I don't know if I've ever told you this before, but, wrong as you may be on this particular issue, I've got a very high opinion of your talents. We could use more young men like you in the Labor Party."

He tapped the inch-long ash from his cigar and leaned back in his chair. "Now tell me, young man. Have you ever thought of joining the Party? If you want to get ahead in Norwegian politics, you can't stick with the losers too long. No offense, Mr. Holt. It was a good way to get started. But I think you're due for a change. With my blessings, I can imagine you'll go far. Well, what do you say?"

Bjørn knew what Danielsen was up to. Afraid or unwilling to accept the truth, he was behaving like a man with a terminal illness who deceives himself about the imminence of death. Bjørn decided the only hope was to shock him out of his stupor. He knew that he risked making Danielsen an enemy for life, but he did not see how that could worsen the immediate situation.

"Mr. Prime Minister, I'm pleased you will have me in the Labor Party. Give me some time to think about it. May I remind you, though, that we met to discuss another issue, that of the Soviet danger . . ."

"Now, now. Holt. About your Soviet danger I've heard just about—"

"Mr. Prime Minister! With all due respect, I'm quite taken aback by your refusal to look the facts in the eye. I understand the potential political disaster that the situation in the north represents for you. You will notice that we have not let a word of our suspicions escape this office."

"All right, Holt, all right. Don't get worked up. You'll get your chance to have your say. Old Skogan talked for an hour nonstop before you came. You'll get your chance. Just keep up the good work plugging the leaks. Talk, I'm listening."

"A domestic political disaster is one thing. It happens to the great as well as the mediocre. The great recover, if not as politicians, then at least as men who still command respect. Take Churchill, for example, or Brandt. But such is not the case, Mr. Prime

Minister, for leaders who, by their own blindness, lead their nations into foreign policy debacles. Chamberlain was lucky he died so soon after Munich. As for our own good Foreign Minister in 1940, he was fortunate enough to have his scholarly work on Ibsen's poetry to fall back on."

Danielsen stubbed out his cigar, took a gulp of Wild Turkey, and turned scarlet. The fat under his chin wobbled as he spoke. "I resent the suggestion that I belong in a category with Chamberlain."

"And I resent your unwillingness to put the fate of Norway on at least an equal level with your domestic political concerns. I am, after all, a Norwegian. Our evidence might not be conclusive, Mr. Danielsen, but it is certainly not insignificant. You act as though it were."

Skogan, ghastly pale, intervened. "Please, there is nothing to be gained by becoming irritated."

"I quite agree," said Danielsen, as casually as if nothing had happened. He licked a fresh cigar, laid it down without lighting it, and fidgeted with his glass. While his gaze drifted haphazardly around the room, he addressed Bjørn. "All right, Mr. Holt, let's say you are right. What would you advise me to do?"

Bjørn sought to sound conciliatory but firm. "Sir," he said, attempting to catch the Prime Minister's eye, "the important thing is that we Norwegians demonstrate a certain willpower to the Russians, especially to Ivanov."

"Willpower?" said Danielsen weakly. Finally his eyes met Bjørn's.

"Yes. If Ivanov or another Soviet representative comes to you —and it is likely that someone will—you must act tough, even angry. You see, Mr. Danielsen, they're trying to determine what we would do if they attacked us. It's absolutely crucial we convey the impression we would fight. If they believe we'll fight, there'll be no invasion. The question is not how we would actually respond to a Soviet attack on our territory. That's another matter altogether. The question, Mr. Danielsen, is how they *believe* we will respond. And, sir, they must believe we will fight."

"Fight?" said Danielsen as he hoisted himself laboriously to his feet. "I thought the days were over when we would have to think

174

in those terms. Well, gentlemen, do keep me posted." He put his index finger to his lips. "And, shhh. We wouldn't want a word of this thing getting around. Just in case you two are wrong." He managed a sheepish smile and left.

"You did the right thing," Skogan said to Bjørn. They stood at the window in silence. The sausage man was grilling across the street. Carefree crowds in gay summer dress clogged the sidewalks and jammed the entrance to the Café Leopold. The traffic was heavy, the air laden with the familiar tangle of city smells.

"Jesus," mumbled Bjørn, "it's like talking to a wall. What are we going to do?"

"I, for one, am going to keep slugging." It was an uncharacteristic remark for the dignified old diplomat. He smiled. "Next on the bill of coming events is Ivanov. We'll have to be good, Mr. Holt, very good. If we appear too tough, he'll go straight to Danielsen. You know what that means. If we come across too weak, he'll have the signal he's waiting for, the signal, God forbid, that the Soviet Union can go ahead with its invasion. Then there's a third possibility, Mr. Holt. We might stage a brilliant performance which that wily Cossack will see through. Things certainly don't look encouraging at this end. Now tell me. Is there any hope with the Americans?"

"Yes, I think so. But it's a long shot. Can we meet this evening to discuss it? You must be exhausted."

"I'm afraid you're tied up tonight."

Perplexed, Bjørn studied Skogan's good-natured smile. "Tied up?"

"I've had to promise you to someone, a very lovely someone indeed."

Bjørn remembered with shock that Christina was to arrive that morning. "Oh, God," he exclaimed, "I forgot to call the airport."

Skogan laughed. "There's no harm done, none at all. She came here. She had forgotten the key to your house. I suppose she knew you kept an extra in your desk. We had just received your phone message and were able to explain your predicament to her. But I did send her off with a solemn promise to have you home at six. I assure you, Mr. Holt, that she wasn't angry in the least when she left."

"Sir," said Bjørn with a grin, "if that's true, you're a diplomatic miracle worker."

"Yes, well, let's hope so. Now give me a full report on the situation in Stavanger and we'll adjourn for the day."

For Martin the whole day had been a disaster. "Who?" "What?" "Which drydock?" "No, no. You're in the wrong place. Drive around those warehouses you see over there, then take a left, cross the railroad tracks, take a right over there where you see that black crane, then another left down by pier nine. I think it might be over there somewhere. Ask again if you can't find it."

He finally located the rusty freighter around noon. By that time everyone was out to lunch except one of the workers. The man sat with his back against a crumbling pile of sandbags, swilling beer and eating from a deep bowl. The odor of fish, sweat, and oil assaulted Martin's nostrils.

"Don't know, buddy. How the hell should I know when she'll be seaworthy? Maybe never. Maybe she never was. I don't do nothin' but work here."

Jesus, thought Martin, this whole transportation business was turning into a real mess. He was beginning to rethink his plans for getting them north when the foreman appeared, whistling. "Back to work, Knut. Lunch has been over for half an hour."

"Get off my ass," growled the worker. "Ain't none of the other guys showed up yet." He slammed his lunch pail shut and trudged up the gangplank.

Martin grabbed the foreman by the arm. "Well, how's she coming?" he asked, trying to sound cheerful.

"Great. Rudder's cracked, bearings in the propeller shaft are shot. She's lucky she got this far." He started to walk away but Martin tightened the grip on his arm. "Heh, pal, how 'bout letting go?" snarled the foreman.

"How 'bout answering a few questions?" Martin released him.

"Questions? Isn't my job to answer questions, mister. Who the hell are you, anyway?"

"I'm supposed to sail to Longyearbyen in that ship," Martin nodded toward the freighter and caught a glimpse of Knut, yawning as he urinated from the bridge.

The foreman warmed up. "So *you're* the loony bird." He scratched his head. "Say, mister, you don't look exactly like the seafaring type. I'd take you for some kind of a paper pusher or something."

"You'll find out otherwise if I don't get some straight answers from you. When's this thing going to be ready to sail?"

"Look here, pal, Mr. Anders has gone off on vacation. He said to tell you everything was set. You're supposed to leave the fare with me."

"Sounds like a great deal." Martin took a hundred-krone note from his wallet and laced it through his fingers. The foreman watched him intently. "Look, I need some information and I'm willing to pay for it."

"Well, how 'bout that? Now you're talking sense, mister. What can I do for you?"

"Tell me when this tub will be ready to sail."

The foreman held out his hand.

"Talk first."

"You won't mention this to Mr. Anders?"

"No."

"Well, we've got problems. Haven't even been able to track down all the parts we need. I'd say she might be ready by early November, not a day before."

Martin let the hundred-krone note flutter to the ground and walked off.

At the hotel an hour and a half later, he found Ulrike sitting at the sidewalk café. She jumped up and waved when she heard the clattering old van pull up. God, how he hated to break the news to her! He stuck his head out the passenger window.

"Come on," she said gaily. "It's a glorious day. Park that wreck and join me for a beer."

"We've got big problems," he said, pulling out a chair and sitting beside her. "Real big problems."

She snapped her fingers at the waiter and ordered two Ringnesses.

"Make mine a Carlsberg," he corrected.

"Martin, I've had the most exhilarating day at the Polar Institute. You'll be impressed when you see what I've brought home. Klaus—"

177

"Yes, fine. I'm sure it was marvelous. But look, we're without transportation again. I'm so furious I—"

"Martin, it's all right." She draped both arms around his neck and kissed him. "Listen, love, with the information I've got, I'm not about to get discouraged again. Half of it was the fever, anyway. Look, we're in Oslo now, not Tromsø. We'll go to every shipyard, harbor, freighting company, fishing fleet owner, and seafaring scoundrel until we've got the passage we want."

She studied him for a moment, then broke into a smile. "Come on, don't be so glum. We're here. The sunshine's a good omen. Let's have a wonderful evening. Then, tomorrow at seven, we'll go to work lining up the trip."

She was probably right. It just couldn't be *that* difficult to get to Svalbard if you went about things systematically. He smiled with relief and drained his mug. "Carlsberg, that's fine beer. Let me have another while you tell me about the information from your friend."

"Have another if you like, but I want to *show* you the stuff. It's up in the room spread all over the bed. I'm so excited for you to see it."

"In that case, let's go," he said, pushing himself to his feet and signaling the waiter. He led her by the arm toward the hotel. Just outside, he stopped and lifted her chin until they looked into each others' eyes. "Did you remember?" he asked.

"Remember what?"

"You know what. To call Bjørn. A promise is a promise."

"No, I didn't remember."

"But you thought about it?"

"What is this, an inquisition or just an interrogation?"

"Both. Now get in there and call him."

"You're being as pushy as a German," she said, grinning.

"Well?" he asked in the lobby.

"Well, what?"

"Are you going to discharge your responsibility?"

She stood on her toes and whispered into his ear. "You'd rather have me tied up on the phone than in bed with you."

"Get over there and make that call. Woman tricks will get you nowhere. Go on, get it over with. I'll wait for you upstairs."

Five minutes later she walked into their room and found him asleep on the bed. He had kicked off his shoes but was still dressed. Bunched up beside him were Klaus's maps of Svalbard with the carefully drawn red and blue areas where uranium was or might be and the larger black patches where there was none. She leaned over and kissed him as she stroked his hair. "You lose," she whispered. "We're having dinner with Bjørn and Christina in an hour."

"What? Christina's in Tromsø," he grumbled, trying to wake up.

"I thought so, too. I guess she and Bjørn have been having some trouble. She got in this morning."

"But why the hell so early? In an hour?"

"Bjørn insisted. Remember what you've been preaching to me: give in on the small points so you have energy left over to make a stand on the big ones."

"But this was a big one. I thought we were going to make love and spend a quiet evening together."

"You're the one who insisted I call."

He shoved the maps onto the floor and took her hand. Laughing, she wrenched it loose and turned to walk away. He sat bolt upright and caught her from behind, wrapping both arms around her waist. She struggled as he pulled her down on top of him, back first. He kept one arm around her, tightening his hold just a little, and began unbuttoning her yellow cotton dress with his free hand. She arched her back and laid her head down beside his on the pillow. Her hair fell over his face. He inhaled its fragrance and, taking a few strands between his lips, he tugged until she turned her head toward him. She lay perfectly still as they kissed.

He slid his hand from around her waist and undid the last button of her dress. She was still lying with her back on his chest. He ran his fingers around her breasts, across her belly and into her panties. He lifted his knees between her legs and gently pried them apart. Her breath began to come more rapidly. "Make love to me," she whispered, rolling onto her side next to him. "I've been late to dinner before."

14

ULRIKE lifted another slice of roast beef onto her plate.

"Don't you want to try the salmon?" asked Christina. "What about the shrimp? You haven't even touched the shrimp."

Ulrike pointed to her glass with her fork. As she chewed, a smile spread over her face. "Doesn't go with the Médoc," she said. In her jubilant mood she was tempted to tell Christina the secret she had kept from her the longest—that she didn't like fish. Or shrimp or oysters or crab.

But this was certainly *not* the time to spring it on her. Christina seemed unstrung.

Ulrike looked at Bjørn. That prick had probably seen through her act long ago. He'd probably ordered the roast beef from Mrs. Erlandsen deliberately just to make a point, just to make it clear he wasn't deceived. Angrily, she speared herself another slice of meat. She had to admit, though—the bastard knew about food —it *was* delicious.

Christina brought out the coffee and liqueurs. The patio behind the house where they sat was enclosed by a high brick wall overgrown with ivy. The garden was a lush tangle of bushes and shrubs, one of the few mildly unkempt areas of Bjørn's life. Finches and sparrows played in the foliage. The air had cooled but was still muggy. The western sky, streaked with high clouds, glowed copper-red.

"Bjørn," said Christina, "if you're going to discuss politics now,

I think I'll run these platters back to Mrs. Erlandsen's. I promised her I'd return them tonight."

"You should be in on this, love. It will put a lot of things in perspective for you." ·

"No, thanks. You can fill me in later. You know how much I hate political discussions."

"Well, if you hate them that much, I wouldn't want to torture you. Tell Mrs. Erlandsen it was superb, as usual."

"Is she all right?" asked Ulrike when Christina had left.

"A little irritated at me, that's all. I haven't told her yet about the crisis. When she learns we might be facing a Soviet invasion, I think she'll—"

"You don't mean to say you've finally seen the truth in what I told you three weeks ago?"

He smiled at her, sipping his coffee. "Let's say I've seen the truth in *some* of it."

"That's a start, at least. I guess I should come right out and tell you that Martin and I are going to Svalbard."

Stunned, he turned to Martin, who was sniffing the bouquet of his cognac and watching the birds. "You're what?"

"You heard me." Her voice was sharp. Martin reached under the table and squeezed her leg. In the taxi she had promised she would remain calm this evening. There was, she had agreed, nothing to be gained by behaving like a fanatic. She pinched his hand to let him know she had not forgotten.

"Look, you can't go to Svalbard, either one of you. There's no way in hell I can allow it. You'll both be in serious danger. They're already clearing the archipelago of foreigners. Martin, you don't believe this uranium story of hers, do you? Why are you encouraging a lot of misdirected, dangerous activity? If you care about her, you'll. . . ."

Martin raised his hand. "Let me set the record straight before you go any further," he said. "Whatever is going to be discussed tonight is between you and Ulrike. But I want you to know where I stand. I don't share her belief that German uranium mining is at the root of the crisis. I'm not even fully convinced there's a crisis. But she's going to Svalbard whether I like it or not. I don't want her going alone. Does that explain my involvement?"

181

"It does. And I still cannot allow either one of you to go. It's just too goddamned dangerous."

"Danger," said Ulrike, "is not going to stop me. You'll have to give me a much better reason. Bjørn, as I tried to explain to you, the Soviet invasion you're expecting is a reaction to *something*. That something, no matter what you or Martin or your bourgeois academics believe, is German uranium mining. By focusing on the Russians you're looking at symptoms rather than causes. Since no one else is willing to get to the bottom of this thing, I'm taking it upon myself. I'm going to expose what Arnheim is doing, regardless of the consequences."

"Ulrike, there's another problem. We can't have you writing anything on this matter just yet, whether you go to Svalbard or not."

Martin squeezed her leg again. She said, "You'll have to give me a damned good reason why I shouldn't. You can't muzzle me."

"Are you ready to listen to what we've been through at the Foreign Office?"

"If you'll allow me to have my say when you've finished."

"Absolutely."

Ulrike was unmoved by Bjørn's evidence. She argued that the search teams he and Skogan had dispatched could not possibly have found the German uranium-mining operations in so short a time. Svalbard was big; uranium extraction could now be done in a manner difficult to detect from the air.

"Which is, Bjørn, why I intend to work my way into Barentsburg. You do remember my tales of Consul Obruchev from my interview with him last spring?"

"Yes," he answered. "I remember quite well." But he was not listening to her any longer. The solution to one of his major dilemmas floated around on the edge of his consciousness but vanished. His mind raced down the wrong track.

He and Ulrike had established something of a rapport, a rapport he needed but feared would not survive his attempt to censor her. But censor her he must. If she sailed to Svalbard, she would see only what she wanted to see. Or worse yet, the Soviets would set her up. One way or another, she would return with evidence of German mining. She would publish something outrageous. Whether the story rested on valid data or not would hardly matter. It would cause a furor in the West. At the very least, it would be enough to encourage the Soviet strike. She must not go!

But if he tried to stop her, he was afraid she would break her story immediately. Again, this might be all the Soviets needed. He must think of something. He decided to play his trump card.

The telephone rang. Bjørn hurried inside, grateful for the interruption: he needed time to consider how he would handle her.

"He seems to be taking it okay," said Martin.

"Don't count on it. I'm sure he's got something up his sleeve. Trust a woman's intuition."

"Where would I be now if I did that?"

"Preparing to sail to Svalbard with me, I suppose."

"But for quite different reasons."

"Martin, it still bothers me that you can't accept my. . . ."

The sound of Bjørn's clogs on the stone tiles in the kitchen cut her short.

"It was Christina. I think she's tipsy. Says she met an old friend at Mrs. Erlandsen's. She'll be back before too long."

"She needed a drink," said Ulrike.

"She most certainly did. And I'm glad she didn't have to sit through this. Shall we stroll through my jungle?"

They walked down the overgrown gravel paths winding through the bushes. Twilight had set in and most of the birds had disappeared. A lone finch hobbled along in front of them. The blue sky had darkened into a velvety purple; the clouds to the west towered in billowy gray heaps. Lightning shimmered in the distance.

Bjørn stopped at the far wall and ran his fingers over the shiny leaves of the ivy. "Ulrike, you're not going to accept what I must tell you," he said. "But I must tell you nonetheless."

"It's getting chilly outside. Do you mind if we go in?"

Martin took off his tweed coat and draped it around her shoulders.

183

"Thank you," she said. "I'm listening."

"Ulrike, as I explained earlier, the Russian Ambassador likewise says German uranium mining is the cause of his displeasure."

"A wise man."

"Or a devious one. I want you to consider the possibility—just the *possibility*—that you are being used as a pawn of Soviet intelligence."

"I resent even the suggestion. I—"

"Let him finish," Martin said very gently.

She ripped an ivy leaf from the vine and tossed it into the air. "I'll try."

"Ulrike, I must know the sources from which you are getting your information. If you're onto something, well and good. But we have reason to believe that the Soviets are planting the uranium-mining stories in the West, hoping to cause an uproar about Arnheim that will justify their attack. Now, don't get me wrong. I'm no fan of your new Chancellor. But if you're being misled, we'd better find out right away. It could spare us all a lot of agony."

Martin was surprised at her calmness. She seemed almost detached. "I have a very dear friend who works out of Budapest. In what capacity, I don't feel comfortable saying. He has picked up word of every major Soviet move long before it has materialized. His analysis of the causes, based on the information he has been able to come up with, has been flawless in each case: Czechoslovakia, Afghanistan, Iran, Poland."

"There are such people, I know. But let's not rule out just yet the possibility that something has changed in some way we don't yet know about. That he, for example, has switched sides. Perhaps he's been forced to. Perhaps he's gotten bored. No reflection on him, you understand? I don't know him. But things like that do happen. Take Philby, for instance, or—"

"That's enough, Bjørn. You've missed the point entirely. I said I was going to Svalbard. I'm not taking anything I hear at face value. If you say I believe the information is accurate, you're correct. But I also know I need evidence, hard evidence."

"Ulrike, if my hypothesis is correct—if the Russians want you to do the story on uranium mining—they'll provide you with *false* evidence that might appear utterly convincing. And they'll do this whether you're here, or in Germany, or on Svalbard. Ulrike, listen to me. It's quite likely they've got you under surveillance right now to see what you'll do. Perhaps you've noticed something already . . . a car, a person. . . ."

She threw her head back and laughed. "Martin, dear, you never told me you were a Soviet spy."

"I tried, but you wouldn't listen."

"Seems we've all got something of a German problem," said Bjørn pleasantly.

"Yours is easier to deal with than mine," she answered.

"I'm not so sure. Think now, seriously. You're positive you're not under surveillance?"

Ulrike nodded. "Positive."

"Martin?"

"No, nothing."

"Well, I would advise you to keep your eyes open. I'd be willing to bet—"

"Can't we just forget this shadowing nonsense, Bjørn? I don't think—"

"It's been dropped. One more question: How do you intend to find evidence on Svalbard that will incriminate Arnheim? Seems to me you would require some sort of professional help."

"Bjørn, I wanted to explain that to you before and you cut me off."

"Sorry. I'm ready to listen now."

"I'm sure you are. I give you the details of my plan which you then use to stop me. Is that it, Bjørn? Or is it just friendly curiosity?"

"All right, let's be frank. I want to talk you out of going, both for your sake and for mine. I want you to level with me on how you think you'll do it. What's your price? What do I have to do to make you talk?"

"When you hear the plan, it won't strike you as absurd. Sure, I'll tell you. We've gone this far. We might as well continue." The prospect of shocking Bjørn out of his blindness lured her on.

"You asked about my price?"

"Yes."

She ground the gravel beneath her foot, then smiled her impertinent smile. "First, you have to take me inside." She held out her hand and caught a drop of rain. The storm had crept up on them unnoticed. Thunder rumbled nearby, and a bolt of lightning spread its luminous fingers across the black sky. She walked slowly toward the house, kicking the gravel as she went. They followed. "Second, you have to make me another pot of coffee. Third, you have to put on the Brandenburg Concerti."

Lightning struck nearby with a bright flash and the brittle crack of thunder. The sky opened up, dumping hail in sheets. "Deal," yelled Bjørn as they all scrambled for the back door.

Bjørn adjusted the bass and treble on the stereo. Martin heard the water come to a boil in the kettle; a shrill whistle drowned out the opening notes of Concerto No. 1. Ulrike and Bjørn rushed to the kitchen, leaving him alone in the living room.

He glanced at the walls: two of Wassily Kandinsky's abstract watercolors, an August Macke with bright blue and red horses, a cheerful Miró, a despairing Edvard Munch. Near the door hung three black and white photographs of a big wooden house.

The effect was pleasant and unpretentious. One mistake, thought Martin—for example, a Picasso in place of the photographs—and the whole room would have been a disaster. But Bjørn Holt didn't seem to make those mistakes. How the old boys at Stanford would detest him! He was as intelligent as they but hadn't been trapped by their dreary formalism. He led an influential and elegant life, a life that somehow made a difference. They would sneer at him with self-righteous contempt, but their contempt would be nothing but a pitifully transparent cloak for their envy. He realized how long it had been since he had thought about the world from which he had come, the abstract, judgmental, inert world of academia. He felt elated to be out of it for now, to be doing something palpable and concrete, something that might make a difference. . . .

"I've met my part of the bargain," said Bjørn. He set a brass stand on the coffee table and put the pot on it. Ulrike filled the cups. The second concerto got off to an undisturbed start.

"Yes, you have," said Ulrike, tasting her coffee. "Ah, Bach. One of our good Germans."

186

"He probably beat his wife," said Martin.

Ulrike shot him an indignant glance.

"As I was saying, Bjørn, we plan to work our way into Barentsburg on some pretext or other. I know the Consul. If you think he won't receive me, you're quite wrong. The slightest hint that I might be available to him and he'll sell his soul to me, secrets and all." She settled back in her corner of the sofa, smiling triumphantly.

Martin said, "It's hard to tell just which of you will be making the pact with the devil."

Bjørn said nothing. He wanted to tell her she was being foolish, but he realized her strategy might work. A Russian official stranded in an arctic outpost . . . why wouldn't he be almost desperate to lay his hands on this fine specimen of capitalist feminity?

"He'll give me the information I need," continued Ulrike. "I'll trick it out of him in one way or another. Then, my dear Mr. Holt, my colleagues in the German press will shovel every resource they've got into mounting an expedition. And that is how I plan to nail Arnheim."

The idea, when it struck at last, dazzled Bjørn by its simple perfection. "In the U.S. they call it horse trading," he said out of the blue. "You do me a favor, I'll do one for you."

"What in God's name are you talking about?"

"Ulrike, I can get you to Barentsburg more safely than you can get there by yourselves. Are you interested?"

She felt a surge of excitement along with her apprehension. Of course she was interested! Her major frustration had been her inability to arrange transportation to Svalbard. But she was suspicious of Bjørn's motives. She saw him putting her aboard a ship bound for nowhere so that she could not get her message to the world. She would listen, but she would be damned careful not to get tricked. "Describe your horse," she said coolly. "But if it's not a stallion, I'm not interested."

Bjørn was all business. "I'm working with a group of CIA agents. Our collaboration is fully illegal. Neither American nor Norwegian intelligence knows anything about it. You realize our 'third way' has put an end to our cooperation with Central Intelligence."

"Of course. Go on."

187

"The Americans are blind to what you and I both see as a very real danger of a Russian invasion. Never mind that we disagree on the causes for the Russian move. At least we both recognize its likelihood. The Soviets have a strong suspicion that Danielsen won't oppose them with military force if they attack. Unfortunately, they're correct. Which means they could have the invasion over and done with in a day instead of several days . . . a greater distinction than you might think. Because an operation that swift will allow them to confront the Americans with a *fait accompli*. Given the mood of the American people and the weakness of American forces on the Northern Flank, it's unthinkable that the U.S. would attempt to dislodge the invaders."

"I'm missing your point."

"The point is this: American military and political leaders know how crucial the Svalbard Passage is for the security of the United States. The public knows only that Danielsen has turned his back on Norway's former protector. Initially, at least, the leadership and the public would be at odds on how to confront the Soviet Union. As Martin knows, the average guy will be gloating for a time that Danielsen got his just desserts. It's thus absolutely essential that the American leadership learn of the Soviet threat *before* the public does. If we can bring this off, we might get an American show of strength in the North Atlantic which would make the Soviets less certain about how the U.S. would respond to the invasion. In this instance, I think that uncertainty would deter them from going ahead with their plans.

"Unfortunately, Danielsen has blown our credibility with the Americans. Without the old nonpolitical channels between our two intelligence services, we have no way to get our message to the people who count in Washington without going public. But if the thing goes public, as I've pointed out, we cannot succeed.

"Luckily, I have an acquaintance in the CIA who was willing to listen. He's agreed, unbeknownst to his superiors, to sail into Barentsburg with two of his men. He's going to try to gather enough evidence to alert his own people. It's not much, but it's our best hope."

"All right, Bjørn, that's perfectly clear. But why the hell do you want us along?"

"Our problem has been finding a way to get the men into and

out of Barentsburg. You'll help immensely. It only occurred to me a moment ago."

"You mean, because Obruchev knows me?"

"In part. You'll be a sort of passport for the whole crew. Let's say we were to set it up something like this. The three CIA men disguise themselves as oil people on their way to do some seabed sounding work in the Barents Sea. The logical stopover is, of course, Longyearbyen. They sail in a trawler belonging to an old Norwegian sea captain with whom they work."

Ulrike tried to hide her excitement. Bjørn's words were sweet, sweeter even than the notes of the Brandenburg Concerti. "Go on, go on."

"There you have it!" exclaimed Bjørn. "On board are not only the three oilmen—that alone might be suspicious. But there are two other passengers as well: a German journalist who is continuing work begun months ago and an American professor who just can't seem to let the German journalist out of his sight. A nice, motley, innocuous crew."

"Quite plausible," said Martin, "especially the part about the professor."

"Anyway, as you suggested, the ship breaks down outside of Barentsburg. Ulrike convinces the captain to nurse it into the harbor. After all, she knows the Consul. You dock. He admits you to the town. If he says only Ulrike can enter, you refuse to go ashore without the others. If he's as interested in you, Ulrike, as you say, he'll take you all in. If not, you've still got a good chance. He won't want to stir up your suspicions by acting overcautious. You'll get your information, my people will get theirs, and then you'll all get the hell out."

Ulrike smiled thinly. "What's the rest of the bargain, Bjørn?"

"That you wait to publish anything on uranium mining until you've returned and discussed it with me."

"Martin?" she asked.

'Sounds acceptable to me."

"Then, Bjørn, I would say that the horses have been traded."

Martin watched the sheets of rain in the yellow streetlights. Bjørn and Ulrike huddled in front of the bookcase arranging how they would keep in touch over the next two weeks without using channels that could be monitored either by the Norwegians or by the Soviets. "Or the Germans," she said. "If I really am being shadowed, it's Arnheim. He knows my political views from my writing, you can be sure of that. And he knows exactly where I am. If he thinks I'm onto something, he's the one who'll have me watched. Or eliminated. Funny I never thought of that before."

A tan Saab 900 sloshed to a stop in front of the house. Christina jumped out and slammed the door. The car lurched off. By the time she reached the porch, she was soaking wet. Water streamed down her cheeks, and her light green dress clung to her breasts and legs. "Serves you right for staying out so late," said Martin laughing.

"The evening was punishment enough. Unbearable, really. Well, are you finished with your politics?"

Bjørn wrapped his arms around her. Suddenly, he felt wretched: he stood face to face with the realization that what he had just done might cost him his relationship with the woman he loved. He knew that Christina would accuse him of involving her best friend in a dangerous mission for his own political ends. She would never understand that Ulrike was going to Barentsburg anyway, that linking her up with the CIA mission would make things *safer* for her. She would not buy the argument that Ulrike's role might help avert a major catastrophe in the North Atlantic.

But she would have to accept his decision. She would have to see the *real* significance of what he was doing. One simply could not reduce the world to individuals alone; the political dimension was just as important. Politics shaped people, determined how they lived, whether there was peace or war. . . . Not to see this— as Christina and most of her colleagues in the Department of Nordic Languages and Literatures insisted on not seeing—was to limit oneself to a simplistic and ultimately destructive view of reality.

When he told her what had been agreed upon tonight, her perception of what was taking place would be hopelessly distorted. She would see him as some sort of a monster, and this would hurt him very much. He could understand why she would feel that way. He could even empathize with her. But he could not allow his behavior in so crucial a matter to be influenced by *her* misperceptions.

"Well, who was this drinking partner of yours tonight?" he asked.

"Jon Lellenberg, of all people. A dreadful bore. An insatiable drunk with an insatiable urge to talk. And a crazed fool on the subject of Ulrike. I'm so sorry I ever mentioned to him that you were in Oslo. That's what I was doing tonight. That's why I was gone so long. I wanted to mislead him in every way I could think of. I don't believe I succeeded. He still believes you're here. God, Uli, I'm so sorry. I could kick myself."

Ulrike kissed her cheek and led her into the kitchen. She wasn't concerned in the slightest about Jon Lellenberg. Bjørn had put himself in a hell of a position trying to help her out, and she meant to do all she could to convince Christina it was not his doing that she was going to Svalbard.

Bjørn and Martin stood at the window.

"If you can do anything to stop her," said Bjørn, "please do. I can't warn you enough about the dangers involved. It's a good scheme for getting my men into Barentsburg, but if you can talk her out of going north, I'll gladly find another."

Martin turned from the window and looked at Bjørn. His face was tense, drawn, and very alive.

"No, Bjørn. Tonight has been a turning point for me. I've spent twenty years as a 'peace researcher,' whatever that means, but I feel I've never really *done* much. I want to go to Svalbard— I'd go now even if Ulrike decided not to. Something's going on up there, something very dangerous. I don't know what. But I want to *find out*. I've been *talking* about peace, about the nature of political reality, for the better part of my adult life and suddenly I feel a need to *act*, to do something, no matter how small, something I can see and feel. . . ."

Ulrike snuggled close to him in the taxi. "Damn it, Martin, do you suppose it's possible?"

"It makes sense to me. What does your woman's intuition tell you? Have you had the feeling he's really that desperately in love with you?"

"I haven't even thought about it. I've been too concerned with steering clear of him. But . . . but . . . oh, I don't know. It all seems so bizarre."

They stood for a moment in front of the hotel entrance watching the last distant flashes of lightning on the horizon. Headlights appeared at the intersection to their left. The car turned and did not pass in front of them, but its shape and color were unmistakable.

"Go up to the room and pack," said Martin. "This is the wrong place for us to be."

She looked at him, puzzled.

"Go on. I'll explain later."

At the desk he checked out hurriedly, and paid in cash. For the first time in years he felt thoroughly frightened.

PART FOUR

15

THE SKY over Oslo was cloudless and blue as it had
been for the better part of August. But summer was over: the air
on that Friday afternoon, the fifth of September, bore the unmistakable hint of a chill. Men in business suits hurried from office
to office as if caught up in a sudden collective urge to get back to
work. The city's women, too, looked earnest and brisk. Gone were
the halter tops and shorts, the jeans and sandals. In their place
were dresses, skirts, jackets, and high-heeled shoes. The noisy
street corner crowds had vanished, children were once more in
school, and the colorful droves of tourists had left. The capital
was again in the judicious hands of the middle-aged and middle-
class.

As Bjørn and Skogan approached the Foreign Office, a gust
of wind rattled overhead in the trees and sent the first leaves of
fall scurrying across the sidewalk. Skogan breathed a sigh of relief. At last the heat wave of August was over.

The diplomatic heat wave around Svalbard also seemed on
the wane. Russian Ambassador Ivanov had postponed the critical
meeting with Skogan until today. For the two Norwegians, this
represented a clear sign that the Soviet Union was having second
thoughts about its invasion plan. Why, they weren't sure. Perhaps
Soviet leaders were puzzled by the failure of rumors about German uranium mining to catch fire in the Western press. Perhaps
the Kremlin had simply gotten cold feet. But whatever the case,
Bjørn and Skogan felt the tide of events had taken a benevolent

shift in their favor. Over a lengthy lunch at Blom's Restaurant, they decided that a firm stand with Ivanov today would deter the tottering Soviets once and for all from their Svalbard venture. Thus, they walked into the meeting later that afternoon tactically and psychologically unprepared for what awaited them.

Ivanov bounded into the small conference room followed by his interpreter. While Oslo had become more somber in mood and dress with the approach of autumn, the Russian Ambassador had evidently decided to swim against the current. He wore a yellow shirt, a garish blue necktie, and a tweed sport coat. He greeted his hosts with hearty handshakes, his booming, jubilant voice a portent of things to come. He crashed down into his chair, rubbing his fat, liver-spotted hands together. "Gentlemen, I wish to apologize for my part in the unfortunate misunderstandings we have had in the past weeks. I admit I was quite incensed. I thought, quite wrongly, that your government was displaying an utter lack of goodwill. You will, I hope, forgive me a mistake in judgment."

It was already clear something had gone dreadfully awry. Skogan squirmed in his seat, trying to hide his discomfort. His entire strategy had been built on a well-thought-out response to the attack he expected from Ivanov. Was there to be no attack? And if not, what was he to do? In a split second he opted for turning the tables, for playing the role of irate aggressor himself in the hope that Ivanov would be caught off guard.

"Sir," said Skogan with cold dignity, "this is hardly a time to speak in banal generalities. Forgiveness is not the issue. We have reason to believe serious violations of Norwegian law are taking place on Svalbard. These violations have nothing to do with your sinister fabrications regarding German activities on the archipelago. They are crimes, Mr. Ivanov, which your government is cynically perpetrating, crimes we shall no longer tolerate."

Ivanov smiled politely. "A serious and most unfortunate mistake on your part, Mr. Foreign Minister, to attribute these things to the Soviet Union. I do assume you are referring to the fate of that glaciological expedition which was so copiously written about in your press. A pity, indeed! The climbers were German, I understand. Poor chaps no doubt knew nothing of the reckless work of their own government not far from where the dreadful accident took place. Or perhaps, gentlemen, they knew too much. . . ."

Bjørn saw Skogan gasp for breath and turn ashen. He took over. "Mr. Ivanov! You know as well as we that what happened was no accident."

Ivanov looked at Bjørn with amusement. He enjoyed revenge and was taking his time. "I do, Mr. Holt, to be quite honest with you. Your Prime Minister said I mustn't mention our little talk this morning, but I think you're due an explanation."

Bjørn winced. Danielsen! After all they had told him, it was hard to believe. Hard to believe, but sadly, indisputably true. The Prime Minister had folded. To save his career from a backlash against his "third way," he had sold the Foreign Office—and his country—down the river! He must have scraped and bowed through the whole meeting with the Russian, a meeting Ivanov had been shrewd enough to arrange. Now the Russian knew beyond a shadow of a doubt that Norway would not fight. He could return to the Kremlin with news that would free the Soviet leaders to move ahead with their invasion plans. Bjørn shuddered. His entire intricate stratagy of conveying to Ivanov the impression Norway would resist had fallen flat on its face. The delicate web that he and Skogan had spun had been torn to shreds by a few cowardly and self-serving words. He tried to block out Ivanov's voice but the Russian blabbered on mercilessly.

"You see, gentlemen, as I informed your Prime Minister this very morning, we share quite identical interests on Svalbard. We no more than you wish a murderer running around up there on the loose. After all, we do have our own scientific expeditions to worry about."

He bestowed a smile on his vanquished adversaries—as gentle as it was false—gave a faint, almost feminine sigh, and resumed his torture. "As for the German outrage whose existence you seem so unwilling to admit, I've at last found a sympathetic ear in your Prime Minister. Unlike the average Western Laborite—a disgrace, if you don't mind me saying so, to the Marxist heritage —your leader demonstrates a sincere concern for some very fun-

197

damental human rights. He has, gentlemen, convinced me that he too wishes to see an end to capitalist-inspired military interventionism on Norwegian territory. He has promised his full support in countering the German neo-fascist menace. He has offered. . . .”

It all happened so quickly. Less than five minutes after Ivanov's departure, Skogan stood at his favorite spot at the window in his study. Bjørn was about to offer some words of comfort when Skogan suddenly collapsed. Frightened, Bjørn gathered some cushions from the sofa and propped up the stricken old man. In seconds, he had telephoned for an ambulance and alerted Marianna.

Skogan looked as if he might topple over at any moment. His face turned gray, his forehead dripped with perspiration. His white hair stood out in a tangled knot. He looked grotesque and vulnerable.

Marianna rushed in with a wet towel and a glass, gasping when she saw him. While Bjørn loosened his tie, whispering words of comfort, she wiped Skogan's forehead, brushed back his hair, and tried to get the glass between his bloodless lips.

Groaning, Skogan fumbled in his vest pocket and pulled out his watch. It tumbled from his trembling fingers and dangled helplessly at the end of its chain. There it hung until Bjørn dropped it back into the Minister's vest pocket. “Five-twenty,” he whispered.

Skogan opened his eyes. “Five-twenty?” He looked at Marianna, who was fighting back her tears. “Five-twenty? Dear, get me my double Scotch, would you be so kind? You see what happens when you're late with the afternoon drinks.”

She squeezed his arm and left the room. Bjørn heard her sobbing as she dropped ice cubes into a glass.

“A treasure,” mumbled Skogan, his voice sounding stronger, “that woman's a treasure.”

“Shhh. Don't strain. Help's on the way.”

Skogan grabbed Bjørn's shoulder and pulled him closer. “Mr. Holt,” he groaned, “I *order* you to get to Washington. Tonight. I'll . . . I'll hang on until. . . .” He stopped when Marianna re-

198

turned with the Scotch. She knelt and helped him take a few swallows. Again, he reached out and tugged weakly at Bjørn's shoulder. "If something happens . . . to me . . . Danielsen . . ."

"Will have me replaced in hours," said Bjørn.

"Yes. We've got to . . . we . . . we . . ."

"Please, Mr. Minister," pleaded Marianna, "you must not exert yourself." She lifted the towel but he waved her off.

"Give me another drink, dear. It helps. Loosens this vise." He placed a palm on his chest. "Helps me breathe. I'm all right if I can breathe."

He drank. A tract of color returned to his cheeks. "Mr. Holt, listen carefully." He grimaced in pain but went on. "In Washington there's a man named Caskey. He's on the White House staff. We received a complaint from him today. It's over there, on my desk. No, no. Leave it for now. But take it with you." Suddenly Skogan was flushed. He spoke more rapidly, as if unsure how much longer he would be able to go on. "Caskey says American oil companies drilling in the North Sea are being treated unfairly by our government." He stopped, bit his lip. The vise tightened around his chest. He managed a smile. "Funny thing, they probably are. It's . . ."

"Please," begged Bjørn, fearing the Minister's mind was wandering. But Skogan shot him a glance of healthy irritation.

"Mr. Holt, I'm asking you to listen. No more interruptions." He sputtered, coughed, and groaned but refused to stop.

"Get to Washington. Look up Caskey. Use him as a pretext for being there. Danielsen must suspect nothing. Draw the thing out as long as you must. Give Caskey some sort of satisfaction. Keep yourself involved with him. It wouldn't surprise me if Danielsen uses the Norwegian Ambassador in Washington to check up on you. He mustn't find out that you're trying to involve the Americans. I don't know where to tell you to start. You know Washington better than I. It's our only hope, Mr. Holt, our only remaining hope."

Bjørn assured him he would carry out his wishes. He was helping him with the last of his Scotch when four medics rushed in with a stretcher. "Heart attack?" asked one of them.

"Yes, I think so," Marianna answered, bursting into tears.

They gave him oxygen, laid him on his side and gently slid him onto the stretcher. Bjørn went with him to the door, holding him tightly by the wrist. "I'm on my way, Mr. Skogan. May God be with you." He regretted his words at once, for they rang in his ears like a dirge. But the Foreign Minister was smiling. He clenched his fist and, twisting his arm from Bjørn's grasp with surprising strength, raised it.

"Let's forget God just now," mumbled the old man. "What we need, God is not going to supply. We need an ally. Get us that ally, Mr. Holt."

Bjørn watched the stretcher disappear down the long corridor. He wept for a moment, then restrained his emotions as he so often did. He dialed SAS and made two first-class reservations to Washington. Minutes later, he slipped, unobserved, out a back entrance of the Foreign Office.

16

THE LIMOUSINE sped down the four-lane access highway that links Dulles Airport to the American capital. Traffic was sparse that Saturday morning, the sixth of September. The woods on either side of the road were lush and well groomed, and the rolling countryside beyond was dotted with neat red farmhouses. Bjørn had forgotten how pretty the drive was.

"I don't see why I can't go directly to the Embassy," said Christina. "I know Halvorsen and he likes me."

"Of course he likes you. That's not the point. I don't want him to find out I'm here until I've had the chance to see several people."

"Which could take a few days."

"Christina, it's been years since you've visited Washington. We'll be at a hotel downtown. You can sleep as long as you like, then see the city."

"In this heat?"

"Jesus, Christina, everything's air-conditioned. Take a cab over to the East Wing of the National Gallery. You've never seen it. Go to Georgetown and have lunch. You always adored—"

"You know I don't enjoy going out alone. At least I'd have someone to talk to at the Embassy. How long is this sneaking around going to take? And Bjørn, why didn't you tell me before we left that you were going to shut me up in a room? You knew damned well I'd be expecting to stay at the Embassy. I should have gone back to Tromsø. I don't like the business of your arranging my leave anyway."

"Christina, please! You know you can't go back to Tromsø until the danger passes."

"What about my friends? You don't seem concerned about them."

"I'm very concerned about them. That's why we're here. I asked you to come because I needed your support. In Washington we have a chance to deter the invasion. If you're concerned about what happens to northern Norway, you'll quit bitching and try to help me."

"Bitching? Is it bitching not to want to be cooped up in a room in a foreign country when the Norwegian Embassy would be more than happy to receive us?"

"Christina, how many times do I have to explain it to you? As soon as Ambassador Halvorsen knows I'm here, he'll have his paws in my business. It won't take him long to realize I'm involved in more than a minor negotiation with a member of the White House staff. He's likely to contact Danielsen on the spot. Danielsen will order me back to Oslo, and my chances of accomplishing anything here will go up in smoke. We're not dealing with everyday politics."

"No, I guess not. You wouldn't go around sacrificing my friends to your political ambitions if we were. Or would you, Bjørn? I'm starting to see a pattern in the way you treat people, and I don't like it."

"For God's sake, you're not going to bring *that* up again, are you? I thought we had finally agreed Ulrike was—"

"Nonsense! You know you could have stopped her if you had wanted to. It might not have been easy, but you could have done it. Instead, you worked her into that crazy scheme of yours because it suited *your* political needs. Very courageous, Bjørn. You do all the armchair theorizing about good and evil, then take advantage of someone with an obsession. You've used her. You've gotten her to do your dangerous work for you. Since when, Bjørn, is some abstract political goal more important than the safety of one real, living, flesh-and-blood human being? If anything happens to her, I'll—"

"Shhh. Nothing's going to happen to her."

Christina did not answer.

The driver, an elderly black man with white hair and a matching moustache, swiveled around and grinned. "They told me to take you to the Mayflower. That right?"

"Yes."

"You know Washington?"

"Fairly well. I worked here for five years."

"Five years, I declare. Listen, mister, there ain't much traffic this time of day. Any particular route you'd like me to take into town?"

Bjørn reflected for a moment. "Sure. If it won't slow us down too much, why don't we take the Dolley Madison Highway through Langley and cross at the Chain Bridge. I always liked that drive."

"Okay by me. Say, what language ya'll been speaking?"

"Norwegian," said Christina, "we just got off the airplane from Norway." Her English was as crisp and clear as her native tongue, although she spoke with an accent.

"Norway," sang out the driver. "I declare. Way back before the war, I had a friend from Norway. He worked up on the Hill for a paper . . . a fine gentleman. Hope you enjoy your stay in Washington."

"Thank you," said Bjørn.

He squeezed Christina's hand. He was worried about the downward spiral of their relationship.

She jerked her hand away and continued to stare ahead. He could not deal with her just now.

They sped under the big sign indicating the turnoff to the CIA building. He was again struck by the conspicuous public facade of that vast private organization. They drove across the narrow spans of the old Chain Bridge: the water picked up the rays of the early morning sun and mirrored them back in bright, iridescent patches. A jet rumbling by on its final approach to National left a grimy exhaust trail across the clear morning.

They were soon in an exclusive residential neighborhood. A young couple in tennis dress strolled arm in arm toward a waiting Mercedes. A lawn boy on the other side of the street was setting

203

up his equipment on the green lawn of a Tudor mansion. An elderly, proprietary-looking woman stood beside him, under a great elm. She watched him with a critical eye, fluffing her silver hair and restraining the two toy poodles dancing on their leashes. Bjørn put his head back on the leather seat and dozed.

When he awoke, the limousine had stopped for a red light in the middle of a black neighborhood. A group of young men stood on the corner, talking and laughing. The dilapidated front porches swarmed with children and old people. The buildings were run down, the trees scraggly, the signs on the corner storefronts warped and faded.

That, he mused, was America. You closed your eyes on a dreamland of prosperity and self-assurance and opened them minutes later on a nightmare of poverty and squalor. He wondered how this perplexing land—this land that he loved and sometimes despised—would react to the crisis in the north. But none of the scenarios he imagined were even remotely similar to what awaited him.

They pulled up in front of the Mayflower.

"Here we are," said the driver.

"Thank you. What do I owe you?"

"Not a thing. Mr. Millet paid me already. He just told me to pick you up at the British Airways desk and bring you here and gave me a hundred bucks. Know what?"

Bjørn raised his eyebrows. "What?"

"He sure gave a good description of you. I recognized you right off."

Christina went up to the room alone. He wanted to have a long talk with her now but there wasn't time. He was already ten minutes late for his meeting.

From the door of the Mayflower's coffee shop, he saw his old Harvard classmate at a table by the far wall. Arthur Millet was reading a newspaper. Between sips of coffee, he toyed with sugar cubes on the table, pushing them about with quick nervous fingers like a Greek playing with worry beads. He looked heavier and older. But as he read, he smiled the same ironic, slightly guarded smile Bjørn remembered so well from their graduate school days, the smile that had sent lofty Professor Kutschnik into a childish rage in front of the entire Politics and Ideology seminar.

Millet was a large, olive-skinned man with unruly black hair and a hooked nose. In his Chemise Lacoste and khaki slacks, with his scuffed leather briefcase beside him on the floor, he could have passed for an older graduate student.

Millet stood when he saw Bjørn. They shook hands warmly. "Well, Holt, you look better than you sounded on the phone last night. Good to see you again, old man."

"Good to see you, too, Art. A pity it takes a crisis to get us together."

"We'll just have to arrange more crises. How long's it been?"

"Let's see. Last time was when I was still in Washington. So about seven years. You're a lousy letter writer, Art. Know that?"

"Hell, yes, I know it. I just ordered breakfast." Millet pulled a chair out and motioned to Bjørn. "Care to join me for some good old American eggs and bacon?"

"No, thanks. Just coffee will be fine. I'm a light eater when I haven't had much sleep."

"Just the opposite with me," said Millet, patting his paunch.

He flagged the waitress, who promptly turned and walked off. "See what kind of service we get these days? I tell you, Bjørn, this whole country's in a mess. No one gives a damn anymore. It's even worse than when you were here."

The waitress, who had taken Millet's wave as a sign he was in a hurry, appeared with a large plate of bacon and eggs and a fresh pot of coffee. "There you go, sir," she said cheerfully. "And for the other gentleman?"

"Just coffee," said Bjørn.

Another customer signaled and she hurried off.

"Art, don't you think you were a little quick to judge her? I hope you'll give me a better hearing."

"Look here, wise guy," said Millet, wolfing down a mouthful of hash browns, "if you knew what I'd done in the last twelve hours, you wouldn't be talking like that. I thought I told you on the phone I was convinced you were onto something." He laughed and took a gulp of coffee. "You see, Bjørn, it takes a lot to convince me when the evidence is as scanty as yours. But you did it. So relax, pal. I've been up all night, too. Laying the groundwork for you, if we want to be specific. I've stretched the old-boy net as far and wide as possible and I've used every other connection I've got in this goddamned town. And I think, Bjørn, that if we decide to move, we'll have the contacts."

"Art, that's terrific. If I'd gone through official channels. . . ."

"Yes, I know. You'd have been lucky to get the ear of a desk officer at State."

"That's about it. Who have you been able to contact?"

Millet looked around. "Let's get out of here. Why don't we take a cab to the Mall? I don't like whispering, and I could use some exercise. We've got a full day ahead. Meetings scheduled from noon till midnight. You and I should get our facts straight before we see the big boys. A united front is what we've got to present. Well, what's wrong? Jet lag catching up with you?"

"No, it's not that, Art. I've got someone with me. A woman."

"Still after the women, huh, Holt?"

"No, not exactly. Christina and I have been together for—"

"So you want to go up to the room and make amends for trying to hold back a Soviet attack on her time? Jesus, Holt, go on and get it over with. I've still got half the *Post* to read. Well, go on. But make it brief."

"I'll call from downstairs. Give me five minutes. We were just having a nasty row and—"

"Okay, man, okay. Get it taken care of so we can do some work."

Bjørn phoned from the reception desk. He wanted to comfort her. She was, after all, in a most unpleasant position. She had put up with his erratic schedules and his political preoccupations for over a month now. And in some respects she was right: if he had not exactly "sent" Ulrike to Svalbard, he had nevertheless done very little to discourage her.

There weren't many women like Christina. She spoke her mind and took the consequences. What did he want, anyway? A pretty face? A good lay? An obsequious hausfrau? He knew what he wanted: Christina, just as she was. It wasn't a question of choosing between her and another woman. That other woman, he was convinced, did not exist. If there was any choice at all, it was between a deep, lasting relationship with Christina and an endless series of casual liaisons with women whom he could keep at a distance. And that, really, wasn't much of a choice.

She answered. "Yes?"

"Listen, love, things are very hot already. I'm going to have to—"

"Look, Bjørn, there's no need to map out your schedule for me. I've got my own plans."

"Christina, do we have to go on like this? It really isn't what either of us wants."

"I don't think you really care what I want. If you do, then leave me to myself for a while. I'll let you know when I'm ready to talk. I've got to go now. My bath's running over."

When Bjørn looked up, Millet was waiting for him at the front entrance. He hesitated for an agonizing moment, then joined his impatient friend at the door.

"All set?" asked Millet.

"All set."

They flagged a taxi and drove off.

Half an hour later they were walking around the reflecting pool in front of the Capitol. Joggers were out in force, and the summer's last tourists wandered about like the tattered remnants of a great army. The day was already sweltering. A lambent haze had replaced the blue sky of the early morning, and a fat band of rust-colored pollution lay along the horizon. Bjørn was sweating profusely. He took off his coat and tie and unbuttoned his collar.

"Not used to the Washington weather, what, Holt?"

"No. And I was naive enough to think it was hot in Oslo this summer."

"It's pretty damned miserable, all right. Hell of a site for a great nation's capital. You know what happened, don't you? We built the place right on a swamp back when we expected to go under anyway. Then things started to look up, we got involved in all sorts of great-power problems, and we never got the son of a bitch completely drained. Speaking of problems, we're going to have our share. Let me start with—"

"Art, will you do me a favor first?"

"Glad to, old man."

"You've never quite told me what your work is here. Nor have you told me anything about your politics. You understand what I'm getting at? The Harvard liberal goes to D.C. to work for HEW and twelve years later he's involved in intelligence work. What's happened, Art? I like to know where my allies stand."

"How much did Johnson tell you about me?"

"Not much. I don't think he knows much. But he did say you had a 'bizarre' kind of 'influence' in the CIA."

"Right, Bjørn, I've become a veritable latter-day Rasputin."

"Good. Now really, Art, what the hell are you up to?"

"You've heard of Chet Willard, the CIA Director?"

"Certainly."

"Well, he came up through the organization. I joined about six years ago and had the chance to work with him on a number of critical assignments before he landed the big job. I happened to call a few things right. My work is actually what got him where he is now. He thinks I can do no wrong. I'd say, old man, that he even thinks a little *too* highly of my talents. Answer your question?"

"Part of it. What's happened to your liberalism?"

"Bjørn." Millet stopped and looked his old friend in the eye. "I hope you're not buying the European stereotype of the CIA. A democracy needs a good intelligence service as much as it needs a comprehensive social policy. I felt my skills would be most valuable in intelligence work, that's all. Of course, the Agency has its share of jerks—Willard and your friend Johnson among them. But if anything, Bjørn, that's all the more reason for getting in there. When some of our weirdos start to become a little trigger-happy, it doesn't hurt to have a few liberals around. My convictions are about where they were in the old graduate school days, although I'll admit to proselytizing a hell of a lot less."

"I'm satisfied. Maybe relieved is a better word. I hope you didn't mind my asking."

"Not in the least. Ready to listen?"

"Ready."

"Bjørn, we've got several very powerful people in this town who are itching for a pretext to use the bomb on the Soviets. I know it sounds like so much hogwash. I wish it were. But there's a growing conviction among well-placed conservatives that something drastic must be done to redeem what they call 'America's honor.' It occurred to me just after you called last night that they might consider Svalbard a perfect spot for letting fly with the tactical nukes."

"I don't see the problem. We avoid the hawks entirely—"

"No, Bjørn, that's the hitch. We can't avoid them. They're the ones who'll be sympathetic to our cause and they're the ones who have the ear of the President. But if we bring them in, I fear we risk having them put together a plan that hinges on the use of nuclear weapons. On the other hand, if we don't bring them in, we risk getting no action at all. I'm going to leave the choice to you. But, Bjørn, don't take my warning lightly. I have access to a lot of information. Believe me, I'm not exaggerating."

He patted his stomach again and hung his arm around Bjørn's shoulders. "Come on, let's walk a stretch. Aerobics or death."

They turned toward the Washington Monument and started off down the gravel walkway at a brisk pace. Millet was soon winded and sat down on one of the ubiquitous green benches. Bjørn remained standing.

"Art, seriously, aren't you overestimating the influence of these men? It seems to me that as soon as we establish conclusively the existence of a Soviet threat, the more rational heads will prevail. That's the America I know."

Millet sprang to his feet and resumed his march. "The America you know, I'm afraid, is an endangered species. This country has lived through too many humiliations, Bjørn, humiliations that your 'rational heads' allowed to come about. We've got a President now who won the election with his pledge to give America back its self-respect. The man is of a different caliber from his predecessors. He's not an evil man, but he sees very complicated issues in the simplest black and white terms. So far he's had the advantage of good advice. But, Bjørn, here's what worries me. If we alert the men who have the influence to get an American *response* over Svalbard, we might risk having the same men program the President in the direction of a *nuclear* response. Maybe we could drop a few more subtle hints and see if your rational

209

types don't sooner or later pick up on the danger. I'm just afraid too much talk of a Soviet attack will give the warmongers too goddamned much time to work on the President . . ."

"Are you trying to tell me you want out of this whole thing?"

"No, Bjørn, not in the least. I'm willing to go balls-out on this if it's what you want. But I want you aware, *totally* aware, of the risks."

Bjørn might have answered differently had he known how prophetic Millet's words were. "We've got to risk it, Art," he said. "The invasion could come any day. A gradual approach is as good as no approach at all."

"Okay, pal, let's get with it. If the afternoon brings in the catch I'm anticipating, we'll have a meeting tomorrow with some of the most influential men in town. Now, one little word of advice. We'll be seeing a lot of aides at this point. We've got to make our case without divulging too much. Information here is currency, a more coveted—and stable—currency than the dollar. People hoard it. If we pass out too much too early, we may not get to the top at all. Just enough, Bjørn, to whet the appetite."

"I understand. Which fish are we after?"

"The trophies. My boss, Clark of the Joint Chiefs, the National Security Adviser, Secretary of State Barker, Secretary of Defense White—"

"You don't mess around."

"Not in these matters. Either you go to the top or you go nowhere. One more question, Bjørn: Is there anything you've withheld from me, anything that could come out later and drive a wedge between us in our dealings with the big men? If there is, we'd better get it out into the open now."

Bjørn described how he had arranged for the CIA mission to sail to Barentsburg.

Dismayed, Millet listened. "Jesus, pal, if that comes out, we'll both be knee-deep in shit."

"What do you want to do about it? The CIA has to know that its own people are on their way to Svalbard. They're not going to trust the findings of Norwegian intelligence. Besides, Norwegian intelligence doesn't know much more about this than your own boys. That's how well the Soviets have covered themselves."

"Tell you what, Bjørn, leave this one to me. Let me mull over a few ideas. Whatever happens, though, don't *you* bring it up. Get the picture? Foreigners aren't supposed to be ordering the CIA around."

17

THE OLD TRAWLER *Utsira* plowed northward. From time to time, the steep, green mountains of Norway's western coast came into view. The sea was blue-gray and glassily calm. The overcast had thickened; the sky became a vast opaque dome. The air began to grow cold.

On the third day of the voyage Turk announced the approach of the seventieth parallel; Tromsø was slipping by off starboard. Martin and Ulrike stood on deck, scanning the horizon in search of land. Not more than twenty miles of island-specked ocean separated them from the town in which they had met. But the Institute for Disarmament, the Peppermøllen, Christina's old wooden house, the abandoned peasant cottage where they had first made love—these things all seemed so far away, as if they belonged to a world set apart in space and time from the one they had now entered. They stood in silence and watched the melancholy swooping of the gulls.

At dinner that evening, the six discussed for the last time their plan for entering Barentsburg. When the *Utsira* reached the mouth of the Ice Fjord—the waterway that leads up to the Russian settlement—Turk would replace the main generator wire with a faulty duplicate. The ships's electrical system would soon run down, forcing an emergency stop. The Soviets would board, Ulrike would ask to see Consul Obruchev, the status of the ship and its passengers would be clarified, and—if all went according to plan—they would go ashore.

They expected the ship to be searched during their absence. Johnson had taken special precautions. He had installed a simple marine radio in place of the ship's sophisticated monitoring, transmitting, and decoding equipment. In a small back cabin he had rigged up the type of sonar device used in sounding the seabed for favorable drilling sites. Sounding, after all, was supposed to be what the *Utsira* was doing up around Svalbard. Finally, he had stored all their modern weapons in Stavanger, leaving them with only an emergency stock of old rifles and hunting knives that could be found aboard any trawler plowing arctic waters. The tents and sleeping bags which Turk kept aboard the *Utsira* were stashed away in a storeroom.

Johnson explained how the absence of modern weapons or sophisticated monitoring equipment increased their mission's chances for entering and leaving Barentsburg safely. But a greater burden was now on the agents themselves. Johnson stressed that the drift of modern intelligence work had been toward the use of technology. This, he said, had resulted in a very costly neglect of the "human factor" in an agent's training. The present mission was a case in point: his superiors, infatuated with the new technology, would have been unable to gather the data he intended to harvest. But he and his men, while expert in the newest equipment, had not forgotten that in the end it comes down to the man. This, he said, was why they would succeed.

Johnson brought out a bottle of champagne and proposed a toast. Their scheme, he said, was as good as any they could hope to devise. Bizarre but good. Jim Duncan ran to the galley for a fresh bottle of coke. Ulrike watched in disbelief as he bounded out of the cabin in his high-water pants. Andy Wheeler was watching her, amused. He screwed up his eyes and thumbed toward the door through which his colleague had vanished. "You haven't seen anything yet," he said. "Wait till you come to Oklahoma."

Shortly before eleven, Martin and Ulrike again went out on deck. They wore sweaters and windbreakers, for it had become very cold. The sun was somewhere below the horizon, but not far enough below for complete darkness. The sky glowed eerie white. The clouds were low, and Martin could see their rapid movement as they rolled down from the northwest. A stiff breeze was blowing; the trawler rose and fell in the waves. Mist from the sea and from the light drizzle moistened their hands and faces as they clutched the deck railing and stared out into the night. Martin slid his arm around her waist and pulled her tightly against him. He kissed her windblown hair, and its fragrance mingled with the raw and briny smells of the sea. It was, he thought, one of the happiest moments of his life.

She broke the silence. "I had that awful dream again," she said sadly.

"Which dream?"

"The one I told you about the first night we were together. Don't you remember?"

"Yes, of course I do."

They fell silent again and listened to the thrashing of the swells against the prow. He felt the tension in her body grow.

"It was the same as before," she continued, biting her lower lip. "The same as before, except that I noticed something I hadn't noticed earlier. The drummer, the one in the procession of soldiers that surrounded our car . . . that horrible man who leered at me and drummed while they beat up my father. . . . Do you remember?"

"Yes."

She grabbed his arm and held it with all her strength. "That drummer was Mikhail Obruchev. It was him, Martin, to the last detail. The two gold teeth, the bald head, the big stomach. God, I dread seeing him again."

"I'm sure you do. But Ulrike, this drummer of yours is the key to your whole mission. The unconscious does odd things in dreams. He wasn't really there when your father was beaten up. Besides, I don't think he'll be as hideous face to face as he was in the nightmare. From what you've told me, he sounds like a rather interesting fellow."

"Martin, don't be so patronizing. Of course I know all that." She grasped the railing with both hands. "It's obviously not *him* I'm afraid of. It's all the things he reminds me of. It's just a feeling I get whenever I picture him, a feeling that something terrible is about to happen. I'm scared, Martin. Not for me. No, I don't believe it's me I'm frightened for. It's us. I feel something is about to happen to us. . . . Martin, you won't ever leave me, will you?"

214

Her words hung like an echo above the sounds of the sea. He pulled her to him once more. "No," he said, "never."

By the time they reached the Ice Fjord, the sea was frothing angrily and the driving rain flung down the first particles of sleet.

Turk warned that the storm could get much worse, with temperatures falling close to zero Fahrenheit and waves growing large enough to rip open the seams of a small vessel like theirs. This, he said, was probably an advantage in getting the *Utsira* into Barentsburg without arousing too much suspicion. But what about getting out again? A northwester could last for days, and, in the span of a few hours, conditions could worsen drastically. How would they explain their departure if the northwester were howling at full strength when they had finished their work in the town?

Johnson admitted this was a serious problem. Every extra hour spent in Barentsburg meant more risks. For a while he toyed with the idea of waiting out the storm in Longyearbyen. But he soon decided it would be foolish not to use the advantage afforded them by the weather. If worse came to worst, they would play on Soviet perceptions of the "brutal American entrepreneur" to justify their departure. They would contrive a timetable according to which they had to be back in Stavanger. They would explain that if they were late, they would be fired. There was, they would say, no such thing as a "legitimate excuse" as far as their boss at Caltex was concerned. Better to take their chances with the weather than with that bastard.

"Flimsy," said Turk.

"Weak," said Martin.

"I once had a boss like that," said Duncan.

"Can't we think of something better?" asked Ulrike.

But they could not. So on they sailed toward the hornet's nest, confident they were on their way to gaining crucial information but unsure how—or if—they would be able to escape with it.

When they were within a couple of miles of the Soviet settlement, Ulrike went on deck in full raingear. Martin, who had been chatting with Turk on the bridge, came down to join her. The sleet stung their faces as they squinted into the mist. Barentsburg gradually came into view behind diaphanous curtains of blowing spray. Martin shuddered and shouted something which Ulrike could not hear above the roar of the wind and sea.

The town was perched high on a bleak greenish-brown hill which rose directly out of the churning gray water. The treeless slope was traversed at intervals by horizontal plateaus, giving it the look of a great ugly staircase. The harbor was cut into the lowest plateau. A tall crane was unloading a freighter. Several trucks bumped their way between the piers and the giant warehouses with corrugated steel roofs that lined the waterfront. Bulldozers were widening one of the many blackened roads which cut across the face of the hillside like scars.

Above the harbor were several massive coal-storage bins, connected to the docks by long chutes with elbow curves. One of the bins was full; the coal glistened jet black in the rain. Directly behind the bins stretched the town's gloomy buildings: long rectangular two-story apartment houses with mauve walls and rows of tiny matching windows; slightly higher office buildings of sooty concrete; and on the outskirts of the tiny town, a desolate green stucco house. Just beyond the highest row of apartments, the hillside disappeared into the thick blanket of clouds. The mine shafts—which the CIA men thought might hold Soviet intercontinental ballistic missiles aimed at the American heartland—were hidden by the overcast.

Ulrike tugged at Martin's arm. She pointed. Two small patrol boats were approaching at high speed, leaving parallel wakes on the rough water which looked like torpedo trials. They pulled up alongside. Turk signaled engine problems, and the patrol boats led the ship to a point inside the jetty where the water was calm enough for boarding. Two Russian officials in brown greatcoats and fur hats marched across the *Utsira*'s deck without a word and entered the captain's quarters. Turk offered them a drink, which they refused. A brief exchange took place in broken Norwegian. They demanded to search the boat. Turk agreed, on the condition they first meet with his passengers and explain why the search was necessary. The larger of the two Russians said "no" but his smaller colleague overruled him. This time Turk's offer of drinks was accepted. The Russians waited with stern faces while Turk rounded up Martin, Ulrike, Johnson, Duncan, and Wheeler.

216

Duncan spoke for the Americans, careful that his Norwegian did not sound too polished. "We are American citizens," he said. "We are employed by the American oil company Caltex and are involved in the search for good drilling sites in the Barents Sea. You may see the sonar equipment on board which we use in our work. I see no problem with that. Do you, William?"

"No, no. None at all. Glad to explain how it works if you're interested. Give him your card, Jim."

Duncan handed the Russian a business card. It was in English. They studied it, grumbled something to each other, and handed it back.

Duncan continued. "Mr. Trygve Torsvik is our captain. This is his ship. We lease it from him along with his services."

"Free enterprise," said Wheeler. "It works very well. You boys ought to give it a try."

Turk lit his pipe and refilled the Russians' glasses with aquavit. They drank in unison as the ship bobbed up and down in the swells. "And the woman?" asked the smaller Russian.

"I'm a West German journalist," answered Ulrike. "This is my friend, Dr. Martin Dodds, an American who is teaching in Norway. We are on our way to Longyearbyen. A mutual friend arranged for us to sail with Captain Torsvik. We have nothing to do with the oil operations of the other gentlemen on board."

She pulled down the hood of her rain parka. Both Russians ogled her, stunned by her striking good looks.

"I am also a friend of your Consul, Mikhail Obruchev," she said. "I trust he will allow us to come ashore as his guests while repairs are made on our ship. Please tell him I'm most anxious to see him again."

The two Russians stared at each other dumbly. "Yes, we must get permission from him anyway before you dock. We will tell him you are here. Name, please?"

"Von Menck."

"Yes, good. Remember that, Comrade. Monsikk."

"No, von Menck."

"Yes. Excuse my pronunciation. One more thing, and we will go ashore for instructions. What sort of problems are you having with the ship?"

"Seems to be the generator," said Turk. "It shouldn't be too hard to track down, but we don't have the equipment on board to do it. I don't want to risk the run to Longyearbyen in this weather until it's repaired."

"Yes, we understand. Anchor here and wait. We will return as soon as possible with our orders."

18

WHEN Bjørn returned to the hotel at one-thirty in the morning, he was elated. The meeting was set for three o'clock the coming afternoon at the State Department. Except for National Security Adviser Holzhauer, all of Millet's trophies were in the bag. And it looked as if Holzhauer could be brought around with a little more wooing.

He peeked into the bedroom. Christina was asleep on her back with the sheet pulled up around her neck. Her blond hair was loose on the pillow. He slipped into the bath and showered. At last, he thought, he would have a chance to talk with her.

He came into the room naked, drying his hair with a towel. She opened her eyes and looked at him with indifference. He sat on the bed beside her and ran his fingers over the sheet the length of her body. "Christina, can we talk?"

"Later, Bjørn, please. I don't have anything to say."

She closed her eyes again, but a slight tremor in her leg ran up through his fingers like an electric shock. He pulled back the sheet and leaned over her, kissing her neck and breasts. She did not move, but he could feel her body grow tense. She turned her head to avoid his kisses.

He slipped down, ran his tongue along the soft skin above her sex, reached up and took her breasts in his hands.

"Enough, Bjørn." She rolled onto her side and tucked her legs up toward her chest.

Gently he kissed her back, her calves, her thighs. She squirmed and twisted until she lay on her stomach. He caressed her buttocks with his hands and kissed the nape of her neck.

"Please, Bjørn, not now."

He put a knee between her legs and moved it upward. "Christina, I want you," he whispered.

"Bastard."

"Christina!" She lay very still, her legs slightly parted.

"Bastard," she said again, sliding her ankle over his.

They made love. Soon she was crying out so loudly he had to hold his hand over her mouth. "Bjørn," she said. "Bjørn." Her voice held all the tenderness of happier times.

"Please, Christina, can't we talk this thing through? I want so much—"

She placed a finger over his lips. "Bjørn, I love you, you know I do. But something's wrong. Something's really wrong. I can't talk yet. I can't. Please, you've got to respect me in this. You can't—"

His kisses swallowed her words.

When the telephone woke him at eight o'clock, she was already dressed. "I've phoned Ellen at Harpers Ferry. She's coming into the city to do some sightseeing with me. Good luck, Bjørn. I hope everything goes well."

"God, Chris, how long are you going to keep this up?"

"I don't know. When will you be back?"

"Should be around six. We've got a big meeting at State at three. Wait for me, will you? We can go somewhere special for dinner—if nothing catastrophic comes up. If it does I'll call you. And tomorrow we can move over to the Embassy. That should make—"

The phone interrupted him. Christina answered. "Yes," she said, "I'll be right down." She hung up and turned to go out.

"Christina, you'll be here tonight, won't you?"

She paused at the door. "I don't know. Goodbye, Bjørn."

He jumped out of bed but she was already gone.

Undersecretary of State Richard Olsen's office on the seventh floor of the State Department was paneled in oak and offered a fine view of the city. The furniture was mostly early American; there was no conference table.

Olsen had placed several chairs in an informal circle for the meeting. He had moved the room's three marble-top coffee tables so that each man would have an ashtray and a glass of water.

Bjørn stood chatting with Olsen and Millet. From the window he could see the Washington Monument and the green expanses of Arlington National Cemetery across the river. He glanced at his watch: ten till three. The nineteenth-century portrait of an undistinguished-looking American notable stared emptily past him.

"On loan from the National Gallery," said Olsen. "The curators are very good about making us look cultured."

"Who is it?"

"I haven't the slightest idea."

There was a sharp knock at the door. In strode General Harry Clark of the Joint Chiefs, square jaw protruding, crew cut bristling, his barrel chest adorned with a glittering array of medals. The next quarter hour saw the arrival of CIA Director Chet Willard, Secretary of State Theodore Barker, Secretary of Defense Jerome White, *and* National Security Adviser Paul Holzhauer. Bjørn felt a fresh surge of admiration for Millet. It was no easy task to assemble this distinguished and powerful group of men on less than two days' notice.

Millet, in the same khakis he had worn yesterday and an open sport shirt, began the meeting.

"Most of you have already met Mr. Holt. You've heard bits and pieces of the distressing evidence he has brought to Washington. If there are no objections, I'd like to ask him to present his evidence now in its entirety. After that, I think we'll have plenty to discuss."

"Just a second," grumbled General Clark. "I had a short talk with Mr. Holt yesterday, but he never did reveal the exact capacity in which he was here. Could you do that for us, please?"

"Of course, General. I'm the chief adviser to the Norwegian Foreign Minister, Kristen Skogan."

"Why didn't he come himself?" snapped the General. "If the affair's as bad as you say, seems he ought to have taken the trouble."

221

"He was planning to come. Unfortunately, Mr. Skogan suffered a massive coronary Friday afternoon. A result, I would guess, of the pressures he's had to face recently."

"Sorry to hear that, Holt. I met the old codger here last winter when our two countries were on better terms. A good Joe, that Skogan. He'll pull through, won't he?"

"I called this morning. His doctor is hopeful."

"So you're officially representing your State Department? Or did your President send you?"

"I'm glad you brought that up, General. I'm not representing Prime Minister Danielsen. As far as he knows, I'm in Washington on another matter."

"So who the hell are we dealing with, Holt?"

"You're dealing with a representative of the Norwegian Foreign Office."

"Who is not the official representative of his government."

"Correct."

"And a little strange. Wouldn't you say so, Mr. Holt?"

"Perhaps. Also most fortunate for you, General, and for the others in this room. Because if I *were* the official spokesman, you would not get the information I'm going to give you. Take your choice, General. Between form and substance. A crisis is building which threatens both our countries. If the awkwardness of my diplomatic position is more important to you than my message, I'm sure I can find a sympathetic ear elsewhere."

"That's the spirit, Holt. Just checking your colors. Sure we've got to shovel all that political and diplomatic crap out of the way once in a while. Otherwise, what we call 'Western civilization' would sink in its own muck. Well, what are you waiting for? Get on with your presentation. What kind of a mess has that pinko President gotten you into now?"

"Fact of the matter is, Prime Minister Danielsen has made a horrible mistake. The reasons are not important, although I would feel more comfortable having you know that he does not dislike Americans or the United States. His 'third way' was largely the result of his myopic attempt to cater to recent trends in the Norwegian electorate and in his party. But the mistake is no less serious for that reason. The Soviets are planning, as I have said, to move into the power vacuum created by the 'third way.' They intend to acquire for their naval forces on the Kola Peninsula a secure window to the Atlantic. They'll get it, too, if they succeed in annexing Svalbard and the northern provinces of Norway. You're all aware, of course, of the shift in global power relations which would result from Soviet possession of the Svalbard Passage."

"Quite aware," interjected CIA Director Willard.

"Our dilemma, yours and mine, boils down to this. If the Soviets invade—and in just a minute I want to explain to you why we feel such an invasion is imminent—Norway will offer no resistance. This is because of our Prime Minister. If Norway would fight, the northern provinces could hold out for at least a few days, maybe longer. This would give you time to mobilize world opinion behind you, time to establish publicly that the rumors which will provide the Soviet pretext for the invasion—rumors of West German uranium mining on Svalbard—are nothing but cynical fabrications. But Norway will not fight. The Soviets, I'm very sorry to say, know this. They're assuming that the United States will likewise offer no concrete resistance. They intend to confront your country with a *fait accompli* and challenge you to dislodge them."

"A frightening scenario, Mr. Holt," said Secretary of State Barker. "But before we speculate any further, could I ask you to give us your reasons for believing the invasion is imminent? As far as I know, all of our intelligence reports are in disagreement with your prediction."

Bjørn wove the events of the last weeks into an artful tapestry of incrimination. When he had finished, there were no skeptics in the room. "All we need before we take some sort of action," said the CIA Director, "is incontrovertible proof, proof of our own. Mr. Millet, why haven't our men in Scandinavia been on top of this thing? Is Wilson slipping?"

"Sir, we've got a group sailing for Barentsburg right now. If all goes well, they'll be in and out in a couple of days. . . ."

"So Wilson did know something was in the offing?"

"No, sir. Mr. Holt called me from Norway two weeks ago and asked me to alert our men. I had trouble reaching Wilson. He's involved in something in Finland right now. So I personally arranged to have a team put on site. You know William Johnson, I believe. He's in charge of the mission. I have absolute confidence in his abilities as an agent."

Astonished, Bjørn listened to his friend concoct a lie likely to put an abrupt end to his career. *That* was courage, he thought.

"Mr. Millet," said Willard, "that's hardly acceptable practice. Why wasn't the matter brought to my attention?"

"An error in judgment on my part, perhaps. But you were vacationing in Nag's Head until yesterday. I wanted to wait for the report from Johnson before disturbing you. You realize that the affair seemed considerably less urgent until Mr. Holt arrived with this latest evidence."

The CIA Director looked him over suspiciously, then said, "All right, we'll drop it for now. I suppose it's a little like Holt's status. Do we go with form or substance? Now then, gentlemen, let's assume the message from our own people confirms the threat of a Soviet invasion. What then?"

General Clark stuffed a cigar into his mouth, lit it, leaned back in his chair and rubbed his crew cut. He was a brilliant but eccentric military thinker who was presently on the best of terms with the President. Some considered him a genius, the hope for the future of the American military. Others saw him as a dangerous adventurer. But everyone, even those who detested him and what he stood for, paid him the highest form of respect: they listened to him.

"Holt," he boomed, "I like you. You've impressed me with the way you've handled yourself here today. I think you've come to the right conclusions regarding Soviet motives. But, Holt, you've made one big mistake. You fail to see that a Soviet takeover of the areas in question would be highly favorable to the United States. For your country, of course, it would be the disaster you describe. But for us, not in the least."

Secretary of State Barker, a refined, elegantly dressed man in his late fifties, sat up straight as a rod. Barker had been in his new job since early March—the President's only substantial concession to the liberal wing of the Republican Party. He seemed ill at ease in this company. "General Clark, I would appreciate it if you would cut the theatrics and get to the point. You know as well as anyone the significance of the Svalbard Passage for our long-range security. You yourself briefed me on the Northern Flank before my confirmation hearings."

Harry Clark leaned back in his chair again. The cigar was still between his teeth and the condescending smile lingered on his lips. "Patience, Barker, patience. The truth often lurks in dark caverns far beyond the reach of conventional thought. Especially when the politicians are doing the thinking. You see, gentlemen, conventional thinking is what got us into the bind we're in today. Military history is strewn with the corpses of once-great nations that have been strangled, not by the enemy, but by their own unwillingness to part with outmoded ways of thinking. The best modern example is France. With her huge army, she wasn't even able to give Hitler a fight. Why? You know damned well why. The military leaders clung to notions of trench warfare made hopelessly obsolete by the rise of the armored division and its accompanying tactical air force. And what, gentlemen, does this murderous conventional wisdom preach to us today? Meet each Soviet move with a balanced and rational countermove. Correct? And what, gentlemen, is the result? I'll tell you what: a gradual gobbling up of the free world by the Russkis. Because Ivan can always predict just how we'll react, can always plan just how he'll deal with our reaction."

He held his cigar in his left hand now, waving it about like a conductor's baton. "The Russian advance, gentlemen, has been proceeding uninterrupted for ten years now. A little here, a little there. But it all adds up. And even more important is the psychological factor. Ivan's starting to think of us as a dying power with little will to reverse the trend. To him, we look like a stinking carcass. I warn you, the collectivist vulture is preparing to feed off our remains.

"Now, gentlemen, I must admit that the stench of death is there. We've had some bad luck, some weak leadership, some domestic problems. But all that's beginning to change. We're still a great country. It's about time we start to act like one. If we wait too much longer, it might be too late."

"General Clark!" interrupted the Secretary of State. "Please spare us. We all know your philosophy of international relations. Would you kindly stop talking about carcasses and smells and get to the point."

"Well, well, Barker, you certainly are on the rag today. I'm coming to the point just now."

He waved his smoking baton at Secretary of Defense Jerome White, the quintessential technocrat. White looked bored. He doodled on his pad while the General addressed him.

"Now, Jerome, suppose the Soviets moved on the areas in question. How many men would it take to stop them or to dislodge them if they beat us to the punch?"

White, for once, did not give an exact figure. "General, assuming we had a million men, a million *motivated* men who were neither high on drugs nor too dumb to read the instructions on crates, and assuming we had the means to get them to the site of the battle . . . assuming all those things, we could still do nothing. Murmansk is right there. It and the surrounding Soviet installations on the Kola Peninsula constitute the largest concentration of military force in the world. Whatever force we could bring to bear, the Soviets could counter with a far superior force. If we wish to mount a defense of that area, our only option is the employment of tactical nuclear weapons."

General Clark took a swallow of water and jammed the cigar between his teeth. "Yes, Jerome, quite correct. Now, Mr. Olsen, before you were made Undersecretary for Political Affairs, you were at one of the Scandinavian desks, weren't you?"

"I was."

"So you know something about Norway?"

"Yes."

"Good. Roughly how many people live on Svalbard and in the northern provinces which the Russians are likely to annex?"

"General, I know where you're going with your questioning and I object—"

"I don't give a goddamn whether you object or not. You loafers at State are paid so the people who are doing something can get some information when they need it. Who in the hell—"

"Roughly thirty-five thousand," interrupted Bjørn. "Perhaps twice that many if we draw the line south of Tromsø." He wanted to help the General finish up so the meeting could turn to more realistic considerations.

"Thanks, Holt. A measly thirty-five thousand. From the military point of view, *uninhabited*."

He laughed. "I don't want to give the impression I'm callous. I'm as concerned about human life as the next guy. But the truth is this: sometimes the sacrifice of some is necessary to preserve the lives of others. That is, after all, the meaning of war. Correct, gentlemen? We send out X number of soldiers to die so the majority of us may continue to live. Let me give another example. Let's return to the Frogs. When the Germans marched into the Rhineland in '36, they should have met some vicious French resistance. In '36 the Frogs were still by far the stronger nation. Now they'd have lost some men, some damned good men. . . . Frogs aren't all faggots. But they'd have broken Hitler's back in the process. Instead, they dallied around and did nothing. The result was a world war which claimed forty, fifty million lives. Now is there anyone in this room who would argue that it was more humane to save those few Frog lives in '36 than it would have been to prevent the holocaust? Which, gentlemen, brings me back to Svalbard."

The room remained silent as Clark cut the end off a fresh cigar and lit it. He slapped the marble-top table beside him, causing the water glasses, the ashtray—and Richard Olsen—to jump. "I'll sum up now. I know Mr. Barker would like to get back to his golf game. But please, gentlemen, listen to me very carefully. How we deal with the present situation is going to have a critical impact on the future of our country.

"As I have said, the decline of America is underway. We *must* reverse the trend. If we fail, gentlemen, the writing is on the wall. Now, the Northern Flank offers us a godsend. We let the Soviets take it. Then . . . then, gentlemen, without speaking a word, we unleash a barrage of tactical nukes. We clear out the whole goddamned area. After all, no one invited the Russkis to step in there in the first place.

"Sure, there'll be some damned unfortunate casualties. All of the Norwegians in the area, to be exact. But, gentlemen, consider the benefits. In military terms. In human terms. We reverse the trend of our decline at last. The Russkis won't dare lift a finger for decades. Their certainty that we will respond to future aggressions with 'rational caution' will go up with the first mushroom cloud. The balance of terror between the superpowers will be restored, the danger of an all-out nuclear confrontation will vanish. *That* will be the result of the 'surgical' employment of tactical nukes at this point. Stability will return to our world. The flowering of civilization beneath the umbrella of peace will take up where it started to wither a decade ago. America will again be the symbol of strength and morality she was before we lost our nerve. Gentlemen, what I'm proposing will take some courage. But it will pay off in the long run. It's the only humane thing to do. Hell, it's the *only* thing to do."

Looking at the faces around the room, Bjørn felt a stab of panic. Too many of these men seemed under Clark's spell, and he, Bjørn, could understand why. The General's argument was a masterful synthesis of truth and delusion; it would appeal to certain types—types Millet had warned him were the powers behind the scene in Washington. Worse, Clark's scheme probably would appear successful at first: it would force a Soviet withdrawal. There was, of course, the slim possibility that the Soviets would escalate the conflict. But that, in Bjørn's view, was unlikely. As he saw it, Russian foreign policy was a paradigm of patience: win one here, lose one there. The Russians took risks, of course, but they never put themselves in a position where they could not back down.

Yet even if Clark's plan were to succeed in the short run, it was an outrageous proposal. For the unspoken foundation of the international order since 1945—the number one rule of the game —was the agreement that nuclear weapons *not* be used. To break that agreement was to plunge the world down a new and uncertain course which would surely end in the very conflagration Clark maintained he would avoid.

Bjørn tried to convince himself that most Americans shared his own view, that his fears were irrational. Clark was nothing more than a frustrated General who needed to blow off a little steam. . . .

His equanimity was just returning when National Security Adviser Holzhauer's words shattered it for the rest of the day—and for many more to come.

"Very perceptive, Harry, very perceptive, indeed. This time I think you've hit on something."

Holzhauer, the President's most trusted adviser on foreign affairs, straightened his bow tie, clearing his throat as he smiled. As always he wore a gray suit and a white shirt with pearl cufflinks. His sparse brown hair was combed straight back, his bony face was framed by gold wire-rimmed glasses, and his ears—which seemed to move up and down when he spoke—were a little too large. Bending his slight torso forward as if to tie his shoe, he laced his fingers over his knee.

"Just one problem, Harry. One minor problem."

"Yeah?" grumbled the General. "Don't tell me you, of all people, are going to object. What's wrong, Paul? Losing your balls?"

"Harry, I don't think my balls are the issue here. You know as well as I that the American people are tired of seeing us defend ungrateful countries. Now, if the people's perception of Norway—"

"Okay, Paul, got you," shot back Clark. "What you're saying is that if we could pull it off politically, you agree that it should be done?"

"Yes, Harry, I agree very strongly."

The atmosphere in the room was now so charged that everyone seemed to have forgotten a foreigner was present. Everyone, that is, except Art Millet. He gritted his teeth and glanced at his Norwegian friend as if to say, "Do something!" But Bjørn felt too weak to move, much less to object to what was being discussed in front of him with such blatant disregard for his country.

Chet Willard, Director of the CIA, spoke. "I don't make policy but, like everyone else, I have my opinions on what it should be. . . ."

"And?" urged the General.

"And I think we'd better take a close look at how the American people will react to something this extreme."

"For Christ's sake," thundered Clark, "why 'extreme'? I've explained it's the most humane approach, however you look at it. That's not *my* definition of extreme."

"Harry, I'm not objecting to your logic or your strategy. You know very well how I feel about the weak leadership that has allowed our power and prestige to sink to their present levels. I'm merely asking you to consider the long-range impact of your plan on the domestic political scene."

"Correct," said Holzhauer. "We should also look at it from that angle."

"All right," said the General, "but let's not start using domestic political necessity as an excuse to get soft."

Willard continued. "Let's say, Harry, that we use the tactical nuclear weapons before the American people have become unified in their anger at the Soviet Union. As Paul, I think, would agree, the average guy will just then be saying that it serves Norway right to be overrun by the Russians. People don't know anything about the Svalbard Passage and its immense importance to us. What they do know is that Norway has thumbed her nose at our attempts to protect her. We'll be coming to the aid of Norway with nuclear weapons—now wait, this is how the average guy will see it—just at the moment Norway is getting what it deserves. What I want to say is this: We might for a time succeed in stopping the Russians and in restoring global stability. But if the American people are not clamoring for some kind of drastic action, I think our use of the bomb might cause a backlash. We might, in other words, unwittingly pave the road back to power for the liberals. And under the worst conditions. They'll put controls on our intelligence operations, they'll let our attempts to revive the army stagnate, they'll undermine the rescue of America before we've had a chance to succeed."

"You're wrong," grumbled General Clark. "The American people always respect a no-nonsense, courageous show of force."

"Perhaps," said Holzhauer. "But let's get down to the nitty-gritty. The President's not going to buy the use of nuclear weapons unless the people are shouting for a big retaliation. We all agree this is the perfect opportunity to use the bomb. Why don't we just decide how we can create a public-opinion climate that would justify its use? We need to operate like Roosevelt before Pearl Harbor. He knew the Japs were coming, but he let them come anyway. The result was a furious nation that gave him what he wanted: the freedom to strike when, where, and how he chose." Holzhauer cracked his knuckles and rubbed his hands together. "What about this, Harry? What about letting the Soviet attack transpire, perhaps without the President's foreknowledge? In the days after the aggression, we use the media to paint it as a move directed primarily against the U.S., not Norway."

"Which it is, in any case," added Willard.

"Right. We don't even have to lie on that one. Anyway, we depict the Soviets as having taken advantage of us, of having used the average American's lack of knowledge of the Northern Flank to humiliate us. It won't be long until the people are crying for revenge if we orchestrate this thing just right. And revenge they'll get. Under those circumstances, I'm certain we can sell the President on Harry's plan."

"Won't do," said Clark. "If the pressure builds slowly on the Soviets, we'll be playing their game. They'll say, 'If you do that, we'll take Berlin. If you touch Cuba, you'll regret it in the Middle East.' No, gentlemen, that's how they expect us to escalate. Our hope is with the quick, unexpected shot. We've got to catch them totally off guard and stun hell out of them. The counterstrike must come directly on the heels of the invasion. Which means that we've got to get public opinion turned around pretty goddamned fast. Unless, of course, you take my stand that. . . ."

Olsen left the meeting in protest, slamming the door behind him. Secretary of Defense White also took his leave, citing the wish to let the others "handle the nontechnical side of this thing." The discussion among the three hardliners on how to manufacture the domestic climate which would make possible an American nuclear strike dragged on for another hour.

Bjørn was suffering from a severe case of shock. The whole affair had taken on a surrealistic quality which his superbly analytical mind could not absorb. He sat thunderstruck, wondering how he, the brilliant theoretician and practitioner of diplomacy, had managed to set the stage for so ruinous an event. He felt utterly and irretrievably helpless.

Indeed, that last hour of the fateful Sunday meeting was the most unpleasant of his life. Dark thoughts slipped through his

231

consciousness like the shadowy forms of fish gliding below deep water. He saw Skogan on his deathbed, crying out in pain when he learned of the catastrophe that his adviser had brought down on his beloved country; he heard his father curse his son's name with loathing; he saw Christina at the window of her house in Tromsø, a blinding flash illuminating her face—reproachful even in agony.

Barker's words did little to restore Bjørn's confidence.

"I'm sorry, Mr. Holt," said the Secretary of State, "that you had to listen to such barbaric nonsense. But it pays to let them talk. You see, Mr. Holt, they're all so brilliant that they never fail to cancel one another out. Let me assure you . . . as soon as we have word from our own men of an imminent Soviet invasion, we'll get you the kind of deterrent you need. And we'll get it before your land and people are ravaged, not after."

Bjørn took leave of Barker and Millet in the corridor, too shaken to utter more than a few bewildered words. When he came out of the State Department it was almost seven o'clock. A humid southwest wind had come up, pushing into the city the smells of the American South. The sky to the west was dirty pink. He felt an urgent need to see Christina. He ordered the taxi driver to speed up and almost forgot to pay him when they arrived at the Mayflower.

Blood throbbed in his temples as he walked to the reception desk for his key. He hoped beyond hope it would not be there. But it was.

When he unlocked the door to their room he saw the note on the dresser at once. His stomach contracted with anxiety as he read:

Bjørn,

Forgive me. I should not have come to Washington with you. Under the present circumstances, I thought it better for me to return to Norway. No point complicating my error still further. I didn't want to discuss my decision with you, as I know talking about it would only trouble both of us. (I had already made up my mind before you came home last night.) This doesn't mean I've given up our relationship; I only need some time alone to mull things over.

I've called Professor Hansen. I start teaching again Wednesday morning. To save you the trouble of trying to track me down, I left at three this afternoon on TWA flight 420. I'll be on SAS from London to Oslo, then fly directly to Tromsø.

Best of luck resolving the crisis. I have no doubt you'll succeed or, coward that I am, I wouldn't be on my way north. (Your *political* skills I've never for a moment doubted.) Do call me at home when and if you wish. I've got to run now. It's almost noon and I haven't finished packing.

Christina

He sat on the edge of the bed and took a deep breath, then grabbed the phone and called Dulles. Perhaps flight 420 had been delayed . . . perhaps she had missed it and was waiting for another. If not, he might still be able to get the British Airways Concorde to London and intercept her. Realizing the futility of it all, he hung up before anyone answered.

He stretched out on the bed, an arm over his eyes, and waited for the blackest despair to engulf him. It did not. Rather, he felt a fierce determination to stop the insane course of events today's meeting had set in motion. For the first time in his life he realized that Skogan, that old Jens Holt, that Christina were the things that really mattered. His politics had ceased to exist in a vacuum.

19

MIKHAIL OBRUCHEV had been riding high for several weeks. Koznyshov had been very impressed with his success in driving the glaciological expedition off Svalbard, and ever since his triumph, even Karnoi and Nikovski—now stationed in Barentsburg—had gone out of their way to curry favor with the Consul.

But yesterday all that had changed, cruelly and abruptly. Koznyshov had received distressing news from Moscow via a messenger. Evidently, the Soviet Ambassador to Norway, who occupied a position in the Party hierarchy much higher up than his ambassadorship would suggest, had just returned from Oslo in a rage. Alexi Ivanov had reported that the Norwegians had found a bullet hole in the rib of one of the expedition's climbers. Now he was demanding an explanation for the sloppy job done by Soviet intelligence, and Koznyshov was on the spot. Not that the blunder was yet of crucial significance. Ivanov had made clear that it was not, thanks to the credulity of the Norwegian Prime Minister. But there were a couple of persistent bastards in the Foreign Office who knew what was going on. If the invasion did not come off soon, they might somehow throw a wrench into the Soviet plan.

The messenger had also conveyed Ivanov's displeasure over the absence of the promised rumors about German uranium mining in the Western press. He had even sent Koznyshov a short sealed letter in his own hand which hinted darkly at a possible investigation of the KGB leadership if things did not shape up.

At the lower end of this pecking order was, of course, Mikhail Obruchev. Less than twenty-four hours ago, he had been chewed out by the General for what seemed to him an eternity, and he was not taking it lightly. News of the *Utsira*'s arrival in Barentsburg thus reached him at the worst possible time.

Would Koznyshov, he wondered, interpret the ship's undetected approach as still another sign of his, Obruchev's, incompetence? Perhaps he should try to get the ship to leave without informing the General. But what if he were found out, as he no doubt would be? It was just no use trying to outsmart Koznyshov; it couldn't be done. He felt trapped, as he had so often felt since those mainland shitheads had come into his town and started ordering him around. He would just have to hope for the best.

His hands trembled as he picked up the phone. As he dialed, he thought of his old friend Belov, whose office Koznyshov had taken over. What wonderful, untroubled days those had been! Hunting, drinking, showing that slut Olga a good time, building furniture behind his house with a gang of vodka-happy workers, bartering with his Norwegian friends for all sorts of Western luxuries. Why had they come and taken all this away from him? What had he done to deserve the tortures they were putting him through?

"Mikhail Obruchev," repeated the General, "it's not your fault. You had no way of knowing about the ship's approach in this weather. And I told you yesterday it wasn't the fate of the climbers that infuriated me. It was your failure to inform me. We can handle most situations if we have the data. So, Comrade, relax. I still have confidence in you. Let's look at this new little problem of ours with open, creative eyes. Who is on the ship?"

Obruchev was as unnerved by the General's tranquility as he would have been by the great man's wrath. It confused him and made him think he was in for something he couldn't foresee. "Three American oilmen," he said hastily. "Also a Norwegian captain, an American teacher or doctor or something, and a West German journalist. Von Menck, the one who wrote the article on Barentsburg you liked."

He heard the click of Koznyshov's lighter and the sound of his drawn-out exhalation.

"I see. Very good. Yes, that's most fortunate indeed."

Again he paused. Obruchev, of course, had no way of reading Koznyshov's mind. Nor was he privy to the KGB's strategy of planting rumors of German uranium mining in the Western press, a strategy in which Ulrike was an unwitting accomplice.

"Well, General, what should we do with them? Tow them out to sea?"

Koznyshov continued as if he had not heard Obruchev's question. "Very, very good. Von Menck, eh? It'll be a pleasure to meet her at last." That fool Norwegian, Jon Lellenberg, he was thinking. His men were going to have to improve their recruiting skills. He chuckled for a moment over his luck . . . and the luck of the fool who had let her get away. This was almost too good to be true.

"Mikhail Obruchev!"

"Yes, sir."

"Get down to the harbor. Escort that woman to your office at once. Treat her civilly. Chat with her, answer her questions. Entertain her however you wish until she mentions uranium or anything vaguely related to uranium. Then send her over to me that instant. Tell her I'm your man in charge of that area or some such thing. Understood?"

"But General, what if she doesn't mention uranium? She didn't mention it when she was here before."

"Listen here, Obruchev, I'm not an idiot. She'll mention uranium as sure as you're standing in your office. Don't ask questions. Just do as I say."

Obruchev—who was in fact standing—was baffled. "But, sir—"

"No more questions. How does the town look? Are we expecting any SS-20's today? Is there anything intelligence men might spot? I always assume the worst, Mikhail Obruchev. It's safer that way. . . . Well?"

"Two of the missiles came in last night. Our teams have already sunk them in the mine shafts. We might get some third stages, but they'll be in crates. Otherwise, everything is as usual. There's a freighter with food supplies being unloaded at the harbor, and I think they're going to try to get one more coal barge out today."

"Good. Have Dimitrov take the others to the Workers' Center. Tell him to implement Plan White immediately. Send Karnoi and Nikovski over with them as well. No . . . no, on second thought, we'll spare our guests that. Let those two put a search party together. Have them make a list of every item on the ship and every item in possession of the passengers. I want them to be most thorough. Also, have Karnoi get a team of mechanics on the ship's problem. If we do let them out, we'll want them out *fast*. Clear?"

"Yes, General."

The Consul pulled a bottle of vodka from his desk and downed a swallow to brace himself. He walked down the stairs to Olga's old office. The two men who had boarded the *Utsira* rose when he entered.

"Let's go," barked Obruchev, yanking on his hat and rain parka.

"Are we bringing them ashore?"

"Yes. But first we've got to find Dimitrov. Know where he is?"

"Yep. Then to the pier?"

"No. Not until we've gotten in touch with Lieutenant Karnoi. But first, Dimitrov."

"Right, sir."

They climbed into the jeep and headed down the muddy road. On the way they passed a young man who grinned and flipped Obruchev an obscene gesture.

"Know that idiot, Consul?" asked the driver, shouting at Obruchev over his shoulder.

"Watch yourself, Comrade," boomed back the Consul. "If you could do anything as well as that man flies a chopper, you wouldn't be worrying about your next promotion. Speed up. There's no time to waste."

The driver glanced in his rear view mirror and almost ran off the road. Lydov had pulled off his fur hat and, one hand on his hip, was twirling about on the wooden sidewalk in a frenzied Ukrainian folkdance.

"Sir!" he shouted at Obruchev, "that pilot of yours seems a bit off his rocker. He's dancing around out there like a faggot."

"Shut up and drive."

The driver grumbled something under his breath and, swerving to avoid a deep puddle, pulled up in front of the Workers'

Center. Obruchev, agile in spite of his age and portly build, jumped down and ran inside.

Ulrike was the first to come ashore. Obruchev pulled off his hat when he recognized her, letting the cold rain and sleet pelt his bald head. He waited, awkward and self-conscious, while she maneuvered down the swaying gangplank.

"Consul Obruchev, what an unexpected pleasure to see you again. I told our captain there would be no problem docking in Barentsburg. Thank you for being so kind."

Obruchev devoured her with his eyes as though he could see through her thick, loosely fitting raingear.

"Delighted, also," he mumbled to Ulrike. "The others. The others are to go to the Workers' Center. You and I will talk in my office." He fumbled with his hat and pulled it over his soaking head, angry at himself for having taken it off in the first place.

"Comrade Dimitrov," he roared.

The driver of the small olive-green transporter waiting on the pier looked out his window. Turk and the Americans were coming down the plank.

"Comrade Dimitrov, take these guests to the Center and see that they get something to eat and drink." He glanced back at Ulrike, this time shyly. "You come with me," he said, starting up the pier to the waiting jeep.

Ulrike followed without looking back. Martin watched her lean into the wind. That woman, he thought, that woman had gotten under his skin. He had never in his wildest dreams imagined that something like this could happen. He was alive again! The world seemed utterly changed. Little things he wouldn't have noticed a few weeks ago struck him as beautiful; he felt things he hadn't felt since his youth; and this stirring and awakening, this emotional springtime, was all because of her.

"Please come with me," said the Russian named Dimitrov in a loud but pleasant voice. "Let's get out of this storm and have a drink."

"Sounds great," answered Wheeler. "Got any real Russian vodka on tap?"

Dimitrov smiled. "Only Coca-Cola."

"Really?" said Duncan, wishing it were true. Maybe Wheeler was right; maybe he should practice a little nightly until he could pour down a healthy drink without grimacing. After all, in this business you had to be tough.

"Where did you learn your Norwegian?" asked Dimitrov as they walked into the large café on the second floor of the Workers' Center. Several Russians taking their afternoon coffee looked the foreigners over and returned to their newspapers.

"We deal with the Norwegians almost every day," said Johnson. "Not that they don't speak English. They all do, of course. But our boss at Caltex—that's the company we work for—is a stickler. Among other things, he likes his people to know Norwegian. He even requires it of some of us. We three all got sent to Berlitz—"

"Berlitz?"

"Sorry. That's a language school. We had a pretty good background before we came over, and we've all been here quite a while now. How about yourself? Your Norwegian sounds excellent to me."

Dimitrov gave a slight bow. "Thank you. I also was sent to language school. We've got a lot of business with the Norwegians up here. I often act as the interpreter, although the Consul does all right too."

Dimitrov was a large, heavy-set man with horn-rimmed glasses and medium-length brown hair. He seemed used to dealing with Westerners. "Here, here," he went on, "let's sit over at that big table by the window. We can see the harbor from here. I'll show you what goes on in Barentsburg. Not very interesting, really. A lot of coal mining and not much else. But I suppose it's better than staring at the walls. My, this is going to be some storm, isn't it?"

Huge wet snowflakes swirled past the window. Martin thought about Ulrike and what she must be doing at that moment. Duncan forced down his vodka, Wheeler joked with the Russian, Johnson asked an intelligent question from time to time, and Turk gazed about in silence and smoked his pipe as the northwester tightened its grip on the town. Workers came in in small groups, shook out their wet clothes, drank coffee and vodka, shouted at each other

239

and at the plump, cheerful young woman behind the bar, stared at the unusual visitors, and went out. Some had hands and faces blackened by coal. Others were grease-stained from working on machinery. Still others, about to begin their shifts, wore clean work clothes. Turk and Martin, with Dimitrov's blessing, took a short stroll down to the game rooms. Then the Russian took all five on a guided tour of the center.

Koznyshov, having prepared for all contingencies—including a penetration into Barentsburg by Western intelligence—had done his job well. Johnson and his colleagues, though suspicious, noticed nothing unusual. The soldiers stationed in the town dressed as ordinary workers. The remaining contingent of miners preserved the appearance of business as usual. And nothing at the harbor indicated the stockpiling of military hardware. Only Turk, who had been in Barentsburg many times before, noticed something specific.

Obruchev helped her out of her parka and wondered what he should do while she unzipped her rainpants. Embarrassed, he walked to his desk and hauled out the vodka. "Drink?" he asked, glancing furtively at her, then looking quickly away.

"Of course," she answered. She almost felt sorry for him. She slipped off her galoshes and tossed her rainpants over the coat rack. While he dug through his drawer for a second glass, she dragged a heavy green chair close to his desk and sat down. He stood up as if called to attention and muttered a clumsy apology. She smiled when he poured the two glasses full to the rim.

"Cheers, Consul Obruchev. To our reunion."

"Cheers."

"Did you by chance get to look at the article on Barentsburg in my paper? It came out right on schedule, the second week in June."

He realized he was still standing and sat down heavily. God, how he hated situations like this. He felt like a caged animal on display, powerless and humiliated. If only it weren't for Koznyshov, he could take her on a tour of the town as he had done before. They could walk around, he behind her most of the time, while he answered her questions. He could look at her without feeling he would be caught doing so and despised by her. He could even tell her some stories that would make her laugh.

"Oh, no," he said, "I didn't see the article. I can't read German. But there is a man here who can. He said it was very accurate. Maybe you will meet him later today."

"Well, I'm glad you weren't displeased with it. It was certainly very generous of you to show me around."

"Yes, well . . . well, of course. I will show you some more things later that I forgot before."

Ulrike took a sip of vodka. It burned all the way down but the sensation was not unpleasant, at least not when you were chilled halfway to the bone.

"That would be most kind of you," she said. "By the way, Consul Obruchev, would you be so kind as to answer a few more questions for me now that I'm here? I was going to try to reach you in the next day or so from Longyearbyen in any case." She looked directly into his eyes, her expression probing, a little coquettish, and wondered why this poor bumpkin was so terrifying in her dreams.

He refilled his glass and emptied it with a gurgling noise like water draining from a nearly empty tub. "I will be glad to answer all questions."

She studied her fingernails for a moment, then raised her eyes and spoke. "Consul Obruchev, to get right to the issue, I've gotten hold of some distressing evidence. I've become convinced in the last weeks that my government has begun a dangerous action. I think, Consul, that the West Germans are secretly mining uranium on Svalbard. Do you know anything about this?"

She watched closely for his reaction. "Well," he mumbled, "that's not something I wish to talk about just now." Koznyshov! he was thinking. That bastard knew too much! And he, Obruchev, had spent the last three weeks believing he had him figured out and under his thumb. That was a mistake, a very serious one, one he wouldn't repeat. God, would that man ever leave, that man who divined all your secrets, knew your past as if it were his own, saw through your lies as if he could monitor the inner workings of your brain? How did he know that this woman who just walked in from a howling blizzard would mention uranium?

241

"Consul, please. This is no small matter."

"Yes, I know." He didn't know, of course, but his lack of knowledge gave his replies an uncertainty that was hard to interpret. Ulrike assumed he was trying to make a decision on whether to confide in her. She leaned over his desk and placed a hand on his arm.

"Consul, it's very, very important that I find out the truth."

Obruchev glanced at her, shocked, then stood and walked to the window. She could see the snowflakes swirling by. The storm seemed to be intensifying; she hoped she could squeeze the information from him before it got bad enough to make their departure from Barentsburg a problem.

"I will help you," he said at last.

A wave of relief swept over her. "Thank you, Consul. I can't tell you how much I appreciate this."

He marched to the desk and picked up the phone.

"What are you doing?" she asked, but he didn't answer. His attentions seemed focused on the receiver.

The phone rang three times before Koznyshov answered. Obruchev knew he had handled the situation well to this point. He concentrated on what he was saying. He didn't want to blow it with those shitheads this time. "Comrade Velovsky, you've been informed by now of the Norwegian ship we've taken in for repairs? . . . Yes, that's correct. No, Comrade, but one of the passengers on the ship is a West German journalist. . . . No, no, it's a woman." He gave her a clumsy smile which exposed his two gold teeth. "I would like you to see her at once. She has some questions concerning uranium which I would like you to answer for her. May we come now? . . . Yes, very good. Thank you, Comrade."

"Consul," said Ulrike, "I would really rather talk to *you* about this. After all, we know each other a bit. I thought—"

"I'm sorry. I think you will get more precise information from Comrade Velovsky. He has the details."

"Well and good. But will you promise me that we can talk again if I'm not satisfied with the interview?"

Obruchev paused, perplexed. He didn't want to infuriate the General by making pledges he couldn't keep. He said, "I think you will be most satisfied." He waited outside the door while she slipped on her raingear.

242

The Consul drove the jeep himself this time. He pretended he could not hear the questions she shouted at him, and before she could press him further they had arrived.

"Improvise" was a word Koznyshov loved. He had always told his people that the key to successful intelligence work was the ability to improvise. The unexpected, he liked to say, was something that always came to pass. And it was the unexpected that either made or broke you.

Ulrike's visit was the unexpected event that would bring victory to his country and the KGB on Svalbard. He did not believe her landing in Barentsburg was an accident. Rather, he was convinced that she had come to document the rumors about German uranium mining with which she had been supplied. So much the better! He would see to it that she took with her a story the West could not ignore. Just how he would do this, he wasn't yet sure. He would have to wait until she sat across from him. Then he would size her up . . . and improvise.

He paced back and forth in Belov's tiny office, uncomfortable in the baggy wool suit he had had his Moscow tailor make for him. He chuckled, remembering how the proud old craftsman had at first refused to create such an abomination. "It's for a costume party," Koznyshov had assured him, "and it must be made exactly as I say." To dispel the tailor's lingering distaste for the job, he had even had himself measured for an elegant dinner jacket at the same fitting—a quite unnecessary addition to his vast wardrobe.

Koznyshov's attention to detail in his policy of "total disguise" made him confident that the strange landing of the *Utsira* could do him no harm—and potentially a lot of good. Even if the worst happened, even if the entire crew of the ship worked for Western intelligence, the affair would end nicely. The SS-20 missiles which were sunk in the mine shafts were as yet without warheads; the most sophisticated monitoring equipment could not distinguish them from the normal machinery used in mining. Only the human eye could reveal their existence in Barentsburg, and none of the mysterious "guests" was going to be lowered into the bowels of the earth to look. All other military hardware was neatly stacked away in the huge warehouses along the waterfront, and the amphibious craft which would be used to take Longyearbyen was hidden inside fake coal barges moored in the harbor.

As for the town itself, well, here Koznyshov had to give his underling, Dimitrov, credit. The man had kept the appearance and the rhythm of the town so similar to the way it had been that even old inhabitants would have been hard-pressed to detect the changes. The thought of Dimitrov keeping the Westerners distracted at the Workers' Center reassured the General that nothing would go wrong. They would see only what he wanted them to see.

He stopped at the window and watched the violent storm. Memories of the heroic defense of Moscow in '41 came back to him. Mother Russia, he mused, how well Mother Russia knew how to turn the elements to her advantage, how deep and mysterious was her communion with nature. He, as a Russian, felt he shared in this communion. Where the weather was concerned, he was almost superstitious. Looking out into the blizzard, he could feel its power pulsing through his veins: the storm was his hereditary ally, a vicious and loyal protector.

As usual, however, Koznyshov's superstitions possessed more than a kernel of rationality. For he knew that the storm provided him with the backup he needed in the present situation. If the unexpected somehow led the intruders to his secrets, he would simply eliminate them. Their ship would be towed out to sea and left to the mercy of the northwester. It would be impossible for anyone to prove that she had not broken up in heavy seas. He was covered, he had the flexibility he required to devise brilliant and subtle tactics of deception.

Through the blowing snow he watched Obruchev pull up to the wooden sidewalk in a jeep. The Consul climbed out and helped a shapeless form in raingear to the door of the Mines Administration building. Serene and confident, Koznyshov waited.

"Consul?"

"Yes."

"One moment." Koznyshov opened the door.

"Miss von Menck, Comrade Velovsky," snapped Obruchev. "Comrade, answer her questions. Call me when you have finished." He felt odd ordering the General around, even though he had been "ordered" to do so. "Good day," he said, and beat a hasty retreat.

Koznyshov–Velovsky closed the door and watched Ulrike as she slipped off her parka and galoshes. He lent her an arm, helping her step out of her rainpants.

"Well, sir, where shall I put this mess?"

She shook her head a few times. Her long hair fell back into place. She examined him coolly. Her mind was still on Obruchev, on why he had washed his hands of her, on what she would have to do to get back to his office. The meeting with this stranger she considered a time-consuming formality she would have preferred to avoid.

"Here, give them to me. I'll lay them out in the room next door." She had spoken Norwegian, but he answered her in German. He went out with the soggy bundle.

Ulrike walked about the office, suppressing her frustration. A single low-wattage light bulb pulsed feebly at the end of a twisted cord. The walls were the color of tobacco-stained fingers; the linoleum floor was scuffed and faded. Soviet leaders, whose portraits hung everywhere, peered at her through the gloom with implacable sternness. The room's only window looked out on a cluster of unsightly apartment complexes and another bleak office building.

Koznyshov strode back into the room. "Here, here. Sit down, please." He slid one of the metal chairs around the desk opposite him and gestured toward it with an open hand.

"Thank you, Mr. . . . I'm afraid. . . ."

"Velovsky," said the General, circling the desk. He remained on his feet. "The clothes will be dry when you leave. I've hung them near the stove."

"A lot of good that will do." She nodded toward the window. A torrent of water from the roof was splashing against the glass.

"It's a nice feeling to start out with, though. A comfortable illusion. Care for a drink?"

"No, no more vodka, please."

"Now, Miss von Menck, let's not be the prisoner of Western stereotypes. There are those of us who drink other things. I, for one."

She noticed for the first time that his German was very polished. It didn't sound like the prison-camp German that so many Russians his age had learned during the war and that she had so often heard as a child in Dresden. She began to take him more seriously. "In that case, Mr. Velovsky, a cognac. But just a touch. Your Consul almost drowned me in vodka."

"Ah, yes. Mikhail does love his vodka." He pulled two snifters and a bottle of Rémy Martin from his makeshift bar in the file cabinet. He poured them each a small measure, handed her a snifter, and sat down.

Koznyshov had known from the moment she had taken off her raingear that she would discount anything he told her if he played the role he had intended to play—that of a lower-level functionary under Obruchev's command. He was improvising now, working up to the new identity the situation demanded. "To your stay in Barentsburg. I hope we can make it as pleasant as possible. Sorry we've got so little to work with." He raised his glass.

She smiled but said nothing.

"Now, Miss von Menck, I understand you wished me to answer some questions."

"You understood quite wrongly, Mr. Velovsky. I had a few very specific questions for the Consul. I didn't want to speak to one of his subordinates. He sent me here quite against my will."

"I see." Smiling again, he withdrew a pack of Russian cigarettes from his breast pocket and gave it a nonchalant toss into the wastebasket. He opened his desk drawer and produced the unmistakable light-blue package. "Smoke?"

"No, thank you." She eyed him guardedly. Strange, she thought. This was looking more and more like a setup all the time. But why would they set *her* up? They could not possibly have known she was coming. "French cigarettes, I see."

"Yes, Gauloises." He took his gold lighter, which he had been careful to stash away in his desk, and lit a cigarette. "We Russians have changed," he said, repeating one of his favorite remarks. "We're no longer afraid to give credit where credit is due. If the French make better cigarettes, we smoke them. The paranoia, the xenophobia—those were the growing pains of a new socialist order. I'm happy to say such things now belong to the Soviet past."

She nodded toward the wastebasket where the Russian cigarettes had landed. "No longer afraid, Mr. Velovsky? Then why this charade?"

"Miss von Menck, I've got work to do in Barentsburg. I won't be here long. But while I am, I don't like to stir up the resentment of those around me. As I'm sure you know, we also have our class barriers in the Soviet Union. I'm dealing with people here whose paths I would not cross in ordinary life. I do what I can to put them at ease."

"Then you're not working for Consul Obruchev?"

"Let's say, Miss von Menck, that I'm working *with* him. But I honestly don't see why this should concern you."

"Nor do I see why you should try to conceal your identity. Or do you have something to hide?"

"Perhaps, although hide might be the wrong word. Miss von Menck, what are you doing in Barentsburg? I'm not naive enough to believe your arrival was entirely accidental."

"Whether you're naive or not doesn't interest me. My arrival *today* was indeed accidental. I was to disembark in Longyearbyen. But, Mr. Velovsky, in the most important sense, you are correct in your suppositions. I intended to come to Barentsburg as soon as I could arrange to get here from the Norwegian settlement. I am here for a reason."

"Yes?"

"Mr. Velovsky, as the Consul mentioned to you on the phone, I have certain questions regarding the behavior of my own government on Svalbard."

"Perhaps you could be more specific."

"Need I be? Surely you must know something about Arnheim's outrageous secret attempts to mine uranium right under your nose. Certainly, you're not naive. . . ."

"If I remember correctly, my naiveté—or lack of it—was not one of your concerns."

"Mr. Velovsky, I have some urgent matters to discuss. If you only wish to play little word games, I see no reason to continue this discussion."

"All right, Miss von Menck. We'll stop the games. What are you doing in Barentsburg?"

"I have every reason to believe German uranium mining is

247

taking place on Svalbard. I want to expose this to the world. We've all suffered quite enough from the excesses of the German Right. If that mining is not stopped. . . ."

"I couldn't agree with you more. In fact, Miss von Menck, precisely the same concerns have brought me to this miserable outpost. Now, what may I do for you?"

The snow was sticking now and drifting around the sides of the buildings. The blizzard was beginning to bury some of the town's ugliness. She looked out the window, struggling to hide her eagerness.

"You do know about it, then?" she asked.

"Yes."

"Has the Soviet government lodged complaints in the West? Has the United Nations been notified?"

Koznyshov took a last drag on his Gauloise and immediately lit another. "I'm sorry, Miss von Menck, but it should be quite obvious to you that I cannot discuss such policy matters with a foreigner. Even the Consul does not participate in discussions on this level."

"Then it is correct for me to assume that you are a higher official?"

"Higher than what, Miss von Menck?"

She brushed the hair nervously from her forehead and took a sip of cognac. "High enough, let's say, to take part in making decisions of national importance?"

"I think that would be a safe assumption."

"And you are informed about the mining activities of the West German regime on Svalbard?"

"Yes."

"And you are going to tolerate them?"

"For the time being."

"Why?"

"Because we would like to find a peaceful solution to the problem."

"Mr. Velovsky, if I told you I could get you just such a solution . . . and do it in a way that would expose Arnheim to the world for what he is . . . if I told you this, what would be your reaction?"

He smiled at her and poured her another cognac. "Miss von Menck, I would say that you had a rather overinflated assessment of your own capabilities."

"All right, good. You're not the first to feel that way. And you're not the only one who'll be proven wrong. I'm asking you to cooperate with me in a venture that cannot possibly do you any harm. Tell me the location of the mining, and I'll get this thing cleared up in a most conclusive manner, a manner that will benefit the Soviet Union as well as everyone else."

"If you wish. But I want one thing perfectly clear. Soviet intelligence is monitoring the mining activities in a most thorough fashion. The situation is complex enough as it is. I'm sure you understand that we cannot take any special precautions to assure your safety. If you're caught by our agents in the area, you'll have a lot of explaining to do."

"I think not, Mr. Velovsky. I won't be going alone, but with an expedition consisting of many members of the German press. Svalbard is, after all, not Soviet territory. We'll be perfectly within our rights."

Koznyshov's mind raced jubilantly ahead. A team of German journalists! That would be superb! He would have his own men set up a fake mining site. If the journalists saw through the scheme, there would be ways to get rid of them *fast*. Back home in Germany, it would look as if Arnheim's own people had knocked off the members of the press who had found him out. There would be a furor. Or, if the journalists fell for his ploy—and he suspected they would—the press would soon blossom with stories of Anrheim's insidious activities. In *either* case, he would have his pretext for a Soviet invasion.

"Well, Mr. Velovksy," she said sharply, "what about it? A team of journalists will hardly be a threat to your security on the Northern Flank. Especially since they'll be working for your cause as well as mine."

She was taking the bait like a hungry fish, he thought. He gave her a little more line to make sure she swallowed the hook. "I must warn you again, Miss von Menck, of the acute danger—"

"Mr. Velovsky, I'm not interested in risks and dangers. These are of no consequence to me at this point. I can well imagine the outrage your people feel toward Arnheim's Germany. I feel much the same thing. Now, please. Give me an indication where the mining is taking place. What I do with that information is my business. I take full responsibility for the dangers."

Koznyshov thought: It would be a stroke of genius to set up the phony operation near the spot where Obruchev had felled the climbers! More subtle minds in the West would race to conclude that the climbers had been shot off the cliff by Germans. They would assume that the glaciological expedition had wandered too close to the clandestine uranium mining operations and had therefore been driven away. The one remaining flaw in the Soviet story—the bullet hole the Norwegians had discovered in one of the climbers' ribs—would thereby be removed!

Laying his delicate hands, palms down, on the desk, he leaned toward her. "On the east side of the Newtontoppen," he whispered.

She sat up straight in her chair, flooded with horror. *The entire area around the Newtontoppen was the one Klaus at the Polar Institute had told her she could forget about!* Bjørn had been right all along! She was being programmed, lied to, manipulated!

The danger of the situation instantly blocked out her hot, sickening guilt. Her instinct for survival told her that this man, whoever he was, must *not* find out she had seen through him. If he did, she and the rest of the *Utsira*'s crew would never leave Barentsburg alive.

She took both his hands and poured her terror into a desperate show of false gratitude. "God bless you," she stammered. "God bless you, Mr. Velovsky. You've done more than you'll ever realize to . . . help us . . . vanquish a common enemy."

Two hours after the *Utsira*'s departure from Barentsburg, Obruchev burst into Koznyshov's office without knocking. The General stood at the window staring into the storm. He spun around as if assaulted. His eyes flashed with anger.

"Sir!"

"Obruchev, what's gotten into you? Forgotten how to knock?"

"Sir, Dimitrov reports that one of the soldiers from Regiment

Thirty-Six is missing. A Comrade said he thinks he saw him crawl aboard that Western ship."

"A defector?"

"Dimitrov thinks so."

"Who was it?"

"Tushkevich, the electronics man. A member of the team that searched the ship."

Koznyshov stood and began to pace rapidly. Ever since the ship had left, he had had the haunting feeling that something was wrong. He had gone over every detail of the odd visit—his meeting with von Menck, Dimitrov's report on his time with the Americans, the lists compiled by the search party. But he had been unable to find anything, any reason for his uneasiness. Now he had one.

"Comrade Obruchev, you are to find Karnoi, Nikovski, and Lydov at once. You will meet me at the helicopter pad in fifteen minutes for your briefing. That ship must be sunk, Comrade. It must be sunk during the storm. The job must be done with precision and speed. There can be no time for them to get off a message. All on board must be eliminated. Eliminated, Consul. Is that clear?"

"Yes, sir. But, sir, it's not possible to fly a helicopter in this weather."

"Not possible, Consul? Not possible? You'll fly the goddamned helicopter. You'll find the trawler and you'll put a five-hundred-pound bomb right through the deck. You will, Consul. I should think that a man in your position would be a fool not to try. Well, do you fly or don't you?"

"The ship will be sunk, sir."

"Good. Meet me at the helicopter pad in ten minutes."

"Yes, sir."

Lydov maneuvered the heavily laden craft up into the battering winds of the worst northwester to hit Barentsburg in half a century. The Consul breathed easier as they entered the low swirling clouds and headed out over the Ice Fjord. This was his world. He was boss. Wind, snow, sea—these things were frightening. But at least they behaved in ways he understood. He could pit himself against them with a prowess few could equal; he could feel his strength as a *man*. Gone were the uncertainties and humiliations of dealing with Koznyshov. Gone was the iron hand that had turned his beloved town into a prison. If only for a short time, he was free, and all the danger in the world could not kill his joy.

20

HEAVY SEAS battered the *Utsira* until her old bones began to creak. Again and again, her prow emerged from the giant swells—shuddering, dripping, straining upward toward the heavens. For an agonizing split second, the old ship would hold that position, as though she feared the imminent plunge into the trough between the waves. Then she would crash forward so steeply that her screw would surface and set her vibrating furiously.

Clinging to whatever they could, they huddled around Turk on the enclosed bridge.

"What do you think?" shouted Johnson over the roar.

Wheeler clapped a hand over his mouth and stumbled toward the metal staircase.

"You, Duncan! Impressions!"

"Didn't like it. Can't say why. Just didn't like it."

"Got the same feeling," yelled Johnson.

Ulrike grabbed Martin's arm for support and moved closer to the CIA man. "There's no mining. I've been duped."

"Well, Jesus Christ, about time you—"

"Let's not forget who got you into the town," shouted Martin.

"All right, she helped get us in. Granted. But we still don't know a goddamned thing about what's going on. Let's have *your* impression, Dodds."

Martin wanted to smash him in the face. He knew Ulrike was suffering, knew how much courage it took to admit she was wrong. She didn't even attempt to make excuses. God, how he admired her!

"Why don't you listen to how Ulrike discovered the setup? You'll find out more than the CIA could find out in a month."

"Drop the insults, buddy. I'll listen to anyone who's got anything to say."

Ulrike spoke in a rasping voice. She coughed; it racked her body. But her hoarse, frenzied words rose above the crescendo of the storm.

When she told them what had happened, Johnson stared at her in disbelief. Duncan moved closer to her, and Turk, fighting the stubborn wheel with his powerful hands and arms, craned his neck to listen.

When she had finished she began to cough in spasms and held a hand to her throat. Martin pulled her close to him.

"You okay?"

"I hope so."

"Fuck," bellowed Johnson. "They're doing just what Holt said. But we need evidence. We can't put Washington on alert because some German woman—"

"I've got your evidence," interrupted Turk.

"What?"

The old captain scanned the close horizon while he battled the lurching wheel. "Better send someone to check on Wheeler," he said.

Martin nodded silently and disappeared down the heaving stairs.

"Well?" urged Johnson.

At last Turk spoke. "I had me a good friend once, a fellow who used to work up in Longyearbyen. Made himself quite a fortune up here, he did. Now how d'you suppose a man makes a fortune in a place like this?"

"Crime?" rasped Ulrike.

"You guessed it, sweetheart. Smuggling with the Russkis. And he was good enough to want to cut me in."

Johnson tried not to show his irritation.

"What did you do, Turk?" asked Ulrike.

"Well, I made myself a pretty nice fortune, too. By an old

sailor's standards, anyway. Wouldn't want to give you the wrong impression, young lady. I never looked at the stuff myself. Always said a man can't do nothing with a picture. But the Russkis seem to be of a different mind. So every couple of months, my friend and I'd make a run down to Copenhagen. We had a third partner down there, a big old friendly Dane, who'd load us up with bales of them dirty magazines. All the newest stuff, mind you. Never any repeats, and always guaranteed to please the Russkis."

Jim Duncan looked at the captain, disappointed. "Turk, you never struck me as the common-criminal type. I thought you had more class than that. Were you really a porn dealer?"

"Son, you got lots to learn. If I was to tell you all I done, you'd jump right overboard. What I was trying to tell all of you is this. Ever since I can remember—and that's been since back before the war—them Russians in Barentsburg been crazy for Western pornography. Hell, I was just up there last April and they was swarming around me like flies asking for pictures. Now tell me, fellas, how many men asked you for pictures today? None, you say? None? Now why d'you suppose that is, fellas? Well, there's only one answer. Cause them men ain't the usual miners. Nope, what you were seeing up there today were soldiers. Now I got to give it to them. They put on a hell of a show. But not good enough to fool this here old man."

"Shit," bellowed Johnson. "Is that all?"

"Those are soldiers, boy. What more d'you want, their mothers' names?"

"Goddamnit, Turk, don't you see that won't do? We already *know* they're soldiers. Otherwise that Velovsky character wouldn't be up there. Wouldn't surprise me from the description if that wasn't KGB chief Koznyshov himself. But I can't put D.C. on full alert because the Russians in Barentsburg have stopped buying dirty magazines. I need evidence, concrete evidence. Otherwise, all I can do is go back to Stavanger and try to get Wilson to look into this whole situation further. And by then it will probably be too late."

When Martin opened the door to the small cabin, he saw a figure move in the shadows behind the sonar equipment. He

255

made his way across a stretch of open floor, fighting to stay on his feet. Wheeler, he thought, must be very sick indeed to have come in here.

He rounded the corner, peered into the musty darkness behind the useless device, and froze in terror. A man in a Russian greatcoat was on his knees in the passage between the tracker and the wall; he seemed to be scratching at the floor like a demented rat. He twisted his neck at Martin, staring at him with huge glazed eyes. He began to crawl backwards, choking and trembling.

Too frightened to think clearly, Martin leaped on the man before he could rise and smashed his head against the metal floor. When he offered no resistance, Martin dragged him to his feet. He whimpered, trying to embrace his assailant while he muttered pleading, incoherent words in Russian, then collapsed. Martin hoisted him to his feet once more and pushed him out of the cabin and down the corridor. At the stairway, the ship bucked, sending the wobbly man to his knees. Martin kicked him weakly. "Climb!" he ordered. The man inched up the stairs on all fours.

Ulrike saw him first and gasped. Wheeler, who had made his way back to the bridge, grabbed Duncan, and the two headed for him. Johnson opened a small compartment under his seat and pulled out an old pistol and a rusty hunting knife. The three agents surrounded the Russian, who lay blubbering on the floor.

Martin appeared at the top of the stairs. "Found him in the sonar room. I don't think he's dangerous, but he scared the hell out of me. Roughed him up a little before I knew what I was doing."

"Bravo, Professor," mocked Johnson. "Glad to see you recognize the limits of pacificism."

"Fuck off. I shouldn't have hit him. Who the hell is he?"

"A Soviet agent. Who the hell do you think he is?"

"A defector," said Martin.

"Likely chance. Duncan! Wheeler! Get the Professor an answer to his question." He handed the hunting knife to Duncan.

The man went limp. Wheeler searched him as if searching a corpse for loot, then rolled him onto his back. Duncan sat down on his chest and held the knife to his throat. The blade was chipped near the end, and the rust made it look more like a trowel than a weapon.

"Well, boy," he growled in English, "let's hear your story. Fast and accurate." Duncan slid the dull blade along the man's throat, then moved it back and forth in front of his eyes. The man responded with a gagging sound as he choked out a few words in Russian.

Ulrike lost her temper and lunged at Duncan, shrieking hoarsely at the top of her lungs. She planted her fingernails in his forehead and ripped into his skin. He tossed her from his back without taking his eyes off the Russian.

"Arschloch," she screamed. "Ihr seid alle Arschlöcher. Nazis seid ihr. Lasst den armen Kerl in Ruhe!"

"Deutsch?" stammered the Russian. "Sie deutsch?"

Ulrike bent over him and took his hand. "It's all right," she said in German. "They won't hurt you. They just want to know who you are."

"What are you saying?" demanded Johnson.

"I'm telling him we won't do him any harm. Don't you see how you've frightened him? God, why? I was just beginning to believe you might have a little humanity in you in spite of your fascist work."

"Shut up. You'll interrogate him as I say. Word for word. Got it?"

Martin knew from the way she looked that he needn't interfere. She put her arm around the terrified Russian.

He was just a boy, twenty years old or so, slightly built, with dark, sensitive features. For a moment she had a vision of his mother and father as children, suffering under the Nazi occupation of Russia. Must he meet the same fate at the hands of these men, different only in appearance from Hitler's puppets? This boy wouldn't hurt a fly. Why were they torturing him?

Johnson seized her arm and jerked her up. Without the slightest warning she slapped him in the face so hard the clap reverberated through the cabin. Turk spun around at the wheel, his expression one of rare anger.

"Let go of me this minute," she hissed. He did.

Johnson either returned to his senses or realized he had better

257

take another tack with Ulrike if he wanted to get a word out of the Russian.

"Sorry," he said. "It's a tense situation. We might be dealing with a spy."

"William, it's a tense situation for everyone. He's no spy, I assure you. Now quit acting like a Nazi and I'll interrogate him."

Martin looked at Johnson's puffy, crimson cheek and felt a surge of pride. Ulrike coaxed the Russian to sit up. She made Duncan put away the knife and fetch the man a Coke. She sent Wheeler below for the Russian–German dictionary from her duffle bag.

For the next half hour, the Russian stuttered on in broken German with the help of the dictionary. He explained how his unit had been sent up to Barentsburg from the Caucasus, its soldiers disguised as miners or, like himself, as petty officials of the mining community. He was an electronics specialist who had been sent aboard the *Utsira* with a search party and had sneaked back onto the ship later.

Had he been seen? He didn't think so. The storm had been so intense, the visibility so poor. How many soldiers were in Barentsburg? He didn't know, but almost everyone there was with the military. What about the real miners? A few had been kept on, but most had been sent away. What types of military equipment had been brought in? Just about everything: amphibious craft, hidden inside fake coal barges; heavy artillery to protect against attacks from the sea; light tanks and all-terrain personnel carriers; and huge missiles which had arrived with special teams of technicians and had been sunk in the mine shafts.

The CIA men gawked at each other. The interrogation continued. How could he prove he was with the military? He showed them his dog tag, which Johnson said was authentic. Did the search crew suspect the *Utsira* of spying? No, he didn't think so. Largely because the radio was so old and weak and not outfitted with coding equipment. Would he be missed? Yes—but when, he couldn't say. And finally, why had he defected? Because he hated military life, hated war—which he was convinced was coming in a matter of days—hated the cold and the sea, missed his family. . . .

The pitching of the ship became worse as they approached

the mouth of the Ice Fjord. "Enough," yelled Johnson. "Duncan, get down to that radio." He scrawled a message and handed it to his subordinate:

Soviet invasion of Svalbard imminent. Data indisputable. Attack possible any day. Troops and equipment in position inside Barentsburg. SS-20's with possible third stages in mine shafts. Relay to highest level at Langley at once.

"Keep trying. Do your best. I know there's not much chance we can reach Jan Mayen in this weather. But we've got to try. With that defector on board, we can be damned sure it won't be long until our friends from Barentsburg are after us."

"But, William, our transmissions will make it easier for the Russians to find us. Don't you think we should ride out the storm in silence?"

"No. They'll find us anyway with that new radar of theirs. Go on, start beaming. In good, clear, midwestern English."

"I wish we had the coding equipment and the good transmitter with us."

"Duncan, with that stuff, we'd never have gotten out of Barentsburg. Now go down and start transmitting. Don't come out until you've got something to report. Something positive."

"I gotta seal up ship and sail north," yelled Turk. "Never seen nothing like it. Not even in '42. She'll break up if we don't take her direct into the storm."

He pointed to the map. "This here stretch of water between Spitsbergen and the Prins Karls Forland is what we gotta cover. It's called the Forland Sound. Unclean water. A graveyard, my boy, without no gravestones. Gonna be hell to navigate, but we can't take her onto open seas. She'd come apart at the seams."

He ran the stem of his pipe across the map, tracing the projected route through the Sound and into the Kongsfjord. "If we make the mouth of the Kong, we'll make Ny-Ålesund. Nothing else within hundreds of miles unless we head back toward Longyearbyen."

"What are our chances of making Ny-Ålesund?" shouted Martin.

"Son, if we don't hit a rock, they ain't too bad. Unless the temperature drops a few more degrees. With this wind, the wind chill factor goes way down. When it drops too low, that ice you see out there on the deck'll start to thicken up real fast. If that happens, you lay the ship on the weather and get out there and chop. If you don't get some of it off you'll sure as hell get swamped. That's how most of them've joined the graveyard up here."

"And if we turn around and head back up the Ice Fjord for Longyearbyen?"

"Nope. We're better off taking our chances with the weather than with the Russkis. You heard Johnson. They're gonna be after us. If we sail right back under their noses, we're done for. Now listen here, Mr. Martin, if the icing starts, we got a pretty good crew. The ice stays nice and soft for a while. Salt water don't freeze the same as fresh water. Gets hard as a rock, but not right off. You get out there with your picks and axes and it comes off in chunks the size of mattresses. We got all the stuff on board to tie us to the rails. Ain't the first time it's been done."

Martin watched the mighty gray waves crash across the deck. "You're the boss, Turk. Let's hope the temperature doesn't drop. I'm going down to the cabin to check on Ulrike."

"Go right ahead, sonny. And get some rest, too. You might need all your strength later on."

Ulrike lay sleeping on the narrow bunk. Martin peered out the porthole. The furious sea pitched the ship around like a balsa wood toy, plunging it into a valley one moment, lifting it onto a great mountain of water the next. From the top of one of the water mountains, he stared down sixty feet into a frothing trough and glimpsed the jagged teeth of a rock.

A rift appeared in the clouds. He watched it rush toward the southeast where it briefly exposed the vertical granite cliffs of Spitsbergen. The sea was venting its force against the rock walls with such savagery he imagined the walls themselves disintegrating. It seemed incredible the old trawler could withstand the beating much longer.

An alarm sounded. There was pounding in the passageway. Martin floundered out of his bunk and unlocked the door. The ship jolted; he and Johnson careened across the cabin and landed on the floor. They braced their backs against a corner wall. Ulrike woke with a start.

"We're going down!" Johnson shouted.

"A rock?"

"No. We're icing!"

"Icing?"

"Bad. Temp must have dropped ten or twelve degrees. Come on! We're going on deck to chop. All of us."

Ulrike looked questioningly at Martin but there was no time to explain. Johnson helped them both out of the cabin as if they were all best of friends. In the face of possible death he suddenly seemed relaxed, almost gentle. Strange man, thought Martin. Unpredictable, the kind you'd better keep at a distance.

They bounced against the corridor walls. "Cheer up, Dodds," shouted Johnson.

"What?"

"The message. We think the boys in Jan Mayen have gotten it. Washington will know soon."

"Good," said Martin, "damned good." He was too numb to feel anything.

Ulrike pulled at his arm. "I dragged you into this, Martin. If anything happens, I'm—"

"Shhh. You didn't drag me anywhere. Don't start sounding like we're done for."

"Right, Dodds," Johnson interrupted. "The Russians picked up our message, too. They're after us. They might not understand English, but they know that goddamned defector's aboard. They know he might spill the beans. That squirrely coward's put us all in danger. I'd like to get rid of that goddamn Slavic whimp. I'd—"

"Johnson, without him, we'd have had no message to send."

The Russian sat, ghostly pale and seasick, in a corner of the galley among broken dishes and stray kitchen utensils. Duncan and Wheeler were preparing the ropes as Turk had instructed. The storeroom door banged back and forth with the motions of the ship. Inside the cubicle, rusty picks and axes clanged against tools and cans. A pile of raingear lay on the floor. The agents were untangling odd-looking masses of rope.

"Quick," yelled Johnson. "Everyone put some rain stuff on. Won't do much good, but it's better than nothing. First the rain-gear, then the harnesses." He kicked a rope harness from the pile, then seized the end of a long anchor rope. He sorted out several short ropes with his free hand—each rope had a carabiner-like clip at both ends—and pushed them aside. "Hurry up and get the raingear on. Then I'll explain."

Du musst das Ding anziehen," explained Ulrike to the Russian, who did not seem to understand what was going on. "You have to put this thing on."

"Okay, now the harnesses. Like this." He picked one up and slipped it over his head, tying the cords tightly round his waist and chest. The others did the same. Ulrike helped the bewildered Russian.

"Now, see these clips on your harnesses? Grab one of those short ropes and hook it to you . . . no, Wheeler, the other end. The big clip's for the deck rail and nothing else." He held up the fat anchor rope which was already secured to a steel beam in the galley and shook it.

"Okay, good. Now listen. Duncan ties himself onto the anchor rope, goes out on deck and fastens it to the rail up front on the prow. That way we've got a safety line to move back and forth on. Then he hooks himself onto whatever point of the deck rail he can get to, using that small rope hanging from his harness. Then the rest of you go out one at a time, sliding along the anchor rope with that big loop on your harness clipped around it. When you get to a good spot on the rail, unhook from the anchor rope. But first make sure you've clipped the small rope onto the rail. Otherwise, goodbye.

"You'll be under water half the time. Hold your breath, and when you come up, come up swinging that goddamned ax. We've got to get some ice off the deck. Turk says he can run us aground in a mile or so, says there's a gravel beach. But at this rate, we'll go down before we get there. All right, *move!* Grab a pick or ax from that storeroom, clip onto the big rope Duncan's hauling out there, and MOVE!"

Ulrike was still helping the Russian.

"MOVE!" bellowed Johnson again. "Get that fucking Russian out right behind Duncan."

Duncan threw open the door two steps up from the galley and hauled out the anchor rope. A frigid wind sliced through the opening, followed by a cascade of water and a swirl of snow. The deck broke out of a swell and shot upward like the glistening peak of an iceberg. The Russian took a step forward, stopped, buried his head in his arms. The torrent of water rushing through the door swept his feet out from under him. He slid back into the galley like a quivering fish washed ashore by the tide.

Johnson drew the dull hunting knife and glowered. Ulrike came at him. "No," she screamed, "leave him here."

He pushed her back with his free hand. "You crazy, woman? Alone with Turk? The man's a basket case. For all we know, we'll come back and find ourselves without a captain."

Martin wrapped both arms around Ulrike and yanked her back. He was beginning to see the killer in Johnson and feared he might turn on her. She struggled for a brief moment, crying out in German, then looked on in silent horror.

Johnson kicked the Russian in the side of the head and pointed with the knife toward the door. Duncan had already secured the anchor rope to the prow and clipped himself onto the rail. As soon as he lifted his head, the Russian saw the waves crash over the man on deck. At the sight he collapsed into an inert, whimpering mass.

Insane rage disfigured Johnson's handsome face. Slowly, he circled the prostrate boy, his eyes gleaming. He kicked him again, harder this time. The Russian extended his arms full length and spread his quaking fingers. His gestures seemed to madden Johnson still more. "Coward," he growled, "filthy motherfucking coward." The Russian sloshed around on the floor, already several inches deep in water, and staggered to his knees.

Johnson smiled and lowered the knife as if it had all been a joke. Then, with horrible suddenness, he hurled himself at his victim, knocked him flat on his back, and plunged the twelve-inch blade into his throat. The Russian thrashed and choked, his blood spurting in all directions. Johnson sat astride him, working the

263

knife down through the spinal column until the shorn tip of the blade grated against the metal of the floor. When the man began to go limp, he unclipped him from the anchor rope and shoved him away like a hockey puck. Rocked by spasms, the body came to a stop at Ulrike's feet.

"Okay, move it!" ordered Johnson, straightening and pulling the straps of his harness tighter. Without a word, Wheeler clipped into the anchor rope and went out. Ulrike and Martin followed; Johnson was close behind.

They were on deck less than two minutes, but all the horror of a lifetime seemed packed into those brief moments. The roar of the sea was deafening. The heaving deck was too slippery for a foothold. The force of the giant waves washing over the ship knocked them breathless, and the icy water numbed their bruised, prostrate bodies. But the ice on deck was not yet hard. A few solid jabs with a pick or ax, and the next wave carried off the ice in great, greenish-white chunks.

Again and again, they found the strength to struggle back to their feet. Choking and coughing after each onslaught of the water, they managed to get their picks up for one, two, three more blows before the next dam burst.

A wave crashed into Martin while his pick was still in the air. He landed on his side; his head smashed onto an area of deck he had cleared; another wave hurled him across the ice to the end of his safety rope. He felt he was losing consciousness. The snow had let up. The clouds swirled in from the northwest at a dizzying speed. Shaggy fingers of black hung down onto the waves. He saw the snouts of rabid wolves . . . tattered ears, sharp vicious teeth, matted fur, great lapping tongues. . . .

Duncan had been on deck the longest. He decided on one last feeble jab with his ax before inching his way back inside. To his surprise, a sheet of ice several feet square broke loose and slipped into the torrent. One more good blow, he thought, letting his ax sink in just behind Andy Wheeler.

It all happened before Duncan realized what he had done. The ax severed Wheeler's safety rope, the next wave charged like a bull, another huge sheet of ice—the one Wheeler was standing on—broke loose, and both the ice and Wheeler disappeared into the raging sea.

Johnson managed to get Martin and the others attached to the main rope. They hauled themselves back into the galley and bolted the hatch. Martin and Ulrike fell in the bloody water near the Russian's body, then gathered their last strength and made their way back to their cabin. Too numb to speak, they collapsed in their bunks.

When they awoke, the ship was no longer tossing. They struggled into dry clothes. Martin rolled closer to the porthole and looked out. His right knee and shoulder ached and a sharp pain shot through his rib cage, but he felt surprisingly strong. Fifty feet away, he saw a mammoth granite spire rising vertically from the the frothing water. In the distance he could make out a smooth meadow of gravel, swept clear of snow by the tide. The gravel beach faded into the fog about two hundred feet away. Two hundred feet of water, he thought, is all that separates us from safety. Two hundred feet! Perhaps they would be able to reach shore when the tide went out.

The sea around the grounded ship was rough but not nearly as rough as it had been. From the patterns of the falling snow, he knew the gale had weakened. There were still angry gusts which sent the snowflakes charging frantically this way and that, but the storm seemed momentarily to have abated. He turned to awaken Ulrike. She was already up on an elbow looking at him.

Johnson entered without knocking. "We lost Wheeler," he said. "I guess you saw that."

"Yes," said Ulrike, coldly. "Wheeler and another boy whose name we don't even know. Where are we?"

"Turk managed to run us aground here. He says there's nothing but cliffs ten miles in either direction. Just in time, too. The ship looks like an iceblock. We should be able to walk ashore in about two hours."

"What then?"

"We've got to get over a pass to reach Ny-Ålesund. Our people will take care of the rest. I can't radio from here. We've gotten our message through, and we don't want to give the Russians any more help than necessary locating us."

"Please go and leave us alone," said Ulrike.

265

Johnson again seemed relaxed, almost gentle. "Of course. I'm sorry you had to see all of that. I know it's difficult. But this isn't civilian life. There are situations where you just don't take chances. We couldn't be *absolutely* sure he wasn't a spy. We've seen stranger disguises than that." He turned and went out.

A few moments later, Turk entered, smoking his pipe. He moved no faster—or slower—than usual. "You all right, sweetheart?" He sat on the bunk beside Ulrike and took her hand.

"I'm all right, Turk. Thanks."

"She's not, really," said Martin.

"That cough?"

"Yes. And I believe she's coming down with a fever."

"Nonsense," she said.

Turk put his hand to her forehead. "Whew. You've got a fever, all right. A good one, too. Well, don't you worry, neither of you. We've got a sled on board somewhere. We'll tuck you in and give you a first-class ride."

"Lock the door," she whispered, as soon as Turk had left. "I want you."

"Now?"

"This second . . . Martin?"

"Yes?"

"It may be the last time."

She was right and he knew it. He didn't contradict her or try to comfort her. After the utter horror of the last hours, that would have been false and trivial—an insult to the passion he felt for her, a passion now stripped of all pretense. He loved her more than he had thought it possible to love; he desired her more than he had imagined it possible to desire. He locked the door and went to her.

She moaned quietly. The waves lapped rhythmically against the hull of the ship. He talked to her. She smiled.

Anguish suffused their lovemaking, for its very intensity seemed to presage a kind of farewell. They felt the knife that had ripped into the Russian's throat, they felt Wheeler's lungs filling with icy water, they felt all the agony of their pasts—and felt all of these things in one great tidal wave of compressed experience. The world in all its anger and tempestuousness, in all its heart-rending sadness, in all its warmth and beauty, simply swallowed them up.

21

"TAKE a look at this, kid. A blip on the periphery."

Lydov examined the radar screen while the helicopter bucked around in the squalls.

"That's nothing, boss. What you're seeing is right about at shoreline."

"Go on in. Let's have a look."

"Love to, boss, but it's no use. We're picking up some kind of debris the storm's blown ashore, an oil drum or something."

"What's wrong, Lydov? Scared?"

"Of flying? Shit!"

"Then get down there. But real easy. In this overcast, we could hit one of the granite spires before we saw it."

"How high are they?"

"Along this part of the coast, I'd say around two hundred feet."

"Whew! Let's play it safe, boss. I'll stay up around five hundred till we're over your oil drum and then let her down straight and slo-o-ow. Sound good?"

Obruchev nodded. His eyes were bloodshot, but this time it was fatigue instead of vodka. The crew had been in the air for hours under impossible conditions. And even worse than the weather was the frustration. Repeatedly, they had picked up a faint and garbled English-language transmission. Obruchev was convinced it was from the *Utsira*, but hadn't been able to locate the vessel on radar.

Had he made a fool of himself again? How had that old tub eluded him and managed to slip away? He doubted that they had yet gotten through to anyone with that ancient radio of theirs, but now the storm was subsiding. It wouldn't be long until someone tuned in on one of their transmissions. He glanced again at the radar screen. That solitary blip was his only remaining hope. It *had* to be the *Utsira;* it was as simple as that.

Karnoi leaned forward from his seat behind Obruchev. His strident, jangling voice slashed through the clatter of the engines. "Comrade, the blip is too close to the shore to be a ship. You heard our pilot. Why are you wasting fuel by going in?"

"Comrade Karnoi is correct," yelled Nikovski. "Look at the gauge. We've emptied both auxiliary tanks. We'll be lucky to stay up another hour."

"The conclusion is obvious," resumed Karnoi, emboldened by Obruchev's recent fall from grace. "We can make it to Ny-Ålesund. They will have fuel there. We will either buy it or acquire it by other means. That way we can complete our mission and return safely to Barentsburg. It's either that, Comrade Obruchev, or crashing out here with our mission still not completed. That would be worse than your blunder of last month. It would be unnecessary and quite stupid."

Lydov was closing in on the blip. He thumbed at the Consul. "Well, the boss here's pretty stupid, so I guess we'll be going in."

"Goddamnit, Lydov, shut up and fly."

"Easy, boss, easy. Just kidding."

Obruchev twisted in his seat and faced the two agents. "What you see on radar is the ship we're after. She's run aground. We've got to get to her before another message goes out. Jettison the bomb, Lydov. We won't be needing it anymore."

"*No!*" howled Karnoi. "If it's not the ship, we've disarmed ourselves. The KGB does not operate like that. You'll be court-martialed, you'll be—"

"Lydov, jettison the bomb."

"Love to, boss. Never did much like flying with them hot potatoes."

While Karnoi smoldered, Lydov let out a joyful cry and pushed the red button. The craft jumped upward, suddenly

269

lighter by five hundred pounds. "Too bad we ain't down there with nets to pick up the fish," he exalted.

Karnoi jolted forward as if he wanted to strangle the youngster, but a threatening stare from the Consul stopped him cold.

At eighty feet they broke through the overcast. They all saw it simultaneously. "Damned good guess, boss," said Lydov.

The *Utsira* rose from the beach like a bizarre ice castle. It was just beyond the churning surf. Its passengers could have escaped without taking to the water, but blowing and drifting snow made it impossible to tell if there had been footprints. The wind, not as strong as earlier, gusted erratically. The chopper heaved and quivered.

"They're on board," yelled Karnoi, "and you were foolish enough to waste the bomb."

"Look, I'm beginning to think you're stupid. If they're CIA people, they know damned well someone's hot after them." Obruchev tapped his window. "They're up there somewhere, trying to hide from us."

"And if they're not intelligence officers?" ventured Nikovski.

"That's why we're going aboard," answered the Consul. "If they're not agents, we've got nothing to fear. And it will save us a miserable search."

"But *they've* got something to fear, agents or not," snarled Karnoi. "You know what our orders are, Consul. I assume you don't intend to try to second-guess General Koznyshov?"

Obruchev did not answer. "Get dressed. Lydov, can you land on the beach?"

"Rather not, boss. Those gusts can tip us too easy. We'd better hover at fifty feet and use the rope ladder."

"Right. That way you can let us down on deck and we won't have to worry about climbing the hull. You two ready?" He glowered at the agents, who were struggling into their parkas. "I'll go first. Come down behind me."

Lydov pointed the helicopter into the wind and brought it to a jerky hover above the ship's aft deck. Unarmed except for the pistol in his breast pocket, Obruchev started down the rope. As he approached the deck, a gust hit him and started him swinging like a pendulum. He cursed into the wind and roaring sea; then, controlling his temper, he surveyed the deck for a drift into which he could jump.

Lydov saw the problem and inched lower. Another gust struck. The helicopter lurched fifteen feet to the right and Obruchev careened like a wrecking ball into the side of the bridge. The ice which had formed on the metal wall shattered from the impact and dropped in fragments. Stunned but uninjured, the Consul clutched the rope a split second longer, then lost his grip and plunged into the deep snow on deck. Growling and blaspheming, he floundered to his feet, brushed off the seat of his pants, and signaled Lydov to come down a bit more.

Soon the rope ladder was flapping off starboard just beyond Obruchev's reach. Skillfully, Lydov maneuvered the helicopter ahead. When the rope was close, Obruchev grabbed it with a cat-like swipe and fastened it to a rail. He looked up, grinning. The ladder formed a graceful bow between the helicopter and the ship, held taut by a wind which, for the moment, had become steady. In seconds, it was coated with ice. He laughed aloud: what fun to watch those two shitheads trying to climb down.

But suddenly the wind died, the rope ladder straightened, and the ice which had formed all along it fell around him like pieces of a broken chandelier. Lydov took on a little altitude so the next gust would create less of a bow in the ladder; he left just enough slack so an unexpected movement of the helicopter would not tear the rope from its mooring on deck. Disappointed, the Consul looked on while Karnoi and Nikovski scampered down unharmed.

Nikovski was the first to stumble upon the dreadful sight in the galley. He could not suppress a gasp of horror, in spite of all the death he had seen. The Russian defector, whom he recognized but did not know by name, lay on his back, frozen in a deep slab of ice on the floor. The ice around him was pink from his blood, and the jagged wound in his throat gaped up like a second terror-filled mouth.

Nauseated, the agent turned away just in time to witness the Consul's cheerful arrival. "No high-powered transmitting equipment on board," sang out Obruchev, "and no coding devices. Just like the search party in Barentsburg reported. Nothing but that sick old radio we've been picking up. Good news, Nikovski! I doubt if they're even agents, and even if they—"

In that instant, he saw the young Russian encased in the roseate ice. His reaction was different from Nikovski's: he unleashed a stream of profanity which neither wind nor sea could drown. Now there could be no doubt he was dealing with CIA men! His foolish hopes that Koznyshov had been wrong, that the Westerners were not spies, were shattered. They would try to make their way to some settlement or other. From there, they would get the message off. *He had to find them fast and get rid of them!*

Suddenly it occurred to him. Ny-Ålesund! Of course. There was nowhere else they could go. They would be heading for Ny-Ålesund over the pass. He would cut them off with the helicopter, storm or no storm. There was no way in hell they were going to get out of this one, especially that two-faced little Kraut whore. He grabbed Nikovski by the elbow and pushed him toward the door.

On deck, another shock awaited the Consul. The gusts had become more violent; the lull in the northwester was over. Lydov made a slight mistake trying to straighten the rope ladder, the helicopter jumped up a trifle too high, and the rope pulled loose —not from the ship's railing but from its mooring inside the chopper.

"Land, you fucking idiot!" shouted Obruchev. "Come on, Karnoi. Right here. Jump. Jump! I said. Over the edge. Onto the beach. You too, Nikovski. We've got to get somewhere the kid can land."

They sprang from the deck into the massive drifts and hauled themselves away from the trawler. Huddled together, they waited for Lydov to land. But the chopper rose into the clouds. Beside himself, Obruchev leaped up and down, shrieking obscenities until his voice gave out. Karnoi and Nikovski watched his outburst for a second, then looked away in disgust.

In the meantime, Lydov was holding the controls with a knee, a foot, an elbow while he spliced together a makeshift ladder of straps, ropes, cables, and clothing. Soon he was finished. He dropped through the overcast, just missing a granite spire which jutted up behind him. Fastening his contraption securely to a seat bracket, he tossed it out the door.

The Consul watched in amazement as the odd, fluttering macramé unfolded in the wind. So that was it, he thought, the kid was using his head, putting together a ladder so he wouldn't have to risk setting down. Jesus, he was a good kid, that boy, a damned good kid. There weren't many like him around anymore.

Tilted slightly forward, the helicopter poised ten feet off the ground and some hundred feet ahead of them. "Go!" shouted Obruchev. He watched the agents trudge across the drifts, glanced at the angry, rising tide, and hurried after them.

He had almost overtaken Karnoi and Nikovski when a vicious gust blew in from the sea and knocked him over. He brushed the snow from his eyes just in time to see it happen.

The helicopter lurched to the side and tilted, causing a blade to strike the beach. The craft righted itself momentarily, as if the blade had slashed through a snowdrift and emerged without damage. But it began to vibrate violently. In the next second, it careered out of control in great bounding leaps. Still lying in the snow, the Consul screamed at the agents at the top of his lungs. "Get down! Get down!"

His senses went numb. The ghastly scenario unfolding before him seemed to slow down, forcing him to watch each minute detail. The two agents stood as if frozen in place, gaping at the errant chopper. It headed away from them and out toward the sea, staggered, abruptly changed course, hesitated like a snake coiling to strike, and lunged directly at them in a savage pirouette. Slowly, ever so slowly—or so it seemed to the Consul—Karnoi and Nikovski began to dive toward the ground. But it was as if gravity refused to pull them earthward rapidly enough. Before they had landed on the beach, the only remaining blade of the giant propeller reached them. It sliced through them just below the shoulders, sending their heads—with necks, chests, and truncated arms still attached—in a steaming arch across the frigid sky.

Obruchev watched the snow labor to bury the bright-red blotches which spread from the lower halves of their bodies. The heat of the corpses was melting the snow, the red would not go away. . . . Why, in God's name, was it taking so long? Why was he being forced, on top of everything else, to witness *this?*

The helicopter came to a stop nearby. A geyser of flame from the cockpit area shocked Obruchev into action. He raced toward Lydov, who was struggling to open a jammed door. Yanking a twisted length of propeller from the snow, Obruchev pried at the door, oblivious to the flames lapping at his arms. The aluminum around the doorframe bent until the latch sprung. Lydov slumped forward, muttering and gasping. With all the strength he could muster, the Consul dragged him away from the wreckage, counting as he ran. Halfway to the trawler, he slammed his friend to the ground and buried his own face in the snow.

He waited, unsure of his ability to judge time, for the five-hundred-pound bomb to go off. Five minutes must have passed before he remembered they had jettisoned the thing before approaching the ship. He felt no relief. There was no time to squander on feelings of any kind. He needed the supplies in the burning chopper. He was going to have to overtake his prey on foot . . . snowshoes, his rifle, a tent . . . and Lydov. What the hell was he going to do with Lydov? He tugged at the youngster's arm. "How bad are you hurt?"

"I couldn't help it," screamed the pilot, writhing in the snow. He looked at Obruchev with glazed and empty eyes. "Boss," he choked, "it wasn't my fault. The wind. I couldn't . . . I. . . ."

The tongues of flame which darted and flickered behind them suddenly dimmed and went out. The Consul raised his head. The helicopter was still intact—damaged, twisted, but intact. "Come on, son. We're in luck. The gusts that knocked you over just blew out the fire. Let's get you inside the chopper, get you some coffee and vodka."

Lydov fell back in the snow, wailing like an infant. When the Consul tried to help him up, he jerked his arm away. "Where are we?" he stammered. "What happened?"

"Son, get hold of yourself. We've had an accident. It's all right. It wasn't your fault. Now, come on. I'll help you."

"Don't need no help," said the pilot. He stood and limped to the helicopter. Obruchev gave a mighty sigh of relief. It was premature.

Lydov climbed into the cockpit and patted the seat beside him. He began to giggle. "An accident! What fun! Heh, boss, let's have a party." His eyes glittered.

Obruchev hopped aboard. "Look here, Lydov, we've got to get a move on it. Now put on your parka and gloves. I'll get the snowshoes ready. Hear that roar? Tide's coming in. If the cold doesn't get us, the ocean will."

The pilot stared blankly at Obruchev. "A PARTY," he drooled. "I want my party."

"You'll get your party, pal." He fished under the seat for a bottle of vodka, wondering what he would do if the kid's madness didn't pass. "Here, Lydov, try this. Best party drink in the world."

Lydov examined the bottle, opened it and began to pour out its contents like a naughty child. Obruchev grabbed the bottle and stared angrily at him. He forced himself to slap him in the face. "What the hell's wrong with you? How long you going to keep this up?" Lydov gazed at him without the faintest glint of recognition in his eyes, then snatched the bottle back and resumed his pouring.

The wind whistled through the holes in the damaged fuselage, bringing with it puffs of snow and bursts of spray from the surf. Obruchev climbed back to where the supplies were stored, hoping against all odds that Lydov would recover soon enough for them to leave together. He packed for both of them: a tent, down bags, dried foods, a butane stove, ammunition, rifles, and three bottles of vodka. When he returned to the cockpit dragging his half of the gear, Lydov was still sitting at the controls, pretending to fly.

The Consul decided on a new tack. "Well, kid, coming or not? I've packed your stuff. It's piled right back there if you want it. Want me to get it for you?"

Lydov pulled off his leather flying hat and shook out his flaxen hair. Obruchev thought he was coming to his senses. "Sure, boss," said the kid, "why not?"

In the back of the helicopter, the Consul found a crate of explosives and a radio detonator. He thanked his lucky stars that the stuff hadn't gone off in the crash, and started back to Lydov. Abruptly he reversed his course: the explosives, he realized, might come in handy on the pass. He made three more trips, one for Lydov's gear, one for snowshoes, and one for the explosives and detonator.

When he settled into the seat beside Lydov, the pilot was staring blankly ahead and making an odd hissing noise. He tugged the hat back over his ears and began once more to play with the controls.

Obruchev forced himself to take a long, detached look at his predicament and soon decided he had no choice. He would have to abandon him. At this point, it was either the kid's ass or his. If he wanted to get to the pass in time to intercept the CIA people, he couldn't drag along one hundred fifty pounds of resisting madman, as well as all his gear and the heavy explosives. Just getting there was going to be hard enough.

He smashed open the jammed passenger door and tossed out his pack. "Listen, Lydov," he hollered. The door blew shut with a crash, then swung open again on its own accord. Snow swirled into the cockpit and covered everything with a light dusting which did not melt: the temperature inside the wreck had already dipped below freezing.

"Lydov! I'll be back for you. Now listen. For God's sake, quit playing with that thing and listen! Take a tent and some snowshoes. Snowshoes, got it?" He clapped his own pair together and pitched them out the door. "You've got enough supplies back behind your seat to last you a week. Do you hear me? Make camp up there. Two, three miles inland. Don't go around that ship. There must be no trace of us around here. Got it? The chopper'll wash out with the tide. Look, Lydov, look at the surf. Ten minutes and it'll be on you." He grabbed his shoulders and shook him. "Now, get ready and get out of this thing. I'll be back for you."

The Consul jumped down, strapped the snowshoes onto his feet and, struggling into the heavy frame pack, charged up the beach. If that didn't bring the kid to his senses, he didn't know what would.

When he had gone a little over a hundred feet he stopped and looked back. It was snowing harder again. He could barely make out the silhouette of the helicopter. There was a motion. He thought it was Lydov. But it was only the broken door blowing back and forth in the wind.

22

News of Skogan's death reached Bjørn Tuesday evening while he was dining as the guest of Norwegian Ambassador Knut Halvorsen.

"Thank you," said Halvorsen to the staff assistant who brought the telegram to the table, "leave it right there. And please don't disturb us again during dinner."

It wasn't until after the lobster newburg that the Ambassador tore open the brown envelope. There was a moment of silence during which he filled the wine glasses. Bjørn was sure what the message would be. "Skogan?"

"Yes, correct, Mr. Holt. A pity indeed. I didn't know him very well. I realize how respected he was in diplomatic circles, but he always seemed a little standoffish to me. Good boss, I suppose?"

Bjørn nodded. He forced himself to stay on through dessert and coffee, evading the question of when he planned to leave for Norway. After a listless stroll down Massachusetts Avenue, he called a cab and returned to the Mayflower.

He stood for a long while on the walk in front of the busy hotel, feeling none of the things for which he had prepared himself: no anger, no bitterness, no grief. A limousine pulled up and several distinguished-looking men jumped out. They gave brusque instructions to an elderly bellhop and, engrossed in conversation, cut a cheerful swath across the crowded sidewalk.

Traffic streamed by. Taxis wove their way in and out of the

torrent, honking and braking. The clammy air blossomed with the stench of exhaust; the void inside him yawned out at the night. He went up to his room. Loosening his tie, he drew the curtains on the glittering city.

Minutes later the telephone awoke him.

"Holt! Jesus Christ, where the hell have you been? Are you part of this circus, too?"

"Art? Sorry, I'd just dozed off."

"Dozed off? It's only nine-thirty. Listen, we got problems. Grave problems. The message has come in. All just as you say, invasion imminent and so on. That son of a bitch Holzhauer is trying to block us from getting to the President. I'll be there in fifteen minutes."

"I'll be waiting."

"Good. Get ready for combat. Real combat." There was a click at the other end of the line.

The last forty-eight hours had been hectic. Caskey of the White House staff had insisted on several lengthy meetings with oil company representatives, and Halvorsen had demanded Bjørn's presence at two supremely inane diplomatic luncheons.

There had been little time for devising a plan of action to deal with the new developments in the Svalbard crisis. But he had one. Or so he thought before Millet's visit.

His plan—which Millet and Secretary of State Barker endorsed with a good deal of enthusiasm—called for arranging a visit to Longyearbyen by a group of high NATO officials. This would have a double impact: it would make a Soviet invasion unthinkable for the duration of the team's stay and it would convey to the Soviets the impression that the West might indeed be capable of a united stand. Just to be sure the message was unequivocal, Bjørn also suggested that the U.S. Navy order several Trident subs to sail into the northern Norwegian fjords in a manner clearly detectable to the Soviets.

Barker had personally checked into the matter of arranging the NATO visit. With the greatest care, he had compiled a list of NATO officials he could recruit. Next to each name, he had included a brief career sketch and detailed instructions on how and when each "candidate" could be reached. The plan, he estimated, could be put into effect in less than three days.

Once the CIA message came through, Bjørn, Millet, and Barker were certain they could convince the President that their plan was the cheapest, safest, most promising way to head off a major confrontation. The President had the well-earned reputation of a man who was easy to influence until he had made up his mind, but nearly unmoveable thereafter.

True, he was a conservative, and his views on many things bordered on the medieval. But on foreign-policy issues, he was not—at least not yet—as hawkish as many of his closest allies and advisers.

The knock at the door rumbled like a drumbeat.

"Evening, Art. Fill me in."

"All as you said, Holt. Invasion imminent, SS-20's sunk in the mine shafts. Incredible, but not as incredible as what's happening at this end."

"Your people and the others—are they out safely?"

"Don't know, man. The boys in Jan Mayen who picked up the message said something about a nasty storm. But let's not worry about that now. We've got our hands full right here in the old swamp city. Listen here, Holt. You're not going to believe this. We're out, excluded." He glanced at his watch. "They're going in to meet with the President in a little less than two hours—"

"Okay, Art, so they don't want me, a foreigner, and you, some sort of CIA Rasputin, at a national policy meeting. I wouldn't jump to conclusions. Barker's got more going for him than you think. He'll present our case with—"

Millet threw up his hands in a mighty gesture of distress. "Hell, Bjørn, Barker doesn't even know there's a meeting."

Millet plopped down in a chair and pressed his hands to his temples. "Look here, man, we're being confronted with a conspiracy, plain and simple. I happen to have been in Willard's office at Langley trying to bring him around when Holzhauer called. That was before Willard knew I was *out*. He told me about the message from Johnson *and* about the meeting with the President. I only learned later that I wasn't invited. Just top-level people, Willard said. I asked about you. Same response. So I stopped right there, suspecting the rest, went to a pay phone and called Barker's house. This was only about an hour ago."

"And?"

"The housekeeper answered. He's at the Kennedy Center with his wife. I wonder who supplied him with the tickets, Bjørn. He's being excluded, too. Seems to be a common practice around here these days, keeping the Secretary of State away when there's anything important to be decided. I pumped the housekeeper for more information but she suddenly got suspicious and clammed up. Probably thought I was an assassin."

"You probably sounded like one. You think he really is at the Kennedy Center?"

"I hope so."

"Okay, Art, listen. We catch him at the Center, get him to the White House when the others are supposed to go in, then let him walk in with them. I don't see how they can chase him away if he's right there."

"Hold on, pal, hold on. You're leaving out one critical little detail. You don't know Barker like I do. He's a gentleman. I promise you he will *not* barge in on the President uninvited. Maybe he'll try to schedule a later meeting, but by then he might end up talking to a wall."

"Art, we've got to try all the same. Come on! Let's get over to the Center and find him. Once he knows what's going on behind his back, he might be mad enough to *do* something."

"Calm down, Holt, will you? Aren't you the one who always stressed the importance of working from a solid plan? Change it if you have to, but always have it out in front of you as a point of reference. Gives you the image of knowing what you're doing. . . . It was you, wasn't it, who used to say that?"

"Maybe, Art. But in this case—"

"Goddamnit, Bjørn, just hang on. You wouldn't listen to me earlier when I tried to warn you about these men. This time I'm going to force you. I've got something worked out I think we should consider."

"Not without Barker. We're nowhere without him."

"Agreed. It includes him. Order me some coffee, will you? He'll be in the theater another hour and a half. Let's take a few minutes and go over my plan. If you don't believe it will do the job you came here to do, we'll see if we can't herd Barker into the White House with the others."

Bjørn dialed room service. "I think," he mumbled, as he waited for an answer, "that we should do both. Hear your plan *and* get Barker into that meeting. . . . Hello? Yes. Coffee in 614. Correct."

"Have them send up a couple of hamburgers. I haven't eaten since—"

"And two hamburgers. What? No, no, just hamburgers. How long will that take? Twenty minutes? Can't you speed it up? Okay, thanks. And please send the coffee right away."

"And french fries," grumbled Millet, walking to the window and peeking nervously through the curtain. But Bjørn had already hung up. "We can't do both at once. My plan uses the Secretary *during* the meeting. Where the hell's the coffee? This goddamned place couldn't win a race against the Senate—"

"Art, it hasn't been thirty seconds since I called. Your turn to calm down."

"Calm down? Fat chance." He fished in his shirt pocket and pulled out a rectangular gray box the size of a pack of cigarettes. He flipped it onto the bed.

Puzzled, Bjørn watched the flight of the mysterious projectile. "Well, don't you want to open it?"

"No, Art. I'll take your word for it. What's inside?"

Millet's face looked drawn and wrinkled in the artificial light. He moved slowly to the bed and picked up the box. "Ironic, Bjørn, most ironic. The White House has been damned worried about leaks at State. The boys over at NSA got the assignment this time and got a little carried away. They even bugged the office of Undersecretary Olsen."

Bjørn was beginning to piece things together. He watched Millet intently.

"Well, Bjørn, we tracked down the offender without ever activating the bugs. But someone evidently forgot to take them out. After you and I talked Saturday, it occurred to me that a transcript of that meeting with the bomb slingers might come in handy some day. I knew it would probably mean my career in the Agency was over, Bjørn, but that Rasputin ESP of mine told me to go ahead. Since I've done so much liaison work for Willard, the boys at NSA didn't ask questions. Mewes turned on the device from noon till midnight Sunday and delivered this little jewel to me this—"

There was a knock at the door. "Room service," announced a faint female voice. Millet stashed the container under a pillow as if he expected Willard to rise out of the coffee pot like a genie. Bjørn took the tray and slipped the young girl five crisp dollar bills, pleading with her to hurry up the hamburgers.

"Right here, Bjørn, right here." Millet waved the little gray box containing the tapes. "The whole goddamned Sunday meeting. Every last goddamned warmongering syllable of it. And the machine that'll play these babies back is in the trunk of my car." He gulped down his coffee and held out his cup for more. "How, old man, do you think these would affect Petrovich?"

"Petrovich? Which Petrovich?"

"*Which* Petrovich? How many are there?"

"Ahhh, got it. You mean the Soviet Ambassador to the States."

"Precisely. Eugen I. Petrovich, bless his heart. We find Barker. The three of us pay the Russian Embassy a late-night call and insist on an immediate talk with Petrovich. We explain what's going on, play him the tapes of our little Sunday surprise, offer them to him. . . ."

"He'll be suspicious as hell."

"Which, Bjørn, is why Barker *must* be with us. We'll be with Petrovich at exactly the same moment that nasty, nasty conspiracy is taking place at the White House. Barker informs Petrovich of what's happening; the Russian, shrewd customer that he is, has the White House watched—and *bang*. Russian intelligence spots Clark, Holzhauer, and Willard slipping out of the President's chambers in the wee hours of the morning—the same three men who, on the tapes, are calling for luring the Soviets into a nuclear trap. Get the picture?"

"It's coming into sharp focus, real sharp focus, Art."

"It should be. When Petrovich puts two and two together, he'll be off for Moscow before those blowoffs in the kitchen get my hamburgers off the grill."

"And Barker. Will he cooperate?"

"You bet your life. First, it's a damned good strategy for preserving the peace, something that Barker truly cares about. Second, it will give him an opportunity to get back at Clark and his boys. Imagine, they'll get the President all primed to use the big one to counter a Soviet move that never materializes. The President will be a little more cautious in the future when a bunch of bombsters descend on him. Third, the pricks'll have no way to get back at Barker, even if they find out what he did. What are they supposed to do, accuse him of preventing a nuclear war?"

"But, Art, they'll find *you* out."

"Fuck 'em. I'll move to Norway and chase those pretty uninhibited blond women around for the rest of my life. It'll still be there if we succeed."

"Art," said Bjørn reverently, "I can't believe it. If you're willing to put yourself in that kind of danger, I think we can pull it off."

"Not only willing, pal, not only willing. Shall we get over to the Kennedy Center?"

"By God, Art, you've really done it this time. I mean *really* done it." He grabbed his friend's arm and tugged him to his feet.

In the corridor, they almost collided with a girl carrying a tray.

"Who for?" asked Millet.

"614, sir."

"Good. Put them on this gentleman's bill." He snatched the two hamburgers, wrapped them in a napkin, and walked briskly to the elevator. Grinning, he pushed the "down" button with his elbow.

In ten minutes they were speeding through the capital in Millet's old blue Chevrolet, the worn-out shocks, sloppy steering, and shuddering brakes not slowing them down one second.

23

From his sheltered perch high up on a cliff overlooking the pass, Mikhail Obruchev watched the moon break through the clouds. Its pale-yellow light flooded vast expanses of peaks, glaciers, and snowfields. Far to the west, a sliver of inky-black sea glistened between two jagged summits. The gale had died to a whisper, leaving the night utterly silent.

The thought crossed his mind that the fugitives might try to move before dawn. If the moon stayed out, he could not afford to doze off. He cursed his fate as he had so often during those last weeks, for he knew how badly he needed sleep. Why did it have to clear up just now? Why the hell couldn't it hold off a few more hours? What if he fell asleep in the moonlight and let them slip by? Just a few hours of darkness . . . was that too much to ask?

As if his entreaties had been heard, the flaw in the clouds mended itself. Darkness returned in stages, and the vista of glowing desolation which stretched out before him faded from view.

He sighed. The storm was over—that much had been evident to him since midday of this, his third day in the wilds. But it looked as if the cloudiness was going to linger a little longer, long enough for him to get some sleep.

His body grew heavy, but he could not still his thoughts. What if they had some sort of a radio with them? If atmospheric conditions got much better, they might yet get their message off. Or perhaps they had gotten it off already? Was it possible that his Herculean efforts to overtake them would be in vain?

But no! What was he thinking? They had all been searched in Barentsburg, as had their ship. Most thoroughly, too, as Koznyshov had ordered. Only one radio had been found, and that radio he had seen with his own eyes aboard the beached *Utsira*. Why was he plaguing himself with idiotic, groundless fears? Not only did they have no radio with them; they couldn't possibly have reached the pass yet. The northwester would have seen to that. And now . . . well, now that the explosives were in place on the steep snow-covered mountainside above the narrow gap through which they must climb, he really didn't have to worry. All he needed was to await the right moment and flick the detonator switch, and they would be buried forever under a million tons of rock and snow.

Now he must sleep! Fatigue was the only thing that could still trip him up. The cold, the exertion, the short September nights which allowed him only two or three hours of fitful rest were beginning to catch up with him. He must sleep so that he would be in top form when dawn broke around two o'clock. He pulled the last bottle of vodka from his pack and downed half a pint. Leaning back against the cold rock, he luxuriated in the warmth it kindled in his stomach and limbs. A mild euphoria replaced the tension in his neck, and he closed his eyes.

The vision of the berserk chopper tore into his peace of mind. For the third night in a row, his tranquility was shattered. He growled in agony. So what? he asked himself bitterly. So what if those two idiots had gotten it? Christ Almighty, he wouldn't have minded slitting their throats himself. They were the kind of pricks who made a guy's life miserable. All they cared about was making sure you paid a price for having a little fun. For three days now he had been completely free of them, and he had enjoyed it! No one to tell him how to conduct his affairs, no one to question his judgment, no one to interfere when he was doing a job only he knew how to do, no screeching voice to upset the melodies of the wind and sea, no despicable little worm slithering along behind him keeping a mental record of his every move. . . . What the hell did it matter to him that they were gone?

Confused and agitated, he yanked out the bottle and tossed down another mighty gurgling swallow. The sky ruptured anew. A probe of moonlight caught him, bottle in hand, as if revealing his excesses to the world. He felt naked and betrayed. A little drunk, he watched the frayed edges of a sleek black cloud skirt across the lower half of the moon. The eerie silence, the strange play of light and darkness, unsettled him. To calm himself, he focused on the shadowy craters of the moon's face—and saw an apparition of Lydov's sallow, sunken visage.

He shut his eyes, but the apparition became more distinct. The face peered at him through diaphanous sheets of blowing snow. The surf raged. Between him and his friend, a twisted aluminum door moved back and forth in the wind with hypnotic regularity. Panic-stricken, he opened his eyes. But the moon again retreated behind heavy clouds. Lydov's face would not go away. It stared at him from the black arctic overcast, it stared at him from inside his burning eyelids, it gave him no escape. He slapped his cheeks, poured down the remaining vodka, held snow to his forehead, banged his back against the rock. But nothing could induce Lydov to depart. He was like a ghost over whom the Consul had no control. "Kid, I'm sorry," pleaded Obruchev. "For Christ's sake, I'm sorry. Why didn't you walk up the beach? I left you everything. Why? Why? What was I supposed to do?" Lydov lingered a bit longer, his gaze full of hurt and reproach. A wall of water crashed over the helicopter, knocked it on its side and sucked it under the hungry sea.

Obruchev growled a few drunken obscenities, ran his hand over the detonator beside him, and fell into a deep and dreamless sleep.

Less than three miles away, William Johnson crawled out of his tent to check on the weather. He studied the clouds, calculated the average wait between the brief periods of moonlight, and decided it was time to move. It would, he realized, be hazardous to venture forth at night. The glaciers they must cross, like the ones they had already struggled over, would be riven with deep, narrow crevasses hidden beneath the snowdrifts. Even in full daylight, it was difficult to detect them; at night it would be next to impossible.

286

But the alternative to moving on was infinitely less attractive. With the storm breaking up, they would be sitting ducks for the Russian helicopters he assumed would be looking for them. He must not waste these three hours of uncertain light even if they only covered several hundred treacherous yards. He lit the butane stove inside his tent and, after instructing Duncan to make some strong coffee, hurried off to rouse the others.

Their campsite below the pass was a good one. A slanting rock formation towered overhead like the roof of a chalet. The wind had swept clear an area fifty feet square around the base of the wall, enabling them to pitch their tents on solid ground. An occasional tuft of brown mountain grass poked up through the cracks in the stony earth, and a lonely cluster of wildflowers near the far extremity of the clearing was still in bloom. Six-foot snowdrifts surrounded them on three sides.

When Johnson entered Martin and Ulrike's tent, he was surprised to find Turk with them. The old seaman was holding a silent vigil while Martin pressed a damp cloth to Ulrike's forehead. She lay in the padded sled where she had spent the last two days and nights since her collapse. She tossed and sobbed quietly.

Martin glanced up from his crouching position and returned to Ulrike. Turk remained silent.

"My, my," said Johnson, "friendly crew. I told you, Dodds, she'll be okay. We've got to get her—and us—to Ny-Ålesund, that's all. Another of couple of days. You should all be catching up on your sleep."

"What are you doing here?" asked Martin.

The CIA man held open the flap to let the moonlight pour into the tent. "We've got to move. Duncan's got the coffee on. Pack up. I want to break camp in ten minutes. See for yourself. The sky's beginning to clear. There's enough light to find our way. If we're lucky, we'll be over the pass at daybreak. We might have to hide again if it stays clear . . . might have to move at night. But we *must* keep moving. We don't know when the Russians will find the *Utsira* and mount an all-out search. The closer we are to Ny-Ålesund when that happens, the better our chances."

"Ulrike can't be moved again until her fever breaks. Look at her. First she's burning up, then shivering like—"

"Dodds, let me have a word with you outside." Reluctantly,

287

Martin followed him to the edge of the clearing, where the drifts began. The shadow of the rock formation under which they were camped pointed like a faint arrow across an endless meadow of white. The wan silhouette of high peaks draped in ragged layers of clouds loomed on the distant horizon.

"Look here, Prof," said Johnson, his voice shattering the windless stillness of the night, "the girl's not going to make it. You've got to face the facts. She's a goner whether she goes or stays. Drag her along if you want. It doesn't matter to me. But for Christ's sake, don't sit here and. . . ." He look up in that instant and found himself talking into the vast arctic emptiness.

When Martin slipped back into the tent, Turk was at Ulrike's side. They leaned over her. She stopped shivering for a brief moment and smiled. "He wants to go now? That's all right, Martin. Forget what I said earlier." She paused to catch her breath. "Please forget it. I didn't know what I was saying. I'll be fine on the sled. It hasn't really been that bad. No worse than lying here. Please don't worry. If you have the strength to pull me, I have the strength to make it." She pressed their hands weakly and closed her eyes.

Martin had no illusions about the toll the sled ride had taken on her. Twice, the sled had jerked loose on a downhill grade and careered out of control, slamming into a boulder the first time and dumping her into a snowdrift the second. Then, yesterday, the snow beneath it had given way, leaving her hanging over a narrow, bottomless crevasse.

Worse, after the pneumonia had choked off her breath and made her delirious with fever, she had begun to blame herself for the terrible things that had happened. It was impossible to reason with her. She felt that if they dragged her along on the sled, it would be the difference between life and death for the others. That feeling, thought Martin, might finish her off. His mind was made up: they were staying.

Johnson burst into the tent. "We're ready. I'll give you five more minutes. I. . . ." He stopped, dumbfounded, when he saw Turk at the girl's side. "Heh, old man, heh! Come on! Hop to it! You're part of the team, and the team's leaving."

Turk pulled his pipe out of his pocket and scraped around the bowl with the pointed end of his ice ax. "William, I lost my ship." He paused while he packed in a pinch of tobacco. He struck a match. The light from the tiny flame danced on his grave, wrinkled face. "I lost a lot more than just a ship. The *Utsira* was part of me, boy, a friend. She and I had been together a long time. A long, long time. Now, I ain't blaming no one. But to my way of thinking, I've lost about all I care to lose just now. So, William, I'll be staying here with the girl. Go on. Git. You two can take care of yourselves. All I ask is that you find us some help as soon as you arrive. Seems to me you owe us that much, William, that much at least."

Johnson shrugged his shoulders. He lifted the flap of the tent and disappeared into the night.

Obruchev awoke with a start. "Goddamnit," he hissed, looking out on the cold gray morning. Of all the idiotic things, he had overslept! What was worse, he couldn't tell by how long. The overcast had thickened again, and he could not find the sun. It could be three . . . or seven . . . or even nine. It would be just his luck, he fumed, to have snored away like a blasted fool while the quarry he had come all this way to catch slipped over the pass unseen. Furious with himself, he focused the scope of his rifle on the rise leading up to the pass. But in the flat light, he was unable to spot any irregularities in the surface of the snow, even those he knew were there.

What now? Jesus! If he climbed down for a closer look, he would litter the whole area around his artfully constructed trap with his snowshoe prints. That was out. He had been lucky enough to get the explosives in place and get up here while it was still snowing. That was his trump, and in a fight against six of the enemy, even *he* needed a trump.

He was calm long enough to reconsider the courses of action still open to him. He weighed the advantages of staying where he was, of gambling that they had not yet reached the pass. But what if they had? He imagined himself sitting in his little nest in the cliff for two days while his enemies—the same bastards who had been in his grasp before he had overslept—made their way unobstructed to Ny-Ålesund. To hell with that, he thought. The uncertainty would drive him mad. Besides, he was out of vodka. A man had no business up here without his vodka. . . .

289

He scanned the horizon. His view of the sea was obscured by a curtain of snow squalls. Already, the highest peaks had vanished into the sagging gray sky. Another reason he could not sit up here like an idiot carved in stone. If it snowed again—which it looked like it might—the footprints would be gone forever. Assuming, of course, that there were footprints at all. He was growing confused. If he could only get *behind* the pass without leaving tracks, his problems would be solved. If they had crossed, he would stalk them; if not, he would still be able to detonate the explosives with the radio device. And there would be no snowshoe tracks to give him away. But, unfortunately, he couldn't fly. He leaned out from his perch and looked up the vertical cliff which disappeared into the clouds several hundred feet above his head. *That* was the only way to get behind the pass. The thought of the climb made him dizzy; the image of the ice climbers he had shot off the glacier wall swam up before him. He doubted he could do it; he dreaded the thought. But what other choice did he have?

Racked with anxiety, he surveyed the terrain in front of him once more. He was stalling for time and he knew it. So convinced was he that the climb was inevitable he almost didn't see two tiny, white-clad figures with heavy packs trudging toward the pass. He wiped the condensation off his scope and looked again. For a moment, he felt jubilant.

It wasn't long, though, until his confusion returned. Where the hell were the others? Had they perished out here in these brutal wilds or had they taken the long way around? This galling uncertainty was reducing him from a man to a trembling coward!

He ran his fingers over the detonator as he groped for a way out of his newest dilemma. Then, suddenly, he had an idea. The long way around was not something the others would have attempted with the girl. If they had chosen to split up that way, the girl would be with the two men just now entering his cunningly constructed avalanche zone. With the change in the weather, the others must have branched off somewhere just below the pass and headed for the coast. Of course that's what they had done! It was what he himself would have done: sent part of the group down to the sea to try to alert a passing ship.

The rest seemed easy. After he got rid of these two fools, he would follow their tracks down to where the others had split off. From there, he would pick up the new trail and take it to its end. He would approach them down around the coast and . . . well, the best method would suggest itself when he found them. There was one person to worry about, that was all: the third young man. Otherwise, there was only a girl, a professor, and an old sailor.

The thought of seeing Ulrike again filled him with anticipation. His anger at her for the way she had tricked him mingled with a powerful desire to possess her sexually. He chuckled aloud. In more ways than one, the time had come to even the score.

Glancing through his scope, he found the two agents on the outer edge of the zone. He waited until they had covered another fifty feet, clicked off the safety and pushed the detonator switch. There were several muted explosions, then a thunderous roar as tons of snow and rock shook loose from the mountainside and rumbled into the gap.

He stood and stretched, content with the perfect execution of his plan. His elation returned; he felt invincible. Those two were out of the way; soon the others would meet their deserved fate. He scrambled down the rock wall like a young man, stretched and grunted, then strapped on his snowshoes and headed down Johnson and Duncan's tracks in the direction from which they had come.

24

"I DON'T CARE if it's the President himself," growled Petrovich to his aide. "Tell the Secretary of State I'll see him in the morning. First thing if he wants. It's after midnight, I've had my drinks and I'm ready for bed."

The Soviet Ambassador to the United States was downing his final bourbon and water in his library. He had just finished reading the *Washington Post* and was drowsily recollecting how pleasant his three months in the American capital had been. He knew that this was about to change. But not yet . . . not just yet. The warm glow of the bourbon, the satisfaction that he, and not his old archrival Denisov, had landed the coveted Washington job, the serene approach of sleep had created in him a contentment he savored. The thought of a meeting just now—no doubt some kind of political ruse to catch him off guard—was more than he could stomach.

"Well, get back to the phone and tell him. What are you waiting for?"

"Mr. Ambassador, he's at the door."

"What? Here? In the middle of the night?"

"Yes, sir. Standing right out front with two other men. He says he must see you at once."

Petrovich smoothed his bushy eyebrows with the backs of his hands and sighed. "Right here, you say? At our door? Who are the other two?"

"A tall blond man named Holt. He says he's with the Norwegian Foreign Office. He assured me he knew you from Moscow. He said you had met him several times at the Norwegian Embassy there in the late seventies."

"Holt? Holt? Don't recall anyone by that name. Don't even recall visiting the Norwegian Embassy. Oh, well, you know how diplomatic life is. Maybe I do know him from somewhere. And the other one?"

"Arthur Millet from . . . well, he said you probably knew where he was from."

"Millet. Why, yes. Just read an intelligence report on him the other day. Those KGB boys over here *are* on the ball. Millet . . . he's no small fry. I think they said he worked right under the big boss. Millet, eh? Not just one of those political lackeys. We'd better let them in."

Petrovich rose clumsily, buttoned his maroon silk pajamas where they had separated over his thick hairy chest, and pulled the sash of his robe tighter. "Bring them right in here. Make sure they are who they say they are, especially the Secretary. Have someone in the Political Division meet them in the lobby, someone who would know or have pictures. Make sure they pass through the X-ray scan. If they notice anything, tell them . . . tell them it's a matter of policy. Like getting on an airplane over here . . . necessary because of the rise of terrorism in the West. Seat them right here and tell them to wait. Clear?"

"Yes, sir."

When Petrovich re-entered the library, he was still wearing his robe and pajamas. His hair was freshly combed with water.

"Go on," he snapped at his aide. "And send up Sergei. We'll need something to drink."

The young man pointed to the case in the corner.

"What's that?" asked Petrovich.

"A recorder," said Millet. "We've brought along some tapes we would like you to listen to."

"Very well." He brushed off his aide with a flick of the hand, hoping that the new X-ray scan had not malfunctioned. "Go on, now. These men are trustworthy." He shook hands with the three mysterious visitors and muttered a few gruff words. He recognized Secretary of State Barker from the one or two occasions when they had met, and felt both reassured and perplexed. This entire episode, he hoped, had nothing to do with Svalbard.

"Please sit down, gentlemen," began Petrovich. "I don't know what the habits of my predecessor were, but I can tell you right now that a visit at this hour does me little honor. We shall keep it brief. If the reason for your coming is as important as your mode of approaching me makes it appear, I will be glad to meet with you first thing in the morning. Sergei will be here directly to take your orders for drinks. Now, please. What's this all about?"

"Mr. Ambassador," replied Barker, "we've learned of your country's intentions on the Northern Flank." Bjørn cringed; he found the Secretary's words much too direct and provocative— no probing, no sparring, no jockeying for position. For Christ's sake, the point wasn't to raise Petrovich's ire but to get him to cooperate.

"I must say," continued Barker in the same harsh voice, "that I'm shocked and deeply disappointed that the Soviet Union has chosen a return to its previous policies of naked aggression."

Predictably, Petrovich remained unruffled. He smiled.

"Just what are you referring to, Mr. Secretary? I'm sure you're mistaken. Bad information, perhaps? It happens to us too, on occasion. The Soviet Union, let me assure you, has no thought of changing the defensive policies it has pursued for many decades in the region of which you speak. Or for that matter, in any region. If you would be kind enough to enlighten me as to the reasons for your absurd charges. . . ."

"Mr. Ambassador, I'm not asking you to confirm or deny the charges. I'm asking you to listen to—"

"Listen? Why should I, sir? Sit and listen while you accuse my country—quite rudely and at a dreadful hour of the night—of some silly intentions she does not and never will harbor?"

Bjørn could scarcely believe his ears. How had Barker, good man that he was, managed to get the crucial encounter off to such a bad start? How he longed to take over, using his intimate knowledge of the Soviets to bring Petrovich around. But his hands were tied; he had agreed with his cohorts on the way here that this must be a wholly *American* initiative in order to achieve the desired impact on the Russian Ambassador.

"Why should you, Mr. Petrovich?" erupted Millet. "Why

should you? Because it's part of your job. I can't imagine you'd want to lose your job because you failed in your duties."

"And what, sir, is that supposed to mean?"

Bjørn waited, tense as a bowstring, for Millet's reply. This was it. If his old friend failed to find the right tone, they might all be out on the street.

"What I mean, Mr. Petrovich, is that an Ambassador and his staff act as a conduit for information. It is your duty to convey to the Kremlin important news regarding developments in the country in which you are serving."

"I don't think I need to be instructed as to my duties."

"In which case, I assume you'll listen."

"Talk."

"Mr. Petrovich, I'm not one to beat around the bush. As Mr. Barker said, we know of your invasion plan. But, sir, that is not the reason we're here. We know something in addition, something even your leaders in the Kremlin do not know. You see, Mr. Petrovich, there are those in Washington who are aware of your intentions and *want* you to move, nonetheless. They *want* you to blunder into an area that is almost unpopulated. The Northern Cape is quite unique, Mr. Ambassador. It, unlike Berlin, unlike the Middle East, is an area the United States could defend *with tactical nuclear weapons* without destroying what it set out to protect. Perhaps your policymakers in the Kremlin have overlooked. . . ."

The entrance of Sergei, Petrovich's sleepy valet, silenced Millet.

Just in time, thought Bjørn. He had noticed a flicker of confusion in Petrovich's eyes. That was the exact point to suspend the attack. You didn't want to drive a man like Petrovich into a corner. It never did any good.

Millet resumed as if he had read Bjørn's thoughts. "In any event, Mr. Ambassador, it isn't our goal to accuse you. We only want you to help us. We're dissidents, Mr. Petrovich. We don't want a nuclear confrontation. We disagree with some of the most powerful men in Washington on just this issue. Which is why we've come to you. Merely by conveying the information we will give you, you can avert what we believe to be a pending nuclear disaster—a disaster for us, for you, and, of course, for Norway."

Behind his implacable facade Petrovich was indeed awash with confused thoughts and feelings. How the hell had the West gotten onto the plan? Or had it? Perhaps it was this wily Norwegian. (Oh, yes, he remembered him very well now, this Holt fellow. He was the one his friend Alexi Ivanov despised so, the one who had humbled old Alexi in front of a distinguished international gathering during the Barents Sea Conference.) Perhaps it was Holt who was behind all of this. Look at him sitting stoically over there as if he were a powerless observer! Perhaps Holt had a hunch about the Soviet invasion which he was trying to sell in the United States. If he, Petrovich, seemed interested in the "facts" his American visitors intended to divulge, would that not incriminate him and his country? Would he not be letting the cat out of the bag? Would he not be falling into a trap which this scheming Norwegian—as yet without the ear of the Americans or even his own government—was trying to set for him? He had better get these jerks out of here before he slipped up.

On the other hand, what if they were telling the truth? What if the Soviet Union went ahead with its planned invasion only to be met with a response that, God knows, the men in the Kremlin were not anticipating? It would come out sooner or later that he, Petrovich, had been too blind—or too stupid—to pass on what he knew. *That* would be a real debacle, a blazing, ignominious end to his brilliant career.

He weighed his alternatives and decided he'd better listen. "All right," he said patronizingly, "there's no invasion planned. Utter nonsense. The matter is academic. But I'll listen. It might give me some insight into how your policymakers view my country. But listen only, you understand. I see no reason to carry this information beyond the walls of this embassy."

Bjørn breathed a quiet sigh of relief. The drinks arrived. The Ambassador pushed Sergei out of the room and closed the door behind him.

"Mr. Petrovich," said Barker, "if I might continue where Mr. Millet left off."

"Yes."

"Thank you. Let me say first of all that we're quite in Mr. Millet's debt. To get word to you of the pending disaster, sir, he took some very courageous steps, steps that will cost him his career, at the very least. You see, sir, Mr. Millet was able to procure tapes of the entire fateful meeting which took place at the State Department Sunday afternoon. The three of us who are here with you now were present at the meeting. But the participants who determined the outcome were General Clark of the Joint Chiefs, National Security Adviser Holzhauer, and CIA Director Willard. I'm sure I needn't point out the influence of these men in this city and nation, nor the special relationship they enjoy with our President."

"Continue, please," ordered Petrovich, as if by listening he were discharging a burdensome obligation.

"Mr. Ambassador, after you hear the tapes—tapes on which these three men lay the foundation for baiting the Soviet Union into a nuclear trap—you will understand the significance of what I am now going to tell you. Clark, Holzhauer, and Willard are meeting at the White House this very moment, meeting with the President of the United Sates to convert him to their insidious plan. I was excluded from that meeting, Mr. Ambassador, because I do not believe the present situation need be handled with nuclear weapons. All who share my belief will likewise be excluded for as long as possible. Mr. Petrovich, the three men who wish to use nuclear weapons against you have entered into a conspiracy to block the President from any views other than their own. They might succeed. If they do, our two countries will be on a nuclear collision course—unless you convey our message to the Kremlin. May we play the tapes for you?"

"If you insist," said Petrovich, irritated, "Excuse me for one moment first." He left the room.

Millet winked. "He's going to have the White House watched."

"Or to relieve himself," said Barker, who was rapidly becoming discouraged.

As they listened to the long tapes, Petrovich's mood vacillated. At times he would be convinced of their authenticity and of the truthful intentions of his visitors. Then he would reproach himself for his naiveté. It was just too farfetched to be true! These high officials acting against the will of their superiors? No, not a chance. It was this goddamned Norwegian who had laid the trap and enlisted the support of a few members of the Washington establishment. And he, Petrovich, had almost been fool enough to walk right into it!

His fatigue fed his irritation until, at last, he could stand it no longer. This was an insult to his intelligence. The time had come to end this little farce.

But annoying shadows of doubt remained. He grumbled something, stretched and left the room once more. He checked by radio with his men watching the White House. Nothing yet. He went back to the library room, determined to act.

Millet clicked on the recorder. Holzhauer and Willard were explaining the manipulation of public opinion that would be needed to make Clark's proposal more palatable to the President. Petrovich listened another few minutes, unable to control his curiosity. When Millet shut down the recorder to begin a new spool, however, Petrovich cleared his throat and pronounced a firm "Enough."

"Just listen to this part that's coming up," said Millet. "Then you'll have the crux of it."

"Enough, I said."

"But, Mr. —"

"Enough! It's all academic anyway. We're not planning an attack on Svalbard and we already know you're a bunch of lunatics when it comes to the bomb. Look what you did to Japan! Now please leave. I've listened to as much as I can tolerate." His voice soared to a crescendo. "Go home and let me get some sleep. Matter closed. Machine off. Out! Out! Out!"

Bjørn's desperation erupted when Petrovich started for the door. He leaped to his feet and blocked the Russian's passage. Aghast, Barker and Millet watched. Petrovich lifted his huge arm and pushed it into Bjørn's chest. "Out of my way," he growled.

But Bjørn did not move. He grabbed the Russian's arm, slinging him around until he crashed into the wall with a reverberating thud. Petrovich, stunned, tried to sidle away. Bjørn halted him with an iron grip on the lapels of his pajamas. Petrovich, furious now, tried to wrench free. Bjørn shook him wildly. "Look here, Petrovich! Get this goddamned information to Moscow and get it there *fast!* It's yours. The tapes. The recorder. Let others vouch for its authenticity. Just get it there. Otherwise, Petrovich, otherwise, you'll go down in Soviet diplomatic history as the greatest idiot yet."

Petrovich gave a mighty heave toward the door. His escape was accompanied by indignant curses in his mother tongue and the sound of tearing silk.

They left the recorder and tapes where they were and waited. Upon Petrovich's booming order from his bedroom, Sergei appeared and escorted them out.

The air was fresh and cool. The first shimmering of an opalescent dawn stretched across the eastern horizon. A lone bird chirped in the distance. Two giant street-sweeping machines rasped along the pavement and a single taxi sped by in front of them. Without a word, they got into Millet's car and drove off.

At the Mayflower, Bjørn packed his bags and called for a seat on the first flight to New York. There was no reason to stay in Washington any longer. He had played his last card: for him, the game was over.

25

EARLIER, before her condition had become so grave, Martin had considered the possibility that she might die. He had caught a glimpse in his mind's eye of life without her. It was a vision as desolate and cold as Svalbard in autumn. It was more than just a simple vision of the future; it was also a somber and painful memory of what his life had been before. He had not recognized the emptiness then, for he had never known how different it all could be.

He could not, would not, face it, After all they had been through, it was inconceivable that a simple, treatable illness would snuff out a life so vivid, so full. Such things did not happen.

"She's going to make it, Turk. I don't know how, but she will. You wait and see. There's nothing—"

"Martin, will you listen to me?"

"Yes. But we can't take her on that sled again. Help will be here in two days. We'll wait, Turk, we have to wait."

"Son, there will be no help."

"What? Johnson—"

"Johnson's a strange man, my boy. Don't know if he has any feelings at all. He don't really care if any of us gets out of this alive. Fact is, Martin, it would be better for him if we didn't. Especially if she didn't."

"But—"

"Listen here, Martin, she's seen too much. Bjørn's told us about her reputation as a journalist. That's why he was real keen on not having her publish nothing on Svalbard. Now how d'you think Johnson's feeling about her after all she's seen him do? Nothing but trouble, he's thinking, if she gets out of this alive. That's why I say there'll be no help."

"But what about you, Turk? After all those years you've worked with him?"

"They know I'm done with 'em. I'm not of any use to 'em anymore. They couldn't care less, boy. Just the way they are. Or Johnson is, at least. That's why I'm saying we've got to do something to get her out of here."

"All right, okay. But what? She can't go two or three more days on that sled. Look at her. She's soaking wet again. She gets like that every few minutes. What happens out there in the cold?"

"Son, the coast's only about seven miles that way." He gestured toward the west with the stem of his pipe, then picked up his ice ax and began scratching a map on the floor of the tent. "See here, lots of canyons starting a mile or so from where we're camped. They all run down to the sound. Problem is to find one that isn't too steep to climb down. If we can get to the coast and set up the tent, we'll have a chance of alerting a passing ship. Now that the weather's come around, there'll be a few of 'em sailing. I've got flares with me. We'll get her on a ship. Maybe they'll have antibiotics on board. If not, they can at least get us to a spot where we can radio for a helicopter. I think we'd better try it, sooner the better."

"All right. But let's give her a few more hours just to see if the fever breaks. We can't take her out in this condition."

"Then go. Go now and scout out them canyons. I'll stay and watch after her. I'd go myself, Martin, but I think you can do it faster. These old legs of mine are about to give out. Legs never was meant for land."

"I'll be back as soon as I find something." He grabbed his pack and snowshoes, knelt for a moment beside Ulrike, and hurried outside.

Turk hobbled after him. "Martin, take your rifle. Bears can be a problem."

"No. It's more important to me to be able to cover ground. Never did learn how to carry one of those things comfortably. I'll

301

be all right." He snapped on his snowshoes and started up the drifts. "Take good care of her," he called back over his shoulder.

"Damned right I will," muttered the old man.

Martin was near panic. Two hours had passed, but it seemed an eternity. The three canyons he had been able to reconnoiter were deep, ugly gashes surrounded on all sides by vertical rock walls. The couloirs which connected them to the high plateau were much too treacherous to descend without ropes. And even if Johnson had not taken the ropes, it would have been unthinkable to lower Ulrike in her present condition. The decision on what to do would have to be taken all over again.

A premonition that she would die grasped him. He plodded ahead toward the tent, his eyes fixed on the snow, his stomach in knots, a heartwrenching pain in his chest. Images of their time together cruelly forced their way into his consciousness. He saw her as clearly as if she were there before him, snuggled into the window sill at Christina's on the night they had met. The wind from the open window ruffled the lace on her blouse and kicked up the ends of her honey-blond hair. She gave him a longing smile, as if they had already experienced what was to come in the next weeks, and sprang, laughing, to her feet. He saw her leaving that night, walking toward the big wrought iron gate with her black umbrella pointed into the wind. This time she stopped at the gate and looked back, as if pleading with him to follow. For some reason he was unable to move. She brushed the hair from her forehead, gave him one last smile, and disappeared into the soggy night. But soon she was back, sitting on her heels in the peasant cottage where they had first made love, naked to the waist, the orange glow of the fire shimmering on her slender arms, shapely breasts, delicate throat. The narrow gold chain around her neck sparkled cheerfully. Her eyes were so direct: she was so enigmatic, yet so scrupulously honest! He could feel her skin against his as he pulled her toward him . . . all exquisite warmth and tenderness until she was seized by a passion so intense it almost frightened him. He saw her in Oslo. She was approaching an intersection on the other side of a busy street carrying a shopping bag. Crowds of pedestrians streamed by.

Behind her was a lush green park. The rays of the late-summer sun filtered through the trees. Children, swans, foliage . . . he never knew until that moment how much one could yearn for the ordinary. She saw him, smiled and waved. He longed to rush to her, but a caravan of trucks rumbled by, blocking her from view. He could hear the gears gnash and the brakes squeal; he could feel the pavement vibrate beneath his feet. The light changed, the little green man appeared on the traffic signal, and she bounded forward to meet him, radiant and beautiful. . . .

He walked a little longer, listening to the snow crunch beneath his feet. When he looked up he could see the campsite. Off to the left, a movement in a boulder field caught his eye. Turk relieving himself, he guessed. But it seemed a long distance for Turk to have gone.

Instinctively he hid behind a nearby rock, riveted to his spot by a sudden compelling dread. He was about to force himself to continue when a squat man with an extended rifle crept out from behind the boulders, crouched and began to move with cat-like agility across the snowdrifts which stretched between him and the clearing. Aghast, Martin watched, trying desperately to decide what to do. Not fifty feet from the clearing, the man stopped and dug himself down into the snow. He pulled off his fur hat and wiped his brow with his arm.

The drummer! Martin felt as if he were experiencing Ulrike's nightmare in all its terribleness. He felt utterly helpless . . . no rifle, nothing but a hunting knife.

Obruchev, with his massive bald pate, his short stout legs, his two gold teeth—Martin could see the teeth when the man leered in the direction of the tent and broke into a smile—this awful man was after her, the person he loved above all else in the world.

He must not let her see him! Her life must not end so horribly. She had suffered too much.

But what the hell could he do? He cursed himself a thousand times for leaving the tent without the rifle. A hunting knife against this bull of a man? Fat chance.

Obruchev left him no more time to think. He started again for the tent, disappearing over the edge of the high drifts which surrounded the clearing. Martin raced toward the rock formation, momentarily losing sight of the tent. He circled the granite wall counterclockwise and, yanking off his snowshoes, climbed along the little ridge to the rock's edge. Holding his breath, he glanced around the corner. Obruchev had just slipped off his pack and set it next to the solitary clump of wildflowers. His rifle lay on the ground beside him. Slowly, soundlessly, he was bending over to pick it up.

Clutching his knife, Martin sprang forward. He dropped six feet and landed just behind the stooped Russian. With more strength than he knew he had, he flung an arm around the Consul's neck and plunged the blade into his side.

Obruchev spun around like a cornered beast, his violent motion ripping the knife, buried in his rib cage, from Martin's grasp. In the same motion, he lashed out with a savage backhand to his assailant's jaw. Martin stumbled sideways, yelling to alert Turk, and caught his balance just in time to receive the full force of Obruchev's knee in his groin. As Martin slumped forward, the Consul smashed a mighty fist into his solar plexus. He dropped to the ground, unable to catch his breath. Through the blinding flashes behind his eyes, he saw the Russian pull the bloody knife from his side and lunge with it into the tent.

The world seemed to stand still. His legs would not move, his breath refused to come, his head whirled and throbbed. He heard a spine-chilling, guttural howl and watched, paralyzed, as the Consul fell backwards through the tent door. His fur hat jarred loose when he landed. Martin saw the gash on the top of his great bald head. Turk slipped out behind him with his ice ax still in hand, crouched warily, and moved forward.

"Martin, get the gun! Get the gun!"

Obruchev's rifle lay not two feet from him, but Martin could not move. He watched in horror as the Consul rolled toward him and grabbed the rifle. In a split second, he raised it, aimed it at Turk and fired. Martin closed his eyes.

The blow on his head must have distorted the Consul's vision. He missed. He growled and struggled to his knees while the old man bobbed and weaved like a prize fighter. Obruchev managed to steady the barrel. Turk jumped to the side and hurled the ice ax, catching him squarely on the forehead. Obruchev's rifle danced crazily in his hands and fell to the ground. Turk rushed behind him for the ax. Obruchev seemed to recover instantly. Still on his knees, he snatched the rifle and tried to aim.

Martin thought he heard Ulrike scream. With all the strength he could summon, he staggered to his feet and fell on the Consul with weak, outstretched arms. Obruchev crumpled, his body suddenly limp. The rifle fell beside him. Turk bent over him with the ax and waited. But the Russian did not stir.

Martin knelt beside her and took her face in his hands. It was wet with tears. She was so weak she seemed barely able to open her eyes.

"Martin," she whispered. "Martin, I knew you'd come back."

"I've come to take you home. There's so much we're going to do."

A slant of light from the tent door fell on her neck and chin. She winced when he stroked her cheek. He took her in his arms and held her tightly to him, but her shivering grew worse. She managed a smile and tugged her stocking cap from her head.

"Martin, I want to sit up. Help me sit up. I haven't sat up in two days."

Holding her hands, he pulled her upright and hugged her. But when he lowered her again with infinite gentleness, the shivering began, more violent than before. Her long blond hair lay tousled about her in wild disorder and perspiration glistened on her forehead.

"Martin, please, please. Don't let me die. I don't want to die. I don't want to lose you."

"Shhh. You're not going to die. I promise. It'll only be a few. . . ."

For a long time he lay beside her, utterly numb. Later he began to weep. Turk must have heard him, for he entered the tent and led him outside.

26

Turk and Martin sat on a promontory overlooking the Forland Sound. A Norwegian trawler plowed southward not far from the coast. Turk shot off a flare. Martin watched the ship slow down. He gazed beyond it into the distance. Snow clouds poured inland above the rough gray-green water. A few gulls swooped and circled to the monotonous roar of the sea. The air was as fresh and pure as any on earth, but the wind was icy and chilled him to the bone.

Bjørn's plane was about to touch down in Tromsø. He had little time for the visit. There might still be a role he could play in this whole mess. But he doubted it. The crisis seemed beyond the control of nations, much less individuals. He had come only to tell Christina that he loved her very much, that their living apart had been a disaster, that he wanted her to be with him from now on.

The American President was on national TV. He read the cue cards Holzhauer had prepared for him to a stunned nation. He put emphasis on the underlined words so the subtleties of the crisis—subtleties he did not entirely grasp—would be clear to all.

In Moscow, stern men in dark suits and military uniforms conferred behind great wooden doors. Koznyshov took out his gold lighter, lit a Gauloises and listened. Ivanov, he thought, was speaking quite well today. Petrovich slid the tape recorder farther

306

under his chair, wondering if this was the right moment to stick his neck out.

Danielsen poured himself another Wild Turkey and called in the press. There were elections coming up, and certain points needed a little clarification.

Fall came early to Oslo that year. Outside the window of Skogan's study, the trees along the boulevard were splotched with brilliant patches of orange and red. Across the street, the waiters at the Café Leopold were taking down the last umbrellas. The sausage man was still grilling away, undaunted by the cold. His guess would have been as good as anyone's on how the crisis might end.

Printed in the United States
19323LVS00004B/187